Lynne Graham was bo[...]
has been a keen romanc[...]
is very happily married, [...]
who has learned to cook since she started to write?
Her five children keep her on her toes. She has a very
large dog who knocks everything over, a very small
terrier who barks a lot, and two cats. When time
allows, Lynne is a keen gardener.

Louise Fuller was once a tomboy who hated pink
and always wanted to be the Prince—not the
Princess! Now she enjoys creating heroines who
aren't pretty pushovers but strong, believable women.
Before writing for Mills & Boon she studied literature
and philosophy at university, and then worked as
a reporter on her local newspaper. She lives in
Tunbridge Wells with her impossibly handsome
husband, Patrick, and their six children.

HIS CINDERELLA'S ONE-NIGHT HEIR

LYNNE GRAHAM

CONSEQUENCES OF A HOT HAVANA NIGHT

LOUISE FULLER

MILLS & BOON

First Published in Great Britain 2019
by Mills & Boon, an imprint of HarperCollins*Publishers*
1 London Bridge Street, London, SE1 9GF

His Cinderella's One-Night Heir © 2019 by Lynne Graham

Consequences of a Hot Havana Night © 2019 by Louise Fuller

ISBN: 978-0-263-27355-7

MIX
Paper from
responsible sources
FSC® C007454

This book is produced from independently certified FSC™ paper
to ensure responsible forest management.
For more information visit www.harpercollins.co.uk/green.

Printed and bound in Spain
by CPI, Barcelona

HIS CINDERELLA'S ONE-NIGHT HEIR

LYNNE GRAHAM

CHAPTER ONE

DANTE LUCARELLI, BILLIONAIRE renewable energy entrepreneur, roared down the private road on the powerful motorbike, revelling in the wind against his skin, in the rare sense of freedom. For a very short space of time all his problems evaporated. And then that magical moment was over and he was recalling his duties as a guest and slowing down to enable his host, Steve, to overtake him.

'You let me win!' Steve growled, punching the taller male's arm in retribution as they parked the bikes. 'Where's the fun in that?'

'Didn't want to show you up in front of the locals,' Dante tossed back, his thick blue-black hair tousled, white teeth glinting in the sunlight against his lean bronzed features as he grinned down at his former schoolmate. 'Anyway, it's your bike... And so this is it? Your latest venture?' he added, glancing through the overhanging pine trees at the restaurant surrounded by decking and overlooking the swimming lake. Sited above the sandy beach, it had a funky, carefree, Caribbean vibe. 'Kind of small, isn't it, for a guy who builds skyscrapers for a living?'

'Knock it off,' his friend urged, a burly blond man with the build of a rugby player. 'It's seasonal and does very well when the weather's good.'

'And employs a lot of those locals you like to take a paternal interest in,' Dante mocked, knowing Steve's sense of civic responsibility all too well. Steve Cranbrook was a kind man and one of the very few men Dante trusted.

They were in the south-east of France, a rural, far-from-touristic area where Steve had bought a chateau on a hill as a summer home for himself and his family. His all too numerous family, Dante reflected with a near shudder. Steve had four of the little blighters, two sets of twins under five, and they had been crawling over Dante and demanding attention ever since he had flown in earlier that day, which was why the break from the chateau was welcome. It wasn't that Dante disliked children, just that he wasn't used to them and weathering Steve's sociable kids was like trying to stand in the path of a hurricane armed with innumerable arms, legs and chattering tongues.

'It's not like that,' Steve protested. 'I just invest when I see the chance and contribute if there's a good cause. There aren't many employment opportunities around here.'

Dante took a seat at a wooden table hewn out of a giant tree trunk. Shrewd dark-as-pitch eyes swept the colourful bunting fluttering in the breeze as he picked up on the rampant beat of the music coming from the speakers and noted the youthful gathering at the bar. 'I bet this is the only party place in the neighbourhood,' he commented.

'Pretty much, but the food's good too. We get a lot of family trade when the beach is busy. So, tell me, when are you meeting with Eddie Shriner?'

Dante's lean, darkly handsome features tensed as the bite of his biggest problem sank its teeth into him afresh. 'In two weeks' time, and I still haven't got a woman on board to keep Krystal at bay.'

'I thought Liliana was stepping up as a favour,' Steve incised in surprise.

'No, that fell through. Liliana wanted an engagement ring as an inducement,' Dante admitted with an exasperated frown of recollection. 'Even though it would be a phoney engagement, I wasn't taking the risk of travelling down that road even with her.'

'An engagement ring?' Steve queried in surprise. 'Why on earth would she need a ring to pretend that she was your girlfriend again for Krystal's benefit?'

Dante shrugged a lean shoulder. 'She said it was a matter of pride, that she would lose face in front of Krystal if she didn't have a ring, because why else would she have reconciled with me when we broke up years ago?'

'Your love life…' Steve groaned, raking a rueful hand through his floppy blond hair. 'If you didn't dump so many women and leave them bitter and angry, you wouldn't be in this situation.'

Dante compressed his eloquent mouth in silent disagreement. He had no intention of ever marrying and producing children, and he had never lied to a woman on that score. He was upfront about his sex life and there was no room for love in it. Any woman who thought otherwise soon learned her mistake. He didn't get attached to women—never had, never would—and Liliana was the only exception to that rule. She was an ex who had become a friend and he genuinely respected and liked her, but he had still not been able to love her or want a more serious relationship with her.

Even trusting Liliana had initially been a challenge because Dante had never had quite the same view of women since he had caught his deceitful mother in bed with one of his father's closest friends. His snobbish mother, who stood in social judgement over others for their smallest mistakes and was quick to turn her back on them. He had soon realised that his parent regularly slept around. His indifference to Liliana had, however, told Dante all he needed to know about his own essentially cold heart. Without a doubt, he had inherited that ice gene from his unloving parents, he acknowledged grimly.

His sole experience of love had been his deep attachment to his older brother, Cristiano, and when Cristiano had died a year ago, it had shattered Dante and left him tormented with guilt. He often thought that had he been less selfish he might have saved his brother. Tragically, however, Cristiano had taken his own life because he had never been able to stand up for himself. Placed under intolerable pressure by their demanding parents and trying desperately hard to please as the eldest son and heir, Cristiano had crumbled and ultimately snapped under the strain.

And now the best that Dante could do in memory of his late brother was strive to buy back that little piece of woodland heaven where Cristiano had gone whenever life became too much for him. Sadly, in the wake of their firstborn's death, their parents had immediately sold that piece of land for the highest price possible to Eddie Shriner, a resort developer currently married to Dante's most embittered former lover. Even since marrying Eddie, Krystal had made several unashamed attempts to get Dante back into her bed. The woman was incorrigible and the last thing Dante needed was Krystal coming on to him while he was trying to make a business deal with her husband.

'You should hire an escort to play your girlfriend. *That* sort of a woman, someone you *pay*,' Steve disconcerted him by suggesting, his voice dropped to a discreet level across the table lest he be overheard.

'Sounds dodgy and dangerous,' Dante countered with a grimace, his attention stolen by the petite young woman standing by the bar with a tray.

Her hair was as multicoloured as a Halloween bonfire, a vivid curling mass of untidy copper, red and glinting gold anchored by a clasp to the back of her head. She had the porcelain pale skin of a true redhead and the legs and breasts of a goddess, Dante decided, following the slim shapely length of those fantastic legs down into the scuffed cowboy boots she wore teamed with a floaty short floral skirt and a fitted top, above which the swell of her lush breasts foamed like a desert mirage. Quirky fashion sense though, decidedly *not* his style.

'That's Belle. Er…ground control to Dante?' Steve joked when Dante failed to even look his way.

With difficulty, Dante dredged his attention back from those ripe, enthralling curves and the classic shape of the oval face above the display, and glanced wryly back at his companion.

'That's Belle,' Steve repeated with amusement glinting in his frank brown eyes.

'What's a looker like that doing waitressing in a place like this?' Dante demanded as he shifted restlessly on his bench seat, reacting to the all-male punch of pure lust pulsing at his groin.

'Possibly waiting for an opportunity like you to come knocking,' Steve mocked. 'Look, she's trying to save up enough money to get back to the UK and set herself up there again. You could step in like a good guy and fly her over to London with you.'

'Is this why you brought me here? Since when do I do anything for nothing?' Dante demanded, lifting his sunglasses to get a better look at that glorious oval face, only to discover on that closer inspection that it was unexpectedly dotted with freckles. He was almost relieved that there was a flaw in all that perfection. He wondered what colour her eyes were. Big eyes, *too* big?

'Of course not. It just occurred to me this minute that you could both do each other a favour. Why not *hire* Belle? She's in a jam… Oh, and there's a dog in the story too. You like dogs, no? Well, by all accounts she's a very *nice* girl, probably not your type at all. They've been running a book behind the bar all summer betting on which guy will make waves with her.'

'Charming,' Dante breathed, his nostrils flaring with disgust as he looked away. 'I don't do nice girls.'

'But this isn't one you would plan to *do*,' Steve pointed out very drily. 'You need a fake girlfriend, not a lover, and *she* needs the money. I offered her a loan but she wouldn't take it. She's got pride and she's honest. She told me she couldn't take the money because she didn't know how she would ever pay it back.'

'And she's a waitress. End of story,' Dante responded sardonically. 'I don't mess around with waitresses.'

'You're a snob and I never knew it,' Steve remarked in wonderment. 'Of course, I knew about the blue blood, the family *palazzo*, the title and all the rest of those trappings you claim to despise.'

'What would a waitress do if she was plunged into my world?' Dante enquired with biting derision.

'What you were paying her to do, which is more than you can say for most of the entitled women we both know,' Steve pointed out levelly. 'It would be a simple hire-and-fire situation but I'm not sure she would go for it. I hear she can be a bit of a hothead.'

Dante said nothing because he collided with the eyes of the woman coming to serve them. Yes, the eyes were big and they were a sparkling, unusually dark blue that verged on violet, very noticeable against that ivory freckled skin of hers.

While Belle was on her break she had watched the two men walk in from the car park. Everyone knew Steve, the British owner of the restaurant, a friendly and unassuming man in spite of his wealth and success as an award-winning architect with a string of international offices. Steve was also an unashamed family man with four beautiful kids and an even more beautiful Spanish wife, but his guest was as physically different from him as night was from day.

He was very tall, lean and powerful in build and

he moved with the lithe precision of a man very much at home with his own body. His luxuriant wind-tousled black hair, falling almost long enough to touch his broad shoulders, blew back in the breeze, accentuating his hard, sculpted features. Even in jeans and an open-necked shirt, he was as sleekly magnificent as a black panther, physically beautiful in a wild, natural way and probably equally dangerous.

Several women peered out from the bar to admire his progress. Belle went back inside to do her job, silently listening as the bartender, a keen user of social media and a business student, identified the stranger as Dante Lucarelli. Evidently, he was some mega-rich Italian, a tycoon in the field of renewable energy. She walked over to serve Steve and his guest and as the Italian glanced up at her from beneath long black curling lashes that were wickedly wasted on a member of the male sex, she collided with vibrant dark golden eyes. For a terrifying split second, she froze as if a detonator had gone off inside her and her whole body burned as if he had set her on fire.

Flushed and filled with discomfiture, she took their drink orders and hastened back to the bar to fill them. She shouldn't have looked at him, shouldn't have looked anywhere near him, she scolded herself fiercely. He was extraordinarily good-looking and he knew it. Of course he did. Nobody saw a face like that in a mirror every day and failed to notice its lack of flaws and, even if he didn't look in mirrors much, every woman under sixty was studying him with appreciation and he could hardly be unaware of the amount of attention he attracted.

Belle's face was red and she hated that she couldn't

stop that rush of self-conscious colour that turned her the colour of an overripe tomato. It embarrassed her as much at the age of twenty-two as it had when she had been at school and the butt of unkind jokes. Diminutive in height, red-haired, freckled, as well as overly endowed in the chest category, she had been very, very low on the cool scale of popularity at school.

Dante was hugely amused by the top-to-toe blush that had enveloped Belle. When had he last seen a woman blush? He could not remember, but then he didn't make the mistake of associating blushing with either shyness or innocence. He was much more inclined to link it to sexual attraction and awareness. He was accustomed to women looking at him and wanting him. After all, it had been happening since he was sixteen, when he had lost his virginity to one of his mother's friends, his rebellion after being confronted by his mother's extramarital fling. At the age of twenty-eight, he took it for granted that ninety-nine out of a hundred women would say yes to sharing his bed if he asked. And rarely did he even *have* to ask. Sex was frequently offered to Dante on a plate and without the smallest encouragement.

Belle delivered the drinks without once looking in Dante's direction and that overheated feeling in her body began mercifully to fade, allowing her to breathe again. It was normal to notice an attractive man, she soothed herself, and it wasn't her fault that she blushed fire-engine red. Just an unfortunate fact of life and she needed to learn to deal with it, as she had learned to deal with so many other unfortunate facts.

Predictably, her mind strayed back to the bad luck that seemed to thread through almost every wrong decision she made. She had been born to a woman who didn't want her, and a father who wanted nothing to do with her and told her so without embarrassment. Her grandmother, Sadie, had told her that that lack of interest was her parents' problem and not something that Belle should take personally. Her grandparents *had* loved her, she recalled with a prickling sensation behind her eyes, but her gran and grandad were both gone now and thinking about their loss only made Belle feel sad because it reminded her all over again that she was alone in the world with nobody and nothing to fall back on when things went wrong. And in France, things had gone very, *very* wrong for Belle.

Dante studied Belle as she moved round the bar, striving to imagine her dressed in haute couture, and that was a challenge when for some juvenile reason his brain only wanted to picture her naked. Clearly, a new wardrobe would make her infinitely more presentable but, of course, she would have to stop biting her nails. Such a disgusting habit, he reflected with distaste.

'What's she doing in France?' he asked Steve carelessly, angling his chin in Belle's direction.

'I only know local gossip. Word is she came out here about three years ago as a housekeeper/ companion for an elderly English widow living in the village. The widow's family hired her in London and left her to sink or swim as the old lady drifted into dementia. Eventually the local doctor got a little help for her but Belle was basically left to struggle.'

Dante slanted up an ebony brow. 'She sounds like an idiot. Why didn't she just walk out and go home when the job got too much for her?'

Steve frowned. 'She was attached to the old lady by then and didn't want to let her down or abandon her.'

'How did she end up working here, in the bar?'

'The widow had a heart attack and died and as soon as the funeral was over, her family sold her house and left Belle homeless and without sufficient money to get home on. They also threw out the old lady's dog… Charlie,' Steve murmured as a small raggedy mutt badly in need of grooming nudged up against his leg for attention before moving on to eagerly greet another regular customer, who was more likely to offer him food.

Dante paid no heed to the dog, his attention resting on his friend. 'And then?'

'The guy who rents this place offered Belle an old campervan to live in. It's parked in the overflow car park behind the trees and she and the dog moved in. Then he gave her a job here.'

'So, she's pretty much one of life's losers,' Dante surmised without surprise. 'I'm more into winners.'

'But losers are undoubtedly easier and less demanding to negotiate with,' Steve remarked with cynical acceptance. 'And when have you ever been shy about profiting from other people's misfortunes?'

Dante grinned. 'Being ruthless is in my genes.'

'Except when it came to your brother. I lost count of the times you dragged Cristiano out of trouble,' Steve murmured, unimpressed. 'And you say you're not sentimental and yet look at the lengths you're willing to go to, simply to buy that woodland back.'

Dante's high cheekbones and strong jawline clenched hard. 'That's different.'

'It must be, particularly as I seem to remember that the first time you stayed in Cristiano's log cabin, you hated it like hell.'

'I don't enjoy roughing it, but Cristiano was always a back-to-nature freak,' Dante recalled abstractedly, his attention locking back on Belle as a couple of young guys flirted with her while she delivered their drinks. She wasn't blushing for their benefit, she was brisk and professional, he noted with helpless satisfaction. He signalled her with a graceful brown hand to order another set of drinks.

'Not for me,' Steve demurred with regret. 'Sancha will have dinner on and she hates it when I'm late for meals.'

'It's only nine,' Dante pointed out incredulously.

'Well, to be honest, my wife doesn't really like me out of her sight for too long,' Steve admitted with quiet pride.

Dante winced at the very idea of his freedom to do as he liked being curtailed in such a fashion.

'Listen, don't knock being married until you've tried it!' Steve protested in his own defence.

'I am never ever going to try it,' Dante assured him with a grim look of amusement. 'But I am in the market for a girlfriend I can employ and I may be late back tonight.'

Dante returned to watching Belle, his attention drawn involuntarily to the bountiful swell of her breasts as she bent down to lift drinks off the tray, not to mention the enticing curve of her bottom thrust out and the skirt rising to expose the backs of her slender bare thighs. He shifted in his seat again, his even white teeth gritting with irritation. He wasn't a horny teenager. Why was he reacting like one? She brought him his drink and he tossed a note down, telling her to keep the change.

'It's too much,' she said uncomfortably.

'Don't be silly,' Dante advised succinctly. 'I'd like a word with you in private when you finish your shift.'

'I'm tired. I'll be going straight to bed,' she told him swiftly. 'Sorry!'

'Don't blow me off before you hear what I have to say,' Dante urged. 'It's possible that I could have a job for you, a job that would eventually get you back to the UK.'

Belle tensed like a greyhound fired up at the starting line. Her eyes lifted from the table they had been carefully studying and surged up to his lean, darkly handsome features instead. There she clashed unwarily with stunning dark golden eyes and she took a very slight step back, gooseflesh tingling on her exposed skin. 'A job? What kind of a job?' she questioned.

A lazy grip on his beer bottle, Dante lounged back gracefully against the balustrade surrounding the decking. 'Later,' he murmured silkily. 'That is…if you can contrive to stay awake that long.'

Belle reddened at the comeback. He was so sure of himself he set her teeth on edge. He dangled the bait and then waited for her to jump. Well, she wasn't going to jump, was she? What sort of job could *he* possibly offer her? Aside from waitressing, her only work experience was in housekeeping and caring, and it was unlikely that he would seek to hire her for domestic work. Intelligence told her that a wealthy man would use an agency to fill such positions. On the other hand, she had no reason to suspect that he could be on the brink of offering her anything immoral. She was not irresistible, she was not the sort of bombshell that men moved mountains to impress or entrap, she acknowledged impatiently. No, the only sort of sleazy offers she got came from bored married men and randy young ones, thinking that a foreigner might offer a taste of something more exciting than a local. Though surely it wasn't beyond the bounds of possibility that Dante Lucarelli could have an elderly relative in need of care?

Then, even in that line, there were plenty of people with the paper qualifications for caring that Belle ironically lacked. Fate had forced her into a caring role after her widowed grandfather had become sick. She had had to drop out of school to look after him when he was diagnosed as terminally ill. But it would have been unthinkable for Belle to do any less when her grandparents had loved and cared for her since she was a baby.

Tracy, Belle's mother and her grandparents' only child, had been a fashion model in love with the high life, and when Belle's father had refused to marry Tracy after she fell pregnant, Tracy had refused to become a single parent struggling to survive. At only a few weeks old, Belle had been dumped with her grandparents. On the only occasion when Tracy *had* chosen to take Belle home with her, it had proved a disaster for both mother and daughter. Tracy was a man's woman and the man in her life always came first. That was why, in the end, Tracy had satisfied her maternal instincts by making regular payments to her parents in return for which they had raised Belle for her.

Between the ages of five and fifteen, Belle had not seen her mother once, merely following her parent's jet-set progress round the world with the aid of a map and infrequent postcards. It had been a huge source of disappointment and hurt to Belle when she was fourteen to be invited to live with Tracy and then just as swiftly be thrown back out of her mother's life again. Tracy's lover had made a pass at Belle and Tracy had caught him in the act. Although she had forgiven the man involved, she had not forgiven her daughter for the sin of having attracted his attention. After that episode, Belle had not laid eyes on her mother again until her grandfather's funeral, when Tracy had only come home for long enough to collect the proceeds of her parents' estate.

'For goodness' sake, you're old enough to be keeping yourself now!' Tracy had complained bitterly when Belle had asked her for financial help. 'Don't be looking for any more handouts from me! Your father stopped paying his dues for you years ago and now, *finally*, it's my turn to be free of you.'

Yet Belle had sacrificed three years of her life and the education she had badly wanted to nurse her grandfather. She had also conserved Tracy's inheritance by ensuring that her grandfather, Ernest, did not have to sell his home to fund his own place in a care home. Ignoring those unwelcome realities, Tracy had sold everything that could be sold and had left Belle penniless and sleeping on a friend's couch in London. Ironically, back then the advertised job in France with Mrs Devenish had looked like manna from heaven, Belle conceded ruefully.

Belle had needed somewhere to live, and London had been too expensive. In addition, the very idea of working abroad had seemed to promise adventure, something that Belle's life had sorely lacked. She had leapt in with both feet, believing that all she would have to do was cook, clean and shop and provide occasional companionship to a lonely elderly woman. She had assumed that she would have free time in which to explore and had never dreamt that she would end up trapped and working round the clock in a dull rural village without even a café.

As Belle helped to collect the last glasses, she glanced down at the beach, where she could see Dante Lucarelli poised below the pine trees. Was he waiting for her? *Of course* she was going to ask him about the job! She was not in a position to ignore even the vaguest chance of getting back home again because the restaurant would be closing for the season in another few weeks and then where would she be? She wasn't a French citizen and couldn't sign up for welfare or anything like that. At least in London, if she had no other choice, she could fall back on the benefits system.

Saying goodnight to the other wait staff and with Charlie faithfully following her, Belle trudged down to the beach. Dante was a dark silhouette below the trees and then he stepped into the moonlight, which made his black hair gleam blue and lit up his lean, strong features, highlighting his high cheekbones, classic nose and hard jawline. He needed a shave. A shadow of dark stubble accentuated his wide sensual mouth. With his eyes glittering colourlessly over her as he awaited her arrival in silence, Belle could feel herself getting hot again, as if her body was burning up inside her skin. Suddenly she was grateful for the darkness, knowing she was tomato red again.

'Belle?' Dante queried. 'What's it short for?'

'Tinkerbelle,' Belle admitted with extreme reluctance. 'Unfortunately, my mother thought that was a cute name for a baby girl but my grandparents called me Belle. Belle Forrester.'

'Tinkerbelle? That's out of a kid's movie, isn't it?' Dante breathed in surprise, studying her where she stood as stiff and still as though she were on the edge of dangerous quicksand. She had released her hair from the clasp and it foamed across her shoulders in an untamed curling mane.

'*Peter Pan.* Tinker Bell was the fairy, but *Belle* is a movie name too,' Belle told him with compressed lips.

'I guess if you'd had wings you'd have flown yourself back home,' Dante remarked very drily.

'So…er…the job?' Belle prompted tautly.

'The job would be a little unusual but completely above board,' he assured her and then, as though suddenly recollecting his manners, he moved closer to extend a lean hand. 'My name is Dante Lucarelli.'

'Yes.' Belle barely touched the tips of his fingers. 'The bartender identified you before you'd been seated for five minutes. He's a business student.'

'Tell me about yourself,' he urged.

'There's not a lot relevant to tell,' Belle retorted uncomfortably, wishing he would just get to the point instead of keeping her in ignorance. 'I'm twenty-two. I left school at sixteen with a bundle of GCSEs and I haven't had any educational input since then. I'd like to change that when I get back to London. These days you need training and qualifications to make a decent life.'

'If you know that why did you skip that opportunity until now?'

'I never *had* the opportunity,' Belle countered wryly, settling down on the concrete bench beneath the trees. 'My grandmother died and then my grandfather fell ill and needed looking after. After they were both gone, I took a job here, which was basically housekeeping but which turned into full-time caring as well.'

Dante lounged back against a tree trunk, all lithe, lean power and thrumming masculinity. He was as relaxed as she was tense. 'Is caring for older people what you want to do going forward?'

Belle stiffened. 'No, definitely not. I think professional caring's a job you need a vocation for and I don't have that.'

'Fair enough,' Dante murmured, increasingly surprised by her cool, unapologetic self-containment, because at the very least he had expected bubbly encouragement and flirtation from her. In his experience women came on to him whether they thought they had a chance with him or not, but Belle wasn't making the smallest effort in that direction. 'You may not have a vocation for the job I'm about to offer you either, but it *would* eventually get you back to the UK and I would *pay* you handsomely to do it.'

Belle twisted round to get a better view of him, wishing he would step out of the shadows so that she could see him better. 'Tell me about it…'

'I need a woman prepared to pretend that she's my live-in girlfriend. Faking the part would be *all* that was required from you,' Dante assured her with calm emphasis. 'The job would only last for a couple of weeks and then you would be free to pursue your own plans with the cash I give you. It would be a win-win proposition for both of us.'

Belle was rarely deprived of speech, but the shock of the nature of his job offer was sufficient to glue her tongue to the roof of her mouth because such an exotic possibility wouldn't have crossed her mind in her wildest dreams. 'But…er…you don't even know me,' she protested weakly when she could find her voice again.

'Why would I need to know you? Steve vouches for your trustworthiness. It's a job, a role if you want to call it that. It's casual and temporary but also financially rewarding,' he completed smoothly.

'But pretending to be someone's girlfriend would mean knowing stuff about each other, that sort of thing,' Belle protested in a rush. 'And we're complete strangers.'

'I'm sure a simple question and answer session would cover the basics you would need to know,' Dante fielded without hesitation. 'Think about this from my point of view.'

Belle's eyes widened. 'I don't know you well enough to do that.'

'Then let me do it for you,' Dante responded silkily. 'I'm offering you the job purely *because* you're a stranger and I will be paying you to provide what I require. As a stranger, you'll walk away afterwards without a problem. You won't cling or believe that I have any further obligation towards you, nor will you assume that having helped me out makes you special to me in any way.'

Belle stared back at him, stunned by that revealing little speech. 'Do women often cling to you?'

Dante tensed, glittering dark eyes locking to the pale troubled oval of her face. 'It's been a problem in the past. If there's a stage-five clinger out there, I've met her!'

'I'm not the clingy type,' Belle whispered abstractedly, marvelling at the impact of those compelling dark eyes of his even in low light. 'But you still haven't explained why you need a fake live-in girlfriend.'

'And I won't share any more of my private business unless you first express an interest in accepting the job,' Dante incised impatiently. 'Sleep on the idea. I'll see you tomorrow morning at eleven and you can give me an answer then. But be warned... I am a demanding employer with high standards. If you take the job, you'll have to meet all my requirements. That will mean wearing the clothes I buy for you, breaking the nail-biting habit...and ditching the dog. I'm not keen on dogs.'

Belle's shamefully bitten nails curled into her palms. He had *noticed*. She always prayed that people didn't notice her bad habit but it seemed horribly typical of Dante Lucarelli that he had noticed her stubby nails, and she was mortified. Almost at the same time she reached for Charlie for reassurance and lifted him up onto her lap, sand from his paws and coat flying in all directions. 'I can't possibly ditch Charlie.'

'He can go into kennels for the duration of our arrangement.'

'No, he needs love and attention, and taken away from everything familiar, he would be frightened!' Belle reasoned fiercely, hugging Charlie to her as if he were a worn soft toy.

'He's not a child,' Dante reasoned in exasperation.

'He's the only family I've got, and he's had a rough ride so far in life,' Belle argued in growing dismay. 'I won't part with Charlie!'

'Sleep on it,' Dante advised again. 'Now, let me walk you back to the campervan.'

'That's not necessary,' Belle told him, springing upright and setting the dog down. 'It's only a hundred yards away.'

'I decide what's necessary, not you,' Dante shot back at her, suspecting that she could be more trouble than she was worth because she was emotional, far too emotional. Cristiano had been full of emotion and very much prone to attachments as well and look where that caring, sharing nonsense had got his brother! Cristiano had left behind two heartbroken, seriously clingy and demanding chihuahuas and Dante kept them in exclusive boarding kennels in the very lap of luxury. He visited his brother's pets religiously once a month. It wasn't quite the same as taking the dogs home with him, but it was the best he felt able to offer dogs who had never been treated as dogs and who probably didn't even know that they *were* dogs. Tito and Carina expected to share beds, sleep on laps and be hand-fed from plates.

Belle breathed in deeply. 'Do you think maybe you're having to *hire* a girlfriend because you're so rude, heartless and authoritarian?'

'I can't remember when a woman last insulted me,'

Dante confided in receipt of that refreshing question and gloriously untouched by the condemnation. A lifetime of criticism from his parents had ensured that he had developed a very tough hide.

'You must meet an awful lot of uncritical women.'

'Very rich men rarely meet with anything else,' Dante imparted with cynical conviction, pausing beside the small rusting campervan below the trees to marvel that anyone could actually be living in the battered vehicle full-time. 'I'll meet you in the bar tomorrow at eleven.'

CHAPTER TWO

IN THE CONFINEMENT of her bunk bed, Belle lay awake well into the early hours, pondering her choices, which only got fewer the more she thought about them. As always, she made lists. A long list of important questions that she *should* have asked but which Dante might not have answered. A list of pros and cons, again full of blanks, owing to her lack of facts on his situation.

'What do you think?' she asked Charlie ruefully as he cuddled up to her. 'We don't like or trust people who dislike dogs, do we? Do you think that's being too judgemental? Unfair? I mean, Steve's a lovely person and he's *friends* with Dante, which says something in his favour.'

Armed with her lists and clad in denim shorts and a light floral top, she walked up to the bar in the morning sunshine. The restaurant was being cleaned and it was time to prepare the tables for lunch. Hips twitching to the beat of the music playing, Belle set out place mats and glasses while she wondered if Dante was even capable of understanding how she felt about her dog.

Charlie hadn't started out as hers, but necessity had

made him hers and they had been together since shortly after her arrival in France. She didn't have any family. She couldn't count the father she had only met once in her life or Tracy, who hadn't stayed in touch once her own parents were both gone. Charlie, silly and scruffy as he was, had become Belle's family. He wasn't the brightest of dogs, but he was always cheerful and loving and a wonderful comfort when the world seemed dark and she felt alone.

Dante, fresh from a late breakfast of kids and toddler tantrums, was in the mood to be charmed and the first thing he saw as he mounted the steps was Belle's bottom swaying in rhythmic time to the music. She had a gorgeous derrière, curvy and firm, and when she was dancing it was a work of art in the making, exactly what the average male wanted to see and take advantage of. Even so, he didn't *intend* to take advantage, Dante reminded himself doggedly, because as her potential employer, he would naturally be immune to her appeal. Sex didn't come into his dealings with employees. No matter how tempted he was, he would never ever make that mistake, he assured himself squarely.

'Sit down with me,' he told Belle as he strode past her.

'I can't. This is work time,' she pointed out, her gaze locking on him as though magnetised. 'I should've told you that last night.'

'I arranged it with your boss. You've got an hour off to be with me,' Dante informed her smoothly.

'But this is one of the busiest times of the day!' she exclaimed.

'I'm *paying* for your time off the clock,' Dante told her without hesitation.

Her face burned, hot as hellfire as she settled down at the table he had chosen. Money talked, she knew that, had long accepted it as an unpleasant fact of life. When people paid, they got to break the rules and call the shots. It turned normal into abnormal and deprived her of personal choice. She sat down opposite but her chin came up in challenge. 'I thought you'd come in earlier than this.'

'I slept in,' Dante declared without embarrassment. 'I travelled all day yesterday to get here.'

Belle was tempted to remark that he had undoubtedly travelled in luxury and could have no idea of the exhausting rigours of cheaper modes of travel, but she swallowed back the cheeky comment, accepting that she wasn't in a strong enough position to make it. She knew how to keep her lips sealed when she had to, knew all about serving in respectful silence regardless of how rude or provocative people were. That was one advantage of lowly labour, she acknowledged ruefully: it taught humility.

'I assume that you're considering taking the job?' Dante lifted his level black brows in question as Belle's colleague delivered coffee to the table.

'Yes,' Belle confirmed, throwing sugar into the espresso because there was no milk available, and stirring it in haste. 'But you have to explain it first.'

Dante dragged in a deep breath and his T-shirt stretched taut as the strong muscles beneath the fine cotton flexed. Determined not to stare at his muscular chest, Belle looked at his face instead for the first time since they had sat down. Dazzling dark golden eyes gripped hers and her tummy lurched as if she had been plunged downward on a fairground ride. 'In two weeks' time I have a married couple coming to stay at my home for the weekend—Eddie and Krystal Shriner. I have a very important business deal that I hope to make with Eddie. The fly in the ointment is Krystal, whom I was fleetingly involved with four years ago. She's been trying to get back with me ever since,' he admitted stonily. 'And I don't want her flirting with me in front of her husband because that would destroy any hope I have of making a deal with him. He's a possessive man.'

Involuntarily, Belle's interest was caught. 'Is Krystal the stage-five clinger you mentioned last night?'

Dante nodded grim confirmation. 'Another woman living in my home with me would be a safeguard and the only possible precaution I can take. Your presence would infuriate her, but I will seem a much less attractive option if I appear to have already found a woman to settle down with. Krystal won't risk losing Eddie until she has a viable replacement in her sights.'

Belle grimaced at such calculation and settled back less tensely into her seat. 'Am I allowed to ask how long you were with this woman when you were involved with her?' she asked curiously.

His black brows pleated and his shapely mouth compressed into a flat hard line. 'One weekend…'

'One weekend?' Belle gasped in disbelief. 'And you've had all this trouble with her after that?'

'I didn't say she was normal,' Dante fielded drily.

'And they're going to be staying with you in London?'

'No, not in London,' Dante cut in. 'They'll be staying in my home in Italy.'

Belle was nonplussed. 'But I *thought* you were offering to take me back to London.'

'After the job's done my private jet will take you anywhere you want in the world, but we won't be travelling to London over the next couple of weeks,' Dante warned her. 'If you accept the job, I'll be taking you to Paris for new clothes. You can't possibly pass yourself off as my girlfriend with your current wardrobe. We will then fly to Italy, where you will familiarise yourself with my home and lifestyle. As soon as Eddie and Krystal have departed, the job will be over and you will be free to leave.'

Belle cringed at the prospect of Dante buying her clothes because that reminded her too much of her mother's financially lucrative and rather sordid relationships with men. Tracy was pretty much a professional mistress whose lovers paid for her expensive clothes, jewellery and cruises. Belle had been ashamed when she'd finally worked out the truth of how her mother afforded to live so well without ever apparently having to work and she was no longer surprised that her birth father had spoken with such derision about her mother, referring to her simply as 'the gold-digger'. Evidently even when she had been much younger Tracy had been busier bedding wealthy men than she had been modelling for a living. Belle was merely grateful that her grandparents had never grasped the truth about their daughter.

'So,' Belle said a little desperately as she trailed herself back out of those unpleasant memories and thoughts. 'The job as such would only last for a couple of weeks?'

'*Sì*... Yes,' Dante translated for her when she looked at him blankly.

Digging hurriedly into her pocket, Belle extracted the lists she'd drawn up the night before. 'I have some other questions for you, if that's all right.'

'I suppose it has to be,' Dante conceded, watching her tiny tongue slide out to moisten her full lower lip with a fascination the exercise should not have commanded. Instantly he was imagining that tongue working a spell on his all too ready body and he gritted his teeth hard, furious with his failing self-discipline. He was spoilt when it came to women, he acknowledged, because it was rare for him to meet a woman he wanted that he couldn't have. But she would be working for him. He would be *paying* her. Adding sex to that arrangement would make it dubious in the extreme.

Belle painstakingly read her first question. '"Why do you not have a female friend willing to do this for you?"'

'I did. She changed her mind and decided it was a matter of pride that she have an engagement ring on her finger before facing Krystal. I wasn't prepared to take the pretence that far,' Dante admitted flatly.

'My goodness, you're so much in demand with the women in your life, you must feel positively *hunted*!' Belle trilled back as sweet as sugar.

Dante played safe by taking the comment at face value and shrugged a broad shoulder in dismissal. 'Next question?'

'Charlie's a big deal.'

Dante frowned. 'Charlie? Who's Charlie?'

Belle bridled. 'My dog. You met him last night.'

'He's a dog, not a person. I didn't *meet* him,' Dante told her drily. 'The kennels I mentioned are not far from my home and I can assure you that they offer the very best of care because they've been looking after my late brother's two dogs for me for over a year.'

Belle studied him, aghast. 'You've left your brother's dogs in kennels for over a year?' she gasped in horror. 'Why haven't you brought them home with you?'

'I'm not a dog-oriented person,' Dante reminded her impatiently. 'Look, I can't even believe we're having this stupid conversation about animals. If you must bring the dog, bring it, but it will be sent ahead of us to Italy. It's not coming to Paris with us!'

Belle decided to quit while she was ahead. The arrangement wasn't perfect, but she could see that he thought he was being very generous with that concession and she didn't want to be so demanding that she talked herself out of the job.

'You still haven't said what you're prepared to pay me,' Belle remarked uncomfortably.

'What did you earn working last year?' Dante shot back at her, annoyed that he was going to have to live with a dog under his feet, no matter how briefly. She was an odd little creature, he decided, and far too attached to the dog, but such human quirks and his apparent acceptance of them could well make her seem more convincing in the role he was giving her.

Taken aback by that blunt demand, Belle blinked and told him before she could think better of such honesty.

'Seriously…that's *all*?' Dante checked in apparent disbelief.

Belle reddened. 'That's all but it *was* a live-in position and those always pay less.'

'Multiply that sum by fifty and that's what you'll walk away with in a few weeks' time,' Dante assured her without skipping a beat.

'By *fifty*? You can't pay me that much and buy me clothes into the bargain!' Belle objected in amazement. 'That's an outrageous sum.'

'Deal with it. It's not an outrageous sum to me,' Dante declared. 'And if you make a genuine effort to meet the demands of the role, I'll give you a bonus as well.'

Belle was almost white with shock at the thought of so much money coming her way. Even frantic on-the-spot calculations screamed that that much cash would turn her life around and give her options for the first time ever. She would be able to come up with the deposit to rent a flat in London and organise some sort of educational course to make herself more employable. In fact, the sky would be the limit with a financial nest egg that decent behind her. She was ashamed of the truth, that his offer had made her mentally tear up her pros and cons list because a risk that would improve her life so radically seemed well worth taking. It was not as though she had anything to lose aside from Charlie.

'It'll be like winning the lottery,' she whispered helplessly.

'No, *I'm* the lottery you have apparently won,' Dante contradicted. 'Start getting into *that* role. What I'm willing to pay you will merely be pocket change when compared to the life you would lead living with me.'

'The pocket change wins though,' Belle told him. 'I think living with you will be a real challenge.'

Dante ignored that comment, rising above the temptation to inform her that having *any* woman living below his roof and invading his cherished privacy would be a punishment for him. 'I'll have travelling arrangements made for the dog and I'll pick you up tomorrow.'

'Tomorrow?' she echoed, blinking in surprise. 'That soon?'

'We haven't got time to waste and you can't have much to pack. Give me your phone number,' Dante instructed. 'I'll text you to let you know when we're leaving.'

As Dante cleared the steps down into the car park in a couple of strides to head back to his motorbike, Belle was left in a total daze. She went back to setting tables because she couldn't quite accept that she was leaving the restaurant and that her life could change so suddenly. On the score of packing, Dante had hit the nail on the head because she had very few possessions and an even smaller collection of clothing, she conceded. Though she would give Charlie a bath and a good brush to ensure that he looked his smartest and that he wasn't mistaken for some unloved and neglected stray. She would also have to thoroughly clean the campervan and pass the key back to her boss.

When Dante arrived to collect Belle the following morning she was in floods of tears over parting with the dog and the pet transporters his PA had organised were hovering beside their van, reluctant to step in and hurry matters along. Fortunately, Dante had no such inhibitions.

'Say goodbye to the dog, Belle,' Dante told her. 'It's only for a few days.'

'He's scared,' Belle whispered shakily. 'He's never been in a cage before.'

'Put him in the cage. How are you planning to get him into the UK?' Dante enquired. 'Presumably at some point of the journey he will have to tolerate a cage. This will be good practice for him.'

Charlie went into the cage and cowered at the back of it like a dog expecting to be beaten. Stifling a sob, Belle handed over the paperwork Charlie had arrived in France with two years earlier. 'He looks so pathetic,' she muttered wretchedly.

'Yes, he's feeling very sorry for himself,' Dante agreed, thinking that Charlie should be onstage because he certainly knew how to work an audience. 'But you'll be reunited very soon. Pull yourself together.'

Belatedly, Belle registered that Dante looked very different. No longer casually clad in jeans, he sported an exquisitely tailored dark grey business suit that showcased his tall broad, narrow-hipped physique to perfection. Staring for a moment longer than she was comfortable with, she hurriedly twisted her head away. 'I am perfectly together. I was just upset,' she proclaimed defensively.

'Crying in public is not acceptable unless you're attending a funeral or a wedding. Saying goodbye momentarily to a dog is not a good enough excuse,' Dante informed her as her single bag was dropped in the capacious boot of the car and the driver yanked open the passenger door for them.

'S-sorry,' Belle said in a wobbly voice, turning her tear-stained face away from him as she climbed into the opulent car.

The car ferried them at speed to Toulouse-Blagnac Airport, where they were rushed through the VIP channel at speed to board Dante's private jet. Eyes wide from her first glimpse of the opulent oyster-coloured leather seating and the sumptuous interior, Belle accepted the pile of high-fashion magazines the stewardess brought to her and tried not to stare while the same woman flirted madly with Dante with loads of hair flicking, smiles and a provocative wriggle in her too-tight pencil skirt that would've caught the attention of a dead man. Dante, however, remained remarkably untouched by the display and flipped open a laptop to work. Belle wondered if women always vied for his attention so blatantly and then asked herself why she was even interested.

He was a breathtakingly handsome guy, rich and sophisticated, as alien to her as snow in the summer heat. Her hormones went all out of kilter around him and she felt uncomfortable in her own body as it betrayed her in ways she hadn't expected. It had never occurred to her before that she could be attracted to someone she didn't like, that a mere flashing glance from tigerish dark golden eyes could make her breasts swell and her nipples tighten and a hot dull ache blossom at the junction of her thighs. That weakness was a revelation because it was new to her, but it wasn't something that particularly worried her.

She was convinced that she would never give way

to that kind of temptation because she was painfully aware that sex meant very little unless it was accompanied by genuine feelings. None of her mother's many affairs had lasted or cured Tracy's essential dissatisfaction with her life. And Belle wanted much more for herself than a fleeting sexual thrill or a luxurious lifestyle. She wanted love, a man who would make her feel whole and safe, and when she finally found him, she would have a family with him, recreating the family she had both lost and never really had, she thought fondly. He wouldn't be a commitment-phobe like Dante, who saw women as clingy and probably didn't like children much more than he liked dogs. He would be an ordinary guy, willing to settle down when he met someone who made him happy.

'Have you ever been to Paris before?' Dante asked, watching Belle peer out of the limo windows like a child on a school trip, afraid of missing out on a single sight.

'No.'

'And yet you've been in France for…how long?'

'Almost three years.'

'Why didn't you travel around?'

'I couldn't leave Mrs Devenish or Charlie to look after themselves and, to be honest, I never really had enough money to go off exploring.'

'Then why did you lumber yourself with a dog into the bargain?' Dante enquired drily.

'He wasn't mine initially. Mrs Devenish's niece brought Charlie out here as a gift for her. Unfortunately, she wasn't well enough to look after a puppy, but she did enjoy seeing him round the house,' Belle confided ruefully. 'She was a lovely old lady but her relatives didn't want to accept that she was ill. They liked coming out here in the summer for their holidays and they insisted that I was exaggerating her condition. It took the doctor to convince them otherwise and by that stage, as it turned out, she only had a few more weeks to live.'

'You need to learn how to stand up for yourself more effectively,' Dante censured.

Belle shrugged. 'Only if you can afford to take the consequences and I had neither another job to go to nor anywhere else to live.'

'You shouldn't have put yourself in that position.'

'Haven't I just done the same thing again with you?'

Dante frowned at her in bemusement. 'What are you talking about?'

'Well, I don't have an employment contract or any safeguards with you either...*and* you've now got Charlie to hold over me,' she pointed out, lifting her chin.

'You can't think I'm likely to hold Charlie hostage? Or ditch you in Paris without money?' Dante breathed in a raw undertone, insulted beyond belief by her suspicions.

'Isn't that what I'm saying?' Belle murmured gently. 'Beggars can't be choosers. I've *had* to take the risk of trusting you.'

Dante released his breath in a pent-up hiss of displeasure and said nothing, his lean dark face grim. He didn't enjoy being taxed with the truth.

Belle stepped out of the limousine onto one of the most exclusive streets in Paris and stared wide-eyed at the even more exclusive hotel that Dante was striding towards. Her strained face flushed, and she smoothed down her floral skirt and studied her scuffed boots with embarrassment. She followed him into the foyer, careful to stay behind him and out of sight, almost skidding on the highly polished floor tiles and horribly conscious of the plush silence and the dulled murmur of well-bred voices. She looked up above the atrium entrance to the serried ranks of colonnaded floors above. Never had she been so aware of her shabby appearance and at any moment, if she wasn't careful enough and drew the wrong person's attention, she expected a hand to fall on her shoulder and someone to ask her what she was doing there, because she felt like an intruder.

'You've got very quiet,' Dante remarked as she shot into the lift on his heels and immersed herself in a corner. 'You have a busy schedule this afternoon.'

Belle looked up at him in bewilderment. 'Doing what?'

'Visiting the spa for beauty treatments. Don't ask me what's included,' Dante advised. 'I told my PA you needed a makeover, especially in the defective nail department. I'm afraid that perfect grooming goes with the territory.'

'I'm afraid you're stuck with my defective nails,' Belle countered snidely. 'There's nothing anyone can do with them.'

'Belle...if I was willing to pay the surcharge,' Dante murmured silkily, 'they'd cut off your hands and give you new ones!'

Belle paled and linked her hands together tightly, wanting to nibble nervously but afraid of the reaction she might ignite if she succumbed to temptation. The lift doors whirred silently back and a man in a white jacket began to bow and scrape.

'Our butler. Anything you want or need, you ask him,' Dante informed her, walking out into the vast space awaiting them.

Dumbstruck, Belle wandered across the floor and straight out onto the balcony to lean against the elaborate wrought-iron balustrade and stare in awe at the superlative view of the slender silhouette of the Eiffel Tower, the glass roofs of the Grand Palais and the bell tower of Notre Dame Cathedral.

'Madam...?'

She swivelled to register that the butler held a silver tray and was offering her a glass of champagne. She swallowed hard, only just resisting an urge to pinch herself to see if she was dreaming and grasped the champagne. Her glass in her hand, she was ushered back inside and up the swirling staircase to her bedroom, which was the last word in over-the-top glamour, from its brocaded walls to its soft and inviting velvet seating and subtle eau-de-Nil colouring. Far above her, ornate lace mouldings decorated the ceiling. She hastened into the bathroom and was disappointed to discover that it contained only a shower, although it was a vast wet-room affair that could have coped with a party and took up a good half of the room.

When she came downstairs again, lunch was being served and a young woman in a very stylish suit was using a tablet at Dante's elbow. 'Belle...this is my executive PA, Caterina. She will be scheduling your appointments here because I have meetings to attend.'

Belle sat down opposite Dante to have lunch. Not having eaten since breakfast, she was starving. Dante and his PA talked in Italian while she ate, and she watched Dante's eyes shimmer pure gold in the sun-light before his ridiculously long black lashes skimmed down to shade them. Her mouth ran dry, her throat tightening, sudden nerves assailing her. Her fingers lifted to her mouth and at the exact same moment, Dante flashed a warning look at her. 'Try it and I'll plunge your hands into bowls of ice water!' he threat-ened impatiently.

Her colour rising, Belle dropped her hand back to her lap. 'Stop threatening me!' she snapped back at him.

'You have to learn sometime,' Dante told her while Caterina watched the byplay in seeming fascination. 'I'll take you out to dine somewhere tonight...' He turned back to his PA. 'Make sure she's camera-ready.'

'Why would I need to be camera-ready?' Belle de-manded.

'Because I expect that we will be papped at some stage of the evening.'

'Papped?'

'The paparazzi,' Caterina explained. 'Dante's social life is always hot news in Italy.'

Caterina escorted her downstairs to the spa facili-ties. Belle endured one treatment after another, finally relaxing into the procedures when the less pleasant ex-periences were behind her. She flexed her fake nails, now long and shaped and a pale, barely noticeable pink. She reckoned not a single hair now existed anywhere on her body aside from her brows and her head. The facial and the massage that followed were soothing and the treatments concluded with an appointment with a hair stylist, who lamented at length over the sun damage to her bountiful tresses and then quietly and efficiently transformed her unmanageable mane into a sleek fall as smooth and straight as silk.

Back in her bedroom she was greeted by three women with mobile racks of clothing and cases of other items. Her size established, she didn't get away with being shy. She donned elaborate silky lingerie while the most senior woman muttered about a good foundation for clothing being very important to an elegant appearance. Then she had to model outfit after outfit while the women argued amongst themselves about which colours and designs best suited her. She had never seen such beautiful, expensive material before or garments put together with so exceptional a finish and fit. But considering that Dante only required her to play his girlfriend for one weekend, she couldn't credit the sheer size and diversity of the wardrobe that he evidently deemed necessary. She recalled that she would have to live her role in his home for a few days beforehand but still rolled her eyes at his extravagance. Only when she saw her unfamiliar reflection in a mirror did she stop rolling her eyes and stop worrying about what he had chosen to spend.

There she was garbed in a very slightly sparkly blue dress that might have been specially designed for her, shoestring straps adorning her shoulders, a superbly designed backless bra restraining her exuberant breasts, the hemline swirling well above her knees, her feet shod in perilously high sandals. She looked taller, slimmer, less overwhelmingly busty and she breathed a little easier, grabbing up the clutch that toned with the shoes to go down the stairs.

* * *

'Very classy...' Dante pronounced approvingly, watching her descent from below, and yet there was the strangest kernel of disappointment at the heart of his reaction. He realised in surprise that on some level he had liked the untamed curls, the youthful eccentric clothes, and that truth shook him. Indisputably, Belle looked more gorgeous than the first time he had seen her but somehow, inexplicably, she had been hotter and sexier in her own natural style.

'You're getting what you paid for,' Belle fielded with an awkward shrug.

His dark deep-set eyes flared with golden highlights. 'Don't dwell on that aspect. It's not important.'

Dante studied her long shapely legs and imagined lifting the skirt and running his hands up those slim, smooth thighs. A very faint shudder ran through him as he stamped down hard on that lusty image and attempted to quell the heat at his groin while reminding himself that he wasn't going to go there, wasn't going to yield to that kind of dangerous impulse. Of course, he would have to touch her. In the roles they were playing, a certain amount of physical contact was unavoidable, but he would ensure that it was only enough to give a superficial if convincing impression.

In the lift, the lustrous glow of Dante's stunning eyes sent tiny little tremors travelling up through Belle's legs. She felt weak, dizzy, and the lift felt claustrophobic. At the very heart of her she could feel a pulse pounding out her tension like a drum while her breasts ached beneath her clothing. Attraction, just stupid body chemistry, she told herself dismissively as she climbed into the back of the glossy limousine awaiting them.

The silence hummed as she gazed back at him, every nerve ending in her body tight with tension. His eyes were brilliant gold, striking, utterly compelling and she swallowed hard. Dante succumbed to a 'what the hell?' prompt, because he had never been into self-denial. How the blazes could they hope to pretend to be lovers if he had yet to even touch her? he asked himself. That was nonsense. That decision forged, he reached out a hand and she clasped it, allowing him to propel her across the seat into his arms. She went without even having to think about it, her heart pounding so fast she felt light-headed.

His big hands framing her face, he kissed her with so much hunger she was blown away by the experience. Her heart raced even faster, her body tense and throbbing on the edge of an anticipation she had never felt before. Her tense fingers clenched into the collar of his jacket. He crushed her lips with a groan and his tongue stole between them, delving deep for a skilful exploration that acted like a wake-up call for every fibre of her being. Nobody had ever made her feel what he was making her feel and it was wildly unexpected and unbelievably exciting, and the experience engulfed her like an avalanche. She was in over her head before she knew it.

'Bad timing, *amante*,' Dante growled, his hips arching up slightly as she braced a steadying hand on a lean masculine thigh, dangerously close to the tented fabric doing a very poor job of concealing his excitement. For the first time in his life he *wanted* a woman to be bold and he waited for a split second; however, frustratingly, she made no move. 'I can tell the driver to drive us around…'

That suggestion spooked Belle. She moistened her swollen lower lip, her attention locked to his reddened mouth, her entire being, it seemed, caught up in the need for him to touch her again and satisfy the surge of need that had come out of nowhere to make her tremble and perspire. 'Er…'

'*Madonna mia… Ti voglio…* I want you,' Dante framed raggedly, claiming her ripe lips with his again at the same time as he pressed her hand to the part of him that most craved her attention.

Her fingers spread across the fabric, hesitantly tracing the long thick length of him through the fine fabric of his trousers, and that suddenly she was into frighteningly unfamiliar territory because she never ever played the tease, never encouraged where she had no plans to deliver, but just then she was dealing with a level of temptation new to her. No man had ever got her to the point where she wanted more than a kiss or even to the point where she truly wanted *him*. In a matter of minutes, Dante had accomplished both feats and shocked her witless because in his arms she was learning that even logical thought was more of a challenge than she could manage.

Her startled eyes flew up to his smouldering appraisal and she burned inside and out, her temperature climbing in direct response to the predatory hunger she saw in him and that on some level she actually craved. 'I thought we were going to eat,' she reminded him shakily, striving with a sense of cowardice to escape a situation that she knew she had helped to create because she hadn't said no and she hadn't pushed him away.

'I can feed you back at the hotel,' Dante husked, catching her hand in his as she backed away from him to prevent her retreat.

'Sex isn't part of our arrangement…is it?' Belle demanded in sudden dismay.

'Of course not,' Dante assured her silkily, smoothing her small fingers in his to keep her close. 'But what we choose to do outside those boundaries is our business alone.'

'Er, well…yes, but I don't think we should be getting *too* friendly,' Belle mumbled in an awkward rush, trailing her hand free of his.

'There has to be a certain degree of familiarity visible between us or nobody is ever going to believe that we're lovers,' Dante countered with reluctant amusement.

Belle hadn't thought of that aspect of their pretend relationship and she wanted to kick herself for not thinking of it sooner because she had literally walked blind into a brick wall.

'You seem very…nervous,' Dante selected, scrutinising her troubled face with a growing frown. 'I may want you but I promise that I'm not going to try to force you into anything you don't want.'

Belle flushed and straightened her spine, embarrassed that she had made him feel that he had to give her that reassurance. 'I know. But to be honest, er… I'm a bit out of my depth with you.'

'How?' Dante shifted lithely back into his corner,

teeth gritting at the biting ache of unfulfillment nagging at him.

'I haven't got a lot of experience,' Belle admitted stiffly. 'I probably should've said no sooner.'

'How much is "not a lot"?' Dante prompted drily.

Belle sucked in a steadying breath. 'I'd rather not go into that.'

'You needn't be shy, nor should you feel that you have to lie for my benefit,' Dante murmured loftily. 'I see women as equals. I *prefer* experienced partners.'

'Well, then, I wouldn't suit you at all!' Belle confided in a tone of stark relief. 'I haven't had a, er, partner yet.'

That statement disconcerted Dante so much that for a split second he simply frowned down at her with astonished dark golden eyes. 'You *can't* be a virgin!'

As he spoke the door beside him was abruptly opened by the driver and both of them were taken by surprise, neither of them having noticed that the car had stopped, and Belle was miraculously rescued from the need to respond to his incredulous statement. In his wake, she slid along the back seat, struggling to keep the skirt of her dress from lifting as she alighted. In what had to be her worst nightmare, just as she was attempting to keep her underwear choices a secret known only to her, the flashbulbs of cameras went off, blinding and disorientating her as she fought to climb out gracefully in her high heels. Mercifully, Dante saved her from a clumsy exit by reaching down to grab her hand with his and he practically pulled her up and out of the limo, giving her the chance to find her feet and discreetly smooth down her rucked frock.

In the crowded entrance foyer, so impervious to

the presence of the photographers that he hadn't even spared them a glance, Dante stared broodingly down at her and said again, proving that his mind was still on the conversation she had gratefully abandoned, 'You can't be…'

And Belle's second-worst nightmare came true with those words. She felt the awful burn of that hot familiar tide of colour sweeping up her body in a mortifying tide.

'And a blushing one,' Dante pronounced in even greater disbelief. 'You're supposed to be as much of an urban legend as unicorns.'

CHAPTER THREE

'WE'RE NOT GOING to discuss this any more,' Belle told Dante heatedly as they were ushered through a crowded room of staring diners to a well-lit velvet-lined booth in the corner.

'Don't kid yourself. When you said we had to know stuff about each other, that is definitely something a man would *need* to know,' Dante fielded grimly.

'Not in our situation, it's not,' Belle argued. 'We're only faking it.'

'What would you know about faking it?' Dante enquired witheringly.

'Stop it!' Belle hissed between clenched teeth in a sharp aside before she took a seat. 'If you don't stop embarrassing me, I'll look like a tomato all evening!'

'You could've told me the truth upfront!' Dante replied, still pointed in tone as he spread open the wine list, signalled the hovering maître d' and ordered wines in fluent French.

Belle pressed the cool backs of her hands to her cheeks in an effort to ratchet down her inner heat source. '*Why* should I have told you?'

'I feel short-changed and like I'm about to throw a

baby into a snake pit!' Dante groaned in frustration, wondering if he had chosen the wrong woman entirely for the role. 'You are manifestly unsuited to pretending to be my sexy lover. How on earth are you going to pull that off?'

'You don't have to have sex to be sexy,' Belle whispered vehemently across the table. 'Not five minutes ago you were all over me!'

'If I'd been all over you, we'd still have been in the limo and I wouldn't be in need of a cold shower,' Dante parried drily. 'I kissed you. Let's not get lost in virginal exaggeration.'

'Just *lose* that word from your vocabulary!' Belle tossed, taking refuge behind her menu and making hasty selections, desperate to change the subject. 'It embarrasses me. I wish I'd lied now.'

Dante ordered the food and lounged back in his chair, narrowed sardonic dark eyes welding to her still-flushed face. 'So, tell me why… Religious scruples?'

'My grandparents didn't encourage me to go out and about when I was younger because we lived in a rough area and they were worried about my safety. Then I was restricted by having to stay home as a carer. It wasn't a conscious decision, but lack of opportunity is certainly part of it,' Belle acknowledged, gratefully sipping the water poured for her, soothing her tight vocal cords. 'And that's all I've got to say on the subject.'

'I'm still not satisfied,' Dante admitted, tasting the wine and indicating that it could be poured.

'It's absolutely none of your business,' she told him quietly when they were alone again.

'You made it my business when you made me want

you,' Dante contradicted ruefully. 'Now it seems clear that you're one of those women who decides to stay as pure as the driven snow until she marries.'

'I didn't say that I was saving myself for marriage,' Belle pointed out. 'And I'm not. But I only want intimacy if it comes with a serious relationship.'

'I won't offer you a serious relationship.'

'Of course not,' Belle conceded. 'Anyway, I'm working for you, so there won't be anything of that nature to worry about.'

Dante reminded himself that he too had believed at the outset of their agreement that there was no room for sex in it. But from the minute he had touched her, something had indisputably changed for him. He had acknowledged that he wanted her, and all his reservations had vanished at the same moment, which he supposed made him a fairly typical male, driven by his libido. He didn't want her to be out of reach, he didn't want to hear that she would only share a bed with a man if she was in a serious relationship and he was still wondering how she would stand up to Krystal, who oozed sex appeal.

'I'm just waiting to meet the right person,' Belle extended quietly, hoping to defuse the tension with that admission.

'And what is that right person going to be like?' Dante asked with helpless curiosity.

'Someone who matches me. Look, I don't want to talk about this any more. It's too private and personal,' Belle told him abruptly. 'Subject closed.'

Frustration gusted through Dante. 'I suppose you mean someone crazy about dogs.'

'That wouldn't be the most important thing, no,' she countered uncomfortably. 'I accept that I'll have to compromise, and that one person can't possibly meet all my expectations.'

'I suppose you have a list drawn up for that too,' Dante guessed. 'A shopping list of requirements.'

'I'm not shopping.' Belle lifted her chin.

Silence fell. The first course arrived and they ate. By the arrival of the next, Belle had relaxed again, refusing to think about what Dante thought of her because it wasn't important. Like a shooting star, he would only be in her life for a very short space of time and it would be foolish to start worrying about his opinion of her because ultimately it didn't matter, she told herself firmly. No doubt she sounded old-fashioned and naïve to him, but she knew what she wanted and needed and she wasn't about to apologise for it.

'You haven't told me a thing about yourself yet,' she reminded him quietly.

'Background…' Dante shifted a shoulder in a dismissive shrug. 'I'm twenty-eight. My family made their fortune in banking. My father married my mother because she is the daughter of a prince and he was born a prince. They set a very high value on their titles even though the Italian Republic no longer recognises those titles. They had two children because they wanted a son to inherit the title—the heir and the spare. I was the spare,' Dante explained tightly, his sensual mouth twisting at the designation. 'There was a lot of pressure on my brother, Cristiano, to be exactly what my parents wanted him to be. So he went into the bank because they demanded it of him even though it wasn't what he wanted to do with his life.'

'And what about you?' Belle whispered. 'What did they want from you?'

'They barely took notice of my existence. I was simply insurance in case anything ever happened to my older brother,' Dante admitted. 'And tragically, the worst happened. Cristiano messed up an investment fund at the bank. Instead of coming to me for advice and help, and feeling unable to face our parents' criticism, he took an overdose...and then he was gone.'

Belle had paled. His pain at that admission had tightened every muscle in his lean, darkly handsome face and his strain was painfully evident. 'I'm so sorry, Dante.'

'Do you know what my parents said to me at his funeral?' Dante breathed in a raw undertone. 'That he was never meant to *be* the elder son, that he was utterly unsuited to the responsibility and that *I* would be much stronger in the role. They didn't grieve for him because as far as they were concerned he was a social embarrassment and a screw-up.'

'That's awful,' Belle murmured urgently, reaching for his hand, which had clenched into a fist on the table-top, and smoothing her fingers gently over his. 'They can't possibly have meant it!'

'Oh, they meant it all right,' Dante contradicted with hard conviction as he pushed his plate away with his free hand. 'I wasn't surprised but I'll never get over the guilt because I *could've* saved him.'

'How?' she exclaimed in surprise at the claim.

'*I* could have stepped in and taken over at the bank.

I was better qualified. *I* could have made the socially acceptable marriage and provided the next generation. Instead I did what I wanted to do and left him to sink or swim. The best advice I had to offer was for him to walk away but he didn't have the heart to do that because he was desperate, always *desperate*, for our parents' approval,' he completed gruffly.

'That's not your fault. He did what he had to do, and you did what you had to do. Whatever happened, one of you was going to be unhappy, and as your older brother he chose to take the hit,' she reasoned ruefully.

'Let's move on to something less contentious,' Dante murmured, taken aback that he had told her so much and disconcerted by the shimmer of sympathetic tears in her big violet eyes. She was the touchy-feely type just as Cristiano had been and being that way inclined, being vulnerable, was like sticking your head up above the parapet to invite a punch in the face.

'Yes, tell me about where you went to school…and I suppose you went to university,' Belle said, unsurprised by his nod of confirmation. 'We'll just stick to easy facts, the sort of stuff I should know about you.'

The rest of the meal went surprisingly well and by the time they were climbing back into the limo, Belle felt calm enough to ignore the single lingering paparazzo with a camera, who stole another shot of them together.

'Your favourite colour?' she pressed Dante again.

'I don't have one.'

'Everyone has one.'

'Blue… You dressed in blue,' Dante said teasingly, highly amused by her interest in trivia like his birthdate, his favourite foods and sports, none of which he considered remotely important or likely to be of use to her. 'Blue brings out your eyes. I'm going to have to buy you some jewellery. Don't men who live with women buy them jewellery as gifts?'

Belle wrinkled her nose. 'Oh, don't spend any more, for goodness' sake! I'll only be leaving it behind me. I couldn't possibly accept jewellery as part of the deal... unless you could buy fakes,' she suggested, looking at him with sudden hope. 'There are very good fakes around now.'

'I'm not putting you in fakes!' Dante told her, studying her with incredulous dark golden eyes. '*Madre di Dio*... You haven't got the sense you were born with, have you?'

Her brow furrowed. 'What do you mean by that?'

'Because a woman wanting to feather her nest would never ever suggest that I buy her fake diamonds. She would want and expect the real thing, even if it was just to sell it at a later date,' he pointed out drily.

'But I'm *not* out to feather my own nest,' Belle argued, her colour heightening. 'I'll be more than content to be paid at the end of this. Anything more than giving me the means to go home and get my life started again would be excessive.'

'Allow me to decide what is excessive.' Dante surveyed her with mounting hunger, his attention lingering on the smooth satiny skin below her throat while he imagined putting his mouth there before toying at his leisure with the sultry curve to her lower lip. He marvelled at how misleading that pouty pink sultriness was. She was a sensual, sexy woman in denial of her nature and she was saving herself up for some no doubt imaginary and perfect hero, who would disappoint her. The idea of Belle being disappointed galled Dante and he asked himself why when he deemed disappointment to be one of life's certainties. Like his current desire for her, he ruminated sardonically. He imagined that once he had her, he would no longer want her. And wasn't that exactly why he should leave her alone and untouched? He frowned because that little moral question reminded him very much of his brother, who had always been kinder and less ruthless than Dante. When had he ever had *anything* in common with Cristiano apart from the blood in their veins?

CHAPTER FOUR

'I'M PLANNING TO have a drink,' Dante announced when they walked back into the hotel suite. 'Do you want one?'

'No, thanks.' Belle wandered restively round the room. 'I wonder how Charlie's doing.'

'He's doing fine. I got a text and a photo earlier. He's eaten and settled in for the night. I meant to mention it,' Dante asserted, tugging out his phone.

Belle darted over to him and stared down at the photo of Charlie in what looked like a very comfortable dog run. He was snuggled up, nose to tail, in a well-padded dog bed. 'He looks sad,' she sighed. 'Have you any photos of your brother's dogs?'

'I'm afraid not.'

'Why didn't you try to find them a new home?' Belle asked ruefully.

'Cristiano left me a letter. He wanted me to keep them.'

'Yes, but he probably assumed you'd keep them at home with you,' Belle pointed out and then winced. 'Sorry, forget I said that. It was totally tactless.'

'But spot on,' Dante fielded, pouring himself what

he imagined would only be his first hard drink of the night. 'Go to bed. I feel like drowning my sorrows.'

'I can't leave you down here alone when you're feeling bad!' Belle protested with a troubled look in her eyes.

'Of course, you can,' Dante asserted. 'I'm not a child you have to worry about.'

She wondered if he had ever got to be a child secure in the love of his parents. They hadn't sounded very loving towards him and his brother. It made her look back on all the years that she had felt sorry for herself because she had neither a father nor a mother who loved her. Yet all along she had had her grandparents loving and supporting her, making up in every way they could for her parents' lack of interest.

'From what you've said about him, I don't think your brother would've wanted you feeling this way,' she murmured uncertainly, fearful of intruding too much.

'And what would you know about it?' Dante derided.

'Nothing,' she agreed apologetically. 'But if he was a kind person, he wouldn't have wanted you beating yourself up about what can't be changed.'

And that was perfectly true, Dante acknowledged grudgingly. Cristiano had always been an optimist who hated dwelling on the darker elements of life. He had made the best of situations, had even tried to make the best he could of the parents he had been born to, tolerating and forgiving their biting scorn and continual demands.

Dante strode forward. 'Stop looking at me with those big sad eyes,' he breathed hoarsely.

'I'm not sad. I just wanted to make you feel better.' Belle sighed.

'Come to bed with me, then. *That* would be guaranteed to make me feel better, *amante*,' Dante growled soft and low, the dark roughened vowel sounds in his voice snaking down her spine like a rough caress.

Belle clashed in consternation with glittering dark golden eyes that made the breath hitch in her tight throat. 'No, that would be a bad idea.'

'Not to my mind,' Dante intoned, catching both her hands in his and tugging her closer. 'You should've got away while you had the chance.'

Her face flamed because she knew that she hadn't wanted to leave him alone. He tempted her as no one ever had and his confession about his brother had made him seem treacherously human and vulnerable, chipping away at her original dislike. It had taught her a lesson too, taught her not to make assumptions about people and assume that wealth cushioned them from the tragedies of life. Going straight to bed, steering clear of spending more time with Dante Lucarelli, would have been the sensible thing to do, but seeing him standing by the windows with a drink in his hand and looking so very alone had bothered her even though there was nothing she could do or say to change anything.

Belle lifted her chin and looked up at him. 'I know you'll let me go if I ask you to.'

'And you won't ask me because you don't *want* me to let you go,' Dante murmured in silken challenge as he trailed a reproving fingertip across a pink cheek, down to the incredibly inviting lush pink of her mouth. 'Well, don't say you weren't warned...'

He leant down and captured her mouth with his, driving her lips apart with the power of his hungry kiss, and she shivered as heat darted through her chilled body, warming every inch of her. She wanted more, she knew she wanted more, knowing that if nothing else when she made no objection to being scooped off her feet and carried over to an armchair where he draped her across his lap without once freeing her mouth again. A quivering intensity of response gripped her as his tongue stroked between her lips to explore.

'The taste of you is sublime,' Dante husked against her throat, his breath see-sawing in and out of his chest. 'But it is also dangerously addictive.'

Belle was amazingly aware of his hand on her thigh, his fingers smoothing below the hem of her dress and moving higher, and she had never wanted anything quite as much as she craved his touch because, even with every muscle in her body taut with denial, a subversive ache between her legs betrayed her with every plundering delve of his tongue. As he skimmed the taut stretch of her panties aside, her fingers speared into his black hair. She didn't know what she was doing, and she didn't care at that moment. Indeed, her only recognisable fear was that he would stop.

And then he touched her, a mere roll of a fingertip against the taut little bud below her mound and her body went haywire, her hips rising in a languorous roll, sweet and frighteningly strong sensation piercing her in a stormy wave. He sat her up and she uttered a little sound of complaint at that moment of disconnection as he unzipped her dress and pulled it down, the unclipped her bra with wicked dexterity so that her unbound breasts tumbled taut and full into his hands.

With a hungry groan, Dante caught a straining pink nipple in his mouth, bending her back over his arm to ravage the bounty he had uncovered. He was fiercely aroused and dimly amused at himself for playing around like a teenager instead of moving single-mindedly from A to Z to extract his own satisfaction as fast as possible. But there was, he was discovering, a shocking satisfaction to be found in her inexperienced responses, in the little gasping sounds she made low in her throat and the increasingly frantic grip of her fingers in his hair. He teased the damp flesh at the heart of her, tracing her body in a caress that almost sent her up in flames in his arms, and then gently exploring to learn that she was even tighter than he had expected.

Belle arched and panted into his mouth, helpless in his arms, her hips rocking instinctively as the pressure in her pelvis built higher and tightened like a band of steel inside her. She was reaching for that perfect moment, blind, deaf, utterly mindless when with one skilful flick of a finger he sent her flying into the sun. She shuddered and cried out, aftershocks of reaction convulsing her as he curved her up to him to taste her mouth one last time. And for timeless moments she lay there in his arms, ostensibly relaxed by the release of all tension but with her brain already leaping back to life to leave her deeply shaken by what she had allowed to happen.

In an instant she was off his lap, gazing down at him, connecting with brilliant dark, glittering eyes.

'The third time you're in my arms, I *will* be taking

you to bed,' Dante murmured slumberously. 'Just putting that warning out there…'

'You know that's not what I want,' Belle began awkwardly, her face burning because she was painfully aware that her behaviour with him was hard to defend.

'You may be a contrary woman, but you want me,' Dante incised with complete assurance.

And he was right, shamelessly, mortifyingly right to the extent that Belle didn't bother staying around to argue with that statement. Her head as high as she could still hold it, she went up to her bedroom and shut the door, a sudden empty hollow feeling assailing her because Dante was still downstairs and every wanton cell in her body wanted him with her. She was learning that nothing was as black and white as she had believed it to be. Desire didn't simply switch off because she didn't want to feel it and desire was a much more significant temptation than she had realised. When Dante kissed her, when Dante held her close, she turned weak and dizzy with longing. Yet longing for and downright *craving* a man who would want nothing more from her than the fleeting pleasure her body could offer him could only lead to *her* unhappiness.

Even so, for the first time she was questioning that she had to love and care for a man before she would have sex with him. Obviously, Dante had no deep feelings for her, and the sense of being close to him that his honesty about his brother's death had awakened in her was dangerously misleading. Was that what had happened to her? Had her sympathy bled over into some strange desire to comfort him that had somehow turned into a sexual invitation? She hadn't meant that to happen and was annoyed that she had failed to call a halt.

Bemusement about her exact motivation and discomfiture over her own conduct kept Belle lying awake for a long time. She accepted that she was discovering stuff about herself with Dante that she would have sooner not known. No matter how hard she tried, she couldn't stamp out her attraction to him, nor could she remain level-headed enough to stay in control in his arms. All she could do now, she reasoned ruefully, was be on her guard and endeavour not to offer Dante any more conflicting signals.

Dante had a cold shower and wondered why he hadn't simply swept Belle straight off to his bed. He was considerably more disturbed by the inexplicable truth that even foreplay with Belle was more exciting than anything he had ever had with another woman. She turned him on, hard and fast, and then she melted with delicious response whenever he touched her. Instead of being furious with her for walking away without giving him the satisfaction he needed, he was already thinking with anticipation about the next time she succumbed to the same hunger that was currently tormenting him. And then maybe *he* would walk away to teach *her* a lesson.

Picturing that scenario, Dante grinned with helpless amusement, knowing that the last thing he would do was walk away. He wouldn't have the self-discipline to walk away because he had let her get under his skin, let her light him up for the first time ever with a fiery need to possess one particular woman. And why was that? Or what was it about her that had penetrated his defences?

What, for instance, had made him talk so very honestly about losing Cristiano? It was true that she would need that background to understand his family set-up and why the land deal was so very important to him. But he had shared details he didn't need to share, drawn out by her warmth and those big compassionate eyes that seemed to offer understanding. In all likelihood it was all an act on her part, he told himself sagely, and she was striving to impress him, possibly hoping to stay in his life for longer than two short weeks.

The following morning, Belle was in a surprisingly good mood. She had behaved foolishly the night before, but she knew that she couldn't turn back time and magically eradicate her mistake. All she could do was avoid getting too close to Dante and start trying to treat him more like her employer. Furthermore, the sun was shining, and she would hopefully be reunited with Charlie soon. More clothing had arrived for her to try and it was a definite treat to skim through the different items and pick a brand-new outfit to wear. She chose a light skirt and top combination, but she frowned at her hair, which was displaying defiant waves again after only one short evening of behaving like her fantasy straight hair. Her true self was fighting to come out again, she thought ruefully, and Dante would just have to accept that she couldn't look perfectly groomed all the time.

'A jeweller is visiting after breakfast,' Dante informed her as she came down the stairs, trying to evade his gaze without being too obvious about it while her colour rose like a banner to advertise her self-consciousness. 'And

then we're heading out to shop for furniture and some
other items. Tomorrow, we'll fly home to Italy.'

'Why would we need to shop for furniture?' Belle
asked as she settled down at the breakfast table with
him.

'You're moving in with me. Presumably a woman
moving in with a man would have items she wanted
to bring with her. You have nothing, so we will have
to buy some stuff. I want us to look like an authentic
couple, to my staff and everyone else in my life,' Dante
admitted calmly. 'That we are only pretending has to
remain *our* secret.'

'Charlie's authentic,' Belle pointed out helplessly. 'I
am moving in my dog.'

Dante lounged back in his chair to study her. In silk
that accentuated the swell of her breasts and somehow
enhanced the satiny softness of her pale skin, she looked
incredibly sensual and very touchable. He watched as
she tucked a stray strand of bright hair behind one small
ear and nibbled at her lower lip and reminded himself
that seducing her would be cruel, because he was never
going to offer her the serious relationship she wanted.
He breathed in deep, recognising the erotic pulse gain-
ing strength at his groin, and he shifted position in outright denial of her libidinous effect on him. 'Charlie's
not enough on his own. We need to buy you some artworks and some presentable pieces of furniture.'

Her smooth brow furrowed. '*Art?* Why would I need
artworks?'

'Part of your new image. You're an art lover like
me,' Dante told her.

'Yes, I do like some art,' Belle conceded thoughtfully. 'But not on the sort of level you would admire. I agreed to do this, Dante, but I didn't agree to pretend to be someone I'm not.'

An ebony brow lifted enquiringly. 'Meaning?'

'The relationship may be fake but, while I'm in it, I'm going to be *me*,' Belle informed him stiffly. 'I'm not going to fake being something I'm not, so I don't want fancy artworks or furniture. I'm an ordinary working woman and I wouldn't know where to begin acting as if I was someone much fancier and richer.'

'That's quite a speech and I appreciate the sentiments you express but I don't see what difference it makes in our circumstances.'

'Well, then, you're not listening,' Belle interrupted more sharply. 'I'm me and I'm *staying* me because that way I'm less likely to make mistakes. I've been a house-keeper, a carer and a waitress, and I won't pretend otherwise.'

'And if you're not part of my world, how am I supposed to have met the *real* you?' Dante asked very drily.

'Make it a funny story. I served you in a bar one night? You met me when you visited someone I was looking after or working for... You picked me up when I was hitchhiking? Use your imagination. Maybe you're moving in with me because I'm *different* from the other women you've had in your life. Don't try to make me hide the real me, as if that is something to be ashamed of,' Belle urged ruefully.

'You're very stubborn.'

'And so are you.'

'Consequently, no artworks?' Dante checked with a

censorious shake of his arrogant dark head. 'But there has to be some furniture, so that you can turn some room in my house into *your* room… Isn't that what women do when they move in with a man?'

Belle shrugged. 'How would I know? And it's an awful lot of fuss and expense to go to simply to put on an act for one weekend,' she reasoned, searching his lean bronzed features with curiosity sparkling in her dark blue eyes. 'Presumably you think getting this business deal is worth any amount of trouble.'

'Pretty much,' Dante agreed.

'Well, then, if it's just one room I could choose a comfortable chair, a small table, bookshelves…oh, and books,' she added reflectively, her eyes warming at the prospect. 'But brand-new furniture won't look very convincing—'

'We'll buy antiques,' Dante incised in a tone of finality.

'But you're not going to expect me to pretend to be something I'm not?' Belle pressed, seeking reassurance.

'No,' Dante conceded, marvelling that he was giving way on that point for in truth he had planned to set her up with an entire false identity, which would have protected his privacy and her anonymity. 'You appreciate that the media will take a much stronger interest in me hooking up with a waitress?'

'I'll be out of your life again before anyone has even identified me,' Belle parried confidently, lifting her head, vibrant waves of copper-red hair shifting across her shoulders and glinting fierily in the light.

'It goes against the grain to admit it, but I liked your hair better before the beauty consultants in the spa got their hands on you. Curly hair suits you,' Dante framed, already questioning what he was saying and frowning at that unplanned dive into personal comment as he sprang lithely upright to greet the older man with a large leather case and his accompanying security guard being shown into the room. 'Monsieur Duchamp, you are very welcome.'

Belle tugged her fingers down from the hair she had involuntarily been touching. He liked her hair better when it was *au naturel*. Well, what did you know? She was astonished but decidedly flattered.

An hour later, she was sporting a designer watch and bracelet, sapphire-and-diamond earrings and a sapphire-and-diamond pendant, the absolute basics without which Dante had insisted she could not perform her role.

The limousine dropped them on the Carré Rive Gauche, which was full of antiques dealers and the kind of esoteric shops haunted by interior designers. Belle found herself much more interested in what was on offer there than she had expected to be because the sheer quirkiness of some of the items intrigued her.

'You're seeing stuff that interests you,' Dante noted.

'I like finding out the history behind them… I like that seat,' she said, pointing at an elaborately upholstered and very comfortable-looking low-slung armchair.

The proprietor, quick to recognise Dante for the rich buyer that he was, hastened over to talk about the chair and demonstrated the weird way part of the arms swivelled back at a touch. Their exchange of French was too fast for her to follow and Belle stared up at Dante in surprise as he began to laugh. Poised there with his dark eyes gleaming with intense amusement, his lean, darkly handsome features relaxed, he was so breathtakingly beautiful and male that she couldn't take her eyes off him.

'What's so funny?' Belle whispered.

'I'll tell you later. We're taking the chair... Come on, keep looking,' Dante urged, one long-fingered hand pressing against her taut spine as he walked her along with him. 'You have a whole room to fill and none of the rooms in my home are small.'

A fat sofa, an Indian carved bookcase, a small inlaid table, a beautiful mirror and an eccentric art deco drinks cabinet followed in quick succession.

'And as an ordinary girl, how am I supposed to have acquired all these valuable items?' Belle enquired with reluctant amusement.

'They are all gifts from me,' Dante teased with a smile. 'I've also ordered a selection of English classics and contemporary novels for you from a bookseller.'

In the limo on the way back to the hotel, he told her that he was taking her out for dinner again and then on to a club. Belle was lazily contemplating the options in her new wardrobe when Dante appeared in the doorway.

'Rain check, I'm afraid,' he murmured quietly. 'There's been a fatal accident on one of my wind farms in Brittany and I have to visit the site. I don't know when I'll get back but it could be the early hours. We'll still be flying to Italy in the morning.'

'Fatal?' she queried in dismay.

Dante nodded. 'A construction engineer fell in one of the turbine towers,' he told her grimly.

'That's dreadful. Will you be seeing his family?'

'Yes,' Dante replied gravely. 'And checking out whether or not safety procedures were correctly followed. There'll have to be an enquiry.'

Belle dined in solitary state at the grand dining table, went for a shower and changed into her pyjamas. Before she returned downstairs, she succumbed to curiosity and entered Dante's bedroom. It was scrupulously tidy with no sign of his hasty departure, but she wasn't there to snoop, she was there to check out whether her suspicions were correct. And they were. There *was* a bath in the palatial suite but it was in the bathroom off the master bedroom. It was the bath of her dreams as well, a huge oval tub with a fantastic view of Paris.

Belle had always loved baths, but she hadn't lived anywhere with a bath for several years. Everyone was putting in showers now. Mrs Devenish's family had had her original bath taken out and replaced with a shower in which she could safely sit. Belle had missed treating herself to the luxury of a bath and she wondered if she dared make use of Dante's while he was out but that idea, tempting as it was, struck her as too cheeky and she went back downstairs and watched television instead.

Around ten, the image of that bath overcame her reluctance and, with a sigh of acceptance, she scrambled up, switched off the television and went to take advantage of it. The bathroom was packed with bath preparations in designer pots and she made liberal use of one of them before pinning her hair up in a clasp and climbing in to lower herself slowly into the deliciously scented warm water. Resting her head back on the padded pillow, she sighed, deciding that she was in heaven as she relaxed, truly relaxed for the first time in months.

She realised that she had dozed off only after a noise startled her into wakefulness again. Water sloshing noisily around her, she jerked up into sitting position, needing a moment even to appreciate where she was. Registering that she was *still* in Dante's bathroom, she froze for a split second until she heard quick steps on the wooden stairs and then, swiftly depressing the plug to empty out the water, she launched herself upright in sheer panic. She almost fell as she raced across the slippery tiles to snatch up a big grey towel, winding it round her as fast as she could. She was cursing herself for invading his bathroom, which she had planned to leave immaculate so that no one would even know that she had used it. All hope of that remaining a secret was now gone with water very noisily draining out of the bath and an array of wet footprints and splashes marking the high-shine floor tiles.

Dante was not in a good mood on his return. Dealing with the man's broken-hearted family had been distressing, and learning that the guy had suffered from vertigo but had concealed it because he had been desperate for a good job had been even less pleasant. And then he saw his bedroom door was lying open and emerging from the en-suite bathroom was a very red-faced Belle, wrapped in a towel and clutching a bundle of clothing to her breasts. She looked so guilty and so embarrassed, it was comical.

'What on earth are you doing in here?' Dante intoned in wonderment, trying very hard not to laugh.

Belle hopped off one bare foot onto the other. 'Your

room has a bath… Mine doesn't. I didn't think you'd mind if you weren't here…but I didn't get around to cleaning up, I'm afraid, because I wanted to be out of here before you caught me.'

'And look how well that turned out,' Dante commented.

'I'll come straight back and clean up once I've got dressed,' she told him apologetically, her face on fire. 'I swear I wasn't snooping or anything. That's probably what you think but I didn't touch or look at anything in here. I just missed having baths and I was tempted.'

As Dante was tempted, appraising her curvy little body in the towel, noting how the tight hold she had on the clothing merely accentuated the magnificent swell of her breasts over the towel. Pale, lightly speckled flesh that he had already touched and tasted, and which had only ignited his hunger for more of the experience. Her hair was piled up in a glorious curly mass, innumerable little tendrils escaping to accentuate the flushed oval of her face, dominated by huge violet eyes and that glorious mouth. It was every fantasy Dante had ever had of her rolled into one and he went instantly hard. She was also the distraction he badly needed after the evening he had endured.

'You look amazing,' he told her gruffly because she did, all bright and flushed and embarrassed in her bare feet but somehow, for all her diminutive size, extraordinarily vibrant, full of life and sass.

'I hardly think so… You're a guy, it's probably just the bath towel,' she deflected tautly, because she was painfully aware that she wanted him to mean what he had said.

'No, it's you…all you,' Dante husked, logic kicking in to demolish his reservations and neatly shift him to where he wanted to be. As they had both acknowledged, it wasn't a normal job that he had given her, and it would also be an extremely temporary one. 'Forget the rules about what you should and shouldn't do, ditch the lists and the expectations. Just *be* with me because you *want* to be.'

Belle was rigid with tension and then a little quiver ran through her, her breathing quickening. She hadn't expected him to be that bold, hadn't been prepared for him to strip everything back to the basics.

'Live a little.' Dante leant back against the door to close it before crossing the room to gently pull the bundle of clothing out of her too-tight hold and drop it to the floor.

'But I'm *working* for you,' she began urgently as she clutched at the precarious towel to ensure that it didn't fall.

'Any court in Europe would deny that our private arrangement has anything in common with a normal job, which is why we shouldn't feel bound by stupid rules,' he argued impatiently. 'Those rules don't apply to our situation and we don't need to consider them.'

Live a little, he had said, and he could not know how deeply those words affected her because Belle was unhappily conscious that she had barely lived at all during her twenty-two years on earth. She had missed out on the supposedly fun-filled years of teenaged experimentation and had felt old before her time dealing with major responsibilities like terminal illness, household bills on a small budget and bereavement. With elderly grandparents, she had always had to be sensible and there had been an awful lot of rules to follow. Rules she was *still* faithfully following, she acknowledged ruefully.

'I know I'm not that guy on your shopping list whom you would choose,' Dante murmured. 'But right now, I'm the one that you *want*…'

And the mad cacophony of warning voices in her head telling her to back away, go to her own bed and sensibly turn her back on the risk he presented, suddenly went silent. Yes, he was the one she wanted, the only one she had ever wanted, and all of a sudden holding out for that one perfect match of a guy who might never come along seemed spineless and sad. Dante had smashed through her defences because the bottom line was undisputable… *I'm the one that you want.*

'That's true,' she framed shakily.

'And it is equally true that I want you,' Dante breathed, bending down to lift her up and settle her down on the bed. 'Let's not make it more complicated than that.'

CHAPTER FIVE

BUT IT *WAS* much more complicated than that, Belle thought helplessly as she watched Dante tugging loose his tie, shrugging free of his jacket. Where did they go from here? Was this a one-night stand, as it was called? Would they move on and act as if it had never happened for the duration of their time together? Would one act of sex kill the attraction between them? How was she supposed to know?

She was lying in a damp towel on a bed and common sense was telling her to throw it off, but she didn't feel brave enough for that. Although she had been half-naked in his arms the night before, that had been different, and her lack of self-consciousness had been entirely due to the heat of the moment when no thought had been required from her and no single sensible thought had occurred to her. No, Belle was very much aware that such thoughts came afterwards, and nervous tension held her fast with Dante providing a very welcome distraction as he stripped.

He was very fit, she conceded numbly, sentenced to silence by awe and shyness as rippling bands of muscle sheathed in bronzed skin began to appear. He shed his shirt, toed off his shoes, peeled off socks, his sleek muscular development on continual display as he flexed and turned and straightened, his trousers hanging low on his lean hips, an intriguing ribbon of dark hair snaking down his flat stomach and disappearing beneath the waistband. He was beautiful, like some flawless fantasy brought to life in the flesh, she reflected, shutting her eyes circumspectly as the trousers slid down. She had felt his arousal, noticed, but she wasn't going to stare while he was watching her like a hawk. Those clever dark golden eyes didn't miss a trick and she didn't want to embarrass herself and be guilty of doing that blushing-virgin thing that he had already mocked.

'You're as quiet as a mouse,' Dante whispered, tugging gently at the edge of the towel as she held on to it. He was as aroused as hell and fighting to stay in control.

'There's too many lights on in here,' she told him, violet eyes flying wide.

Without a word, Dante reached up and dimmed the lights to a more acceptable level. 'Better?'

Belle nodded jerkily. Now that he was actually on the bed, naked and ready to proceed, nerves were swallowing her alive.

'I want you to be sure about this,' Dante breathed abruptly. 'I don't want you sharing this bed with me if you're going to regret it. I don't want to take advantage of you.'

'I know you don't…' Involuntarily, Belle lifted her hand to his lean, darkly handsome face and ran soothing fingers across his brow, where he was frowning, her fingertips skating up into his silky black hair, smoothing down the tousled strands.

It was the warmth she emanated, Dante recognised in consternation. That was what had made him spill his guts the night before, that seemingly natural warmth and affection that had broken through his habitual reserve. That discovery about her and about himself, that he could actually be *that* impressionable, *that* easily influenced by a woman, unnerved him. Yet, in defiance of all the defensive instincts that urged him to back off and steer clear of such manipulation until he could get a better handle on it, he still leant down and kissed her as though his life depended on it.

From zero to ninety in seconds, she thrummed into life like a well-primed engine, Belle thought dizzily as he ravaged her parted lips with the kind of hunger that set her on fire. A jolt of high-voltage electricity shot through her, ensuring she was aware of every inch of her pulsing body and every point of contact where his hot, muscular body connected with hers.

'This is the very best moment of my day, *cara mia*,' Dante confided, undoing the clasp in her hair and tossing it aside before fanning out the tangle of her curls round her face.

The towel was gone and she hadn't noticed it going, Belle registered in dismay as a lean hand travelled up over her ribcage to mould a pale, pouting breast, catching a straining pink nipple between thumb and finger to massage it in a way that sent little tremors down to her pelvis, ensuring that she became insanely conscious of the damp heat blooming there.

He used his tongue to tease her sensitive nipples

and the little tremors picked up pace as he sucked on the swollen buds. Her hips shifted upward of their own volition and he flattened her to the mattress with the force of a sudden demanding kiss. Her hands went into his hair and locked there as he ground his hips into her, sending need rocketing up through her in a heady surge. Her body strained up to his and, by then, all her anxiety had fled because nothing had ever felt so necessary, so right or so good. Even the scent of him, dark and masculine laced with a spicy cologne that had already become familiar to her, was compelling.

He shimmied down the length of her, lean and lithe, parting her thighs, burying his mouth there with a fervour for that intimacy that shocked her. 'You taste so good,' he husked while she trembled all over with reaction, torn between wanting him to stop and wanting him to continue.

As exquisite sensation seduced her, she fought to stay in control, to stop panting for breath, to stop making little noises she couldn't restrain and to still the urge to simply writhe. The pleasure was all-consuming, like a slow burn rising from the heart of her with his every spellbinding caress. Pulsating bands of tension tightened round the dull ache of need at the very heart of her, driving it higher until it peaked and set fireworks rocketing inside her, her whole body convulsing in physical delight.

'If this hurts too much, I'll stop,' Dante swore, sliding over her, tipping her legs back. 'Just tell me.'

'OK,' Belle mumbled, still semi-lost in the waves of bliss that had engulfed her as she felt his surge against her, hard and determined where she was soft and tender and yet, oh, so ready for him. There wasn't a doubt in her head about what she was doing at that moment, not with everything feeling so new and fresh and Dante's experience soothing her insecurities. His dark eyes were pure golden enticement as they held hers.

She skated her hands up and down over his smooth brown shoulders, enjoying the satiny strength of him while irresistible sensation snaked through her as he slowly entered her, stretching her sensitive body. She quivered as the heat of excitement clenched her again and then a stabbing pain hit, and she gasped and he stopped dead.

'I'm hurting you.'

'No, don't stop!' she exclaimed.

'Then try to relax. The more you tense, the tougher the challenge is,' he rasped.

Every nerve in her body still stirred to an edge of breathless excitement, she struggled to relax, and he moved again and it still hurt but this time she buried her face in his shoulder and bore the discomfort in silence. Mercifully, it was fleeting, and she heard his groan of satisfaction as he plunged deeper into her and somehow that lit her up as if she had a thousand-watt bulb burning somewhere inside her.

Her heart rate accelerated as the excitement conquered her again and shot higher with every plunge of his lean hips. A kind of wildness claimed her, and she wrapped her legs round him, urging him on as he pounded into her to finally assuage that insane ache of hungry need at the heart of her. She cried out as the ripples of another climax coursed through her and the wild, sizzling pleasure sent her spinning into release.

Dante shuddered over her with a harsh groan of masculine satisfaction and the world went still for her then.

'Unbelievable,' Dante growled, rolling over and carrying her with him, golden eyes as bright as if flames burned there as he stared down at her. 'That was unbelievable. Are you OK?'

Not feeling up to the challenge of speech or voicing an opinion, Belle nodded.

Dante gazed down at her and smoothed her hair with an unholy grin. 'Your hair looks like I electrified it, *amante mia.*'

He had electrified *her*. Belle gave him a drowsy smile. 'It's called bed hair and it's like that every morning when I wake up.'

'I love your hair,' Dante told her carelessly as he rolled off the bed and headed for the bathroom.

'Where do we go from here?' Belle asked abruptly before she could think better of it.

Dante froze and suppressed a groan, knowing that he should have foreseen that question and should not have overlooked her inexperience. She wanted to know what came next when nobody got to know what came next, he reasoned in frustration. Even so, with him what came next after bedding a woman was usually predictable. He would get bored and move on and she would go home.

'We go on as we have begun,' Dante responded gruffly. 'I'll run you another bath.'

Belle was bewildered. *We go on as we have begun.* What was that supposed to mean? After all, they had *begun* as strangers agreeing to a platonic arrangement. Was he suggesting that they now return to that? And how was she supposed to ask him for further clarification? *That* would make her look a little desperate for reassurance and probably potentially clingy to a man already wary of clingy women. Furthermore, what was the protocol after such an encounter? Should she get up and return to her own room? If he expected that, he wouldn't be running a bath for her, she told herself irritably and smothered a yawn, too sleepy and comfortable to want to move.

'We have a problem,' Dante informed her from the bathroom doorway, something in his voice, something spooked, cutting through her relaxation to make her take notice and push herself up on one elbow.

'The condom tore,' Dante completed grimly.

Belle pushed an uncertain hand through the tousled strands of red and copper spilling across her white brow, her violet eyes stricken, her freckles standing out in contrast to her pallor. *'Tore?'* she repeated shakily.

'It can happen,' Dante breathed tautly, his strong bone structure taut below his bronzed skin. 'But it's never happened to me before. Possibly I was a little too passionate. Are you on any form of contraception?'

Belle went pink. 'Why would I have been?'

Dante shrugged. 'I had to ask. Sometimes women use birth control for other reasons,' he pointed out without any expression at all, and then he turned on his heel and vanished back into the bathroom.

Belle was frozen where she sat and then, in an abrupt movement, she slid out of the bed, wincing at the ache between her thighs, her newly extreme awareness that she had had sex for the first time... And what a disastrous mistake that impulsive and seemingly daring decision was now starting to seem, she reflected wretchedly. It had not even occurred to her that she could use birth control simply to be prepared for such an event. But naturally she had never dreamt that she would end up just falling into bed with someone like Dante. She had assumed that she would be in a serious relationship before she had sex and that there would be time and space to consider such precautions. And why was that?

Because nobody knew *better* than Belle, who was illegitimate and the supposed result of a contraceptive accident, that chance pregnancies should be carefully guarded against and that even the possibility of a child should always be planned to the nth degree.

Belle's father, Alastair Stevenson, hadn't wanted her... For goodness' sake, *neither* of her parents had wanted her! Alastair had had a brief affair with her mother and they had broken up by the time Tracy approached her former lover to tell him that she had conceived. Tracy had sworn that she was pregnant due to a contraceptive failure, but Belle's father had made it painfully obvious to Belle, aged a mere thirteen at their only meeting, that he suspected her mother's pregnancy had been no accident. And in all fairness to Alastair, Belle, knowing Tracy as she did, would have been suspicious too, because it was perfectly possible that, having set her sights on him, her scheming mother had deliberately conceived in an attempt to entrap a well-heeled husband.

Pale as milk, Belle wrapped her clammy body in the discarded towel and dropped down on the foot of the disordered bed, deeply shaken at the mere idea that she had run the risk of falling pregnant. And the last thing she wanted to do was raise a child alone with the father having absolutely no interest in his child. It had done nothing for her self-respect to be confronted by a father who couldn't care less about her, and who indeed seemed to resent her for the simple fact that she had even been born, costing him a small fortune in child-support payments…not that her rich father, a highly successful banker by all accounts, could have found it that much of a challenge to make those payments.

Dante was grateful for the distraction of running the bath. He had never done such a thing for a woman before but felt the effort was required after his less-than-stellar taking of her virginity, which he had hoped to accomplish without hurting her. He was tense and distracted though, already asking himself why he hadn't gone ahead and had a vasectomy when the idea had first occurred to him some years earlier. Cristiano had talked him out of that idea. But Dante absolutely refused to give his parents the heir they craved to ensure the next generation of their precious dynasty. And they had been such dreadful parents that he was convinced he would be equally hopeless in the same role. That was why he had never wanted a child. He lacked heart and affection.

But what if he *had* got Belle pregnant? What would she want to do in such circumstances? If she was even half as fond of children as she was of that scruffy little dog she would want to go ahead and have the child. And then, whether he liked it or not, he would be a father with all a father's responsibilities.

'Your bath's ready,' Dante murmured from the doorway. 'I'm going for a shower.'

Belle stood up. 'What will we do if—'

'We'll deal with it...*if* it happens,' Dante countered levelly, his dark golden eyes veiled. 'There's no point fretting about it right now.'

There was a lot of sense in that wait-and-see attitude, Belle told herself as she settled down into the bath, unable to relax into its warmth because she was too tense and far too busy watching Dante's arrogant dark head shift behind the marble wall that closed off the shower. She supposed she might have considered the morning-after pill had she not been so aware that, had such an option been available to her mother, Tracy, she herself would never have been born at all. And that was a very sobering thought. When Alastair Stevenson had refused to marry Tracy as she had hoped, any interest her mother had had in her unborn child had vanished. Indeed, Tracy had resented being left as an unwed mother and had resented even more the damage pregnancy had done to her previously perfect figure, and she had taken that bitterness out on her daughter.

Belle didn't stay long in the bath. In fact, she crept out of the bathroom like a cat burglar, dropped her towel and donned her pyjamas in frantic haste to get back to her own bedroom as quickly as she possibly could. After all, if there had been an ambience between them, it had died after the mishap. His shuttered face had told her all she would ever need to know about Dante's opinion of her having his child. He didn't want it to happen. He didn't even want to think about such a possibility. And in that, she supposed, he wasn't much different from any other young single guy put in the same position. How else could she expect him to feel? It wasn't as if he were in love with her. It wasn't as if he even knew her that well.

Her dispirited eyes took in the opulence of her bedroom and she sighed. It wasn't even as if she and Dante came from the same world. She was a girl with a mother and a father who ignored her, only casual friends, and she had been sleeping in a rusty campervan and working as a waitress when Dante had met her. Dante was a guy who travelled in limos, wore incredibly elegant designer suits and he had spent more than half his life being educated. She was a nobody, a nothing in comparison, she decided wretchedly.

Why, oh, why had she slept with him? Why had she let herself be tempted like that? *Live a little? Live a little and live to regret it*, she concluded unhappily…

CHAPTER SIX

Dante had been up working since the crack of dawn when Belle finally showed.

She gave him a huge smile from the top of the stairs when their eyes met. It was fake as hell and he liked that he could tell that it was fake because she had a highly expressive face. Faint shadows highlighted her violet eyes and proved that she had not slept much better than he had. Served her right for leaving his bed the way she had, he reflected, dark golden eyes simmering. Dante wasn't used to women taking him by surprise or making moves on their own, and Belle had done both when he had found her gone when he'd got out of the shower the night before. Well, she wouldn't be doing that tonight, he thought with innate satisfaction, because she would only be sleeping in *his* bed while she was in Italy.

'You have about thirty minutes to get breakfast,' Dante murmured softly, watching the sunlight make a fiery halo of her hair and add sparkle to her eyes. Her outfit—striped cropped trousers and a white top, teamed with canvas sneakers—had a nautical air that gave her the look of a sexy sailor. His keen gaze roamed over her shapely figure and he remembered that she had felt like liquid silk and he hardened instantly.

'I'm starving,' Belle admitted unselfconsciously as she dropped down into a seat and the butler appeared to take her order. 'I can hardly wait to be reunited with Charlie.'

'We'll pick him up on the way home. By the way, I've arranged for your packing to be done.'

Belle nodded and smiled as a pot of tea arrived. She was disturbingly aware of the lingering scrutiny of Dante's stunning dark golden eyes. What was he watching and waiting for? She had agreed with his wait-and-see outlook and she wasn't about to freak out over something that might never happen. At the same time, she had had thoughts during the night that would probably horrify Dante because she had tried to imagine herself becoming a mother. For someone who had never had a mother as such that had been a scary prospect, but she had decided that she would cope, somehow, she would cope the way she always had when life threw up unexpected developments.

And the more she had thought about how different a parent she would be in comparison to her own parents, the more she had warmed to the vague image of a baby she could love. A little boy, a little girl, she didn't care, but she *did* like children and the idea of finally having her own family could only warm her heart. That was the right attitude to have, she told herself firmly: turn any negative aspect into a positive so that she was prepared for whatever happened.

'When will we know?' Dante asked levelly.

Belle registered that his mind was in exactly the

same place as her own and she coloured. 'In about ten days—'

'We'll have a test done as soon as possible,' Dante told her in the same measured tone.

Belle demolished a croissant in record time, unnerved by Dante's calm and slightly irritated that he was hiding how he really felt from her, acting all distant and businesslike in the aftermath of the passionate encounter they had shared the night before. Of course, it would be neither civil nor kind of him to admit that he was horrified by their situation, she allowed grudgingly. Really, *she* was being unreasonable in expecting any more from him than a polite pretence.

Dante watched Belle's lips curl round a shred of croissant, the tip of her tongue peeking out as she savoured the pastry with unconcealed pleasure, her head tipping back slightly, lashes lowering, her white throat exposed, her slim body momentarily stretching, the fabric pulling tight across the full firm swell of her breasts. He was fiercely aroused by her sensual enjoyment of her food and he marvelled at the way she could make the simplest things seem impossibly sexy. Thoroughly disconcerted by his reaction, Dante attempted to work out why having Belle once had only whetted his appetite for her and stoked it higher, instead of at least partially cooling his immediate interest.

Glancing curiously across the table at Dante, who had gone very still, his attention locked to her, his lean, strong jawline clenching hard, Belle muttered, 'What's up?'

'I still want you,' Dante breathed in a driven undertone. 'In fact, if we had the time I'd be hauling you back upstairs right now!'

Eyes widening in astonishment at that bold admission, Belle stared at him and a piece of croissant went down the wrong way. Choking, she gasped and coughed, eyes streaming as she took a drink to clear her tight throat. Well, she guessed she had just got her answer about what happened next, but she hadn't expected to receive it quite so directly.

'I'm a passionate guy. I can't change what I am,' Dante murmured huskily. 'But I'm hoping you feel the same way.'

Belle chewed tautly at the soft fullness of her lower lip and could feel the flames breaking out below her skin, an anticipatory warm dampness flowering between her thighs while her nipples tightened in response. 'Er...yes.'

'You see,' Dante pronounced with satisfaction. 'Nothing between us has to be complicated.'

And she thought, *He can't possibly be so clever and yet so stupid at the same time, can he?* Because their relationship had become extremely complicated, not least because of the contraceptive mishap the day before and his desire to continue their intimacy undeterred by that development.

'You think I'll be more convincing playing your lover if I actually am?' Belle queried.

'If I didn't want you I wouldn't be with you,' Dante said drily. 'And I wanted you the instant I saw you.'

Belle shifted in her seat, helplessly gratified by that admission.

'There had to be chemistry for us to do this,' Dante

pointed out. 'I could hardly pretend to be living with a woman who didn't attract me.'

'Obviously not.' Belle squashed down the urge to ask him how often he saw a woman he immediately wanted in the way he had evidently wanted her. Probably ten or more times a day, she scolded herself ruefully. It bothered her that in his radius she jumped like a fish at a hook, overanalysing his every word, quite unable to re-establish the cool, calm outlook that usually guided her around men.

It was different with Dante; *she* was different with Dante. He was *more* in every way than every other man she had ever met, better looking, smarter, more sophisticated and unarguably richer. She recognised her subconscious wish that she was something more special to him than a passing fancy and she almost grimaced with self-loathing. There was no future in their arrangement and the last thing she needed to do was start getting attached to him or developing unrealistic expectations. Cinderella rarely got her prince in the real world.

'Those who know me will be surprised enough that I have moved a woman into my home with me,' Dante admitted, raking impatient fingers through his unruly black hair. 'I have always been very forthright about my lack of interest in marriage and my desire to retain my freedom. So, as a couple, we do *have* to put on a convincing show.'

'You're making me more and more curious about this business deal that is so important to you,' Belle confided. 'It must be something pretty special to make you go to these lengths to attain it.'

'Krystal's husband, Eddie, owns a piece of land that I hope to reclaim.'

Belle frowned. 'Reclaim?' She questioned his choice of that word.

'The land used to belong to my brother and he was very attached to it. My parents sold it off when I was abroad on business because they're not sentimental people.'

'Couldn't you have bought the land direct from them?' she asked.

'No, they would have made other demands of me. I don't put myself in a vulnerable position with them,' he replied in a guarded tone, glancing across the room in relief as a collection of suitcases on a trolley were wheeled towards the lift. 'I believe it's time for us to leave.'

Dante worked during the flight, barely lifting his head from his laptop. Belle pondered the situation she was about to enter, the 'snake pit' as Dante had referred to it as. An array of unappealing characters awaited her, it seemed, the nasty parents, the clingy troublemaking ex from hell. But no, when he didn't get on well with his parents, she would hardly be dragged out to meet them, she reasoned, striking his titled parents from the list of challenges ahead. Instead she concentrated on her reunion with Charlie.

The cluster of shouting and gesticulating press-waving cameras as they emerged from the VIP channel at the airport came as a rude wake-up call. 'Look happy,' Dante urged in her ear as he locked a supportive hand to her stiff spine. Belle smiled and all the cameras obediently flashed. He didn't pause to respond to the questions being hurled at him. Security guards escorted them out to the waiting limousine.

'You're clearly quite a celebrity in Italy. You should've mentioned that,' Belle told him.

'Gossip columnists take a ridiculous interest in my private life and for once I've given them something to report...thanks to you.'

'What have *I* got to do with it?' Belle demanded.

'You insisted that you be allowed to be yourself and I have given you your wish. When my staff were asked to identify you, they admitted that you were a waitress I met in France and the press do love to wallow in a whirlwind romance,' Dante declared with cynical amusement.

'I just wasn't expecting *that* level of public interest in your life,' Belle told him, already beginning to regret her insistence that she go under her own name with Dante as she wondered if her father would read about her in some newspaper.

On the other hand, she couldn't imagine her father reading a gossip column, but what did she know about the man? Very little and hopefully any publicity would be confined to the Italian press. Yet her self-respect cringed at the possibility of her father learning that she had moved in with a very rich Italian because he would no doubt assume that she was faithfully following in her gold-digging mother's footsteps. And she didn't want to give her long-absent father the excuse to believe that he had been *right* not to pursue a more normal relationship with her. His rejection and the injustice of being held accountable for her mother's sins still stung.

Charlie greeted her with rapture at the smart boarding kennels, bounding into her arms as if they had been parted for months. She petted him and calmed him down before turning to Dante to say, 'Let's go and say hello to your brother's dogs while we're here.'

Dante frowned. 'I don't think...'

'Don't be mean, Dante,' Belle argued fierily. 'Imagine how boring it must be in here for them every day and how much it will mean to them to get a visit.'

Incredulous at being called mean for the first time in his life, Dante spread lean brown hands in frustration and annoyance. 'Five minutes...that's all,' he specified. 'And that's all you'll want because they're frantic little beasts with no manners at all.'

'We'll put Charlie into his travelling box and leave him out here while we visit them. It wouldn't be fair to unsettle them with a strange dog,' Belle remarked as she persuaded Charlie into the box. 'You know, Dante...dogs can learn manners. With a little training, you might find them perfectly acceptable. I'm willing to help if I can.'

'They're *not* coming home with us,' Dante swore vehemently, registering that when he gave an inch with Belle she tried to take a mile.

'OK,' Belle conceded, wondering how long it would take to change his mind as he addressed the proprietor and they were led down a corridor giving access to a line of kennels.

'They jump up at you and drop hair everywhere,' Dante complained, angry that he had allowed himself to be shamed into doing something he didn't want to do.

Belle didn't know what breed of dog she had expected Dante's late brother to have owned but she was surprised to see two tiny short-haired chihuahuas, one brown, one black and white, nestled cosily in an extravagant pink basket. As they leapt out of the basket to greet Dante with an enthusiasm he didn't deserve, Belle crouched down and quite deliberately got in their way. In seconds she had an armful of squirming, overexcited chihuahuas in her lap and she sat down on the floor of the corridor below Dante's disbelieving gaze and slowly calmed them down with a quiet voice and an occasional sharp no.

'Do you want to hold them now they've settled?' she asked Dante over her shoulder.

'No,' Dante said flatly.

Belle suppressed a sigh and resisted the temptation to ask him to make an effort. She petted the little animals, wondering how Dante could withstand those little pleading dark eyes. He had been doing it for a year, she reminded herself wryly.

'They've never behaved that well for me,' he confided. 'Clearly, you're the beast whisperer.'

Belle sighed as she returned the dogs to their kennels and they whined and clawed at the mesh in disappointment. 'I suppose I was expecting your brother to have hunting dogs…well, something large and macho.'

'Cristiano was liked cute dogs,' Dante admitted quietly. 'He was gay, and the more our parents criticised him, the more flamboyant he became.'

'They couldn't accept him as he was?'

'Oh, they're very liberal and accepting in public, and they have gay friends, but they still didn't want a gay eldest son and heir,' Dante derided. 'They tried to disinherit him, tried to change the succession rules to prevent him from inheriting my father's title, but there was no legal recourse. Tragically, his death suited them.'

Belle stroked his arm as they got into the limo, Charlie already on board, tail thumping noisily inside his plastic carrier box. 'I'm sorry.'

'As children we were never allowed a pet because my mother doesn't like animals. Tito and Carina were Cristiano's first rebellion. He used to joke that at least the presence of the dogs prevented our mother from making unannounced visits to his apartment in Florence,' he told her gruffly.

Belle smiled. 'He had a sense of humour, then.'

'In the right mood he was the life and soul of the party, but he always suffered from low self-esteem and when anything went wrong, he blamed himself.'

'Does your mother make unannounced visits to your home?' Belle asked apprehensively.

'Not for a long time. Relax... If she shows up, I will deal with her,' Dante assured her confidently.

'How far are the kennels from your house?' Belle prompted.

'A ten-minute drive.' A faint hint of colour flared over Dante's high cheekbones as he met her surprised violet eyes. 'I'll look into rehoming the dogs. It wasn't what Cristiano wanted for them but you're right, it would be kinder.'

He wasn't used to pets, having been raised without them, but her heart ached at the depth of grief and guilt that still tormented Dante. He was so very different from the man she had initially assumed him to be. His emotions ran deep and strong. There was nothing superficial about him. If she discovered that she was pregnant, she didn't believe that he would try to pressure her into doing anything she didn't want to do and that was a relief. She had had a friend once who had allowed her boyfriend to persuade her into a termination. Her friend had agreed in the belief that it would save the relationship, but it hadn't, and it had taken a very long time for her to get over the decision she had made. Belle didn't want to be put in that position, although in her case, she acknowledged unhappily, there would be no relationship to save.

The limo was travelling up a spiralling road with hairpin bends and, almost at the top of the hill, it turned into a lane. Belle was still twisting her head around to catch another glimpse of the staggeringly beautiful view of the Tuscan countryside, green hills and valleys studded with cypress trees, little pale stone hilltop villages, composed of houses with vivid terracotta roofs.

'Welcome to the Palazzo Rosario,' Dante murmured, and she swivelled back to be confronted by the magnificent mansion sited at the foot of the drive and her brows went up in stunned surprise.

'You could've mentioned that it was a Palladian palace,' she whispered in awe.

'How do you know it's the work of Palladio?' Dante enquired.

Belle flushed and her soft full mouth compressed. 'Why? Isn't a waitress supposed to know about stuff like that?' she snapped.

'Few would recognise the fact at first glimpse,' Dante told her wryly. 'I'm curious.'

'My grandfather had a great interest in architecture and a big collection of books,' Belle admitted. 'Growing up he dreamt of being an architect but, of course, it was just a dream.'

'Why?'

Belle sighed. 'When he was young, working-class boys went straight out to work as soon as they were legally able to leave school. It didn't matter how clever they were. Further education wasn't free, and it wasn't an option. Grandad worked as an accounts clerk in an office all his life.'

'But he taught you about architectural history,' Dante gathered.

'It was his personal interest. He would save up to buy these big books and then he would share the best pictures and highlights with me,' she recalled fondly, thinking once again that she had been very fortunate in her grandparents.

'I learned young as well. The *palazzo* belonged to my uncle on my mother's side, Jacopo Rozzi. He was an art historian. He never married and when he died, he left his entire estate to me, which effectively made me independent of my family,' Dante admitted. 'I owe him a great debt for his generosity.'

'Is that how you started out in business?' Belle asked curiously, climbing out of the limo to look up in wonder at the long colonnaded frontage and the perfect symmetry of the rows of tall windows.

'Jacopo invested in my business while I was still at university and got me off to a flying start.' Dante looked down at her, the glow of her usual exuberance drawing him even as he reflected in bewilderment that he had never done so much talking in his life with a woman as he had done with her. She was so natural with him and he had not had that experience with her sex before. Even the attention she was giving the *palazzo*, rather than him, was outside his normal experience and weirdly annoying.

'Belle…?' he breathed silkily before she could rush up the stone steps ahead of him, a newly released Charlie dancing at her heels.

And she turned back to him, wide violet eyes bright below the tangle of red-gold curls on her pale brow. Dark eyes dazzlingly gilded by sunlight, he stared down at her and the hunger she incited surged up inside him with volcanic force. He pulled her into his arms, one hand locking to the back of her head, his fingers meshing into her curls, and he devoured her soft, smiling mouth with his own. Taken by complete surprise, Belle stiffened and then leant into the solid heat of him, the wild, ferociously sweet taste of his hunger melting her deep down inside to create a blossoming ache of need.

Distinctly dazed by that embrace, she stumbled when he set her free and it was all the encouragement he needed to sweep her up into his arms and carry her up the steps with Charlie racing in their wake and barking to indicate his enthusiasm. Belle started to laugh. To say that they made an entrance to the *palazzo* would have been to understate the case, for a group of goggle-eyed staff awaited them there.

Belle slid down out of Dante's arms, flushed and embarrassed by his hot-headed behaviour but immediately soothed by the huge smiles that greeted their arrival. Their luggage was being brought in and she accompanied Dante upstairs. Only belatedly did it dawn on her that that seemingly spontaneous kiss had most probably been driven by Dante's desire to make them seem more like a loving couple. It had been a public statement, nothing more. At that acknowledgement, the bounce dropped straight out of her step again and she scolded herself for believing for one minute that he had simply succumbed to an overwhelming passion.

The first-floor landing was open-plan to the *piano nobile*, the main reception room according to the usual Palladian floor plan. It was certainly a very grand and richly furnished space. Indeed, her brain was already whirling with images of colourful frescoes, classic statues and more architectural detail than she could comfortably absorb in a short space of time. 'Do you use this as the main reception area?' she enquired.

'Only if I throw a party but that isn't very often. I converted rooms on the ground floor for normal life. It's a challenge because Jacopo left me a treasure house and I don't like making changes but, at the same time, I have to actually *live* here, so it has to be made fit for purpose,' he pointed out, following the luggage through a classical double doorway into a simply vast bedroom.

It was only then that Belle realised that naturally they would be sharing a room and that her nights of solo privacy were at an end, but when she laid eyes on the huge canopied bed with its incredibly opulent crimson-and-gold brocaded drapes, she burst out laughing. As if it were not imposing enough, the bed sat on a dais. 'Please tell me I don't have to sleep in that monstrosity...'

'I'll have you know that that is a genuine Louis XIV bed,' Dante informed her with amusement lighting up his lean dark features. 'And it is *very* comfortable... Look, even Charlie thinks so.'

Belle exclaimed in dismay, '*Charlie!* No!'

The terrier had searched out the most comfortable place in the room and had had no problem leaping up onto the bed and making himself at home there. She scooped him up and set him down on the floor again.

'So, you live inside a history book. I would never have guessed that about you,' she admitted truthfully.

'My parents' home is only a few miles away and I've been visiting this house since I was a little boy. I was grateful for my uncle's interest in me because I got very little attention at home,' he admitted ruefully. 'I was brought up by nannies, some better than others, and few of them lasted long because my mother is a demanding employer. Cristiano and I went to boarding school and Jacopo used to come and take us out for the day. He was a very kind man and I think he felt sorry for us.'

'Was he close to your parents?'

'No, and when he left me all his worldly goods, they were outraged because they had always assumed *they* would inherit his estate and to leave it to me, the younger, more rebellious son, was even worse in their eyes.'

'What age were you when he died?'

'Twenty-one.'

Belle shook her head, unable to even imagine inheriting the splendour of such a residence and all that went with it at such a young age. 'You have already lived a most extraordinary life, Dante, and you're not even thirty yet. You may not have been blessed in the parent department, but you were blessed in other ways,' she told him quietly.

'Do you want the official tour now or later?' Dante enquired.

'Later would be fine,' she said. 'I'm a little tired. I'd like a shower and a nap.'

'Dinner's at eight,' he told her casually.

In truth, Belle was thinking that she needed to pull back and wise up fast. She was at the Palazzo Rosario purely to play a role: that of official girlfriend. Dante had reminded her of that harsh fact when he'd kissed her and carried her in like a bride, for goodness' sake! Such a public and exaggerated display of affection would not have occurred to Dante if he hadn't been *faking* it to make them seem more like a real couple. Real couples kissed and laughed and fooled around like that, but *she* had to remember that they were *not* a real couple.

She opened a connecting door and found a bathroom, a gorgeous creation in Carrera marble with a copper bath catching the fading sunlight by the window. Dreamy, she thought, but she was too tired for a bath and would savour its delights some other time.

All her troubled thoughts were concentrated on Dante. The act of sex had plunged their arrangement into a no man's land of confusion, she acknowledged ruefully in the shower. All of a sudden she didn't know how to behave, what was acceptable, what was not. Was he expecting her to be all over him like a rash when anyone else was around? Or did the staff not really matter? Probably not, she decided, not after he had staged that big entrance for them. Now he was probably just expecting her to blend into the woodwork while he got on with his normal life. Her true moment of importance wouldn't arrive for ten days when his guests would arrive…at about the same time as she would be finding out whether or not she was pregnant.

But what were the odds? She winced. She told herself it wasn't likely but she had already calculated that that accident had happened during her most fertile phase, which wasn't good.

The door opened and she froze, telling herself off for not locking the door and ready to curl up in a heap on the shower floor. But it was Dante and he gave her a slow smile over the wall that separated the shower from the rest of the room.

'I decided that I needed a nap as well,' he husked, reaching down to pull up his T-shirt and haul it over his head, a truly spectacular network of muscles flexing to make that movement possible. Her mouth went dry and she knew that he had only been joking about the nap, her colour heightening.

She had assumed he wouldn't come near her again until they were in that big bed later that evening. She was learning that it didn't pay to make assumptions with Dante. He had told her that he was a passionate guy. He liked sex. He liked sex a lot…and he wanted her, had wanted her from the first moment he saw her, and nobody had ever wanted Belle with such immediacy or such passionate intensity. She could live in the moment, couldn't she? She watched the jeans drop, the classic V shape above his hip bones tightening as he got naked in record time. Sensation clenched low and tight in her pelvis and she was literally holding her breath, seeing Dante naked and aroused for the first time. And yes, he definitely had more than a nap in mind.

He stepped in with her, crowding her back against the tiled wall, hunger smouldering in his dark golden eyes, his body taut against her stomach, and she literally stopped breathing. A wild heat gripped her feminine core but that out-of-her-depth feeling was claiming her again. Only the night before she had still been a virgin, still shy, still ignorant of all sorts of things and, while she was no longer that naïve and unprepared, six feet two inches of Dante, naked and bronzed and wet and ready in the shower, was almost too much to handle.

Long fingers pushed up her chin so that he could see her eyes. 'Are you too tired?'

Belle trembled. 'Er…no,' she told him truthfully, barely able to catch her breath.

'Too sore?' he husked.

One of her tomato blushes gripped her from head to toe and she shook her head in urgent negative but even as she did so, she knew she was telling a partial lie. She was still tender, still very aware of what they had done only hours earlier. Yet inexplicably her body now *craved* him like a dangerous drug, as if that one act of intimacy had smashed all her defences, her inhibitions and her misgivings.

And yet, on another level, she was painfully aware that she wanted more from him than he would ever give her, and her insecurities lingered underneath. All he wanted was sex, but he wasn't feeling the magnetic mental pull, the attachment that was tugging at her, no matter how hard she tried to resist it. She was convenient, available, here only to play a role that he was *paying* her for. A role that had somehow become real, only it wasn't real because she was *not* his girlfriend and he hadn't really invited her to share his house with him. In just ten days it would all be over, and she would be gone.

What did that make of her? Did it mean she was like her mother? A woman content to be a man's plaything for a little while and gratefully scoop up the expensive treats and gifts he was prepared to provide in reward? Horror gripped her.

'What's wrong?' Dante breathed rawly, linking her arms round his neck as if she were a puppet and lifting her up against him, feeling the tension in her slender body, the little tremors running through her.

'Nothing,' she protested shakily, fighting that attack of guilty discomfiture, knowing it wasn't the same thing. Nothing that had happened between her and Dante had been planned by either of them. It had all been happenstance from start to finish.

'That kiss…outside…it set me on fire,' Dante muttered thickly, nuzzling his unshaven cheek against her throat, his stubble abrading her softer skin. 'And the thought of you up here, getting naked in my shower was too tempting.'

'So I need to stay fully clothed at all times from now on?' she teased with a little gurgle of laughter.

'No, I'd probably turn caveman and rip them off you!' Dante growled, sucking at the skin between her neck and her shoulder to send an arrow of fiery heat darting down to between her legs.

And as he lifted his wet head, golden eyes molten with desire and framed with spiky black lashes, her arms tightened round his neck and she kissed him. There was no yesterday, today or tomorrow in that hungry kiss, no thought of any of that, no uncertainty. She simply couldn't go another moment without tasting that wide sensual mouth of his and she decided she wasn't going to beat herself up any more about what she couldn't resist. And what she couldn't resist was Dante.

With a stifled groan he braced her against the wall and then he bumped his brow against hers and sighed. 'Need a condom…rain check. Just because we had one glitch doesn't mean I should risk you again.'

'No,' she agreed as he slowly lowered her down the wall again, her body feeling hollow, plunged from the edge of anticipation to what felt like abandonment.

Dante stepped out of the shower and she heard him rifling through drawers as she finished rinsing the conditioner out of her hair, marvelling that the goop in her hair hadn't put him off. She was surprised when a pair of arms closed round her from behind and smoothed up slowly over her full breasts, fingertips lingering to pinch her nipples, reviving that hot liquid burn sensation at the heart of her.

'Had to find my wallet. I don't bring women here. You're the first,' Dante admitted.

'Where do you take them?' she heard herself ask uneasily, hurt at the thought of him with other women, telling herself off for that sensitivity, because of course he had had other women in his life.

'I go to their place…*always*,' he stressed. 'You're unique.'

But only because he hadn't had a choice where she was concerned, she reminded herself. She could hardly play the live-in girlfriend from a distance.

'Unique in every way,' Dante confided, his hands running all over her slippery body, finding the most sensitive spot, dallying there until she bucked and gasped out loud.

He spun her round and lifted her again, stunning eyes glittering like golden stars with intent as he braced her back against the wall again and sank into her with a guttural groan of satisfaction. She was caught up in the excitement, utterly abandoned to the surging sensation gripping her lower body. She needed more and then more, and he gave it to her in spades, all that she wanted until the terrible tension broke and she reached a breathtaking climax of pleasure that wrung her out.

'You see, unique,' Dante told her gruffly in the unbroken silence that followed. 'You don't scream. You don't shout my name. You don't even tell me how fantastic that was. The irony is that I *want* you to do all those things for me.'

And she thought about that confession over dinner, all modest in a neat little dress at the beautifully set candlelit table, and the food, absolutely exquisite. She knew she would never scream for him, never shout his name, never, ever tell him how fantastic he was because the minute he got those responses from her she would be the same as her predecessors and, ten to one, he would no longer want her.

Yet the instant she caught herself having such thoughts, she panicked. Her skin turned clammy. She was thinking like a mistress, withholding on the enthusiasm front in the forlorn hope that such an attitude would help her to hang onto his interest. Her mother had been almost a professional mistress, always hooking up with well-off men, making herself indispensable until they moved her into their homes. Pleasing men had been an art form for Tracy. And Belle was determined *not* to follow in her footsteps, so there would be no scheming, no withholding, no lies. She would be straight down the middle all the way and when he ultimately rejected her, at least she would know that it was her true self he had rejected and not some false image she had put up.

CHAPTER SEVEN

DANTE STUDIED BELLE at breakfast and almost smiled.

She was half-asleep because he had kept her awake half the night. A tinge of guilt infiltrated him as he noticed the shadows below her eyes, the faint slump of her small shoulders. He was a demanding bastard and he knew it but every time he looked at her, he got hungry again. It had never been like that for Dante before. Usually after several encounters he was cooling off and on the way to the exit, but inexplicably Belle kept him coming back for more. He wasn't going to worry about it though, because in another couple of weeks even her originality would have worn off. He liked his own space, hugged his privacy and would, undoubtedly, be glad to reclaim it, which put him in mind of the room he had had prepared for her.

He brushed aside the newspapers he had yet to open. 'Belle?' he murmured. 'I want to show you something.'

Belle blinked and set down her tea, rising slowly by dint of bracing her hands on the arms of her chair. He was probably about to give her that tour of the *palazzo* he had promised, which they hadn't got around to the night before. She ached all over as if she had overdone it at the gym and she had a love bite on her neck. She had toyed with the idea of covering it up with a silky scarf and then had wondered if that uncool bruise was yet another deliberate part of his act to make them look like a more convincing couple.

Dante threw wide a door, and she stepped in and understood then. This was to be *her* room, furnished with the antiques he had bought and still a little bare, but the seat and the books and the promise of privacy were inviting. A wall of glass doors overlooked the internal courtyard, which was an ordered but highly attractive Italianate garden with box-hedged beds. Most of the plants were evergreen and the only colour of flower was white.

'This was once my uncle's office. He liked to be able to walk round the garden when he was working,' Dante told her.

And it was a beautiful room and an even more beautiful garden but it daunted her that she was only to be in his life for a couple of weeks and yet he still apparently felt the need to give her a room of her own. Strikingly, *not* her own bedroom but a room to which she could retreat when…when *what*? Maybe it was just a room she was to use as part of their couple pretence, she told herself urgently. Even so, it was hard to ignore the message he was giving her. He had to be a man who set a high value on his own privacy, had possibly even worried that she would be under his feet all the time when he was around. She would use the room as much as she could, she promised herself, flinching at the idea of being seen as an intruder, a nuisance, possibly even a *clingy* nuisance.

'This is lovely,' she said a shade uncomfortably after the thoughts she had had, and she wandered over to the armchair, smoothing an admiring hand over its soft rich upholstery. 'You never did tell me why you and the dealer were laughing about this chair...'

A slashing smile curved his wide sensual mouth, lighting up his whole darkly handsome face. 'Reputedly the chair is from a *maison close...*'

'A...what?'

'A brothel,' Dante translated gently. 'And the chair was specially designed for ladies to get into more interesting positions for their clients...'

'*Oh...*' Belle said, dumbfounded by the explanation, studying those swivelling arms, trying to imagine and then reddening fiercely.

'Yes...*oh*!' Dante laughed, teasing her. 'But don't worry, I'm not about to ask you to pose for me. I get quite excited enough simply seeing you in my bed... in my shower. You don't need to pose or do anything special to turn me on.'

'Just as well,' Belle fielded with a little snorting giggle as she stared at the chair in wonderment, thinking about its potential history and then laughing more heartily because she really couldn't imagine the sort of stuff that chair might have witnessed. 'Thank heaven I was born into the modern world.'

'I'll organise some more furniture and pictures for in here.'

Belle laughed. 'Don't waste your time. I'll be gone soon enough. It's not worth the upheaval it would cause. Anyway, you said you didn't like making changes to the house.'

The slam of a door and a raised female voice attracted Dante's attention to the entrance hall and he grimaced. 'I think you'd better stay in here. That sounds like my mother is paying one of her uninvited visits.'

Belle, however, was too curious about Dante's mother to take his advice and stay hidden. She moved into the doorway, listening to a female voice ranting in irate Italian and Dante's short clipped responses. She took another step forward and saw a tall woman as thin as a toothpick with ice-blonde hair. She was elegantly garbed in an ivory dress, diamonds flashing at her throat and ears, and in her gesticulating hand she held a newspaper.

'Is this she?' the blonde demanded abruptly, switching to English as she stared at Belle standing at the back of the hall. 'Don't be shy. Shy women don't latch on to men they meet in bars!'

Dante's proud dark head turned, and he extended a hand. 'Belle…'

Belle moved stiffly forward to grasp that lean brown hand and lifted her head high.

'Allow me to introduce you to my mother, Sofia Lucarelli… Belle Forrester.'

Belle didn't bother to offer her hand in greeting because the enraged distaste that made a mask of Sofia's still-lovely face was self-explanatory. She would not be receiving a welcome to Italy from Dante's mother.

'Her Excellency, *Princess* Sofia,' the blonde corrected her son thinly, and then in a dramatic gesture she flung the newspaper in her hand at Belle's feet. 'A *waitress* living in a campervan? Your uncle would turn in his grave if he knew the kind of woman you brought into this house.'

Dante's hand spread in support across Belle's rigid spine. 'No, I rather think that Jacopo would have cheered. If that's all you have to say, Mamma… I suggest you leave.'

'When I think of the women I introduced you to and you have chosen *this* creature!' she flung at him furiously before spinning on her heel and stalking back out again, heading for the red sports car parked at a slant outside.

'And the woman who just insulted *your* morals has enjoyed a hair-raising number of extra-marital affairs,' Dante told her as he walked them into an elegant drawing room. His lean, strong face was forbiddingly hard. 'My father seems to turn a blind eye. Maybe he doesn't care or maybe he plays away too. I don't know and I haven't sufficient interest in either of them to find out.'

Absorbing that admission of his mother's infidelities without comment, because she could see by the darkness of his expression that it was a sensitive topic, Belle murmured, 'You don't mention your father much.'

'My mother is the dominant partner and he supports her in everything she does. She once beat Cristiano so badly that he needed medical treatment,' he said flatly. 'My father stood by and made no attempt to intervene. That's one of my earliest memories.'

'I didn't realise there was physical abuse as well,' Belle whispered with a shudder. 'Didn't anyone ever report her? You said there were nannies.'

'Never underestimate the ability of the very rich to hide their sins and keep their secrets,' Dante said drily.

'Were *you* beaten?' she asked hesitantly.

He jerked his chin in silent confirmation.

She wanted to express sympathy, but he stood there so tall and tense that she regretted asking the question and she simply nodded and turned her head away. 'I think I'll go and have a look at some of my new books,' she muttered ruefully.

The door opened while she was down on her knees doing exactly that and she spun round so suddenly that she lost her balance and tumbled sideways. As she righted herself with a flailing hand, Dante caught her other hand in his and pulled her upright. 'It's past time you told me something about you,' he informed her levelly. 'Or hasn't it occurred to you that, for someone as interested as you are in *my* backstory, I still know virtually nothing about you? And that's not likely to persuade anybody that we're a couple.'

Belle reddened with discomfiture and linked her hands together. 'I was brought up by my grandparents.'

'I know that. What I don't know is why,' Dante pointed out. 'What happened to your parents? Are they dead?'

'No, both are still alive…as far as I know.' Belle tensed even more and walked over towards the glass doors, half turning her back to him because she wasn't prepared to tell him *all* the facts. 'My mother was a model and she travelled a lot. That's why my grandparents took over. My parents broke up before I was born and my father didn't want the responsibility of a child,' she admitted stiffly. 'Perhaps because my mother and I spent so little time with each other, no attachment formed on her side and, once I grew up, she had no desire to stay in touch. I don't even know where she is.'

As he'd listened, Dante's lean dark features had lost their brooding tension. 'Do you *want* to know?'

'Not really,' Belle confided tightly. 'When I was a child I used to be full of anticipation if Tracy was coming to visit but her lack of interest in me hurt. You have this image, this *dream*, and the reality never even came close to the dream, so I suppose I learned to accept that that was just how she was.'

'Did you ever live with her?'

'She asked me to live with her when I was fourteen and I was so excited about it. She was living with this guy who had young kids.' Belle grimaced. 'Later I worked out that she only wanted me there to take care of the kids for her but I didn't want to face that at the time. I'd only been there a fortnight when her boyfriend made a pass at me and she saw him doing it. She packed me up and drove me back to my grandparents the same day.'

'And what happened to the boyfriend?' Dante prompted.

'She blamed me for it, not him, said I must've been flirting for him to behave like that…but they didn't last anyway,' Belle told him wryly. 'I'm sure I got the blame for that too.'

'Sounds like a charmer,' Dante commented. 'Much like my own. Not everyone is cut out to be a parent. I don't think I am either.'

Belle paled, tucking away that unwelcome admission for more private consideration. At least he was being honest about his feelings, she told herself, and she didn't want him to lie. Obviously, if she did conceive he would be an absent father, rather than a parent.

On his way back out through the door again, Dante paused. 'I'm attending an international charity benefit tomorrow evening and I'll be taking you with me. Steve and his wife, Sancha, are flying in for it. It's formal, so you may want to visit one of those salon places.'

'Do I have to?'

'Not if you don't want to… I like your hair fine as it is.' He reached out and lifted one of her hands and then the other. 'But you will have to have these done. They're all chipped.'

Belle swallowed hard and contemplated lying before deciding that that was beneath her. 'I peeled bits off to get at my nails but the extensions are glued on and not very palatable,' she admitted grudgingly.

Dante grinned wickedly down at her, relaxed for the first time since his mother's departure. 'I'll have someone come here to fix them for you. Good to know my solution is working. I haven't seen you try to nibble for at least twenty-four hours.'

'But what am I supposed to do when I'm nervous?'

'Kiss me instead,' Dante suggested lazily, tracing her full lower lip with his forefinger so that prickling sexual awareness spread through every sensitive area of her body. 'I guarantee that that will take your mind off your nails.'

But Belle backed away in haste and sat down on the brothel chair to reach for the Jane Austen she hadn't read in years. The way Dante could make her feel with the smallest touch was terrifying and a frightening reminder that she wasn't in control with him. Boundaries, there *had* to be boundaries, she told herself urgently, and she needed to impose some on herself quickly. This might not feel like casual sex because she was living in Dante's home, but it *was* casual sex and she had to stop forgetting that and coming over all warm and willing and melting every time he got close. And that was not to try to stoke his interest either, that was just to preserve her sanity and her self-esteem. Belle was determined not to be hurt when she was no longer useful to Dante and he sent her back to the UK.

Dante sent her a wary appraisal, wondering what was wrong, missing the sparkle, the teasing, the warmth she usually emanated. He strode out of the room, reminding himself that he had work piling up.

'Dante?'

He spun back to see Belle peering out at him. 'Is it all right with you if I visit your brother's dogs again?'

Dante lost his half-smile and shrugged a broad shoulder. 'My driver is there to be used. He'll take you wherever you like.'

Belle spent the rest of the morning reading and throwing a ball to exercise Charlie in the courtyard.

Dante joined her for lunch in the dining room. She spoke when he spoke but was otherwise quiet. Finally, he couldn't stand it any longer and he said drily, 'Look, I get that you're in a mood but if it's over something I've done I would rather you just told me what the problem is.'

'I'm just uncomfortable with how you're treating me,' Belle confessed.

'In what way?'

'Surely we only have to behave like a couple when

we're in public? It's sort of spilling over into private times as well and *it's*...confusing.' Belle settled for the word stiffly. 'We're not in a relationship as such.'

'Aren't we? I thought we were having an affair,' Dante countered, disconcerted by her criticism and her evasive gaze. 'If we're not or you don't want that, I will back off.'

And there it was, *bang*, flung right in her face, the absolute truth that she meant nothing to him. Pale as milk, Belle nodded. 'I think that might be best for both of us.'

Dante gritted his teeth. Rejection was new to him and the shock of it hit him hard. He breathed in deep and slow. What was so confusing about an affair? But ego insisted he did not ask for further clarification. She was entitled to her space if she wanted it. Sex had never been part of their agreement. But how could she simply switch off like that? What had he done or said that had led to the change in her? Last night, she had been perfectly happy to be in his arms. But possibly he had always wanted her more than she wanted him, he told himself grimly. And possibly she wanted a peaceful night of sleep. Had he been too demanding? Too rough?

Belle shook away tears as she climbed into an SUV to go and visit Cristiano's dogs. Well, he hadn't argued with her, hadn't tried to persuade her to change her mind, which merely proved what she had most feared: she was little more than a convenient sexual outlet on Dante's terms. And she was worth more than that, ex-waitress, formerly living in a campervan, or not, she had to set a higher value on herself.

Tito and Carina were ecstatic to see her again and she took them out to the exercise yard and began trying to teach them to sit and stay, rewarding them with treats if they got it right, but they didn't get it right very often.

'Too old and spoilt to learn,' the proprietor declared in broken English from where she was watching outside the fence.

Charlie ambled into Dante's office without being noticed and strayed into a patch of sunlight where he promptly lay down and stretched on a priceless Persian rug. When he saw him there, Dante ignored him. Charlie ignored Dante, well trained by the experience of the restaurant, where non-dog-loving customers had also ignored him. Dante's afternoon coffee arrived and the minute the tray arrived on his desk and he lifted a biscuit, Charlie shot back to life immediately to assume a surprisingly dainty begging position.

'You're clever,' Dante registered as the terrier fixed imploring eyes on the biscuit.

Rewarded with a tiny piece, Charlie gave him a terrier grin and ambled back, satisfied, to his patch of sunlight.

A knock sounded on the door and Belle glanced in and saw Charlie. 'Oh, I'm sorry. I've been looking everywhere for him. I was going to ask you if you'd seen him.'

'He's a quiet little animal.' Dante believed in giving honour where it was due and watched Charlie bounce up to greet his mistress to be lifted and hugged. 'How were the terrible two?'

'OK. I gave them some exercise.'

'Shouldn't think they would've liked that.'

'No, they did. When they get tired they stop being so frantic.'

Dante studied her. Her hair tumbling round her shoulders, framing the perfect oval of her face, she wore a filmy green top and cropped jeans that were complete with paw prints he doubted that she had even noticed. And she *still* took his breath away. Her pouting pink mouth, buoyant breasts and curvy bottom inspired instant lust in him and the pulsing swell of arousal at his groin filled him with angry frustration. 'Always the optimist. You like to take a positive approach to problems, don't you?'

'Usually,' she agreed.

'But not to me,' Dante derided. 'I've been judged and found wanting without a hearing.'

Belle flushed. 'I'm sorry you feel like that. I was trying to be sensible.'

'Clarify that,' Dante urged, springing up from behind his desk to move forward.

Belle winced. 'Living like this—the clothes, the jewellery, this gorgeous house—it would turn any ordinary girl's head but it's all a bit like the emperor's clothes in the fairy tale. It's not real and it's not mine and it's not going to last,' she reasoned uncomfortably, staring at him, drinking in the effect of all that devastating dark male beauty before bolstering her nerve and biting the bullet of the unlovely truth. 'And I don't want to fall in love with you and get hurt.'

A sizzling silence fell. A woman had never been that honest with Dante before and he was knocked for six by that blunt confession. 'I can't believe you said that.'

'Well, no point in lying about it, is there? After all, you can't want me getting attached to you either,' Belle quipped. 'And what you call an affair is very intense for me because I've never been in a serious relationship... and yes, I know this isn't serious for you, but for me, it *is*.'

'OK...' Dante spread expressive brown hands, taking a step back as if she had mentioned something danger-ously contagious. He had even paled a little. 'But it's not love, it's infatuation because I was your first lover. You'll shake it off fast enough.'

'Er...thanks for that sage advice...' Belle said, eyes wide as she summoned Charlie and walked out again with as much dignity as she could muster.

Dante released his breath in a hiss. He had never been in love. Cristiano had fallen for a long line of users and losers. Cristiano had been on a constant mission to find his one true love, and watching his brother had taught Dante that love was a car crash of insane hope colliding with nasty truths as the loved one revealed one flaw after another. Of course, Belle wasn't fall-ing for him, but she had played a blinder with that ar-gument because he wasn't about to try and touch her again. *She had frightened him off.* Quite deliberately too. For a split second he was amused but that reaction swiftly drained away.

What was wrong with him? He felt as if someone had dropped a giant rock on him. He felt weird. He needed to find another woman to focus on, he told himself fiercely, wipe out the last crazy week and for-get about Belle altogether. How hard could that be? Off with the old, on with the new. That had always been his way.

Belle curled back up with her book and wondered how she would face Dante over dinner. She cringed and pressed hot hands to her even hotter face and groaned out loud. How could she have said *that* to him? How could she have humiliated herself so completely? But it was true that she was developing inappropriate feelings for him and she had to put a stop to that and the only way to stop it was to cut out the intimacy. So what if she was still stuck sharing a bed with him for show?

Belle dined alone and, after a long bath, went to bed early. Dante stalked through his usual club haunts and an exclusive party in Florence, finding something offensive about every woman who paid heed to him until it finally dawned on him that the only woman he actually wanted was, ironically, at home in his bed…and he couldn't *have* her. Was that what made her different and so much more desirable? Was it because she had rejected him? Was it his ego playing up?

Or was he more honourable than he had ever realised? He didn't want to hurt her, he acknowledged over his fifth drink. He checked into a plush city hotel for the night, not trusting himself anywhere near her in the strange introspective mood he was in. He couldn't sleep. He kept thinking about Belle in his bed and remembering how she had made him feel. Weird, she'd made him feel *weird*, he decided around dawn.

Belle woke up in an empty bed and wondered where Dante had spent the night. She felt guilty because she had clearly made him feel uncomfortable in his own home. As she went downstairs for breakfast she saw Dante mounting the steps, looking rather the worse for wear. His tie was missing, his jacket was crumpled and he was unshaven, a dark growth of stubble darkening his already-forbidding features. She bolted into the dining room at speed.

If she had had the nerve, she would have jibed, 'Walk of shame, Dante?' Only, she didn't have the nerve to confront him with a possibility that tore through *her* with the slashing pain of a knife…the very real possibility that he had spent the night with another woman.

The manicurist arrived late morning and redid Belle's nails in a dark blue that she liked much better than pastel pink. Her nails would match the long dress she had selected from her new wardrobe and she promised herself that this time she wouldn't pick at the gel finish and peel it off because she was willing to admit her hands looked much prettier. She would wear the fancy pendant and earrings he had bought and do her very best to look as though she belonged in a formal setting, even though she would be feeling incredibly nervous. She recoiled from the fear of letting Dante down in public. After all, this was what he had hired her to do: act as if they were a couple. No matter how she felt inside herself, she had to behave like his lover without being off-puttingly clingy.

Fully dressed, she went downstairs and from the top step she saw Dante pacing the big entrance hall, tailored dinner jacket shaping wide shoulders, narrow black trousers delineating long powerful legs, with the white of his dress shirt in stark contrast to the vibrant glow of his bronzed skin. Drop-dead gorgeous from head to toe but she wasn't allowed to think like that any more or look at him like that, she reminded herself doggedly.

Dante swung round to watch her descent, and something expanded inside his chest because her beauty had never been more obvious than in that stylish simple dress, her glorious hair tumbling round her shoulders just the way he liked it, a sleek split in the skirt momentarily showing a slice of pale perfect leg. And then she looked at him and her eyes didn't shine any more. He didn't remember noticing that inner glow she had had when she'd studied him but, on some level, he must have noticed because now it was definitely gone. Just as he had forecast, just as he had wished, she was moving on from him, shaking off those silly feelings she was too naïve to understand. He told himself that he was relieved, but his lean hands clenched into fists because he hadn't expected her to get over the notion of him quite so fast, and for some reason that only made his mood edgier and darker.

'Steve and Sancha are saving a table for us. At least with them present, you'll have friends around you,' Dante remarked as if he could sense her insecurities about attending an event patronised only by the wealthy.

Belle lifted her chin, tempted to say that Steve and Sancha had never been her friends, only VIP customers she had served at the restaurant. Friendly, pleasant people, but not people she had mixed with in any social way. She said nothing, however, because she didn't want to draw attention to her nerves.

It was a social gathering way beyond Belle's experience. The benefit was being held in the splendid ballroom of a public building. Wonderful frescoes decorated the domed ceiling, the whole illuminated by giant crystal chandeliers. And everywhere there were people: dinner-jacketed men standing in cliques, superbly groomed women in fabulous designer gowns and jewellery that flashed under the lights.

Dante closed his hand over hers, startling her, and began to trace a path through the crush. Steve Cranbrook stood up and waved from a table at the edge of the floor, his Spanish wife beaming at them both.

'Do they know we're faking it?' Belle whispered, stretching up to Dante's ear.

'Yes, but they're the only ones who know,' he confirmed.

Belle relaxed a little more then, knowing she didn't have to keep up an act with their companions. Sancha chattered as though her tongue had wheels, telling Belle about the international charity and the famine-relief fund. Belle asked the curvy brunette about her children, an adorable mop-headed blonde quartet she had often seen playing on the lake beach with their mother. The crowds thinned as the guests found their seats to listen to the speeches. Belle looked round the room, spotting Dante's mother, the princess, who would never let anyone forget that she was a princess, seated beside a man with greying hair, who had the same classic profile as Dante and was presumably his father.

Her attention roamed to the tables nearest theirs and then her eyes widened, something akin to a jolt lancing through her chest as she stared in astonishment at the man sitting alone at a table and staring right back at her. It was… No, it couldn't be… Could it be her father? Nine years, it had been *nine* years since she had seen Alastair Stevenson. The red hair she had inherited from him had distinguished wings of grey now, but the eyes were no less keen, his face barely lined. He would be in his late forties now, much younger than her mother and time had laid only a light hand on him.

Belle dropped her eyes, suddenly feeling sick and clammy. The father who had bluntly rejected her, who had said he wanted nothing whatsoever to do with 'Tracy's daughter' as if she were not also *his* daughter. The cruel bite of that rebuff had gone deep, and she had no doubt that he had been staring because he could barely credit that his unacknowledged, unwanted daughter could be present at a high-society charity benefit where he, of all people, had to know she did not belong. It was just one of those truly horrible coincidences, she reflected wretchedly, draining her soft drink, and what was more, after nine years, she should be mature enough to handle an accidental glimpse of the man without getting emotional.

The music started up again and as some couples took to the dance floor, Steve grabbed his wife's hand and pulled her, laughing, out of her seat.

'Excuse me,' Belle said tightly and rose from her chair.

'What's wrong? Where are you going?' Dante demanded, reacting disturbingly like a man who would prefer to keep her chained down beside him.

Belle lifted a questioning brow. 'Cloakroom…?'

The fingers closing to her wrist dropped away and he politely sprang upright, but the intense hold of the dark golden eyes below his frowning black brows continued. 'Are you all right?' he pressed, because he had never before seen her so pale that every freckle stood out in sharp relief.

'Of course, I am,' she told him through numb lips as she hurriedly walked away.

CHAPTER EIGHT

FRESHENING UP AND doing a little deep breathing to put the dizziness to flight helped to return Belle to normal.

It had been shock that made her feel ill like that, the sheer shock value of seeing her father after so many years, she reasoned ruefully as she walked back through the entrance hall to thread her passage through the knots of chattering people. And then she stopped dead, in disbelief, seeing the man she had hoped to avoid standing directly ahead of her. Dropping her head, she sidestepped in haste and then froze as a hand fell on her arm.

'Belle?' that almost forgotten deep voice prompted.

Her eyes flashed up into eyes identical to her own and she froze like a woman in front of a steep drop, fearing a fall. 'Er... Mr Stevenson?' she said stiffly.

'Do you know how many years I've been trying to track you down?' the older man asked in a pained undertone. 'How *long* I've been searching for you? And with the first words out of your mouth, you crucify me with guilt. And I deserve it. Yes, I *fully* deserve it, but I am here to ask you for a few minutes of your time. Will you give me that much?'

Belle was stunned that Alastair Stevenson had approached her, stunned by his claim to have searched for her and even more stunned by the emotional charge he was emanating, for the man she remembered had been cold and bitter and hostile.

'*Please...*' he added with emphasis as the silence between them stretched and stretched.

Dante was restless because Belle had been away longer than he had expected and there was something wrong. He knew in his gut that there was something wrong. Was she ill? Or had something upset her? Steve and Sancha reappeared and Steve bent down and said, 'When did Belle get friendly with Alastair Stevenson?'

That vaguely familiar name rang into Dante's inner computer chip of contacts and spat out a designation: high-flying hedge-fund manager, well known in the UK. 'Alastair Stevenson? What are you talking about?'

And Steve angled his head in the direction of the dance floor and Dante was dumbfounded to see Belle with the older man. Neither could be said to be actually dancing. They were swaying opposite each other, heads leaning forward as they tried to talk over the noise of the music, and even as Dante watched the couple with frank incredulity Alastair Stevenson reached for Belle's hand, said something in her ear and walked her off the floor.

Dante swore long and low and inventively in Italian.

'I mean, *obviously* she knows him well,' Steve pointed out helpfully. 'I've never seen him hand in hand with any woman other than his wife. Maybe he's her godfather or some relative or something.'

'I don't think so.' Dante had difficulty vocalising the

words in English, but he was trying to get a grip on the rage licking at him and stay in control. 'She would've mentioned someone like that.'

'They're going outside,' Steve told him helpfully.

'They're… *What?*' Dante exclaimed, leaping upright, just in time to catch a glimpse of Belle vanishing through the French windows standing open onto the terrace to allow a flow of cooler night air.

'Does she smoke?'

'No, she bites her nails.' And if he had to make a choice Dante knew he would still pick the nails for a bad habit because it was an oddly endearing and revealing weakness. Every time her fingers drifted towards her mouth, he knew she was nervous or afraid.

Why would she go off to be alone with a married man? It didn't make sense. She wasn't that kind of woman, was she? At least he had *thought* she wasn't that kind of woman…the type to spot an opportunity and pounce on a rich man for the sake of it. Strictly speaking, she was only obligated to him for another week, he reminded himself grudgingly. He had no official claim beyond that date. Virginity at twenty-two did not indicate sainthood or fidelity or anything else, did it? He was being naïve, he, who was *never* naïve about women and the evils they were capable of.

Belle and Alastair took a table on the well-lit terrace and he signalled the waiter to order drinks.

'Just water for me, thanks,' she said awkwardly. 'So, this private investigation agency you hired to find me traced me through the newspaper photos that were published, but that was only *yesterday.*'

'And I dropped everything and ran, lest you vanish again. Wrangled a ticket for tonight, praying that Lucarelli would be bringing you with him because I didn't fancy trying to visit you at his place.' Alastair grimaced. 'I need more privacy than that to tell you what I have to tell you but I don't want to offend you by being too honest about your mother and the dreadful relationship we've had since your birth.'

'I haven't seen Tracy since my grandfather was buried and you couldn't offend me where she's concerned.'

'When Tracy fell pregnant I was young and naïve. I didn't get a legal agreement drawn up with her because I didn't want anyone to know about our fling. Instead I left myself open to paying every damn bill she sent me, and her financial demands were heavy. When I indicated that I wanted to rearrange the child support through a lawyer, she threatened to visit my wife, Emily, whom I met and married the year after I broke up with your mother. And I didn't want Emily to find out about you. I didn't want anyone to know about your existence because I felt like such a fool for letting Tracy take advantage of me,' he admitted heavily.

Belle's brows pleated. 'Why would her threatening to visit your wife worry you so much?'

'Emily's suffered from depression all her life and she's fragile. Back then her biggest dream was to have a child, but she suffered several miscarriages and then we had a stillborn son,' Alastair revealed sadly. 'I should've told her about you *before* our marriage because afterwards I couldn't face telling her that I already had a child.'

Belle nodded slowly. 'I can appreciate you wanting to protect your wife.'

'But Emily knows about you now. Tracy can't hold that threat over me any longer and once I'd told Emily, I was free to look for you. Unfortunately, I couldn't find you. I had to *bribe* your mother even for the information of where and when she had last seen you,' he told her in disgust. 'By then I had had enquiries made and I had discovered that she had been lying to me and conning me with fake bills practically from the minute you were born. Until recently I didn't even realise that it was your grandparents who had brought you up and that you'd attended a state school with absolutely no frills and left at sixteen.'

Belle was frowning. '*Fake* bills?'

'Salaries for nannies, tuition fees for exclusive boarding schools, riding lessons, ballet lessons, private medical treatment, holidays. Everything your mother could think up she billed me for with false documents and yet you received *none* of those benefits. But I was the idiot who paid and paid and paid even in the early days when I was less affluent and it was a struggle to pay,' Alastair revealed. 'I learned to hate Tracy while she bled me for every penny she could and that was the background to my first meeting with you. I took my bitterness out on you and it was wrong and cruel and unjust. You were only a kid hoping to meet your father.'

'I got over it.' Belle sighed, lifting her hand to squeeze his arm in consolation because she was seeing a complete picture now and it changed everything she had thought she knew about her birth father. Tracy had blackmailed him and lied to him, all to scam money out of him for her own selfish use. 'Tracy *is* a bit of a money monster.'

'A bit? She left you high and dry after your grandfather died and took off with her ill-gotten gains! Not a surprise,' her father pronounced cynically. 'But let's see if we can leave all that and her behind us where it belongs. I very much regret the way I treated you when I first met you. Can we move on from that? I would like to get to know you, and Emily feels the same way. All these years on, am I too late? Or is a relationship still a possibility?'

A wash of stinging tears burned the backs of Belle's eyes as her father reached uncertainly for her hand and squeezed it with a hopeful look on his face.

'I think we could try it, see how it goes,' Belle muttered chokily, tears shining in her eyes even as she gave him a huge smile of forgiveness. 'I know I would like that very much.'

'You chose to bring home a slut,' Princess Sofia whispered in a gloating tone in her son's ear as she brushed past him out to the terrace, where Belle could be seen, apparently so rapt by Alastair Stevenson's attention and their entwined hands that she was blind to Dante's presence only ten feet away.

Dante wanted to launch himself at the older man and beat him to a pulp with his fists. Steve was at his elbow, urging him to stay calm, seek an explanation rather than dealing out hasty words of anger and retribution. Steve was the voice of reason, but Dante was firing on pure animal instinct. Alastair Stevenson was *touching* Belle, and Dante was realising that he could not tolerate that. Being forced to witness that act of desecration was like having someone claw the flesh from his bones. And even worse, Belle was *smiling* at Stevenson, all soft and bright and trusting as she had never once smiled at Dante!

Breaking free of Steve's restraining hold, Dante strode forward, sufficient enraged heat in his condemnatory dark golden eyes to stoke a bonfire. 'What the hell's going on here?'

Alastair frowned and then abruptly rammed back his chair to stand up. 'Sorry, I've been rude keeping Belle all to myself, but I couldn't resist the opportunity to speak to my daughter again. Alastair Stevenson,' he said, stretching out a polite hand.

Anxiously having risen, her hand releasing her father's, Belle had clashed in consternation with Dante's flashing furious gaze and her entire skin surface had broken out in goosebumps.

'Belle just…disappeared.' Dante formed the words through clenched teeth while that entirely baffling word *daughter*, bounced back and forth through his brain, cutting through the violence coursing through his bloodstream to unleash a wave of angry, confused disbelief. 'I was concerned. Dante Lucarelli.' After a perceptible hesitation he shook her father's hand.

'I was hoping that I could call and spend some time with Belle tomorrow morning before I head back to the airport,' Alastair continued pleasantly.

'Of course. You would be most welcome,' Dante responded, smoothly concealing the tempestuous emotions still rattling around inside him, the uppermost being a fierce annoyance with Belle for knowing everything about him while carefully squirrelling away her own secrets.

'I'll see you tomorrow,' Alastair told Belle with a warm smile.

Dante closed his hand round Belle's free one as she finally moved away from the older man. When her fingers flexed in his taut grip, he held on fast. Steve had melted tactfully away but his mother, to whom such diplomacy was unknown, still hovered.

'Well, aren't you a surprising little thing?' Princess Sofia commented with a cold gleam of what might have been approval in her sharp appraisal, because Belle had been upgraded in her estimation with the unveiling of her hedge-fund father.

'Sì...*very* surprising,' Dante growled in Belle's ear, his breath fanning the sensitive skin of her neck and making her flush.

'I wasn't expecting him to be here. I was shocked to see him,' Belle framed.

'Not half as shocked as I was to see you holding hands with him,' Dante bit out in a harsh undertone. 'You've been keeping secrets from me.'

'Why would you have been interested?' Belle said defensively.

'Because knowing about a father is a little more important than knowing your favourite colour or your star sign,' Dante retorted, a whip edge to that tone of dulcet derision.

Annoyance was beginning to spark inside Belle. It had been a tough evening and her emotions were all over the place. She wasn't prepared to be censured for spending twenty minutes with her father in a public place. 'But it's none of your business,' she heard herself say.

And it really *wasn't* his business, she reasoned resentfully, for Dante was merely the man who had hired her to play a masquerade for a weekend, not her husband, not her boyfriend, not anything really. She needed to keep that truth in mind and stop endowing him with an importance he neither deserved nor wanted.

Dante breathed in deep and slow to master his temper. He could never recall being forced to work through so many different emotions in so short a space of time. There had been the concern and then the rage, the amazement and incredulity at her behaviour, followed by the anger that she could have omitted to tell him something so crucial about herself, and then a sick kind of relief he had yet to get his head around.

Some guests were already beginning to leave, and Dante seized on that excuse with alacrity, returning to their table only to say goodnight to Steve and Sancha. Stony silence fell in the limousine and Belle bridled. 'I don't know why you're so angry.'

'Don't you indeed?' Dante scoffed.

'It makes me want to thump you!' Belle told him truthfully.

'It made *me* want to thump your father. You're lucky that he identified himself before I got the chance,' Dante countered between gritted teeth.

Belle studied him in astonishment. 'And why on earth would you have wanted to do that?'

Dante sent her a look of raw disbelief. 'You were holding his hand.'

'*So?*' Belle prodded with a toss of her head and raised brows of enquiry. 'What's that to you?'

And that was when Dante lost control for the first time ever with a woman. 'Because no other man should be touching what's mine!' he virtually snarled back at her.

'But I'm not yours. I'm the woman you hired to *pretend* to be yours.'

'Well, you weren't doing a very good job of it tonight, were you?' Dante raked back at her, startling her.

'I'm sorry if you feel that my behaviour embarrassed you,' Belle fibbed, because she was so annoyed with him that she wasn't one bit sorry and a band of tension was tightening round her temples, warning of the headache to come.

Dante looked heavenward in search of the cool and calm he needed, but instead the limo drew up outside the *palazzo* and Belle leapt out, smoother and even faster than Charlie in pursuit of a biscuit. Dante stalked up the front steps of his home, barely pausing in his haste to follow Belle upstairs and finally find the privacy he craved with her. Somewhere there were no listening ears, no snide remarks from his vindictive mother, somewhere he could talk to Belle and where hopefully she would return to being the Belle he was accustomed to dealing with.

'Did you tell Alastair about our arrangement?' Dante demanded.

Belle whirled round, her shoes already kicked off to soothe her sore toes and increasing the height differential between her and Dante, who was towering over her like a solid column of granite. 'No, of course I didn't!'

she snapped back in wonderment that he could even ask. 'You can't seriously think I would tell my father that sort of thing…what would he think of me?'

'I don't care what he thinks of you.'

'Well, I *do*.'

'There is *nothing* sleazy about our arrangement!' Dante declared in outrage.

'I'm not sure he would agree if he knew the facts, so I'm afraid you'll have to put up with him believing that we're a *real* couple!' Belle fielded tartly.

'We might as well be. We're arguing like a real couple and I'm hoping the angry make-up sex is just round the corner,' Dante confided, watching her rounded bottom wriggle enticingly as she strove to reach the zip at the back of her neck. 'Here, allow me…'

After he had unzipped her, Belle snaked crossly out of the dress and draped it over a chair, mortified to be posing in flimsy lingerie in front of him now that that aspect of their relationship was over. 'There is *no* prospect of make-up sex,' she told him curtly.

Dante stalked forward, all silken predatory grace. His lean, darkly handsome features were taut, his high cheekbones slightly flushed. He stared down at her, stunning dark golden eyes like smouldering honey in the lamplight. 'Even though I want you more at this minute than I have ever wanted a woman in my life?'

Involuntarily, Belle faltered. '*Ever?* Seriously?'

'Seriously,' Dante intoned, framing her hectically flushed face with both hands. 'And I wanted to peel your father limb from limb because I was jealous and that was another first for me.'

And once he had explained that, all the turmoil inside her stopped churning and the oddest sense of peace enclosed her. 'Jealous?' she echoed in surprise and tickled pink by the idea. 'I didn't realise.'

'You must've been the only person in our radius that didn't realise. I almost made a complete idiot of myself assaulting your father,' Dante pointed out grittily. 'You were smiling at him.'

'Was I?' she muttered blankly, quivering as the heat of his big powerful body brushed against her lightly clad frame and his hands slid down from her face to her hips to tug her against him, the fabric tented at his groin, telegraphing his arousal as he ground against her with a low roughened moan that was compellingly sexy.

'Where were you last night?' she asked abruptly. 'Were you with a woman?'

'I got drunk and spent the night in a hotel. No woman. I wanted you but I couldn't have you,' he reminded her darkly.

What remained of her tension drained away.

'Later you're going to explain why you didn't tell me about your father.'

'Later?'

'Right now, we have much more pressing stuff on our agenda,' Dante husked as her bra drifted down to the floor and his hands swept up her ribcage to cup her full breasts, his thumbs teasing at the taut rosy buds that crowned them.

'But we aren't *supposed* to...'

'No rules any more, no boundaries.' Dante claimed her anxiously parted lips in fervent persuasion and a little moan escaped low in Belle's throat as she shivered helplessly against him. 'I can't tell you where this is going, but I can tell you that we're *not* going to stop before we've fully explored it because that would be crazy,' he reasoned thickly.

And in the back of her mind she knew he had a point because she *had* stopped them dead, believing that that was the right thing to do to protect herself. But possibly that decision of hers had come too late in the day to be of any real use and the chemistry and the feelings he ignited were still racing through her like wildfire to wreak havoc with her control. And how could she be anything but secretly flattered when Dante confessed that he had been jealous? Surely that suggested that she meant more to him than a casual lover?

He backed her down on the bed, parting her from her panties simultaneously, backing away a step to strip with an impatience and a burning brilliance in his possessive gaze that could only thrill her. She lay back watching him, wanting him so powerfully that she felt light-headed and almost drunk even though she hadn't had a single sip of alcohol. But then that was what Dante did to her, winding her up so tight with longing that she could barely function. The throbbing ache of need between her thighs was unbearable.

He came down to her, naked and bronzed and hot against her cooler skin, swiftly discovering that she was in such a state of anticipation before he even began to touch her that foreplay was unnecessary. He took the invitation and plunged into her hard and fast and deep. Her whole spine arched as the pleasure rolled over her in a wild, wanton surge. She couldn't fight the hunger and she no longer wanted to. The lusty ferocity of his strong body over and in hers electrified her with breathless excitement. Her heart hammered, the mesmerising rise of pleasure expanding relentlessly as the pace picked up. She soared to new heights, her body clenching tight before the rippling aftershocks of convulsive delight seized her.

Dante slumped down. 'Was I too rough?' he groaned, running his mouth lightly across her peacefully closed lips.

'No, I liked it.'

'Was I fantastic?' he murmured raggedly.

'Nope, sorry, you're never going to get that word out of me,' she told him roundly.

'But I did make you scream,' Dante responded with an unholy grin of satisfaction.

Belle had been too far gone to know what she was doing, so she let him have his moment of glory. Dante leapt out of bed and lifted the house phone, speaking briefly before scooping her up to take her into the shower with him.

'Time to tell me about your father and why you gave me the impression that he wasn't part of your life,' he chided.

'Because he never has been and I only met him once before tonight,' Belle admitted.

'Once?'

'Tracy was always very cagey about giving me any details about him. His name was on my birth certificate though. She told my grandparents that he was a deadbeat dad. She visited us when I was thirteen and she was in a real rage about Alastair refusing to pay for something and accidentally dropped a few details about where he worked,' Belle divulged. 'I faked being sick at school so that I could get out and I caught the train into London to track him down. I was curious…' Her voice died away, her face shuttering.

'Of course you were. *And?*'

'I'll explain *his* side of the story, which I only got tonight, because I don't want you thinking too badly of him,' Belle continued and, while she washed her hair, she told him about her mother's greedy con tricks and threats and her father's marriage.

'I get that he would be hostile after she put him through all that,' Dante conceded grimly. 'But how did he treat you when you first met him?'

'He seemed to think that I was there looking for money from him, which I couldn't understand because I didn't know then that the money Tracy gave my grand-parents came from him and, of course, she was only giving them a tiny part of it. He said he didn't want a daughter, that I was a…a mistake who had cost him a fortune and that he had no interest in having a relation-ship with me,' Belle told him shakily as Dante urged her back to the bedroom where the late supper he had ordered for them already awaited them.

'You were a thirteen-year-old,' Dante remarked curtly. 'That was inexcusable.'

'I was devastated.' Belle shook her head in troubled recollection, her eyes hollow. 'I'd worked out by then that my mother had no natural affection for me, but for my father to be even colder and reject me completely was even worse.'

'I'm beginning to wish I had punched him hard,' Dante confessed grittily. 'I don't care how rough a time he had dealing with your mother. You were still his daughter and once he had first-hand knowledge of what a horror your mother was, he should've been checking up on your welfare, *not* putting his wife first, *not* keeping you a dirty secret, *not* blaming you for your mother's greed.'

'What does it matter? It's all water under the bridge now,' Belle reasoned ruefully. 'I'm willing to give him a chance. I don't have *any* other family, Dante…'

'And if you can give *me* a second chance,' Dante contended reluctantly, 'I can scarcely argue about you giving him one as well. At least he's finally got around to telling his wife about you.'

'Yes, that was a relief,' Belle agreed sleepily, setting down her empty cup and snuggling into him.

She was a snuggler. That was not Dante's style.

He let her sleep before peeling her out of her towelling robe and setting her back below the sheets on her own side of the bed. Ten minutes later she was back snuggling against him and he heaved a sigh, finally and grudgingly acknowledging that he had begun to slide superfast into a relationship of the kind he had always avoided and that he still didn't know how that had happened.

On the other hand, he had Belle back in his bed and wasn't that enough? It was the best sex he had ever had, and clearly, it had brought out a possessive, jealous streak in him that he also hadn't known he had. She wouldn't want him to tell her that, but it was the truth, he reflected as he took stock. He liked her, which was more than he could say for most of his former lovers. She made him laugh. He was even learning to tolerate

Charlie, currently stretched out and dead to the world below the bed.

But he didn't do love and he was never going to do love and yet love, he sensed, was what she would want from him. Did she even grasp that love wasn't something he could pull out of a hat and flourish like a white rabbit? He didn't have that capacity any more. That ability had died in him. He had loved his parents when he was very young. He had loved nannies who'd departed without even saying goodbye. And with the single exception of his brother, Cristiano, he had taught himself not to become emotionally invested in anything or anybody because loving always, *always* led to betrayal or bitter disillusionment.

The following morning, Belle awaited her father's arrival, full of nervous tension.

'So, what do I say to him if he asks about us?' she pressed Dante uncertainly over the breakfast table. 'I mean, he's almost certain to ask. How do I describe us? What do I tell him?'

Black hair gleaming in the sunshine, Dante gave one of his fatalistic shrugs, a flawless fluid movement. 'There isn't a label, a definitive word. Whirlwind romance? Casual? That you'll be back in London and easily able to see more of him soon enough?' he suggested lazily.

Belle dropped her attention to the pristine tablecloth, her complexion slowly turning the same shade of white. Her stomach lurched with nausea. In a handful of words, he had crushed her expectations and she felt as though he had removed an entire layer of skin from her shrinking body. *Casual?* Even after he had said that they would be exploring where their relationship took them? Evidently, it wasn't going to take them very far.

He saw her returning to London, exiting *his* home and *his* life much faster than she had naïvely envisaged. He saw no sort of a future for them. She had seriously misinterpreted his words the night before, had read into them so much more than he intended. Her heart sank.

CHAPTER NINE

DANTE PACED THE elegant waiting room like a caged tiger while Belle averted her attention from him. It didn't help that he looked hauntingly beautiful, even in a blue shirt and jeans, smooth and sleek and sexy enough to attract the eye of every woman they came into contact with, from passers-by on the street to the receptionist who greeted them, to the nurse who dealt with them.

She was praying that the test would come back negative and that she would not be pregnant. When her life felt as though it was on the edge of falling apart, what else could she hope for? Certainly, she didn't feel she had the right to *want* to be carrying Dante's child when he so obviously didn't want her to be.

Her period was only two days late, she reminded herself, but she knew the basic symptoms of pregnancy and her breasts were unusually tender and swollen. She linked her hands tightly together on her lap, wishing that Dante would quell his apprehension and sit down.

A week had passed since her father had visited her at the *palazzo*. Father and daughter had got on very well, but Alastair Stevenson had admitted his concern that she was living in an uncommitted relationship. His questions had made it impossible to avoid telling him the truth. He had also agreed that she was an adult and that it was really none of his business, but it had been obvious that his conviction that she was likely to be hurt had overcome his tact. He had said nothing to her, however, that Belle had not already said to herself.

Belle was painfully aware that when it came to Dante, she had been naïve, impulsive and far too keen to believe what she wanted to believe. Over the past seven days, however, she had coped simply by ignoring the situation. Dante had made his intentions clear and she had to handle that as best she could. It was ironic that he had been incredibly considerate and attentive since he had demolished the ground beneath her feet. Of course, he was probably practising the couple pretence for his guests, Eddie and Krystal, due to arrive that very evening for dinner. Belle was dreading their arrival because she would have to monitor her every word and action in their presence.

The nurse returned with a smile to show them back in to see the English-speaking doctor Dante had sought out to do the pregnancy test. Belle swallowed hard as she took her seat.

'Congratulations,' the middle-aged doctor told them with a beaming smile.

Belle dared not look in Dante's direction and was disconcerted when he reached for the fingers she had raised to her lips and kept her hand in his. For the remainder of the appointment she felt as though she were trapped inside a bubble, detached from the real world. It was shock, she knew that because, even though she had had her suspicions, confirmation and being told the date that she could expect to give birth hit her with the force of a sledgehammer.

'That was interesting,' Dante commented, tucking her back into the powerful sports car he had driven her out in.

Belle blinked, baffled by that as a first comment.

'At least we can still have sex,' Dante added, plunging her deeper into confusion.

'But I won't be here for you to have sex with,' Belle said waspishly. 'I'll be back in London.'

'That's not going to work,' Dante intoned flatly.

Seriously? His first reaction to her accidental pregnancy was 'We can still have sex'?

Dante shot a glance at Belle's pale, stiff profile. She hadn't even giggled, and she usually had a terrific sense of humour. But then she had shown all the animation of a zombie from the moment the doctor had congratulated them. She might as well have been told that she had only six weeks left to live. Maybe she really, *really* didn't like children, he reflected, wishing he had raised that thorny subject instead of carefully avoiding potential obstacles throughout the week. Maybe she was simply appalled at the prospect of motherhood and the changes it would bring.

Dante had spent the entire appointment worrying about Belle's weird response to the news that they would be parents in a few months. He hadn't had the time or space to be shocked on his own behalf. It had crossed his mind that his own parents would be triumphant at the continuation of their precious family line, but that was merely an irritant. Dante had swiftly moved on from regretting the vasectomy he had never had and the promises he had once made to himself in the heat of youthful rebellion and an understandable desire for revenge. He was twenty-eight years old, way past the stage of needing to spite his unpleasant parents to score empty points. After all, nothing could bring Cristiano back and nothing could change his parents into decent people.

How *did* he feel about the news they had received? he asked himself. Apprehensive about the challenges that lay ahead, he acknowledged, for nothing in his own childhood had taught him how a decent father should behave. But he could learn and, in the short term, there was a tiny spark of excitement growing inside him because Belle was carrying his baby. Not only did that increase his possessive attitude towards her, it was also sending images of what their child might look like crashing through his brain. Shock was doing that to him, he reasoned.

'I think that we should leave this whole matter on a back burner until *after* our guests have departed on Sunday,' Dante breathed tautly. 'It's an emotive subject and we don't want to get into it now.'

Belle stared out fixedly at the beautiful Tuscan countryside as the opulent car crested another hill and swept down the other side, that swooping sensation making her tummy lurch with nausea. He didn't even want to *talk* about the baby. Or was it simply that he didn't want to risk her getting upset before Eddie and Krystal arrived? And why his use of that word *emotive*? Dear heaven, was he planning to ask her to consider a termination? She broke out in a cold sweat.

At least we can still have sex. Was there any mood in

which Dante did not want to have sex? The past week was a blur for Belle of being intercepted in the midst of whatever activity she was engaged in and lured away to the nearest dark corner/bed/sofa/shower. Once even in the garden, where she had been playing with Charlie.

Saw you out here... Couldn't resist, cara mia, Dante had groaned hungrily, his hands hard on her hips as he made her rise and fall over him until the world went white and she lost the power of speech.

Dante was insatiable and, admittedly, she couldn't resist him either, but she *had* attempted to give him some space and take a sensible step back from that incessant intimacy. In fact, she had spent a lot of time curled up reading in 'her' room but had soon learned that it wasn't *her* room at all because Dante was always striding in to demand to know what she was doing, even though it was obvious. He would tell her that she shouldn't read depressing books, drag her off on a drive or out to lunch in Florence and once even to meet his 'friend' Liliana, for coffee. Liliana, who wasn't a friend at all! Liliana, a gorgeous brunette barrister, had studied Belle with indignant, envious eyes and had barely spoken to her, saving all her attention for Dante, who had not even seemed to notice the tense atmosphere between the two women.

And then there were the gifts, unsought, unwelcome, even the tiny solid gold replica of Charlie on a chain. There was the cashmere shawl he had purchased one morning when he was convinced she was cold because she had shivered with awareness while he stroked her spine with an abstracted hand and she was too embarrassed to tell him the truth. There was the handbag she had paused to admire in a shop window before she had learned that, with Dante in tow, to look at anything for sale was synonymous with saying, 'Buy it for me, please.' He was generous, far too generous, a good trait for a man to have.

Sadly, however, none of that meant that he was ready to support her in having his child. If she had his child, she and that child would be in his life for years and years and he probably didn't want that, but if she was to choose a termination, his life would return to normal and she would leave it again. That would be that, she conceded sickly. It would sever their connection for good and wasn't that what Dante *always* wanted from a woman?

The freedom to walk away? Wasn't that why he had hired her in the first place?

As a stranger, you'll walk away afterwards without a problem. You won't cling or believe that I have any further obligation towards you, nor will you assume that having helped me out makes you special to me in any way.

A baby was an obligation, a lifelong obligation, one he wouldn't want, she reasoned unhappily, any more than her father had wanted it when he had been a younger man.

'I've got something I have to say to you,' Belle murmured tightly. 'I won't consider a termination.'

'I wasn't planning to ask you to consider that option,' Dante retorted in crisp dismissal. 'That's not on the table.'

'Oh...' Drained by the removal of that pressure from her mind, Belle sagged, suddenly tired but able to think about the baby she was carrying without frightened conflicted responses getting in the way.

Her baby, her little family, she savoured without guilt. It didn't matter that her child hadn't been planned, not the way she had always hoped, it only mattered that her child would be healthy and that she would manage to be a more loving, caring mother than her own had been.

'Where are you going?' Dante enquired as she went upstairs once they had arrived back at the *palazzo*.

'I feel like a nap,' she admitted self-consciously. 'I can't afford to be falling asleep on your guests this evening.'

'*Our* guests,' Dante corrected.

'Yes, I must try to stay in role,' she conceded ruefully.

The happy live-in girlfriend, confident in her position in Dante's life and newly in love, everything Belle *wasn't* feeling just at that moment. She wondered how Dante was feeling and then remembered that that wasn't to be discussed until the weekend was over.

Dante got stuck into work, refusing to dwell further on what they had learned. It had happened. He would deal with it. That was how Dante dealt with challenges. He didn't emote, he didn't rage and he didn't whinge. He would process the development and decide on the best way forward.

Eddie Shriner was a heavily built man in his forties with brown hair and keen grey eyes. Krystal was a tiny blue-eyed blonde with voluptuous curves shown off by a fitted skirt and a low-necked top. She had the low, husky voice of a seductress. Even Belle had to admit that the blonde was a classic beauty but the knowledge that Dante had bedded the other woman made her uncomfortable.

Krystal, however, wasn't the least bit uncomfortable to find herself in the company of her husband and a former lover. Krystal's calculating blue eyes locked onto Dante like a heat-seeking missile the instant she walked through the door and she virtually blanked Belle when she was introduced to her, choosing not to comment on the fact that both women were English born and bred.

Dinner was challenging with Krystal's non-stop attempts to grab Dante's attention with flirtatious comments, which repeatedly interrupted the men's conversation. Krystal liked, possibly even expected, to be the centre of male attention, Belle registered, and seemed to have little time for other women. Krystal pretty much ignored Belle's presence at the table and resisted her efforts to engage her in conversation.

When a member of staff moved to fill Belle's wine glass, Belle covered it and asked for water instead.

Krystal stared and lifted a questioning brow. 'You don't drink?'

'No,' Belle confirmed, because even before she had realised she could be pregnant, she had not been much of a drinker. Alcohol gave her an out-of-control sensation that she didn't enjoy.

'Ah…a problem drinker,' Krystal assumed snidely. 'That must make socialising difficult for you.'

'Actually…' Belle breathed, bristling with the urge to empty a glass of water over Krystal's purring head. Krystal was so smug now, convinced she had identified Belle's fatal flaw and keen to drag it out into the open to humiliate her. A fierce desire to lay an even more basic claim to Dante assailed Belle. 'I'm not drinking because Dante and I are expecting our first child…'

At that spontaneous announcement, Dante's arrogant dark head whipped round in their direction fast, dark golden eyes glittering in the candlelight, his jawline clenching even as Eddie offered them his warmest good wishes. Indeed, Eddie, who was not entirely blind to his wife's penchant for Dante, beamed at the news and relaxed back into his seat.

Krystal, on the other hand, went rigid, her blue eyes locking like knives to Belle, her shapely mouth compressing into a tight line. 'My goodness, that's quick,' she commented. 'From what I understand, you've only been together for a few weeks.'

'Sometimes,' Dante inserted with a glance at Belle's heightened colour, 'that's all it takes.'

'Yes, I knew Krystal was the woman for me the day I met her,' Eddie chipped in cheerfully.

'You should've kept the baby a secret,' Dante censured when Belle emerged from the bathroom later that night.

Clad in the pyjamas she had stubbornly retained and continued to wear, Belle ignored the sexier garments provided as nightwear with her new wardrobe. Even for Dante, Belle refused to dress up like a mistress or behave like one. To her way of thinking, a mistress strove to attract and retain her lover's interest in her body and used that same body to cement her hold on him. And she wasn't prepared to do that.

'You should have told me the baby *was* a secret,' Belle replied with spirit, but, in her heart of hearts, she knew she had blurted out their secret because Krystal had made her jealous and she had wanted to strike back.

'I wasn't expecting you to make an announcement,' Dante imparted.

'A baby definitely makes us look like more of a couple,' Belle argued, engaged in combing her wet hair to tease out a knot. 'Krystal was surprised and furious.'

'And now she'll target you rather than me.'

'Isn't that better? The more attention she gives you, the less her husband likes it,' Belle pointed out, having carefully watched the interplay round the dining table.

'I'm not sure you can cope with her bitchiness,' Dante breathed, snatching the comb out of her fingers with a curse word in Italian. 'Stop that! Let me do it. The way you're doing it, you won't have any hair left by tomorrow!'

Belle stood still while he calmly teased out the copper tangle and tossed the comb down on the dresser again. 'Thanks. I've met a lot of sharp-tongued women in my time, Dante. I'm not a pushover. I can handle anything she throws at me.'

'Fortunately, we'll be busy tomorrow flying out to see the land and you shouldn't be exposed to her that much,' Dante commented.

'I'm tough. This is, after all, what you *hired* me to do,' Belle reminded him tartly.

Dante grimaced. 'I can do without that reminder now,' he told her tautly, stepping back from her to walk over to a table and tear a sheet from the pad there. 'I want to get what I owe you out of the way now. Write down your bank details and I'll organise the payment straight away... OK?'

No, it wasn't OK. Hugely taken aback, Belle stared down at the blank sheet. Her cheeks burned, her mouth quivered, and her eyes were full of pain and mortification. He was *still* determined to pay her, and she didn't want it now, didn't want that reminder of how they had met and what they had agreed to, because nothing had happened the way it was supposed to happen.

'I don't want the money any more, of course. I don't,' Belle confessed wretchedly, looking up. 'It's like you're paying me for sex.'

'I've never paid for sex, so why would you twist everything up and accuse me of that?' Dante demanded angrily, colour flaring over his high cheekbones.

'That's what it *feels* like to me!' Belle argued, refusing to be silenced.

'I pay my debts and I *owe* you it,' Dante framed harshly. 'Let's not make it an issue.'

He sent her a brooding appraisal as she sank down on the end of the bed, his dark eyes aglow with censure, his lean, darkly beautiful face grim with restraint. 'We have enough to worry about without arguing about trivialities.'

Obviously, he meant the baby, she reflected painfully, the baby that he saw as a problem and she saw as a blessing. She supposed she would put the money away for the baby since he was determined to pay it and she printed out her bank details with a heavy heart. He strode out of the room and eventually she slid into bed, too tired to agonise any more and reluctant to greet Krystal over breakfast with the visible evidence of a troubled night. Her phone beeped and her head lifted again because she didn't receive many texts, her friends in London having gradually fallen out of touch when she'd failed to return from France.

With a sigh she scrambled up again and lifted her phone, frowning when she saw an unfamiliar number and then stiffening when she saw the message. It was Tracy, her mother, who had had her number for over three years and hadn't once used it, nor had she ever replied to the occasional text Belle had sent.

Belle's soft mouth tightened, and dismay filled her when she read Tracy's message. Tracy was in Italy and wanted to meet up with her for a catch-up. Belle frowned, unable to imagine anything they would have to catch up on and wondering how the older woman had even found out that her daughter was in Italy as well. Her frown deepened. After what she had learned from her father, she wanted nothing more to do with her mother, but she shrank from meeting up with her just to tell her that. She texted back an apology and said she was just too busy before getting back into bed, troubled by unpleasant memories of her long-absent parent.

While she was trying to sleep Dante was standing in his office with knotted fists. Once again, he had screwed up with Belle because he hadn't foreseen her reaction. Women were so sensitive, or, at least, Belle was, reading stuff into gestures that wouldn't even have occurred to him. He had wanted her to have the money, so that she knew she did not need to feel trapped. He hadn't *wanted* to give her that choice, but he had known he *should*. He didn't think she would wish to rely on her father for financial help. That relationship was still too new and their past history regarding her mother's greed too delicate. He wondered how on earth he had ended up with a woman who treated his wealth as though it were something toxic. She was way too keen to turn her back on everything he gave her, determined to ask for and accept nothing. It did not bode well for the future.

Belle woke up in the morning in an empty bed, a slight dent in the pillow next to hers the only evidence that Dante had joined her late and risen before her. Disturbed that he had kept his distance throughout the night, which would surely give him a new record for restraint, she wondered if the discovery that she was pregnant was already encouraging him to step back from her.

She went down to breakfast, garbed in the prettiest dress she could find in her wardrobe because Krystal was one of those ultrafeminine women who made every female in her radius feel overshadowed. She had expected to see Dante already at the table out on the shaded loggia overlooking the magnificent view of the valley below but the only face that greeted her was Krystal's.

'I think I threw the staff into a panic when I came down, but I've always been a very early riser,' Krystal remarked in the friendliest tone Belle had yet heard from her.

The blonde watched as Belle was served with tea and reached for a croissant. 'I gather you're not suffering from morning sickness.'

'Probably not far enough along yet for that and then maybe I won't get it. The doctor told me that not everyone does,' Belle responded lightly.

'Are you hoping that Dante will ask you to marry him?' Krystal asked baldly.

'No, my mind doesn't work that way. I'm very independent,' Belle fielded smoothly.

'That's fortunate, with Dante being so anti-marriage. He's a total commitment-phobe, which is why I moved on,' Krystal declared with a little shudder of her slight shoulders, implying that her relationship with him had been of a longer duration than it had been. 'Of course, with his history, what can you expect? His brother was badgered practically from birth to marry and produce an heir for the family, and now that he's gone, Dante's expected to take on the responsibility…and he's always sworn that he will *never* marry or have a child.'

'Yes,' Belle agreed quietly as if nothing the blonde had told her was news to her. But she was faking it because she hadn't made that connection between Dante's background, his brother's passing and Dante's strong aversion to commitment or having a child. No, she hadn't put it together for herself even though she had had almost all the facts. After his childhood, the very last thing he would want to do was fulfil his parents' fondest wish and continue the family gene pool. Luckily for Belle, however, she had not once dreamt of Dante proposing marriage and had not even considered that unlikely event.

'But couples don't marry these days simply because there's a child on the way,' Belle pointed out, amused when Krystal's eyes hardened at her lack of reaction.

Dante appeared then with Eddie. Apparently, Eddie had wanted a tour of the *palazzo* and the estate. A helicopter awaited their trip, and as Dante lifted her into the craft, Belle had cause to regret a choice of clothing that was impractical. Before very long, however, she had something more pressing to worry about. While Eddie was enthusing over the hundreds of unspoilt Tuscan acres he had bought up and urging the two women to properly appreciate the spectacular views, Belle was discovering that the motion of the helicopter made her feel queasy and she was finding it a struggle not to be sick.

Her legs wobbly, Belle got out of the helicopter and merely sought the nearest cover to conceal her weakness. She darted behind a concealing tree and was horribly sick. A supportive hand tugged her hair out of the way and stroked her back.

'You turned green while we were in the air. I knew you were ill,' Dante admitted. 'But I thought it better not to mention it…'

Her head swimming, Belle leant back against his lean, powerful body for momentary support. 'How's the deal coming along?' she whispered, desperate to take his mind off what she had just done.

'Eddie wants to sell the whole lot to me, not only Cristiano's piece. I've agreed,' Dante said succinctly. 'I'll turn the majority of it into a nature reserve, but I'll keep my brother's woods private.'

'It's a lovely way to remember him,' Belle murmured softly.

'On the way back we're being dropped off at the cabin. I want you to see it,' Dante told her. 'We can drive home from there, so you won't have to fly again.'

And there he was once more, being considerate when she least expected it, Belle thought painfully, resting her clammy brow against his shirt front, fighting to muster the courage to detach herself from him when she so badly wanted to cling. She breathed in the rich familiar scent of cologne and husky male and the combination made her head swim with longing. Of course, Dante would be in a good mood with Eddie having agreed to sell the land to him. He had got what he wanted out of their arrangement even if he hadn't got what he wanted when it came to Belle. There was no way Dante *could* want their unplanned child. He had always been honest with her but now he would feel forced to prevaricate, for he could hardly admit the truth.

And she hadn't admitted her own truths either, had she? Belle scolded herself as she joined their guests to admire the fabulous landscape from the hilltop. She tried to pinpoint the exact moment when she had fallen headlong in love with Dante. It had begun in Paris, long before she had even seen that her heart was at risk; it had begun when he opened up and told her about his brother and his family. Slowly but surely, she had begun to see that, much like her, Dante had not received the love he'd needed as a child and, because of that, he shied away from any hint of that emotion, automatically distrusting it.

Belle's grandparents had loved her, but as she'd grown up she had felt increasingly guilty that her mother's lack of interest had meant that her grandparents were forced to raise a child in their retirement years. Dante had only known his sibling's love and, without being shown love, it was hard to trust enough to *feel* love. Yet for Belle, the more she had learned about Dante, the more she had loved him. It had been a slippery slope she'd raced naïvely down at dangerous speed, intimacy making her feel deceptively close to him when she wasn't because he didn't return her feelings.

Krystal and Eddie flew on to Florence for lunch while Dante and Belle were deposited in a forest glade overlooking a small tranquil lake. A two-storey wooden structure met Belle's curious gaze. 'It's very modern,' she commented.

'When Cristiano first had it built it didn't have electric or heating. He liked to come here to unwind after a demanding week at the bank. I talked him round and my company installed the windmill and the turbine in the stream and the solar panels.' As Belle gazed around the tall woodland trees and savoured the tranquillity, she said, 'Wasn't it rude of us to leave Eddie and Krystal behind?'

'No. Krystal said she'd seen enough countryside to last her a lifetime and Eddie wants to take her shopping to put her in a better mood,' Dante retorted, unlocking the cabin door. 'It's not very large...'

Belle wandered into the cosy interior, surprised to see a picnic basket and a chilled bottle of wine awaiting them on the table near the stone hearth. 'Who are these for? Where did they come from?'

'The staff brought over food for our lunch. You have to eat,' Dante reminded her. 'Inside or outside?'

'Outside,' she said, glancing round the cabin, recognising that there was little to see but the walls and the furniture because it had been stripped of any personal possessions. 'Anywhere there's shade.'

Dante spread the rug. Belle removed her shoes and sank down cross-legged to investigate the contents of the basket and lift out plates. Breaking open a soft drink, she murmured, 'It's a beautiful place. Did you come here a lot to see Cristiano?'

'Often,' Dante said gruffly, poised between her and the sun, a lean, powerful figure with a shock of black hair and the golden eyes of a tiger. 'He used to sleep outside on the roof during the summer and he made a point of not using the electric I had installed for him. He preferred lanterns. He was at peace here...at his best.'

'The dogs must've loved it too,' Belle mused, wondering why he had yet to sit down and why his lean, darkly handsome features were so tense.

'We have to have a serious discussion,' Dante informed her tautly.

'I thought we were waiting until Eddie and Krystal were gone.'

'Last night I realised it couldn't wait any longer,' Dante incised. 'We have a child to plan for *now*.'

'*I'll* deal with the baby stuff,' Belle parried firmly, nudging the filled plate she had prepared for him in his direction. 'Aren't you hungry?'

'Not really.'

An uneasy little silence fell.

'It's my child too.' Dante, it seemed, was still set on making his point. 'Naturally I want to be fully involved.'

Belle frowned. *'Do you?'* she asked, her incredulity unhidden.

Dante crouched down lithely on a level with her, black denim stretching taut across his muscular thighs, and a current of hunger rippled through Belle, which she tried to suppress. 'A child doesn't have to be planned to be wanted,' he murmured with assurance. 'I want to *marry* you, Belle...'

'No, you don't,' Belle told him with complete confidence, even as her heart squeezed tight with stress and heartfelt regret that that should be the case. 'I know the gossip columnists went mad over you moving me into the *palazzo* with you only *because* you're famous for being a commitment-phobe. A man with that outlook is unlikely to welcome a child into his carefree life, because there is no bigger or more lasting responsibility than a child. Please don't tell me polite untruths to impress me.'

His stunning eyes shimmered, his wide, sensual mouth compressing. 'I'm not trying to impress you. Everything changed when you came into my life—'

'Yes, I screwed it up,' Belle broke in sharply, steeling herself against his arguments. As she saw it, she was protecting them both from the possibility of making a terrible mistake. Marrying a man who only wanted to marry her because he thought he had to and who didn't love her would be a disaster. 'I fell pregnant. You feel responsible.'

A raw glitter lit his eyes. 'I do *not*.'

'You feel so responsible you're willing to go against your own nature and offer a solution you have never wanted,' Belle condemned tightly, anxiety and pain licking cruelly at her because she considered a proposal made out of pity and the conviction that she couldn't cope alone truly humiliating. 'But I am perfectly capable of returning to the UK and making my own life and bringing up my child.'

'Of course, you are, but that's not what's best for either of us. I want to be with you. I want to be with my child,' Dante bit out impatiently, angry that the dialogue was going even worse than he had expected. He hadn't expected enthusiasm, nor had he expected the level of resistance she was giving him.

'You should know me well enough to know that I would never try to keep you away from our child and that I will happily agree any reasonable access arrangements,' Belle protested.

'That's not enough.' Dante vaulted back upright, poured himself a glass of chilled wine and leant back against the cabin to study her. 'I won't give up on this, you know. I'm very stubborn when you challenge me.'

Belle breathed in deep and slow. Her eyes were prickling and stinging with the tears she was holding back. She blinked hard and angled her attention away from him into the trees. She couldn't bear to marry him because she was pregnant, couldn't bear to reach that position in his life and then watch as whatever physical attraction she held for him slowly waned until finally they had nothing left but their child to share. He deserved better than to have to marry a woman he didn't love, and she deserved better than a man who didn't love her.

'You've until tomorrow evening to think over my proposal,' Dante breathed tautly. 'I have a funeral to attend in Brittany tomorrow. I'll be leaving in the morning.'

'The employee who died?'

'Such a waste of a good man.' Dante sighed. 'There were other positions he could have gone for. He didn't need to work at heights.'

And that was why she loved Dante. He genuinely cared about his employees. Even though that workforce ran into quadruple digits, he sincerely regretted the loss of one. He had a heart even though he didn't acknowledge it. That was why she had to withstand his innate desire to do 'the right thing'. He felt he had to marry her because she was pregnant and that was an outdated idea, and unnecessary. She would manage fine on her own. It would make her much unhappier to marry him and then lose him again.

Krystal and Eddie departed early the next morning and Dante left not long after them, a new distance in his attitude to her. He was annoyed with her for refusing to marry him, she conceded ruefully, because he had decided that *that* was the magical solution to the baby he saw as a problem. But a marriage wouldn't solve the baby complication, it would only create more problems.

Belle went to visit Cristiano's dogs that afternoon and arrived back at the *palazzo* to be informed that she had a visitor waiting for her.

Consternation gripped her when she walked into the elegant drawing room and saw Tracy comfortably ensconced in an armchair, flicking through a fashion magazine over a cup of tea.

'Well, you've certainly landed on your feet here,' her mother mocked as she cast down the magazine and stood up, a tall slim blonde in her fifties, who looked a good decade younger than her years.

CHAPTER TEN

'RELAX,' TRACY URGED as Belle parted her lips. 'I was discreet. I didn't identify myself as your mother, only as a friend. I'm quite sure you've glossed over your downmarket background with Dante. It's never wise to remind a man that you come from a lower level of society than he does.'

Belle relocated her tongue. 'What on earth are you doing here?'

Tracy raised a brow, her green eyes hard. 'It's your own fault. You said you were too busy to see me. What did you expect me to do?'

'Take the hint and leave me alone,' Belle said ruefully. 'As I did three years ago when you left me in London broke and dossing on someone's couch.'

'You're still my daughter.'

'The daughter you never wanted,' Belle reminded her. 'And yet you used me to con thousands and thousands of pounds out of my father, which you certainly never chose to share with Grandad and Gran, who were raising me for you.'

'So, you've seen Alastair and listened to his lies?' Tracy assumed angrily. 'And you *believe* them?'

'Yes, I'm afraid I do,' Belle admitted tautly. 'I've got nothing more to say to you and I can't imagine what you're doing here.'

'You're not that stupid,' Tracy told her. 'Naturally I'm here hoping that you will share a little of the pot of gold you're living in.'

'I haven't got any money to share,' Belle retorted sharply.

'He must give you an allowance, at the very least...'

'No, he's terribly stingy,' Belle told her without skipping a beat.

'I wonder how stingy he would be if I threatened to approach the press and sell the whole *sordid* story of your background...and believe me, there are dirty details you know nothing about,' Tracy told her with a sneer.

Belle had paled but she stood her ground. 'I shouldn't think Dante would give a damn,' she countered. 'I definitely don't think he would let you blackmail either of us.'

Tracy swept up her clutch bag with a flourish. 'If you change your mind, you have my number. We'll see...won't we?'

Belle didn't breathe again until her mother drove off in the taxi she had had waiting for her outside. She felt quite sick and dizzy from the stress of Tracy's visit and her shoulders hunched as she registered that her mother had asked her not one single question about her well-being or her relationship with Dante. Tracy simply saw her as a potentially profitable source she was keen to milk. Of course, that was all she had ever been to her mother, the cash cow she used to punish Alastair Stevenson for not marrying her. She blinked back tears of hurt and hated herself for that weakness because it was a long time since she'd had any illusions about Tracy.

But there was no denying that she was horrified at the idea of Tracy approaching the tabloid press with some cooked-up and no doubt sleazy story to sell about her. That would embarrass Dante, and Belle couldn't bear the concept of that because Tracy was her cross to bear, *not* his. In fact, the only way she could protect Dante from her mother was by leaving him because, if she was no longer living with him, nobody would be the slightest bit interested in buying a story about her ordinary self. Dante, after all, was her sole claim to fame.

Perhaps Tracy had done her a favour by jolting her out of her comfortable groove in Dante's opulent home. Belle knew that she didn't belong under Dante's roof. Now her job was done. Eddie had agreed to sell Cristiano's land back and Dante was paying her for her two weeks in his life, paying her handsomely too. That would provide her with a nest egg for their baby.

She needed to leave Dante. Of course, she would get in touch again in a few months, by which time things would have settled down and he would have accepted that marriage hadn't been a very good idea. What was the point in her staying? If she went, he would have his freedom back. Staying, she decided wretchedly, would be clingy, considering that he had never once asked her to stay on and had already paid her for pretending to be his girlfriend.

Furthermore, if she stepped away now, she would hopefully begin to get over him. If she stayed, however, she would probably surrender and end up marrying him while falling deeper and deeper in love with him. Being only briefly his wife and becoming accustomed to the joy of having a proper place in his life and then having to leave that security would ultimately hurt her much more. A short-term shock of severance would be easier for her to bear than getting involved in a marriage destined to die when Dante's interest faded.

But getting back to the UK with Charlie in tow quickly was impossible, for there were all sorts of regulations to be met. Travelling back to France, on the other hand, would be relatively easy and cheap. She would travel by train and return to the campervan until she got Charlie's travel documents sorted out. She didn't have much to pack because none of the new clothes would fit in a few months and, obviously, she wasn't taking the jewellery with her. But maybe she should take it to sell at a later date for the baby? Dante would pay child support, wouldn't he? He wouldn't abandon them, she told herself urgently. He would be relieved, though, when his most pressing problem moved out from under his roof.

Tears tripping her, Belle packed a small case, gulping and swallowing back the thickness in her throat and the increasingly terrifying image of having to live without Dante. He'd only been in her life for two short weeks and he had turned it upside down. He had walked into her heart and taken up residence there and she couldn't imagine her life without him, which probably meant that she was one of those stage-five clingers he had mentioned and despised.

She had managed for years on her own and she would manage again. Two weeks were two weeks and hopefully she could return to the level-headed, practical being she had been before he'd got a hold of her. That belief taking charge, she opened up the laptop Dante had given her for her use to research train schedules.

Dante returned to be informed that Belle had left earlier that evening with Charlie and a suitcase.

It took him a moment or two to process that information. She couldn't have walked out on him, he told himself, because no woman walked out on Dante. He had always been the one to do the ditching and the walking away. Now it seemed it was his turn to see the other side of the fence. There was a note in the bedroom, the jewellery he had bought her stacked neatly beside it, so the breezy, 'Thanks for the money, I'll be in touch' note didn't really have the effect she might have hoped.

Belle had refused to entertain even the thought of marrying him. He had known from early on in their relationship that she didn't have a mercenary bone in her tiny curvy body So, it wasn't a question of her having gratefully taken the money and run. He didn't credit that. Yes, she had been upset by the marriage proposal, but not enough to leave him over it. If he had been in the mood to laugh, he would have savoured the reality that asking Belle to become his wife had upset her rather than pleased her. He, who had long known himself to be one of the biggest prizes on the marriage market and the target of every designing single woman, had been shot down in flames. But, sadly, he wasn't in the mood to laugh there in that empty bedroom without Belle.

He hadn't got halfway to the funeral he had attended before he had realised where he had gone wrong with the proposal. He hadn't said a tenth of what he should've said. He had struck out because he had put his pride first. He hadn't told her he loved her. He had been too proud to put that out upfront. He swore under his breath and attempted to picture his life without Belle. So bleak was the picture he summoned up, he paled. She had even taken the dog with her!

He strode downstairs, all business now that he knew what he had to do. He checked the laptop he had given her, scrolled through her past history and smiled at the ease of discovering her travel plans. She had gone back to France. Why France instead of the UK, he had no idea, but he was enormously grateful for that stroke of luck because he believed he knew where she had gone and he could get there faster than she could to await her arrival.

Late afternoon the following day, Belle staggered out of her taxi outside the restaurant and paid the driver. She was worried about how she was going to eat for the next few days because Dante's payment had not yet reached her account and the long journey had cost her more than she had expected. She released Charlie from his travel carrier and he went bonkers at having his freedom back, tearing around and then letting out a startled bark and changing direction to go pelting down to the beach. Setting the box and her case to one side, Belle stared to see who had attracted Charlie, and then she noticed the tall dark man poised below the pine trees. The terrier leapt and jumped around him in joyous greeting.

Belle knew only one man who her dog greeted with such enthusiasm. Dante might pay Charlie very little attention, but Charlie was, inexplicably, devoted to Dante. But it couldn't *be* Dante, she reasoned, her heart thumping very fast as she walked down to the beach, her shoes crunching in the sand, getting closer and closer. The man moved out of the dappled light into the sunshine and she stopped breathing altogether, disbelieving the evidence of her own eyes. His luxuriant blue-black hair blew back from his bronzed and beautiful face and her throat closed over as he moved towards her.

'Standing here again takes you back two weeks, doesn't it?' Dante intoned. 'We didn't know each other then. We didn't know what was ahead of us.'

'How the heck did you know where I was?' she gasped.

'Looked at your browsing history on the laptop. You should've brought it with you, although I am very glad you didn't because I would've wasted time trying to track you back to England. Why did you come here?'

'I have to make arrangements for Charlie and I don't have the money yet,' Belle admitted, turning red.

'So, only if I keep you as poor as a church mouse can I hang onto you?'

'You don't want to hang onto me.'

'What am I doing here then?'

'Making this split harder on both of us,' Belle told him heavily.

'But I don't *want* to let you go. I have absolutely no intention of letting you go and would go to any extreme, no matter how ridiculous, to *keep* you,' Dante intoned with fierce determination. 'I won't insist that you marry me but I *will* keep on asking… I'm being frank about my ultimate goal.'

Belle shook her head dizzily. 'What the heck are you talking about?'

'You're looking a touch green again,' Dante noted, urging her over to the concrete bench below the trees. 'Sit down. Take a deep breath, and while you're doing that, *listen* to me.'

As she sat, Dante dropped down into a crouch in front of her and reached for her hand. Stunning dark golden eyes intercepted hers. 'I want to marry you because I love you and making that commitment is important to me, but if you can't face the wedding ring, you can still live with me until the day you die. Nothing less is acceptable...'

Wide-eyed, Belle stared back at him, her colour fluctuating. 'How on earth are you in love with me?' she mumbled.

'Your guess is probably as good as mine. I don't know how it happened, but it did happen very fast,' Dante mused reflectively, his lean, strong face serious as he quirked a black brow in self-mockery. 'One day I was planning to live alone for the rest of my days and the next I'd changed out of all recognition. I wanted you with me. I wanted you with me *all* the time. When you weren't immediately in front of me, I had to find you and know what you were doing, which is why you never really got to enjoy that room of yours for very long on your own. You entered my life and became an incredibly precious part of it.'

'P-precious?' she stammered.

'Very,' Dante confirmed, lifting her fingers to his mouth and kissing them and then checking the nails. 'You've been peeling again.'

'Yes…when I'm stressed, I slip,' she said thickly, wondering if she could dare to believe what he was telling her, if it was actually possible for a man like Dante to fall in love with someone ordinary like her. 'But what if you're imagining that you're in love with me?'

'Why would I do that when I didn't want to fall in love in the first place?'

'Maybe…because I'm pregnant?' she suggested uncomfortably.

'Yes, that *did* increase your desirability once I got over the surprise of it,' Dante admitted. 'But I was already in love with you and fighting all these emotions I never allowed myself to feel before—'

'You kept on reminding me that I would be going home to the UK,' Belle protested.

'As I said, I was fighting what I was feeling and in denial, but I wouldn't have gone as far as actually *letting* you leave me,' Dante assured her confidently. 'I was kind of lonely before you came into my life. I've always been rather solitary in my habits, but you pull me in, take me out of myself, make me happy. Before you, only Cristiano could achieve that feat. So, obviously I'm going to fight to the last ditch to keep you. You're mine. I know a good thing when I find it and I'm not letting you go.'

'Oh, Dante…' Belle whispered. 'Walking away cut me in two but I thought it was what we both needed, although if Krystal hadn't reminded me how anti-marriage you were and my mother hadn't shown up…'

His brows pleated. 'Your *mother*?'

'Tracy, yes… Yesterday, she was after money,' Belle

confided in discomfiture. 'I don't know how she found out I was with you.'

'A friend called to tell me that a photo of us together appeared in an English tabloid.'

'Well, Tracy threatened to go and sell some story about me to the newspapers and would probably make up lies to make it sleazy.'

'She threatened you and tried to blackmail you? That is exactly what she did to your father!' Dante interrupted angrily. 'But you don't deal with her, you don't need to. That's my job now. But she can sell whatever stories she wants to the newspapers, it doesn't bother me. If she tells any lies about you, however, she will find herself dealing with the full weight of the law because I *will* sue.'

'But what will your family think about that kind of stuff?'

'Do you think I care? The truth of what went on in my childhood home behind closed doors is more sordid than anything that could be pinned to you,' Dante derided. 'Don't forget that I grew up with my mother's constant affairs with other men and her abuse and that soured my view of women from an early age. The casual affairs I indulged in didn't improve that view...but then, to be fair, I *chose* women who were content to settle for sex and a good time with a rich man. And then I met you and you taught me that there was another kind of woman out there, one who could be warm and trustworthy and caring and who didn't care about my money.'

Tears glimmered in Belle's violet eyes. 'That's quite an accolade. Are you sure you're not seeing me through rose-tinted glasses?'

Dante laughed. 'No, definitely not. You are much too fond of homeless animals. You bite your nails and you are also very untidy and disorganised.'

'I'm not…and I've stopped biting them!'

'You *are*. I keep on tripping over the shoes you leave lying around,' Dante told her without hesitation. 'So, I think we needn't worry about me seeing you through rose-tinted glasses.'

'It's all right to retain a touch of a rose tint,' Belle told him in reproach as he tugged her upright. 'I'm sure I've loads more faults than you've noticed yet, but I do love you an awful lot.'

'And yet you ran away from me!' Dante lamented. '*And* you refused to marry me—'

'I honestly did believe that you didn't *ever* want to get married or have a child.'

'I did think that way until I met you but much of my resistance to those concepts was driven by a powerful need to disappoint and punish my parents for what they did to my brother and me,' Dante admitted wryly. 'But, with you, I *want* a wife and a family, and yes, it's unfortunate that that news will delight my mother but I'm not about to sacrifice my happiness to punish her.'

'Perhaps in time you'll mend fences,' Belle suggested uncertainly.

'Never. I wouldn't trust my mother near our child either. She doesn't like children. No, it will always be safer to keep my parents at arm's length,' he told her firmly.

'So, when did you decide that you wanted to marry me?'

'The minute I recognised that my home felt like a

home for the first time because *you* were in it,' Dante admitted, lowering his handsome dark head to hungrily claim her readily parted lips. He kissed her breathless and her hands closed into his shirt front and then slid up to grip his shoulders, happiness finally daring to take her in a stormy surge as she allowed herself to believe that he loved her.

'You're really not worried about what Tracy might do?' she pressed. 'You see, that's partly why I left. I wanted to protect you from her.'

Dante smoothed gentle fingers through her tumbled hair. 'I'm not worried about Tracy. I can handle her and it's my job to protect you, not the other way round,' he asserted.

'Why did you insist on paying me that money?' she whispered. 'That was very off-putting.'

'I didn't see it in that light. The money was yours and I wanted you to have it. I didn't want you to feel trapped in my home because you were pregnant and financially dependent on me. I wanted you to feel that you had choices because you've *never* had proper choices,' Dante explained feelingly. 'But I wouldn't have parted with a penny had I known you would leave me.'

'How do you really feel about the baby?' Belle asked.

'Excited…but please, no twins, not until I at least learn the ropes of being a decent parent.' Dante sighed. 'Fortunately, we'll be learning together and we both know what to avoid from our own childhood experiences.'

'Yes, we know what not to do,' she agreed, noticing how dark it was becoming and frowning. 'Dante, where are we going to spend the night? I don't think the campervan will meet your standards.'

'What standards?'

'There are probably reigning monarchs in the world today who don't sleep in as fancy a bed as you do,' Belle told him squarely.

'I wasn't planning on us retiring to the campervan,' Dante said gently. 'I phoned Steve. They have a very acceptable pool-house guest suite prepared for us and I'm expecting to have to suffer through a great hail of I-told-you-so when I introduce you as my bride-to-be, because he was always telling me that there was a woman out there somewhere for me. Oh, that reminds me...'

Dante was digging into the pocket of his tight jeans and pulling something out. He lifted her left hand and pushed a ring onto her ring finger without ceremony.

Taken aback, Belle studied the glittering ring on her finger, a fancily cut sapphire surrounded by diamonds. 'I still haven't said yes to marrying you,' she reminded him.

'You want me to get down on bended knee or something?' Dante asked bluntly.

'No, I want you to promise to tell me that you love me every day and I promise to tell you the same thing,' Belle murmured with a huge smile.

'Done. I love you so much more than I ever thought I could love anyone, *cara mia*. I thought I had an icicle for a heart and you took a blowtorch to the ice,' Dante murmured raggedly. 'Now that we're in a serious relationship, does it mean I can drag you under the trees and have my wicked way with you to celebrate that I've finally got you?'

'Nope. I'm not arriving at their chateau with my hair standing on end and covered in sand. I also want the comfort of the pool house. I'm turning into a material girl,' Belle warned teasingly as she bundled up Charlie and they walked to the campervan parked behind the restaurant, picking up her case on the way.

'*My* material girl,' Dante breathed possessively, casting her an appreciative appraisal. 'My woman, soon to be my wife, and I couldn't be happier.'

Belle stretched up to kiss him before climbing into the campervan. 'So, do you think Cristiano's dogs could come home to us now?'

'Yes, I've been resigned to that idea for at least a week and having competition will keep Charlie on his toes, but they are not *all* welcome to sleep in our bedroom,' Dante informed her firmly.

Belle massaged the long muscular thigh flexing beneath her fingers.

'Then again, if your persuasive tactics are daring enough to impress, I'll think it over,' Dante admitted, on fire with pure lust.

EPILOGUE

DANTE WALKED ONE step through the front doors of the *palazzo* and was engulfed, literally, by dogs, kids and an armful of fragrant wife.

'You didn't say you'd get back early,' Belle exclaimed, thrilled that he was home for lunch on Christmas Eve.

'I like to surprise you,' Dante admitted.

'He's lying,' Steve Cranbrook piped up cheerfully from the doorway of the drawing room. 'He gets antsy when he's away from you too long. Five years married and he's still trying to play it cool. Where do you get the energy from, Dante?'

'I'm high on life,' Dante murmured, curving Belle under one arm, scanning the splendidly decorated hall and the big Christmas tree she had ornamented with such care and enthusiasm. In the space of five years, Belle had turned his life inside out and upside down and he loved it.

But their children were the biggest revelation. Luciano had come along first, red-haired and dark eyed, followed by Cristiano, dark of hair and eye, and then little Violet, the chubby toddler sucking her thumb while hanging onto his leg to stay upright, with her mother's hair and eyes and so laid-back in comparison to her brothers' rampant energy that she was almost horizontal. Dante had never expected to enjoy his children as much as he did while he watched their different personalities and temperaments emerge as they developed. And they were each one different, a smorgasbord of their parents and their genes, and he loved them all.

Tito and Carina, greying with age, wriggled as he moved past in greeting. These days they didn't get much livelier than that and hugged their beds in a huddle. Even Charlie had slowed down a little, although the addition of a mate and then a litter of puppies, none of whom Belle initially wished to part with, had led to Dante declaring a moratorium on breeding. They had four dogs, but it was a constant battle to keep the number down with Belle having taken an interest in a local animal rescue society and seeing all too many needy causes. The courtyard rejoiced in two tortoises and the children had rescue rabbits and guinea pigs. The *palazzo* was overrun with animals.

'Dad and Emily will be with us by teatime. They got held up in London,' Belle told him as they mounted the stairs, the hubbub of Steve and Sancha's children and their own squealing with excitement as they played tag falling away behind them.

'I need a shower.' Dante sighed. 'But first...'

'First,' Belle repeated, gazing up at him as if he hung the moon, an expression on her face that he never ever got tired of seeing because he knew he wasn't worthy of it, knew he couldn't possibly deserve the amount of happiness she had brought into his life.

'Shower,' he framed doggedly, knowing that if he

touched her, he wouldn't stop because he had been without her for four days, and four days was a very long time for a man like Dante to go without his very sexy, very beautiful wife.

Belle breathed her husband in like the addict she was. 'You smell gorgeous… The shower can wait, and you look so sexy with stubble.'

And that was it, Dante was all out of fight, backing her down on the bed and claiming her passionately and thoroughly to sate a need that never quite quit. '*Dio*… I love you so much, *cara mia*. I can't get enough of you.'

He vaulted off the bed, naked and bronzed, to grab his jacket and brought out a box. 'Early Christmas present,' he explained, flipping it open to reveal a diamond bracelet that shone like a river of fire across his darker skin.

Belle lay there in a sated huddle, trying to summon up the energy to return to their guests and the million and one things she had to supervise as a wife, a mother and a hostess. The diamonds glittered round her slender wrist and a smile slashed Dante's darkly beautiful features because he loved to see her wearing the stuff he bought her. 'I need a diamond chain to lock you to the bed and then I wouldn't have to share you with anybody.'

Belle lay back, revelling in being quite ridiculously happy, thinking that having lived through all the lonely, stressful times had been worth it when she looked at her current contented life with Dante.

Her father and his wife, Emily, had slowly become part of the family, grandparents to their growing brood of children. Emily was kind and lovable and she adored kids. Belle was much closer to Emily than she had ever been to her mother or even her late gran. Dante had had one meeting with Tracy to warn her off and Tracy had never bothered them again. Belle had got to know her father bit by bit, visiting him and his wife in London when Dante was in the UK for business. In return the older couple had visited Italy and had been waiting at the hospital when Luciano was born, sharing in their joy at the birth of their first child. They had shown the same interest when Cristiano and Violet were born, and Belle truly valued their enthusiastic approach to being grandparents.

Steve and Sancha were equally close to them, looking after their children when, occasionally, Dante and Belle wanted some alone time as a couple and sharing most family holidays with them. For their last wedding anniversary Dante and Belle had spent a glorious week rediscovering each other on a Greek island. Cristiano's log cabin had been extended and in the summer they frequently slept on the roof under the stars, although Dante only did so as long as he had every comfort on the market with him. In the woods, they got back to nature, fishing and exploring and the children and their friends' children absolutely loved those carefree weekends.

As for Dante's mother, they occasionally ran into her at public events and exchanged polite nods of acknowledgement. Dante's father had passed away two years earlier after a severe stroke. Princess Sofia sent magnificent gifts every time her son had another child and had once dared to drop in and seek the reassurance that her grandchildren were being taught their proud history. But although Dante had become a prince on his father's death, he refused to use the title, deeming that snobbish superiority that had tainted his parents and persuaded them to have children they didn't want too dangerous to nurture in his own family.

'We're going to have another wonderful Christmas,' Belle told Dante cheerfully as she emerged from the shower. 'All the family and friends round the table together, healthy and happy.'

'I was never a people person. You're the one who made that miracle possible for me,' Dante told her, appreciative eyes resting on her as she raced around the room getting dressed.

'We *both* did,' she contradicted softly. 'You had to let love in before our life could happen—'

'I didn't so much let love in as get run over by the equivalent of a ten-ton truck!' Dante teased her. 'Meeting you changed my life.'

Belle grabbed his hand, stretched up to kiss his freshly shaven cheek and gave a little wriggle of sheer appreciation as she looked up at him with her heart in her eyes. 'I love you *so* much...'

'Not half as much as I love you,' Dante told her confidently.

* * * * *

CONSEQUENCES OF A HOT HAVANA NIGHT

LOUISE FULLER

To Aggie:
For allowing me to relive the eighties and nineties
(go Buffy!),
and for trying hard at the things you find hardest.
All my love. X

CHAPTER ONE

GAZING OUT AT the sun-soaked, shimmering turquoise sea, Kitty Quested held her breath.

It was strange to imagine that this water might one day be curling onto the shingle beach near her home in England. But then, even now, nearly four weeks after arriving in Cuba, everything still felt a little strange. Not just the sea, or the beach—this incredible scimitar of silvery sand—but the fact that for now this was her home.

Home.

Lifting the mass of long, copper-coloured curls to cool her neck, she felt her throat start to ache as she imagined the small coastal village in the south of England where up until a month ago she'd lived out her whole life.

Birth.

Marriage.

And the death of her childhood sweetheart and husband Jimmy.

Pushing back the brim of her hat to see better, she blinked into the sunlight as a light breeze lifted her hair, blowing fresh against her cheek and reminding her of everything she'd left behind.

Her parents, her sister Lizzie and her boyfriend Bill, a two-month tenancy on a one-bedroom terraced cottage overlooking the sea. And her job at Bill's start-up, distilling what had become their first product: Blackstrap Rum.

She felt a sharp pang of homesickness.

When Miguel Mendoza, director of operations at Dos Rios Rum, had called her three months ago to discuss the possibility of her creating two new flavours for the brand's two hundredth anniversary, she'd never imagined that it would lead to her moving four thousand miles across the Atlantic Ocean.

If she'd allowed himself to think about it she would have refused. She'd been flattered to be asked but, unlike Lizzie, she was by nature cautious, and the hand she'd been dealt in life had taught her to be wary. Accepting the Dos Rios job would not just boost her salary, it would mean leaving everything and everyone she'd ever known. But, five years after Jimmy's illness and death had put her life on hold, change was what she wanted and thought she needed in order to put her grief behind her and start living again.

So, five minutes after putting the phone down, she'd called him back and said yes.

And she didn't regret her decision. Her new home, a white single-storey villa, was beautiful, and only a short walk from the beach. Everyone was friendly, and after three years in Bill's cramped stillroom, working in the vast state-of-the-art Dos Rios lab felt like a treat. In so many ways it was absolutely the fresh start she'd imagined. She'd made new friends and was building a career. But one part of her life remained untouched—

Her throat tightened.

And it was going to stay untouched.

Reaching up, she captured the dark red hair spilling over her shoulders and down her back. At the airport she'd promised her sister that she would 'let her hair down'. It was an old joke between them, because normally she tied it up, here in Cuba though she had started to let it hang free.

But her hair was one thing…her heart was another entirely.

Jimmy had been her first love, and she couldn't imagine feeling about any man the way she had felt about him. Nor did she want to. Love, *real* love, was both a lightness and a weight, a gift and a burden, one that she didn't have it in her to give or receive any more. Of course, nobody really believed her—her friends and family were convinced that it was just grief talking—but she knew that part of her life was over, and no amount of sunshine or salsa was going to change that fact.

Glancing down into the water, she felt her pulse jump as she spotted a cantaloupe-coloured starfish floating serenely in the gin-clear shallows.

Starfish! What was that in Spanish? she wondered. It wasn't the kind of word she'd learned in the lessons she'd been taking back home—the lessons that had seemed less like a hobby and more like fate when Dos Rios had offered her this four-month contract.

Star was *estrella* and fish was *pescado*, but that didn't sound quite right. If only Lizzie was here to help. Her sister had studied Spanish and French at university and had a natural affinity for languages, whereas her own dyslexia had made even learning English a challenge.

Pulling out her phone, she was just about to look up the word when it began to vibrate.

Her lips curved upwards. Speak of the devil! It was Lizzie.

'Are your ears burning?' she asked.

'No! But my feet are soaking wet. Will that do?'

Hearing her sister's burst of laughter, Kitty started to smile. 'Why are your feet wet?'

'It's not just my feet. I'm soaked through. And please don't tell me that you miss the rain!'

'I wasn't going to,' Kitty protested—although she did, actually.

'You were thinking it.'

Kitty laughed. 'It must be quite a downpour if you got that wet going from the house to the car.'

'The car wouldn't start so I had to walk to the station. I missed my train, and then the next train was held up, and the waiting room was closed for renovations, so me and all the other poor sad wage-slaves just had to stand on the platform and get wet.'

'I thought you were going to get a new car?'

'And when we need to, we will.' Lizzie spoke calmly. 'So stop fretting and tell me why my ears should be on fire?'

Kitty felt the tightness in her chest ease. Lizzie and Bill had basically supported her, not just emotionally but financially, for the last four years. When Jimmy had been admitted into the hospice she had moved into Lizzie's spare room, and after his death Bill had asked her to help him with his latest venture—a micro rum distillery.

It had been an act of kindness and love. They hadn't really been able to afford her salary, and she'd had no experience and nothing to offer except a degree in chemistry.

She could never truly repay them, but after all the sacrifices Lizzie had made the least she could do was convince her sister that they had been worthwhile and that her new life was fabulous.

'I wanted to know what the Spanish word is for starfish,' she said quickly. 'And I thought you'd know.'

'I do—it's *estrella de mar*. But why do you need to know?' Lizzie hesitated. 'Please tell me you're not adding starfish to the rum? Bill and I ate them in China—on sticks like lollipops—and I really don't recommend it.'

Kitty screwed up her face. 'That is gross—and, no, of course I'm not going to put starfish in the rum. I just keep seeing them in the sea.'

She heard her sister groan. 'You're looking at one right now, aren't you? Shouldn't you be at work? Or have I got my times wrong again?'

Kitty grinned. 'I'm not in the office, but this *is* work. I'm doing research.'

Lizzie said a very rude word that her mother had once sent Kitty to her room for saying.

'Well, I just hope you're covering up. You know how easily you burn.'

Glancing down at her long-sleeved blouse and maxi-skirt, Kitty sighed. 'The sun isn't that hot now, but I'm wearing so much clothing and sunblock I'm probably going to come back paler than when I left anyway.'

'Who knows? You might not come back at all. Not if that gorgeous boss of yours finally decides to pay a visit to his hometown and your eyes meet across a deserted boardroom...'

Hearing the teasing note in her sister's voice, Kitty shook her head. For all her pragmatism, Lizzie was actually a committed believer in love at first sight—but then she had every reason to be, having met Bill in a karaoke bar in Kyoto on her gap year.

Kitty, on the other hand, had not even had to leave her house to meet Jimmy. He'd lived next door and they'd met before they'd even been able to walk, when his mother had invited her mother over for tea one afternoon when they were just babies.

'I work in the labs, Lizzie. I don't even know where the boardroom is. And even if he does come to Havana, I don't suppose my "gorgeous boss" will even know who I am, much less care.'

After she'd hung up, having promised to call later, Kitty made her way back up the beach to the forest that edged the sand. It was always cooler there than anywhere else.

She wasn't rushing—and not just because the pine needles were slippery to walk on. It was just how people did things in Cuba. Even at work everyone moved at a pace of their own making, and after a week of replicating her typical English nine-to-five day she'd surrendered to 'Cuban' time. It had felt odd at first, but the sky hadn't come crashing down—and, as Mr Mendoza had told her the first time they'd spoken—she was her own boss.

But as she made her way along a path edged with sea grape and tamarind trees, her cheeks felt suddenly warm. What was she talking about?

Like everything else on this untouched peninsula, these trees, the beach, probably even the starfish, were all part of the Finca el Pinar Zayas estate. A private estate that belonged to *el jefazo*—the big boss, as his staff referred to him.

César Zayas y Diago.

His name was not so much a name as a spell. Rolling her tongue over the exotic syllables, she felt her stomach tighten nervously, as though even thinking them inside her head might have the power to conjure the man himself to this deserted woodland.

Some hope!

Lizzie might imagine that she was going to cross paths with the Dos Rios boss, but so far she hadn't even spoken to him on the phone. He'd copied her in on some emails, and she'd received a letter of congratulations allegedly from him when her contract had been finalised, but realistically it was unlikely that he'd even seen it.

Somehow she couldn't imagine the elusive, work-hungry, publicity-shy CEO sitting in the penthouse office of his company headquarters, chewing his pen and trying to find exactly the right words to toast her success. And that signature that she'd spent so long examining had probably been perfected by one of his personal assistants a long time ago.

Not that she was bothered at his lack of interest. In fact, she was quite relieved.

She had moved from the quiet English coast to the pulsing heart of the Caribbean, but she was still a small-town girl, and meeting her legendary and no doubt formidable boss was an experience she was happy to miss.

And he must feel the same way about meeting her, because he had visited the head office twice since she'd arrived, and both times he had left before she had even realised he was in the country.

Truthfully, though, she hadn't been expecting to

meet him. He might have a beautiful Colonial-style home on the estate, and the site of the original distillery was the Dos Rios headquarters, but his business took him all over the world. According to her colleagues, he visited Havana infrequently, and rarely stayed more than a couple of days.

Of course she was curious about him—who wouldn't be? He had taken a modest, family-owned rum distillery and turned it into a global brand. And, unlike so many of his business peers, he had done so at the same time as refusing to play the media game.

She ducked under an overhanging branch, wondering why it was that despite his phenomenal success César Zayas's private life was so private. If he was famous for anything aside from his rum, it was for the way he guarded his privacy with almost pit-bull determination.

Perhaps he was just modest. His biography on the Dos Rios website certainly implied that: it was brief to the point of being minimalist. There were no personal comments or inspirational quotes, just a couple of lines hidden in a more general piece about the history of the company.

Even the photo accompanying the piece seemed designed not to inform but to mislead anyone looking to find out more about the man behind the brand. He was standing in the centre of a group of men lounging on a veranda, glasses of *ron* in their hands, the colour of the liquid an exact match for the huge burnt orange sun setting behind them. It was an informal shot, but it perfectly captured their camaraderie and their glorious masculine swagger.

They were casually dressed, shirtsleeves rolled up, collars loosened, arms resting on each other's shoulders. Some were laughing, some holding the island's other famous export—the Cuban cigar.

All were gazing at the camera.

All except one.

Remembering the picture, Kitty felt her mouth grow dry.

The Dos Rios CEO was turning away, so that his face was slightly blurred, and it was possible only to sense the flawless cheekbones and sculpted jawline beneath the smudge of dark stubble and tousled black hair.

There was no key to identify who was who, but it didn't matter. Even blurred, his features and the clean lines of his buttoned-up and clearly expensive shirt were stamped with an unmistakable air of privilege, that sense of having the world at his feet. For him, life would always be bright and easy and fast—too fast for the shutter speed of any camera.

Only his smile—a smile she had never seen but could easily imagine—would be slow...slow and languorous like a long, cool daiquiri.

She swallowed, almost tasting the hit of rum and the tang of lime on her tongue.

Except she didn't drink daiquiris. Daiquiris were cocktails, and she had never felt cool or confident enough to order one. Not even here in Cuba.

Especially not here in Cuba.

Everyone was so beautiful and sun-kissed and happy. The men had dark, narrowed gazes and moved like panthers, and the women made even the simplest actions—crossing the road, buying fruit at the market—look as though they were dancing the Mambo.

She hadn't dared to face Havana at night, but she had visited three times during daylight and she could still feel the vibrancy of the city humming in her chest—drowsy but dangerous, like a swarm of bees. She'd been captivated not just by the people but by the faded revolutionary slogans on the walls promising *Revolución para Siempre*—Revolution For Ever—and the Pantone palette of gleaming, buffed *máquinas*, the classic nineteen-fifties American cars that lined every street.

Everywhere there were reminders of the past from elaborate, Colonial-style balconies to curving marble staircases. It was vivid, and exhilarating, and she had been tempted to press herself against the hot stucco and absorb some of the lambent warmth of the city into her blood before heading off to explore the tangle of alleys leading off the main squares.

Only she had a terrible sense of direction.

Speaking of which—

She had reached a fork in the path, and she stopped and glanced hesitantly in both directions.

There was no point trying to use her phone—the signal was only strong enough right by the sea—and it was impossible to see over the tops of the pine trees that gave the estate its name. If she went the wrong way it would take for ever. She'd just have to make her way to the track-cum-road that led through the estate and then she'd know where she was.

She felt her heart begin to beat faster.

Her villa was at the edge of the estate. Usually it was home to one of the maids who worked at the main house, but she had gone to the other side of the island to take care of her sick mother, so it was currently empty. She'd been told by Andreas, the head of Dos Rios security, that she was welcome to explore the estate, but she had mostly stuck to the beach and woods around the house. She had never gone as the far as the road before, not on foot anyway.

It took less than ten minutes, and as she stepped between the trees onto the edge of the track she knew immediately where she was. Thank goodness. From here, her villa was only ten minutes away.

Breathing out in relief, she lifted up her hat and fanned her face—and then froze. Half hidden by the dark green vegetation, sunlight dappling their backs, were a group of the wild horses that roamed the estate.

Her heart gave a thump. She knew from conversations with Melenne, who came in three times a week to clean the *cabaña*, that the horses were not wild in the sense of dangerous, they were just not 'broken'. They moved freely, foraging in the woods, and it showed in their satin-smooth coats and toned muscles.

They were so beautiful, she thought, feeling a lump building in her throat, and tentatively, slowly, she took a step closer, holding out her hand to the nearest one. She held her breath as he gazed at her assessingly, and then her pulse darted as his soft, velvety nose snuffled against her fingers.

Breathing out cautiously, she held her hand steady—and then suddenly there was a rumbling growl from behind her, and as one the horses turned and wheeled away between the trees.

What the—?

Turning round towards the noise, Kitty lifted her hand to shield her face as a burst of sunlight hit her eyes. The noise swelled into a roar and there was a gleam of metal. She gasped, the sound choking off as a motorbike and its rider reared up in front of her. She got just the briefest impression of dark eyes narrowing in surprise, and then everything seemed to go into slow motion as the bike swerved away from her, skidding, tilting sideways, sliding smoothly across the coarse-packed dirt until finally it came to a shuddering stop.

For a moment, time contracted to a heartbeat.

Was he hurt?

Was he—?

She couldn't even think the word—and she pushed it away. She was struggling to breathe, her brain scrabbling, her mind stunned, disbelieving what had just happened. And then something opened inside of her chest, and even as panic jostled with fear she was running towards the bike.

The rider was already on his knees, and as he clambered to his feet he glanced up at her and swore in Spanish under his breath—or at least she assumed by the tone of his voice that he was swearing. Her Spanish lessons had been more focused on conjugating verbs than on cursing.

As she reached the bike she stopped and glanced back down the road, stomach clenching. From here it was possible to see clearly in both directions. Had she been standing on this spot she would have seen the bike, and he would have seen her, and the accident would never have happened.

The randomness of it made her head spin. In contrast, the motorcyclist seemed remarkably unperturbed.

Watching him, she felt her skin start to prickle. He was pressing his hand against the chassis of the bike as though it was one of the horses he'd startled, making the muscles beneath his oddly formal white shirt strain against the poplin.

He looked so vivid and real and she hated that he

might have been hurt; hated too that she had unwittingly played a part in his accident. If only she had been standing where she was now. But then she would never have met him—this man.

Her breathing jerked as the thought sneaked into her head from nowhere and refused to leave.

It had been a long time since a member of the opposite sex had even registered on her radar, but this man resonated.

Out of the corner of her eye she noticed the underside of the bike's wheel, still spinning slowly, and she was grateful for the reminder of what had so nearly happened and how she should react, for otherwise her brain might not have remembered what passed for acceptable behaviour.

'Are you okay?'

He lifted his gaze and for a moment she forgot to breathe as dark green eyes the same colour as the pine trees behind her stared at her in confusion. And then she realised she was speaking in English.

She blinked. 'Sorry, I mean...*se hecho daño*?'

He shook his head slowly, his gaze fixed on her face, and she saw that his expression had shifted from confusion to something like irritation. Instantly the sick panic she'd felt at watching the bike's wheels slide from under him was replaced by a bubbling rush of anger.

'*Cómo*—? I mean, *puede*—? Oh, what's the word?' She broke off in frustration. She was too angry to think straight in her own language, let alone in Spanish.

'That would depend, I suppose, on what it is you're trying to say.'

Her stomach clenched. He was speaking English— fluent, almost accentless English.

But clinging onto her outrage, she pushed past her astonishment. 'How could you be so reckless? You could have been hurt. Or worse,' she said accusingly.

'Unlikely. I wasn't going that fast. Besides…' He paused and then almost casually hoisted up the right leg of his trousers and showed her a thin, knotted scar running up from his ankle. 'I've done far worse.'

She gaped at him in silence, too stunned to respond and dazzled not just by the effortless way he switched between languages but by his casual lack of concern for his own safety. A sliver of anger she didn't really understand twisted inside her as she watched him lean over the bike and haul it upright, nudging out the kickstand with his foot.

'How about you?'

He still hadn't turned to face her, but as he glanced over a jolt like a pulse of electricity passed between them as his eyes locked onto hers, his green gaze so intent she felt flushed and dizzy.

'Are *you* okay?'

She stared at him blankly. He sounded businesslike rather than concerned, but she barely registered his words. She was too distracted by his face. Caught in the sunlight, it was beautiful. The straight nose and jaw were outlined in gold, his skin clear and bright like a just lit flame.

Like a just lit flame?

She felt herself tremble as the words echoed inside her head. Thankfully she'd only thought them and not actually said them out loud, but what was she thinking?

Easy question.

Wrong answer.

She was thinking about his mouth and how it would feel pressed against hers.

She frowned, flustered by her unexpected and unwelcome reaction to a stranger—a stranger who had scant regard both for himself and the safety of others. A stranger who couldn't even be bothered to turn and face her.

Her heart began to beat faster, and she had a sudden impulse to turn and dart back beneath the trees. Only there was something in her that wanted to know what would happen if she stayed.

'I'm fine. Although I'm surprised you're bothering to ask.'

She spoke quickly, her words tumbling over themselves, for she was not by nature a confrontational person—a character trait that had only been reinforced by months of sitting in hospital waiting rooms and dealing with a conveyor belt of compassionate but phlegmatic specialists and consultants.

But something about this man…something in his manner…sparked against her like a match striking tinder.

He tipped his head back, his lips parting slightly as though internally questioning what he'd just heard.

'What is that supposed to mean?'

He spoke softly, but there was an edge to his voice that made the hairs stand up on her arms. But remembering how the wild horses had scattered at his approach, her irritation was rekindled and she felt the last of her panic disappear in the face of his level gaze.

'It means that you almost ran into me.'

His eyes flashed, the whites glinting like teeth, but his gaze stayed locked on her face. 'Yes, because you stepped out in front of me. I only came off the bike because I had to swerve to avoid hitting you.'

Her cheeks coloured and she hesitated. It was true, she *had* stepped out into the road... But, glancing back at him, she gritted her teeth. He wasn't even wearing a helmet. How could he be so arrogant, so blasé?

Suddenly her whole body was shaking. She had a sharp, vivid memory of Jimmy, sitting on the sofa in his pyjamas, his face grey with exhaustion, and her heart began to pound with anger. Jimmy had lived his life so carefully, and yet here was this man—this arrogant, reckless man—taking stupid risks, taunting fate, challenging his own mortality.

'Well, you wouldn't have had to swerve if you hadn't been going so fast,' she said hotly, gesturing towards his scarred leg. 'Which is clearly something you make a habit of doing.'

'Like I said, I wasn't going fast. This is a brand-new bike.' He gave her a disparaging glance. 'I only picked it up today, so I'm still breaking it in.' Eyes narrowing, he shook his head dismissively. 'I'm guessing you've never owned a motorbike.'

No, she had never even ridden a motorbike. They were noisy and dangerous: today was proof of that. And yet she couldn't help wondering what it would be like riding a bike *with him*. She could picture it perfectly—knew exactly how it would feel to lean into that broad back, to feel the bands of muscle tense against her as he shifted gear or leaned into a turn.

Her hands felt shaky, and suddenly it was difficult to breathe. Glancing over at his bike, and trying desperately to hang on to her indignation, she ignored the prickling heat rising over her collarbone. Just because it was new, it didn't mean he shouldn't pay attention to other road-users.

'No I haven't,' she agreed, her hands moving of their own accord to her hips, her brow creasing. 'But it wouldn't matter if I had. It still wouldn't change the fact that you should watch where you're going. This isn't a racetrack, you know.'

She frowned, her brain backtracking. How had he got into the estate anyway? The gates required a code. Maybe he'd wanted to show off his stupid bike to one of the staff, or perhaps he was picking someone up—either way it wasn't something she wanted to get involved in.

She glared at him. 'And you should be wearing a helmet.'

'Yes, I should,' he said softly, his green gaze resting on her face.

Something in his simple, uncompromising answer made her blood start to hum. She held her breath.

In the distance she could see the sea. So far she hadn't found anywhere on the estate where it wasn't possible to catch a glimpse of the unruffled turquoise water, and usually her eye sought it out. But today it was him, this man, who drew her gaze. Only why did he make her feel that way?

The situation—lone female on a deserted road with a strange man—should be making her feel uneasy, but she wasn't scared at all. Or not scared by *him* anyway, she thought, her cheeks suddenly hot as her eyes flitted hastily over the enticing curve of his mouth. The only threat was coming from her own imagination.

She felt another twitch of panic.

Her body was aching with a tension she didn't understand, and her hair, already hot and heavy in the early evening sun, felt as though it was crushing her skull, so that it was an effort to think straight.

Crossing her arms in front of her body, she forced herself to meet his eyes, and suddenly she was shaking again—only not with anger this time. There was something so intense in his gaze, so intimate…

Clearing her throat, she said quickly, 'Look, I don't have time for this. I need to get home.' And away from this intense man and the effect he had on her. Only… She glanced down the deserted road. 'But I suppose I can help you move your bike.'

'That won't be necessary.'

He stared at her calmly, and his calmness, his confidence, pulled her in so that her heart was slamming against her chest.

Only that was ridiculous—it was all ridiculous. Him and the effect he was having on her.

Wanting, needing, to escape the unsettling pull of tension between them, she took a step backwards, tightening her arms to contain the beat of heat pulsing in her chest.

'Fine. Suit yourself,' she said, sharpening her voice deliberately, pursing her lips in a disapproval she wanted to feel, but didn't. 'I get the feeling that's what you're best at anyway.'

'Excuse me?'

Now he turned, his eyes narrowing, and she felt a rush of satisfaction at having finally got under his skin.

'You heard me…' she began, but her words died in her throat, like an actor who had forgotten her lines, and breathing in sharply, her eyes dropped to the brilliant and distinctive red stain blooming on his shirtsleeve like a poppy opening to the sun.

Blood.

CHAPTER TWO

'YOU'RE BLEEDING!'

César Zayas y Diago gazed at the woman standing in front of him, frustration momentarily blotting out the pain in his arm. He didn't regret the injury. He never did. No matter how intense, physical pain was straightforward and short-lived. It didn't make you question who you were.

'You're bleeding,' she said again.

She was English, not American—he recognised the accent—and a tourist, judging by her clothes. Probably she'd been sold a boat trip and then just dumped on the beach and left to find her own way home.

He would have to speak to his security team, but right now he needed to focus on the matter in hand—and most especially this titian-haired trespasser.

As his gaze fixed on her face his breath caught in his throat. *No wonder he'd gone head over heels.* She was astonishingly beautiful.

The first few seconds after coming off the bike he'd been too busy picking himself up to notice, his body distracted and tensed against any incoming pain. But now that he had time to look at her he was finding it hard not to stare.

She was slim, maybe too slim—certainly for his taste—but there were curves too beneath her clothes, and he could practically feel the heat coming off the cloud of flame-coloured hair that reached her elbows. But it was the contradiction between that accusatory, grey gaze and the sensual promise of that fascinating, perfect pink mouth that was making his head spin.

His shoulders tensed. Was it deliberate?

Somehow it seemed unlikely. His eyes flickered assessingly over her face. She looked nervous, less sure of herself than when she'd been berating him—or trying to berate him—in beginner's Spanish.

But then she'd just had a shock.

Glancing down at his right arm, he pressed his fingers against the damp fabric, grimacing.

This was supposed to have been a rare, unscheduled moment of downtime. His day had started in Florida. He'd woken early for a five-thirty session with his trainer and moved seamlessly into a four-hour meeting with his lawyers over some cheap import that was using almost identical bottle branding to Dos Rios. The email about the bike had come into his inbox just as the lawyers were leaving, and on impulse, he'd decided to take a diversion to Havana.

He still wasn't sure why he'd even ordered the bike in the first place. Coming to Cuba required both an effort of will and a secrecy he loathed but couldn't avoid—his parents got so upset when he returned home. But maybe, subconsciously, he'd just wanted to make a point to himself that he *could*.

Besides, a motorbike was an easy way to top up his need for adrenalin, a need that he recognised, and embraced in those hours not spent pursuing global domination of the rum market.

And it had felt good—not just the spontaneity of kicking free of his schedule, but the actual act of bonding with the bike. His body and mind had been immersed in the angles of the road and the rush of the wind—and then suddenly she was there.

Like all accidents, it had happened too quickly for him to have any real sense of anything beyond the bike slip-sliding away from him, the earth tilting on its axis, a glare of sunlight and a blur of trees, and then the noise of metal hitting stone, followed by silence.

Even before he'd looked down and seen the blood he'd known he'd hurt himself, but he'd had enough injuries to be able to differentiate between those requiring a Band-Aid and those that needed a trip to A&E. And anyway, after the first shock had worn off he'd been more worried about *her*.

She'd been so agitated and upset that he had deliberately angled his body away from hers so that she wouldn't see the blood—only then she'd fronted up to him, like a skinny little ginger cat, and he'd forgotten all about his arm.

Nothing had mattered except wiping that dismissive uppity sneer from her mouth.

Preferably with his mouth.

He felt his pulse jerk forward.

Careful, he warned himself. She might be beautiful, but he didn't need another lesson in the pitfalls of acting on impulse—and by that he didn't mean taking a bike for an unplanned road test.

Her eyes were wide with panic. 'Why didn't you say something?'

'It's fine.' He held up his hands placatingly, and then regretted it as a drop of blood splashed onto the pale dirt.

'How can you say that when you're dripping blood everywhere?'

She was looking at him as though she'd seen a ghost. For a moment he thought about telling her about the other times he'd come off a bike, but it might backfire and make her panic more. And anyway, it was private. All of it was private. His pursuit of precision, the transcendence of the everyday and that heightened awareness that came with being at one with the machine. How could he explain what it felt like to lose all sense of himself—his past, his position as CEO, all of it—in the heat and speed of the ride? Why would he want to explain that to her?

He glanced past her back down the empty road. Why was she even here? On her own. She was just a tourist and now she was in the middle of a drama. No wonder she looked out of her depth.

It made him feel both irritated and protective. And then he felt angry with himself for feeling anything at all. Feelings—his in particular—were dangerously unreliable. He had the scars to prove it. And he wasn't talking about the ones on his body.

'Look, nothing's broken. It's just a graze.'

'Even if it is you should still get it checked out. It's not worth taking the risk.'

His jaw tightened. It was on the tip of his tongue to tell her exactly who he was, and that this was his estate and she was trespassing, and therefore the risk was all hers. But that would only confuse matters further.

He raised an eyebrow. 'Is that a professional opinion?'

She glared at him, her chin jutting upwards. 'I don't have a car, but I could call an ambulance.'

An ambulance?

Frowning, he shook his head, contemplating all the time-consuming and unnecessary complications of such a step. 'Absolutely not. It can wait until I get home.'

Forehead creasing, she took a step forward. 'I don't think you should wait. What happens if you feel dizzy, or the bleeding won't stop?'

She hesitated, and he could see the conflict in her eyes—doubt at what she was about to suggest fighting with a determination to do the right thing. A long time ago he too had been just as transparent and easy to read. But he'd learnt the hard and humiliating way to keep his feelings hidden, or better still to avoid them altogether.

Her grey eyes rested on his face. 'Look, we can walk the bike back to my villa. It's not far from here. I have a first aid kit and I know how to clean a wound. At least let me take a look before you do anything else.'

So she lived nearby. He wondered where she was staying. From memory, he thought there were a couple of villas beyond the woods, but it seemed an odd place to choose as a holiday home. Most of Havana's visitors liked to be nearer the city centre and all the regular tourist attractions. But there was something about this woman that made him think that perhaps she wasn't here for the Malecón, the Gran Teatro or the Plaza Vieja.

So why was she here?

The answer shouldn't matter, but for some reason it did. Before he had a chance to wonder why, he heard himself say, 'Okay. You can take a look at it. But no ambulance.'

The walk to her villa took less than ten minutes.

Inside, she gestured towards a comfy-looking sofa. 'Sit down and I'll get you a glass of water.'

Sitting down, he felt a sense of *déjà-vu*. It was exactly the kind of traditional Cuban *cabaña* that his grandparents had grown up in, only theirs had been home to at least ten people. Not that they'd seemed to mind. For them—for his own parents too—family was everything.

He shifted in his seat, the ache in his chest suddenly sharper than the ache in his arm. He knew that his mother and father were proud of how he had built up the business, and grateful for the comfort and security he had given them, but what they really wanted—what would make them willingly give up their luxurious lifestyle in a heartbeat—was a grandchild they could spoil. Not that they said so, or at least his mother didn't, but he felt their hope every time he mentioned a woman's name in passing.

His stomach twisted. Children required parents, and typically that meant two people who loved one another, only that just wasn't going to happen for him. Maybe the right woman was out there somewhere, logically, statistically, he knew she must be. But no amount of logic could counteract the fact that he didn't trust himself to choose her, not after what had happened with Celia.

'Here.'

She was back. Handing him a glass, she sat down beside him with a bowl of water, a towel and a large plastic box. When she'd told him she had a first aid kit he'd assumed she meant something she'd picked up at the airport. This, though, looked on a par with the kits at the distillery.

'You're very well prepared,' he said softly.

He felt her tense.

'It's just the basics.' She glanced up at him accusingly. 'You should probably have a kit on your bike.'

In fact he did have one, and he was on the point of telling her that, but he was suddenly too distracted by the way her beautiful red-gold eyebrows were arching in concentration as she rummaged through the box.

Pulling out a packet, she looked up at him, her eyes meeting his, then dropping to the shining patch of crimson on his upper arm. 'I need to see if it's stopped bleeding.'

'Okay.' He nodded, but he was distracted by a glimpse of her feet. She had taken off her shoes, and there was something strangely arousing about her bare toes.

Pulling his gaze away, he glanced back up at her face.

A trace of pink coloured her cheeks. 'So I need you to take your shirt off,' she said huskily.

Kitty swallowed.

I need you to take your shirt off.

As her words reverberated inside her head and around the room her eyes darted towards the triangle of light gold skin at his throat. If only she'd just ignored his objections and called an ambulance. Outside, on the road, with his shirt turning red, she hadn't thought about anything but the fact that he needed help. She certainly hadn't envisaged him taking his clothes off. But how else was she going to be able to deal with his injury?

She cleared her throat. 'Or I could cut the sleeve off?' she offered.

He didn't reply. He just stared at her. And suddenly

she forgot all about his shirt, and even his injury, for nobody had ever looked at her so intently. It was as though he was trying to see inside her, to read her thoughts. Her muscles tightened against a sudden flood of heat. No one had ever looked at her with such focus, not even her husband. It was intimate, exhilarating, both an intrusion and a caress—

'No, it's fine. I'll take it off,' he said.

She watched as he started trying to undo the buttons, but they were sticky with blood, and before she knew what she was doing she leaned forward, batting his hands away.

'Here. Let me.'

Her heart began to beat faster as her fingers pulled at the buttons. She could feel the heat of him beneath his shirt and, try as she might, she couldn't stop her eyes from fixing on his sleek bronze skin as the fabric parted.

Her fingers twitched against the buckle of his belt and, avoiding his gaze, she lifted her hands and inched backwards. 'I'll let you take it from here,' she said.

He shrugged his left shoulder free and then peeled the shirt tentatively away from his injured arm.

For a moment she stared at him in silence, her heart pulsing in her throat. It had been such a long time since she had looked at a man's body. Or at least a body that looked like his.

With broad shoulders tapering to a slim waist his body was muscular, but not overly so, with just the finest trail of dark hair splitting the lean definition of his chest and stomach. His skin was smooth and golden, but it wasn't his skin that drew her gaze, but the two scars running almost parallel up his abdomen.

Clearly he hadn't been joking when he'd said he'd had far worse injuries. But why, having been so badly hurt, would anyone take more risks?

It wasn't a question she could ask a stranger—not even one sitting bare-chested on her sofa.

'What do you think?'

Lost in thought, she was caught unawares by his question and gazed up at him dazedly.

'What do I think?' she repeated his question slowly. Her brain seemed to have stopped working.

'About my arm.'

Dragging her eyes up to the curve of his bicep, she breathed out unsteadily. He had been right. The skin was scuffed, and crusted with grit from the road, but it was just a graze.

'I think it will be fine, but it'll be easier to say once I've cleaned it.' She gave him a small, tight smile. 'Tell me if I hurt you.'

There was quite a lot of blood, but she wasn't squeamish, not any more...not after everything she'd seen and had to do for Jimmy. And anyway it was easier not to think about what so nearly might have happened if there was something practical to do.

'I will.'

His eyes met hers and she felt his gaze flow over her skin, cool and dark and unfathomable like a woodland pool. Her stomach knotted fiercely. Outside, in the aftermath of the accident, there had been so much going on. Now, though, his aura was undiluted—a mix of sandalwood and sexual charisma that made a flicker of unfamiliar heat rise up inside her.

Forcing herself to ignore his body, she focused on trying to be as gentle as possible as she washed away the blood, carefully easing loose the tiny pieces of grit that were embedded in the graze. There was just one last bit now...

She could feel his pulse vibrating steadily beneath his skin, and yet one tiny variable on that road might have stopped it beating for ever. The thought made her shake inside with loss and anger—anger at the unfairness of life, and with this man who wore his beauty and certainty like a shield.

Biting her lip, she leaned in closer, resting her hand against his thigh to help steady herself.

'Sorry.' She'd heard him breathe in and, glancing up, saw he was gritting his teeth. 'Did I hurt you?'

She felt his leg muscle tighten, and quickly she lifted her hand.

'Not exactly,' he said, staring straight ahead. 'Have you finished?'

'Almost.' She patted his skin dry with the towel. 'I don't think it will bleed any more, but I'll put this dressing on, then you won't have to think about it.'

Glancing down, she frowned. 'Oh, I nearly forgot.' Picking up his hand, she washed the smudges of dried blood from his fingers. 'There.'

'Do you have children?'

'What?' She stared at him in confusion.

'I just thought—' He held her gaze. 'You just seem like someone who knows how to care for people, and you're so well-prepared.'

Her heart was pounding. It made no sense, but for one crazy moment she almost told him the truth. This man, this stranger. Only he didn't feel like a stranger. It felt like he knew her so well.

Throat tightening, she stared past him, remembering the months she and Jimmy had spent trying to get pregnant. She had so wanted to give him a baby, but her body just hadn't co-operated. By the time she'd decided to look into it medically, Jimmy had been diagnosed, and then afterwards it hadn't mattered anymore. Although, since arriving in Cuba her cycle had been all over the place, so clearly her body was just ultra-sensitive.

Lifting her chin, she found him looking at her. Meeting his gaze, she shook her head. 'No, I don't have any children. I can't have them,' she admitted.

Before, in England, it had always hurt even to think that sentence inside her head, but somehow saying it now, to him, made it hurt less. How crazy was that? And unfair. To her parents and friends and Lizzie. They had spent so long talking to her, and yet here she was opening up to this stranger—this semi-naked stranger.

Her face felt hot and tight. 'I'm sorry, you don't need to know that that.'

'Don't be sorry. I asked a question and you answered it.'

His words repeated themselves inside her head. He made it sound so simple. But of course it was simple. Everything was simple between them. They had no history, no past, no future. Nothing but a random connection on a dusty road.

And a fluttering pinwheel of anticipation spinning inside her stomach.

Had she been looking for love or seeking some kind of romantic adventure then it might have felt different. But there would never be anyone like Jimmy. What she'd felt for him had been unique, and it was over now—and that was fine, because she knew too how it felt to lose the one you loved, and she never wanted to feel that ache of loss again.

He shifted forward and her pulse boomeranged.

What she wanted now was *him*. This man. This nameless stranger. To feel the hot, languorous touch of his hands and lips warming her skin like sunshine.

His fingers brushed against hers and she tensed, her breath scraping against her throat.

She could smell his cologne, that hint of sandalwood and lemon, and beneath it his own clean, masculine scent, a sensual halo of salt and shade and burning sun. Her pulse leapt forward unsteadily, heat rising up over her throat as his dark green eyes rested on her face.

He was too close, but she couldn't move. She didn't want to move. She wanted to get closer, to touch the curve of his mouth, to feel the tension of his skin, the swell of his muscle. She wanted to hold him close, and be held, to have the warm, solid intimacy of his body pressing against hers.

'You're trembling.' He frowned. 'It's probably some kind of delayed shock. Let me get you—'

She felt suddenly desperate. Her blood pulsed against her skin. She didn't want him to leave. 'No.' Her fingers closed around his. 'No, it's not that.'

Her heart was suddenly beating too fast, and her blood felt as if it had turned to air.

For a second they both stared at each other. He was so close now—close enough that she could feel the heat of his skin and see the flecks of amber in his eyes.

He wasn't a memory or a fantasy.

He was beautiful, full of life and energy, warm and solid and real.

And he was shaking too. She could feel him.

The sound of her heartbeat was filling her head. She felt almost dizzy with longing.

'No, it's not that,' she said again. 'It's this...'

Leaning forward, she pressed her hand against his chest and breathed out unevenly. His skin was warm and smooth and taut, just as she'd imagined. And beneath it she could feel his heart hammering in time with hers.

He sucked in a breath, his jaw tightening. In his narrowed eyes she could see desire fighting with control, and she felt her breath dissolve as he reached up and stroked her cheek.

For a moment their eyes locked, and they breathed each other in, and then, leaning forward, she brushed her lips hesitantly against his, her mouth clumsy with the freedom of touching him.

'I don't even know your name...' he whispered against her mouth.

'It doesn't matter.'

She kissed him again and he pulled back a little, his fierce green gaze trained on her face. She knew that he was giving her space to think, time to change her mind.

Her heart was racing. Should she say something? Tell him that this wasn't who she was ordinarily? That she'd changed her mind. Only she couldn't say that because it would be a lie.

And it would mean stopping, and she didn't want to stop. She didn't want to think or speak or explain. She just wanted to lose herself in this moment, lose herself in him, because right now this *was* what she was, and he was who she wanted.

Threading her fingers through his hair, she pulled him closer. Instantly he pulled her closer too, angling his body, his tongue, to deepen the kiss. His hands slid beneath her blouse, moving over her back from her hip to her waist, up to the catch of her bra.

He stripped her out of her clothing and pulled her onto his lap so that she was straddling him. Lowering his mouth, he kissed her breast, brushing his lips against one nipple and then the other, and in a heartbeat her body turned to liquid.

The intensity of her desire was both a shock and a revelation. Always before it had been a slow and steady progress. This was like throwing a match on gasoline— a pure white-hot blazing urgency that blotted out everything but a need for more.

His hands were at her waist, pulling her down. His mouth was seeking hers now, and instinctively she reached for his buckle.

Groaning, he grabbed her wrists. 'Let's go to your room.' He was fighting to get the words out.

'No.' Tugging her hands free, she pulled the belt open, and then the zip, and felt his body tense as her fingers wrapped around him.

He groaned again, his hands stilling hers. 'I don't have any condoms.'

'I don't either.'

For a moment, she was shocked. In the heat of everything, she had forgotten. But his words reassured her, for clearly he was a responsible lover, and the fact that he was holding back made her feel that she could trust him.

'It's okay.' Leaning forward, she looped her arms around his neck and kissed him fiercely.

Groaning, he raised his hips, shrugging himself free of his trousers, and then he leaned backwards, taking her with him.

His pupils flared and for a second she rode him lightly, teasing the hard, straining length of him, revelling in her power to arouse him. And then, gripping his shoulders for balance, she parted her legs and guided him inside her.

He breathed in sharply. His jaw was taut with concentration, the muscles in his arms and chest bunching as she began to rock back and forth, her breath quickening in her throat as his fingers moved between her thighs, working in time to the fervent, pulsing ache there.

His eyes locked on hers—dark, rapt, blazing. '*Mírame!* Look at me,' he said, his voice hoarse.

She was fighting for control. Heat was gathering inside her and she clutched frantically at his arms, pulling him closer and then pushing him away, needing to let go but wanting to make it last for ever.

Her muscles clenched, her breathless body gripping his. She felt his hands catch in her hair and suddenly she couldn't bear it any longer. Arching against him, she tensed against the heat and the hardness, shuddering helplessly. He groaned, pushing against her, seeking more depth, and then, gasping into her mouth, he thrust upwards.

CHAPTER THREE

SLOWLY CÉSAR BREATHED OUT, his eyes blinking open. For a moment he didn't know where he was—and then he remembered. He must have fallen asleep for a moment, lulled by the languid warmth of her body and the sudden heaviness of his own limbs.

Fixing his eyes on the ceiling, he frowned. It had been a long time since he had held a woman close like this, more than a decade, at least. But then today had been exceptional for any number of reasons.

His chest tightened as he felt the most exceptional of those reasons shift beside him.

Glancing down at her naked body curled around his, he felt his pulse accelerate. He'd just done the one thing he'd sworn never to do again—he'd let his libido dictate his actions.

He grimaced. As if he needed any reminding about the consequences of that youthful, humiliating indiscretion. They were branded in his conscience and he could still feel his parents' shock and disappointment across the years. After he'd made such a fool of himself with Celia he'd sworn never to let a woman get under his skin. And he'd kept his promise.

Until today.

Until…

He gritted his teeth. *Maldita sea!* Thanks to his sudden and completely uncharacteristic loss of self-control he didn't even know her name, but the strength and speed of his desire had caught him unawares. He should have fobbed her off on the road. Better still, he should have called Andreas, his head of security, and let him deal with her. It was his job, after all. But instead he'd let himself be distracted by a curving pink mouth.

He could have called a halt when she'd leaned forward and kissed him with that same perfect, pink mouth, but as her lips had melted against his, his brain, his body, his self-control had gone into meltdown. His past, his promises had been forgotten. Nothing had mattered but her. His whole being had been fixed on the need to touch and taste every inch of her, and even now his still-hungry body was clamouring for more.

But perfect pink lips could still lie and deceive and frankly there was no need for him to go there again. He might have been young, but he was a quick learner— and that lesson had been well and truly drummed into him.

His mouth twisted. So what now?

As though she could hear his thoughts, the woman shifted against him, and instantly his groin began to ache. Reluctant to reveal the hard proof of her ability to turn him on, he started to move. But she was already inching backwards, peeling her damp skin away from his and scooping up the muddle of clothes from the floor in one graceful movement.

Was she practised at this?

The thought snagged in his head and then he pushed

it quickly away. It was none of his business, and besides he wasn't in any position to judge.

'Here,' she murmured. 'These are yours.'

Looking up, he gritted his teeth.

She was pulling her blouse over her head and, catching a glimpse of her pale, curving breast, he felt his skin twitch, his body hardening and aching with a sudden, sharp, serrated hunger. She looked impossibly sexy, and suddenly the heated, passion-filled minutes of earlier felt like just a taster before the main meal.

He wanted more. He wanted to feel that soft skin next to his and the whisper of her breath against his mouth.

He felt another twitch of desire—although this time it might just as easily have been irritation.

Obviously he wanted more.

His last 'relationship' had ended a little over seven weeks ago and, having been flat out at work ever since, trying to resolve this damned trademark dispute, he'd neglected his personal life. Although, given how hard he tried to maintain boundaries, maybe *im*personal life might be a better description.

Either way, to put it bluntly he hadn't had sex in a long time, and this beautiful, uninhibited woman standing in front of him had stirred his hunger.

So what if she had?

It had happened, and it had been incredible. Better than incredible, he thought, his heartbeat jerking as their tangle on the sofa replayed inside his head. And he wasn't going to pretend that he wouldn't willingly pull her back onto that sofa and carry on where they'd left off. Or deny that she was attractive, or that he was attracted to her. But whatever this was—this thing he was feeling, this unruly, insistent enchantment that had sneaked up on him unannounced—he wasn't going to act on it again, no matter how hollowed out with longing he felt.

In fact, his unprecedented physical response only increased his determination to stay cool and detached. For he'd already made the mistake of trusting his body before, and his libido had been proved a poor judge of character.

He glanced down at the scars that ran across his chest and down his muscled abdomen. They might come from a different kind of foolhardy behaviour, but they were honestly acquired, and not the result of emotional weakness or self-delusion.

There would be other women, and next time he would look where he was going.

A breath of cool air drifted over his skin and, leaning forward, he took his trousers and shirt from her outstretched hand and started to get dressed.

In his experience, women normally tried to extend this moment. It was one of the reasons he always preferred to find somewhere neutral to meet. But this woman hadn't even wanted to know his name, and having sex with him didn't appear to have changed that fact.

It was a completely new experience for him—one that in theory he should welcome. And yet he found himself feeling slightly aggrieved by her lack of curiosity.

But then in some ways—although he wouldn't make a habit of it—his anonymity, and hers, was actually a bonus. For the first time in his life he'd had sex with a woman who didn't know or care who he was and, weirdly, he found himself trusting her more because of that.

This hadn't been some carefully planned attempt to seduce him. Nothing was fake. She hadn't told him she loved him or that he was special, nor made any promises. They had both got what they wanted and now they could get back to their lives.

He buckled up his belt and began pulling on his shirt, ignoring the slight tightness in his arm as he pushed it into the sleeve.

'Is your arm okay?'

Looking up, he felt his pulse slow. A lock of that glorious red hair hung loosely across her forehead, and he had to stop himself from reaching out and smoothing it away from her face.

'Yes. Good as new.'

Holding his gaze, she gave him a small stiff smile. 'I'm glad.'

There was a moment of silence, and then she cleared her throat. 'Look, I don't really know what's normal for this situation. I don't usually do this kind of thing, you know—'

He waited a moment, then shrugged. 'Me neither.'

Watching the tic of tension along the curve of her jaw, he knew for certain that he'd got under her skin. What was less certain, though, was why that mattered to him.

She flushed. 'Okay, well… I'm sure you've got things to be getting on with.'

His hand stilled against the top button of his shirt. In other words she wanted him to leave. She was kicking him out.

'Of course.' He felt a twist of irritation, followed by a sudden intense need to dictate the terms of their encounter. Deliberately slowing down the buttoning of his shirt, he glanced assessingly round the room. 'Nice house,' he said slowly. 'How did you find it?'

Her eyes met his. 'It came with my job.'

He felt a ripple of disquiet. 'What job?'

She frowned, not at his question but at the terseness in his voice that he hadn't bothered to disguise.

'I work for Dos Rios—you know, the rum. You might have heard of them.'

His chest tightened. Dos Rios had a policy of providing temporary accommodation for consultants and overseas contractors. His PA would know the details, but obviously he wouldn't have been notified. The comings and goings of his employees was way below his pay grade.

'I should do,' he said. 'As the business was founded by my family.'

He paused, watching her face as he let his words sink in.

'What do you mean?'

The colour had drained from her cheeks. She was staring at him in confusion.

'I—I didn't— I don't...' She was struggling to speak.

'Understand?' He finished her sentence. 'Then perhaps I should introduce myself. My name is César Zayas y Diago.'

In the still, tense silence that followed his remark, Kitty felt her insides loosen. 'No, you can't be,' she said hoarsely.

Her stomach was in freefall.

It couldn't be him. It *couldn't* be, she thought frantically. She'd been in the labs only yesterday, and surely somebody would have said something about his imminent arrival.

He must be lying.

Only her skin felt suddenly too tight, her heartbeat too loud, and as though she was looking at him for the first time she registered the tiny pleats at the top of his shirtsleeves; the expensive dark suit trousers and the handmade black leather brogues.

His eyes rested on her face and she felt a prickle of heat spread over her skin as he held out his hand.

'I assure you I am.'

His voice had grown cooler, its authority no longer like quicksilver beneath the surface but smooth and inflexible like high tensile steel, and with a pang of acceptance she knew that he was telling the truth.

There was only one thing to do and, feeling her breath ricocheting against her ribs, she took his hand and shook it briefly.

His eyes raked her face and then he smiled. Only it wasn't the slow, languorous smile of her imagination. Instead it was cool and assessing and uncompromising. The smile of a CEO...the smile of a boss.

Her boss.

Her heart was leaping against her ribs. Surely there was some mistake? But she knew that there wasn't. No matter which way she turned, the picture and the facts were still the same.

She'd just had sex—wild, unplanned sex—on a sofa with the man who signed her paycheque.

Her head was spinning.

In the five years since Jimmy's death she'd not so much as looked at a man—she certainly hadn't been intending to meet one today. Ironically, if she had been, she would have been taking more care and she might not have stepped out in front of his bike.

But out there on the road there had been more going on than just a near accident. They might not have collided physically, but some invisible chemical reaction had been set in motion.

Her pulse pitched, carried along by another current of panic.

If he'd simply summoned her into his office and introduced himself, like any normal boss, this would never have happened. But, no, he'd had to fall off his motorbike, so she'd had all those unnecessary and confusing and *unguarded* emotions churning around inside her. And that tension between them had kept on winding tighter and tighter.

Remembering the feel of his body against hers, she felt heat wrap around her face. With him she had become another person. His hands, his mouth, had unlocked a wildly passionate woman. Her hunger had been beyond her control—she hadn't known it was possible to feel what he'd made her feel. It had been incredible, and she was still reeling from what had happened. And the fact that she had made it happen.

She had wanted that tumult of touch and release. She had wanted the solid weight of a man's body pressing into her. She had wanted him.

Not love or commitment. Not a future or a soulmate. She knew the void in her heart would never, *could* never, be filled by any man, because she knew the other side of love was loss, and she simply didn't have it in her to deal with that terrible ache of loneliness.

After Jimmy had died the pain had been unbearable, and she'd sworn never to allow herself to be that vulnerable again. It was easier simply to shut down that part of her life rather than risk having it snatched away again.

But she was still a woman, and this man was so gorgeous, and suddenly that had been enough. Enough for her to let go, to let her hair down. Only now she understood that a part of why it had been enough had been their anonymity and the knowledge that she would never have to see him again.

And now it turned out that she was working for him.

She looked up at him, dazed and then out of nowhere she pictured her sister's face. Lizzie wouldn't care that César was her boss. She would argue that desire was a great equaliser. Of course that was hard to do when your skin was still humming from the heat and hardness of your boss's body, but she couldn't change what had happened so she was just going to have to face it head-on.

Her stomach clenched. And becoming a widow had taught her all she needed to know about facing difficulties head-on. 'I didn't know who you were.'

His eyes found hers. 'Clearly. Unless you always try to kill your boss and then seduce him.'

Her cheeks felt suddenly hot. 'I didn't try and kill you. You nearly ran me over.'

He stared at her impassively. 'But you did seduce me.'

She felt her stomach knot. It wasn't a question, and there was no point in lying. 'If I'd known who you were—'

He raised an eyebrow. 'So you work for me?'

'I work for Dos Rios.'

After what had just happened between the two of them it seemed important to differentiate between the man and his business.

The slight curl to his lip suggested that he registered her intent. 'In what capacity?'

'I'm working on the anniversary rums,' she said quickly. 'I'm Kitty Quested.'

They'd already shaken hands, so instead she forced her mouth into a small, stiff smile. Out of the corner of her eye she caught a glimpse of the corner of the sofa, and her pulse moonwalked backwards. This polite formality after the fierce intimacy of earlier felt horribly artificial and unsettling.

Looking up, she met his gaze. He smiled—the kind of smile that made it difficult to swallow.

'I remember,' he said slowly. 'Blackstrap.'

The word echoed like a gunshot around the quiet room. She felt a ripple of panic. He was going to sack her. 'I know what you're thinking…'

'And I know what you're thinking.' He held her gaze. 'But, no, I'm not going to fire you. And, yes, with hindsight, that—' he gestured towards the sofa '—was probably a bad idea, but it's too late to worry about that now.'

He paused, and she felt her face grow warm as his dark green eyes dropped to her mouth.

'In fact it was too late way back when I saw you out there on the road.'

Her breath caught in her throat. She felt her body stirring, and then a swift rush of shame. How could she have such a strong response to a man who, to be frank, she hardly knew? When the man she'd loved, and still loved, was dead. It made no sense, and it was going to stop now.

Whatever connection they had, it would be better, simpler, safer if it existed solely on a professional basis from now on.

'This won't happen again. Obviously.' She spoke in a rush, needing to know that he understood and felt the same way as she did. 'It was just…' She searched for the word.

'Sex?' he suggested.

Her cheeks were growing pinker, but she held his gaze. 'Yes, it was just sex, and what's more important is our working relationship, so I think it would be best if we just put it all behind us.'

He stared at her in silence. Then, 'That won't be a problem,' he said softly. 'From now on you and I have a clean slate. But you don't need to worry about our working relationship, Ms Quested. I really don't spend much time in Havana.'

His words were clipped, his expression impassive.

'Enjoy your time at Dos Rios and I wish you luck in the rest of your career.'

She watched as he turned and walked quickly across the room. As the door closed behind him, she breathed out unsteadily.

He was gone, and that was what she wanted.

Better still, it sounded as though there would be no chance of them ever meeting again, and that was what she wanted too.

It was better that way. Her throat tightened.

All she needed to do now was make herself believe it.

CHAPTER FOUR

HUNCHING OVER THE screen of her laptop, Kitty stared despondently at her notes. She was trying not to panic but there was no point in denying the obvious: after weeks of trial and experimentation, she was stuck.

Straightening her spine, she gazed around the space-age Dos Rios labs, breathing unsteadily, suddenly ridiculously close to tears.

She hardly ever cried. In books and films tears could cure blindness and mend wounds. In real life, though, they just gave you a headache and made your skin all blotchy.

But for the last few weeks she'd kept feeling this sadness. Not like the grief of losing Jimmy—a grief that had made her feel as if she was at the bottom of the ocean, gazing up through black waters. This feeling was nothing like that. It was just frustration that she couldn't seem to do her job.

It didn't help that at Blackstrap the creative process had felt so organic and effortless.

Partly that had been down to the fact that the business had only just been starting up, so there had been no actual deadline and therefore no pressure. And, of course, Bill was so incredibly laid-back.

Now, though, she was working for a global brand that had become almost a byword for rum, and time was running out.

Thinking of Jimmy, and their short, sweet marriage, she felt a lump rise in her throat. She knew all about time running out.

But she was not going to go there and, pushing her memories aside, she closed her laptop and slid it into her bag. She took the stairs down to the foyer and stepped out into the sunlight. After the chilled air of the labs the heat felt like an oven, and she was grateful to get into the air-conditioned cool of the car that took her to and from work.

Leaning back, she closed her eyes. Probably part of the reason she felt so defeated was that she was tired, the kind of tired that felt like an actual weight, physically crushing her.

She sighed. It was her own fault. She'd been sleeping badly and waking early and, although she'd grown used to her own company, the days had started to feel very long. So, without planning it, she'd fallen into a routine of going into the labs and staying late.

Clearly she was in a rut. She needed to forget about rum, put on some sunscreen and get some exercise and fresh air. She couldn't remember the feeling of sunshine on her face—and when had she last gone for a walk?

Her pulse stilled. Oh, she knew exactly when she'd last gone for a walk. It was not something she was likely to forget—or rather he was *someone* she was not likely to forget.

Picturing César Zayas's green-eyed gaze and his hard, muscular body, she felt her skin tighten, and she pressed her thighs together, her muscles tensing against a sudden, dizzying flood of heat.

She had promised herself that she wasn't going to think about him today. It was the same promise she'd made and failed to keep every day since he'd walked out of her villa.

Her cheeks felt hot. It had been stupid to feel that way when he'd been a complete stranger, but it was even more stupid, not to say baffling and pointless, to feel that way now she knew he was her boss.

Only she just couldn't stop herself thinking about his beautiful, masculine face, about his hands and his mouth, and the hard, insistent pressure of his body against hers.

But it was going to stop.

Not because she regretted what had happened. She didn't. It had been amazing. But whatever her feelings had been, they had nothing to do with any kind of reality. Things had just got a little out of hand…

Trembling, she opened her eyes and gazed out of the window at the broad fields of sugarcane.

It was obviously not ideal, him being her boss and everything, but she knew why it had happened. After Jimmy had died she'd stopped eating. Not deliberately—she'd just seemed to forget about food. All she'd wanted to do was sleep. Eventually, over time, her appetite had come back, and even though she was still a little on the slim side her weight was perfectly normal now.

What wasn't normal, though—or healthy—was being celibate for so long.

And it wasn't just sex. Aside from sharing hugs with her family, she now lived a life bereft of physical contact. She didn't even have a pet—a cat or a dog she could cuddle.

She was twenty-seven years old and it had been five years since she'd kissed or been kissed. So she'd wanted to remember what it felt like to have a man pull her close, to feel his warm hands and lips on her skin. Maybe if she'd given in to that need earlier then she wouldn't be feeling like this now, but after years of virtually ignoring an entire gender, was it any surprise that she'd been knocked sideways by that moment of wild, feverish passion that had flared between the two of them?

Back at the villa, she had a long, cool shower, using her favourite body wash, and then sat down on her bed with a book and a glass of mango juice. Normally she hated fruit juice, but for some reason she'd suddenly started craving it.

Twenty minutes later, she hadn't read a word, and she still hadn't shifted the heaviness in her limbs.

She knew it was psychosomatic…that if she managed to find that elusive inspiration everything would change in a heartbeat. Her mood would lighten and she would finally be able to blank her mind to the memory of her mysterious too-attractive boss, and that fierce, involuntary pull of attraction she had felt for him.

If only she could find those elusive notes that would make the rum sing. But nothing she'd tried was working.

She felt another prickle of panic and then, as she glanced across the room, she noticed the dress hanging from the handle of her wardrobe.

It had been an impulse buy.

In the weeks leading up to her flight to Cuba she'd

gone on a shopping trip to London, mainly to shut Lizzie up. Knowing that her sister would be appalled if she came home with nothing but insect repellent and a hat, she'd gone into one of those boutiques where even a basic T-shirt cost as much as her train fare home. Feeling horribly provincial and out of place, she been rummaging through a rail of linen cardigans, trying to look as though she was a regular customer, and there it had been.

Shocking pink, with a riotous pattern of exotic-looking flowers, it had tiny cap sleeves and a flippy little skirt that showed off her legs. It was bright, sexy and eye-wateringly expensive—in short, absolutely not the kind of dress she would ever normally buy. But in her head it had seemed to fit perfectly with her fantasy of a crowded Havana nightclub filled with beautiful dancing couples.

And suddenly, with a dawn-breaking kind of clarity, she knew what she was going to do.

She was going to go out in Havana. She was going to drink mojitos and dance and follow the pulsing salsa rhythm right to the heart of Cuba.

'I'm sorry, Señor Zayas, but the road ahead is closed so I'm going to have to go through the centre.'

Looking up from his laptop, César gazed out of the window of his SUV to where a queue of cars were jostling for position, accompanied by an escalating cacophony of horns and shouts.

He frowned at his driver. 'Is it an accident?'

'I don't think so, sir. It looks like roadworks.'

'It's fine, Rodolfo,' he said. 'I can wait.'

His shoulders stiffened. If that was true, then why

had he turned his entire schedule on its head and ordered Miguel, his pilot, to divert mid-flight to Havana instead of going to the Bahamas as planned?

He was in the process of buying a new catamaran, and had been on his way to Freeport to meet with the architects and the marine engineers when he'd changed his mind. Or that was what he'd told himself and his bemused air crew. The truth was that he'd pretty much been returning to Havana ever since he'd walked out of that villa on his estate seven weeks ago, his blood humming in his veins, his body reeling.

He felt his gut tighten.

Kitty Quested.

For the first few days after leaving Havana he'd resisted pulling her file, but finally he'd relented, assuming that if he answered the questions buzzing round his head the mystery would be solved. Instead, though, his questions had multiplied.

She was younger than he'd realised, and professionally inexperienced. How, then, had she created such an outstanding rum?

Creating such nuanced, complex flavours would have taken patience and persistence—qualities that were rare at that age. *He* certainly hadn't had them when his father had sat him down and told him that it was time to step up and take over the running of Dos Rios.

He felt his chest tighten, remembering his reaction at the time. Shock and disbelief—and then panic. He hadn't been ready, not nearly ready, to do what his father had asked of him. An indulged childhood had been no preparation for the responsibilities involved in running the family business. And after finishing his degree he'd wanted to travel, not work. To have fun, and to be free of his parents' unconditional and sometimes stifling love.

He couldn't blame them for wanting to be so involved in his life. They'd wished and waited for a baby so long, suffered so many disappointments. By the time he was born it had been too late for there to be any brother or sister and his fate had been sealed. He would always be unique, cherished and beloved.

He knew he was incredibly lucky to be so wanted, but his position as their only son and heir was complicated. For years he had prayed for a sibling. Not because he'd been lonely, nor even because he had known it would make his parents happy, but just so he wouldn't have to be so exceptional.

His prayers had gone unanswered, but—incredibly—his parents had agreed to give him a year after graduating from his MBA. A year to make his way alone in the world and make his own mistakes. And that was exactly what he'd done.

And look how that turned out.

He had ended up hurting the ones who loved him the most. The only consolation in the whole sorry mess was that it had taught him a valuable life lesson: that trust was something to be earned, not given.

And yet, incomprehensibly, he had felt as though he could trust Kitty.

But then nothing made sense about that woman. From her sudden appearance on the deserted road to that tantalising passion she'd revealed in that darkening villa.

She was a mystery, an enigma, with a glorious riot of red hair, a pale, serious face and mesmerisingly expressive grey eyes that switched in a flash from concern to fury.

Was it any wonder that for weeks now she had been popping into his head without invitation but with maddening regularity?

Images of her beautiful naked body undulating against his, the last shreds of sunlight spilling across their damp, feverish skin, had hounded his days and haunted his dreams, so that for the first time since adolescence his body had been at the mercy of his hormones.

And so he'd come back to Havana.

For years now he'd rationed his visits—more so since he'd moved his parents to live in Palm Beach—and on arrival he instantly felt that familiar sense of conflict. Relief at being home fighting with regret that he could never truly be himself here. But that was the way it had to be. The open, easy-going young man who had left Cuba to go to college in the States had never returned. Instead, in his place was a man who lived a life of order and restraint.

He gritted his teeth. Most of the time anyway.

That *rollo* with Kitty Quested shouldn't have happened. Normally he was so careful, so considered, plus she was an employee. But something had started out on that road…a spark had been struck.

His muscles tensed as he remembered. Not the impact of metal hitting gravel, but the moment when he'd looked up and she had been running towards him, that incredible red hair flying behind her like a comet's tail. She'd looked so small and fragile, but she had been moving with the same fierce determination as the waves that rode in to La Setenta beach.

He'd felt her panicky fear, had seen it too, for she'd been shaking. Only then she'd started scolding him, and he'd realised that it wasn't fear but anger, and all at once he'd been angry with her for lecturing him and being so impossibly, maddeningly righteous.

But mainly for having that incredible enticingly pink mouth.

And suddenly they had both been shaking. Only not with anger.

Replaying the moment again inside his head, he frowned. At the time there had been so much going on, but of course there was a perfectly logical explanation for that strange weave of tension.

Feelings had been running high.

An accident, anger, and confusion over their respective identities had obviously acted like emotional gunpowder, and his own spiking adrenaline was the spark which had ignited that intense, reluctant attraction he'd felt.

An attraction that he'd confidently expected to fade by the time he walked out of her villa.

Only he'd been wrong.

And that was why he needed to see her again.

His fingers twitched against the keyboard.

Last time he'd had no choice but to leave—to flee, really. Not just from Kitty, but from the past that haunted him, from a weakness he had thought he could only escape by keeping himself away from temptation.

And she had been a temptation. More than that, she had been a compulsion, and he'd been shocked and scared to discover that he still had that same weakness inside him—the weakness that had caused him and his family so much pain.

He'd had no choice. In Cuba, with her so tantalisingly close, there would have been a chance that he might give in to temptation. Clearly he'd needed to put some distance between the two of them—not just to remove the risk of that happening but to get his head in order.

Only that hadn't happened. He'd flown to Florida, then to New York and across to San Francisco. But all those thousands of miles had made no difference. She had got inside his head so that he couldn't think about anything other than her, and it was then that he'd realised that he'd made a mistake.

By leaving so swiftly he'd basically gone 'cold turkey'. His body was suffering withdrawal symptoms. He wanted more, and he was denying himself. Worse, he'd turned her into some kind of forbidden fruit—an illicit, off-limits pleasure—so of course he hadn't been able to stop thinking about her.

Seeing her again would make her real and attainable, and her power over him would simply disappear. Then he would take a new lover, someone who neither worked for him nor lived on his doorstep, and his hunger for this red-haired Englishwoman would be forgotten. Kitty Quested would be just a name on a payslip.

Feeling calmer, he settled back against his seat. The sky was beginning to turn pink and the brash, modern hotels were giving way to grand palm-filled squares and roads crammed with *almendróns*—iconic vintage American cars in a mouthwatering array of pick-'n'-mix colours. The SUV slowed, bumping over the cobbled streets of the Habana Vieja, and he leaned forward, his gaze drawn to the view outside the window.

It was a typical Friday night in his hometown. The streets seemed to swell with noise and laughter, and everywhere there were people. Beautiful, smiling people, chatting, dancing, holding up their phones to take photos. He scanned their faces, remembering how it had felt to be that carefree, so unquestioning of his right to happiness.

And then his gaze snagged on something teasingly familiar.

Hair the colour of damp beech leaves and the curve of a cheekbone, pale and luminous in the fading light.

He frowned. It couldn't be. Not in that dress. Or those heels.

But then she turned and he felt shock break over him like a wave. *It was her.* He watched as Kitty nodded to the dark-haired woman following her, her lips parting in a smile that made his vision go watery at the edges, and then, turning, she ran as lightly as a dancer up the steps into a bar.

It took his brain approximately ten seconds to go from mute disbelief to a memory of her as she had been that evening, arching against him, the curve of her back beneath his hand—

His shock was forgotten and instead he was tensing, his body reduced to nothing more than a swirling mass of instincts and hormones.

'Stop the car.'

'I'm sorry, sir?'

He heard the surprise in Rodolfo's voice but ignored it. 'Just pull over.'

'Yes, sir.'

Feeling the car slow, his heartbeat accelerated.

'I just need to speak to someone,' he said. 'Take the car round the block and I'll call you when I need to be picked up.'

Without waiting to hear his driver's reply he opened the car door and stepped out onto the pavement. The air was sweet and humid, tinged with cigarette smoke, and behind the buzz of chatter and laughter he could hear bursts of reggaeton and salsa from the nearby bars. But he barely registered anything other than the bright yellow door through which Kitty had just disappeared.

He glanced at the sign. *Bar Mango*. He didn't know it, but he didn't need to. He could picture exactly what it would be like: the heat, the hormones pulsing in time to the sound system…the heaving crush of strangers acting like lovers.

Moving quickly through the crowds, he took the steps two at a time, sidestepping a group of American tourists and pushing open the door. Inside the bar the music was deafening and the temperature was several degrees higher than on the street. The room was jammed with people shouting to one another.

'Oye, asere, qué hacemos hoy?'

'Qué vola, hermano?'

He surveyed the crowd, feeling his heart beating exponentially faster as each dimly lit corner failed to reveal her. Surely she couldn't have left already?

His shoulders tensed against an unreasonable rush of disappointment—and then tensed again as suddenly he saw her.

A pinwheel of relief spun inside his chest as he wondered how he had missed her. She was standing next to the bar, talking to the same dark-haired woman he'd seen before, and clearly they were part of a larger group of girls, all about the same age as Kitty—*chicas*, his mother would have called them.

They were all young, beautiful, and confident in

their vivid, lustrous beauty, but he could feel them fading away as he continued to stare at Kitty. She seemed to glow in the darkness, her glossy hair and mouth, the contours of her cheekbones a masterclass in chiaroscuro.

The word whispered against his skin, and he felt his body reacting both to the seductive lure of the syllables and the association in his mind between shadows and silence—and sex.

He breathed out unsteadily.

In another life, with any other woman, he might have hesitated, but watching her lean in closer to the barman, and the man's flirtatious smile, he felt his heart throb in his throat—and then he was shouldering a path through the sweaty, shifting tangle of bodies.

He had no idea what he was going to say, much less how she would react to seeing him there, but there was no time to worry about the unknown. For, as though sensing the gap opening up behind her, Kitty turned away from the smiling barman and glanced over her shoulder.

'Señor Zayas?'

Her grey eyes widened and he felt a swell of excitement as her gaze collided with his. He glanced at her, his spine tensing as it had on the bike just before he lost control. This time, however, it was her, and not the ground, that was causing his body to brace for impact.

'Ms Quested.'

It sounded so formal, so completely at odds with the way he'd been thinking about her just moments earlier, that suddenly he was struggling to find words. His one consolation was that she seemed more dazed and taken aback than he was.

Cheeks flushing, she stared at him uncertainly. 'I didn't know you were back.'

He found her confusion and the blush that accompanied it oddly satisfying. Back in control, he held her gaze. 'I arrived this evening.' Over her shoulder, he could see a trio of women glancing over at him. 'Are you out with friends?'

'Yes.' She hesitated. 'Actually, I met them for the first time tonight. There's an online group for expats. I got in touch and we arranged to get together this evening.'

Her eyes met his and her expression was—what? Defiant? Scared? Tense? Determined?

'How about you? Are you with friends?'

For a moment he thought about telling the truth— how she had got under his skin in a way that he didn't understand, or like, but that he couldn't seem to resist, so that when he'd seen her on the street he'd been compelled to follow her.

And then his brain caught up with his body, and he nodded. 'I've just left them,' he lied. 'I noticed you come in, so I thought I'd come and…you know…say hello.' His body twitched. 'Introduce myself properly.'

Beneath the throb of the music he felt something pulse between them, and he knew from the flare of response in her eyes that she had felt it too.

'About what happened—' she began.

'Kitty? We're thinking of going down the street to Candela. It's another bar, but not so quiet, you know? Is that okay?' Glancing up at him, the dark-haired woman feigned surprise, her mouth curving upwards. 'Sorry, I didn't mean to interrupt.'

'Oh, you're not.' Kitty said. 'Carrie, this is…' she hesitated.

'César.' He finished her sentence smoothly, keeping his voice casual.

'Nice to meet you, César.' Carrie smiled. 'So how do you two know each other?'

Kitty looked startled. 'Oh, we—we're—'

'Friends. We met through work.' He smiled at Carrie. 'Are you from England too?'

Carrie nodded. 'London. Look, you're welcome to join us—' she flicked a glance at Kitty '—but I'll leave you two to talk it over.' She gave Kitty's arm a quick squeeze. 'Just let me know what you want to do, okay?'

As Kitty nodded the crowd pushed forward and she was driven into him by the tide-swell of people, and fleetingly her soft curves were pressed against his groin. His mind blanked but he reacted instinctively, grabbing her elbow to steady her.

Watching her pupils flare, a buzz went through his body like the trembling of an electric storm. Not wanting to reveal his instant uncensored response to her sudden proximity, he let her go and took a step backwards, using his arm to create a space.

'Sorry.'

'It's not your fault—it's crazy in here.' She glanced across the crowded room. 'Is this really a *quiet* bar?'

He laughed. They were both having to shout to be heard. 'For Cuba, yes.'

She smiled, and then her smile stiffened. 'Why did you say we're friends? We're not friends.'

He held her gaze. 'We're not exactly strangers either.'

Her cheeks darkened. 'About that—' She glanced away, then back to his face. 'It shouldn't have happened.'

'Why shouldn't it? We're both grown-ups. And single.'

It wasn't a question, but his stomach tensed as he

watched her small upturned face brace against his words, and then she nodded and he felt his body loosen.

'I know, but I work for you.'

'You work for Dos Rios.'

Recognising her own words, she gave him another small smile and then looked away. 'I just want us to have a professional working relationship, and I know you said that wouldn't be a problem.'

'It's not.' Suddenly, fiercely, he wanted her to trust him. 'And it won't be.'

He knew men in his position who would have taken advantage of Kitty and, yes, he was ruthless in business. But he would never exploit people in that way. He knew what it felt like to be subject to the whims of another, and it was a feeling he would never willingly inflict on someone else.

He glanced past her at the mirror above the bar, his gaze focusing on their reflections, and as he watched the wariness fade from her eyes he quickly closed off his mind against the ache in his groin. It was time to change the subject.

His eyes dropped to the glass of orange juice in her hand. 'You know drinking that is practically a criminal offence in Cuba?'

She smiled. 'I wanted to end the evening with some memories, not a hangover— Sorry.' She shook her head. 'I didn't mean to sound so prim and uptight, it's just… Well, I had this idea. I thought I might find some inspiration—you know, for the rums. But I think I'm just going to end up with a sore throat from having to shout all evening.'

She glanced away and, following her gaze, he met her eyes in the mirror. For a moment they just stared at one another, and then she turned to face him. 'Look, I don't suppose you want to go somewhere a bit less rowdy...'

He felt his heart beat expectantly in his throat. Her voice was light, her expression the question mark that she had left off the end of the sentence.

Behind him the room felt solid against his back, but he could still feel the imprint of her hip on his skin, glowing red-gold like an ember.

There was no reason to say yes—every reason, in fact, to refuse. But he already knew that making her off-limits would simply exacerbate his hunger. His stomach tightened and, remembering that he hadn't actually eaten, he felt a rush of clarity. He'd make this about *that* kind of hunger.

He nodded slowly. 'Actually, I'd like that. Have you eaten?'

Her eyes were dark, almost purple, and he knew even before she shook her head that she hadn't. 'Okay... Well, I haven't either, so why don't you join me for dinner?'

'How do you like your food?'

Putting down her fork, Kitty smiled. 'It's excellent. I really love these—what are they called in Spanish again?' She gestured towards her plate.

'*Boniatos,*' César said softly.

She repeated it carefully, ignoring the leap in her stomach as his green eyes rested on her face. 'They're delicious. Everything is amazing.'

'I hope I didn't drag you away from your evening.'

She shook her head. 'No, not at all. I was beginning to worry that I might have to start complaining about the music being too loud—so thank you for saving me.'

She pulled herself up short. *That wasn't the image she wanted to project.*

'Not that I needed saving,' she added quickly. 'I'm not some damsel in distress.'

He stared at her impassively. 'I should be the one thanking you. You saved me from having to dine alone.'

Her heart was pounding. She still couldn't quite get her head around how the evening had unfolded. She'd met the other girls, as arranged, and walking with them through the streets she'd been struck by how different the city seemed at night. The old-school glamour was still there, but there was also something rawer—a hum of energy and excitement. Everywhere people were talking, flirting and kissing in time to the salsa spilling out of every window.

It had all looked so natural, so easy and uncomplicated, and as they'd gone into the bar she'd wondered how it would feel if she could let her body follow its desires.

Her mouth felt dry. Which, roughly translated, meant César Zayas.

And then, just like that, she'd turned around and found him standing behind her, his green eyes capturing the light like polished emeralds.

Had she imagined such a moment? Truthfully, yes. But the shock had still been electric, her response so visceral in its intensity that she'd actually forgotten to breathe.

And that was how she'd first met this man whose warm lips and urgent hands had filled her head for weeks. Breathless, self-conscious, her eyes wide with shock.

The way she'd behaved that evening had been so out

of character, and the likelihood of seeing him again so remote, she'd convinced herself that meeting him again would be a little awkward but manageable. But the moment she'd turned around she'd realised that she was nowhere near cool or sophisticated enough simply to brush off having sex with a stranger who had then turned out to be her boss.

It had been tempting simply to pretend to ignore what had happened, but she knew from past experience that it would be better to know the worst. Like whether César Zayas's idea of a 'clean slate' meant removing all reminders of what happened that evening—including her.

But of course he had been completely unfazed, and it had been his response that had prompted her invitation, to prove to herself as much as to him that the line they'd crossed seven weeks ago had been a one-off.

Clandestina, the restaurant he'd chosen, was like nowhere she'd ever been. There was no sign outside, for a start, just a doorman in a dark suit who had nodded silently, stepping back to let them pass into the Art Deco apartment block. But as they'd walked out onto the rooftop terrace she'd forgotten to breathe.

She'd been told that Cuban restaurants tended towards the rustic, but this was no homely *paladar*. It was wall-to-wall luxury. Only there weren't any walls—just a polished concrete floor, hot pink velvet-covered chairs and uninterrupted views of the city and the sea beneath a black, silk-lined awning.

She had felt almost dizzy. It was a million miles away from the shabby local pub where she and Jimmy had used to get lunch sometimes. It was pure indulgence—a sensory and sensual overload that bordered on the decadent.

She wondered if that was why he'd chosen it, or whether it was because he was friends with the owners, two brothers called Héctor and Frank. Either way, he clearly felt at home as he was on first-name terms with most of the waiters, and ordered without so much as glancing at the handwritten menu.

Or perhaps it was just the food, she thought, her stomach rumbling as the waiters brought out more plates of the most amazing pulled pork, roast chicken and *frituras de malanga*.

'So where do you see yourself professionally in the next five years? Presumably there's nothing left for you career-wise in England.'

She blinked. She had been a little nervous about the potential for lulls in their conversation, but it had been surprisingly easy and fast-flowing. They had talked mostly about work. And she'd been happy to discuss distilling and sugar cane shortages. But this aspect, her career, was not somewhere she was prepared to go. To talk about the future would risk revealing too much about her past...about Jimmy and their life together.

'I haven't thought about it.'

He frowned. 'Then you should.'

His directness knocked her off balance.

'I don't like to plan ahead.' She swallowed. 'Things don't always work out—'

He frowned, and that mask—the one without expression that he'd worn as he'd left her villa—slipped over his face.

'Dos Rios is a major step up for you. You need to build on that. Your career is international now. Or is there a reason you need to go back to England?'

After all the generic boss-new-employee questions,

his sudden trespass into more personal territory rasped against her skin.

He looked at her curiously and for one terrible moment, she thought he might press her, but after a moment, he shrugged.

It was time to change the subject, she thought. 'So how do you know them? Héctor and Frank, I mean?'

He stared at her so intently in the silence that followed her remark that the greenness of his eyes almost overwhelmed her.

'We used to hang out at the same beaches when we were teenagers,' he said finally. 'And we carried on hanging out through university, and during the holidays, until we all got jobs.'

It was not difficult to imagine the chubby, smiling brothers lolling on wooden chairs on the honey-coloured sand of some palm-strewn beach. César, on the other hand... She stared at him speculatively. He looked poised, unruffled, immaculate. He was dressed in his customary uniform of black suit and tie, although on him it seemed more like armour than clothes.

'You don't seem convinced.'

His eyes met hers and she made a face. 'Well, I can't really imagine you on a beach. Do you tuck your tie into your swim shorts?'

He smiled, and her heart skipped a beat. The table suddenly seemed to small.

'I haven't always worn a shirt and tie,' he said softly. 'I still don't when the occasion requires it.'

The memory of his naked body pressed against hers collided with a 3D image of him rising out of the sea, water trickling down his smooth golden skin. Inhaling sharply, she bit her lip—and then instantly wished she hadn't as his gaze dropped to her mouth.

'But I have to admit it was tricky getting the sand out of my laptop.'

His green eyes glittered and she bit her lip again, but her mouth defied her and she could feel herself smiling.

'Don't you have people to do that for you? I mean, you are the boss.'

The air around them felt hot and tight.

'I'm not always the boss. Sometimes I take the day or the night off.'

Her breathing was suddenly staccato, and she felt her calm mood of moments earlier flee, dissipating in the face of his untempered masculinity and authority like dandelion seeds in the wind. It was time to move the conversation away from the tempting, stealthy undercurrent beneath his words.

'So, what did you do, then, on these beaches?'

'Probably exactly what you did when you were that age.'

Kitty blinked. At 'that age' she'd been trying to fit in lectures around Jimmy's hospital appointments. There had been no time to go the beach.

'Like what?'

He shrugged. 'A whole crowd of us would hook up. You know, have some drinks, make a barbecue, play music, dance.' He raised an eyebrow. 'What?'

'Nothing.'

He shifted forward in his seat so that his knee brushed against hers beneath the table, and she had to clench her muscles to stop herself from pressing back, from leaning in to the heat of his body.

'Why are you smiling like that?'

His mood had shifted, he seemed lighter and more relaxed. It was a glimpse of a younger, less guarded man, and she wondered what had changed him over the years.

She shook her head. 'You can dance?'

'I'm Cuban—we practically invented dancing. So, yes, I can dance.'

His smile beckoned to her across the table, warm, teasing, complicit. She could feel the rise and fall of her breath, hear the sound of her heartbeat inside her head, and she had that sense of standing on the wing of a plane, of freedom and anticipation, as his eyes looked directly into hers.

'Prove it,' she said softly.

CHAPTER FIVE

THEY REACHED THE nightclub just before one. On the tenth floor of the Hotel Bello, the members-only Club el Moré was clearly *the* place to go for Havana's elite.

'You won't find any tourists here,' César said as a waiter guided them to a table.

She smiled. 'Am I not a tourist?'

He shook his head. 'You live here. That makes you an honorary *habanera.*'

A pulse sidestepped across her skin as she sat down, and she felt inexplicably happy at his choice of words. 'So is that why you come here? No tourists?'

His mouth turned up at the corners. 'Yes.'

His blunt answer made her burst out laughing. 'Really?'

He shook his head in time with the smile curving his mouth. 'No, not really. I mean, it can feel a little like you're living in a theme park—with all the cars and cigars—but really I come here because they have the best live music and cocktails in the city.'

As though reading his lips, a waiter appeared at his elbow and expertly slid two exquisite coupe glasses decorated with silver polka dots onto the table. He tapped her glass of orange juice, and then took a sip of his daiquiri.

'I don't normally drink these—' he said.

'Too touristy?' She finished his sentence.

His eyes gleamed. 'A little.'

'So what do you drink?'

'I prefer a highball of eight-year-old Dos Rios with a couple of drops of water to open it up and a little ice to push back the sweetness.' Twisting his glass around, he gazed at it assessingly. 'But tonight a daiquiri feels right—after all, one of your countrymen supposedly had a hand in its creation.'

She shook her head. Some people claimed that in an attempt to ward off scurvy Sir Francis Drake had added limes to the crew's ration of rum, but there were plenty of others who argued that the legendary cocktail had been named after a beach just off Santiago called Daiquiri.

'Anyway, *salud por que la belleza sobra*,' César said, making the usual Cuban toast. Lowering his glass, he pushed it across the table. 'Here, try it.'

He was lounging in his seat, his arm resting against the armrest, but despite his languid manner she sensed that he was watching her, waiting for her response.

Picking up his glass, Kitty took a sip. Her tastebuds exploded. It was divine.

I could get used to this, she thought, her distiller's brain sifting through the classic flavours of lime juice, sugar syrup, and of course rum. And she wasn't just talking about the alcohol, she realised a little guiltily after the first sip.

Heart pounding, she gazed slowly round the room. Both the atmosphere and the decor were completely different from the shoulder-bumping, sweaty tangle at Bar Mango.

Here, everything seemed to gleam and glitter—particularly the men and woman entwined on the velvet banquettes. The women were uniformly gorgeous and sleek. Bare-shouldered and long-limbed, their glossy lips and gleaming white teeth were almost brighter than their jewels. Sitting beside them, beneath a haze of blue-grey cigar smoke, the men looked darkly handsome in their flawless suits.

She glanced over to the dance floor. It was already crowded, and she wondered if and when he was going to respond to her challenge. Thanks to some classes at her local village hall she knew how to salsa, but somehow she didn't think that dancing with Lizzie was going to be much preparation for partnering César.

Her mouth felt suddenly dry, and with an effort she diverted her thoughts back to the drink she was holding. 'It's delicious.'

'It should be. They make it to their own unique recipe.'

She read the challenge in his eyes and tasted it again, trying to pin down the flavour. 'There's grapefruit…'

He nodded, and she felt her stomach grow warm at the approval in his green gaze. Feeling self-conscious, she took another sip, using the glass as a shield against her face.

'It tweaks it, but it's the rum that's making the magic. As it should do, Señor Zayas, given it's one of yours. The four-year-old, I believe?'

He smiled then—a smile that made a pulse beat fast in her throat.

'Bravo, Ms Quested.' Lifting his glass, he tilted it in her direction. 'For someone so young and untrained you have an impressive focus.'

He was only admiring her palate, that mystical ability to detect balance, length and complexity, but, looking up into his eyes, she felt her heart jab against her ribs like a boat bumping its moorings.

It was stupid to let herself be so affected. If she'd been his accountant, and he'd complimented her for reducing his tax bill, would she be feeling like this? Only here, in this beautiful room, with his dark eyes resting on her face, it was hard not to respond, not to bask just for a moment in the spotlight of male attention.

It had been so long. Five years, in fact. And she missed it—missed *him*: Jimmy.

He had always made her feel so special, and now she was alone. Not completely—obviously she had Lizzie and Bill and her parents. But it was a long time since she'd spent any time on her own with a man, and this man made her feel as though she was riding a roller-coaster.

But compliments couldn't change the facts, and he was still her boss. And even if he wasn't she didn't need, or want, a repeat performance.

Her cheeks felt hot.

Okay, that was a lie. She did want him. But a lone sexual encounter with a stranger to remind herself that she was still a woman was one thing... Acting on that desire *again* would be reckless and complicated and stupid.

His position as CEO of Dos Rios wasn't even the main reason why what had happened between them could only ever be a one-off. That was down to her. She didn't want intimacy or commitment, and nor did she have it in her to share such things with someone else.

Not since Jimmy. And nothing was going to change that, whatever people said about time being a great healer.

So, keeping on with all these formalities was not only unnecessary but counterproductive, for surely it implied that without them she was at risk of losing control, when in reality, without the high emotion of an accident driving them together, there was no risk at all of what had happened at her villa recurring.

It had been a one-off, she knew her own mind, and she wasn't looking to be seduced.

She cleared her throat. 'Thank you—but, please, could you call me Kitty? Being called "Ms Quested" makes me feel like I'm in a job interview.'

Her heart skittered in her chest as his gaze locked on hers. Her skin was suddenly covered with goosebumps and she felt her nipples harden.

'If that's what you'd prefer.'

She nodded, and his mouth curved upwards slowly. 'In that case, would you dance with me, Kitty?'

As they walked out onto the dance floor she felt her stomach drop as his fingers grazed against hers. He was the most beautiful man she had ever seen. Everything about him was perfect, from the long dark lashes that grazed his cheeks to those arresting green eyes.

Of course he was a beautiful dancer. Light, fluid…he didn't just follow the music, he was part of it. Like all great partners, he seemed instinctively aware of other dancers, finding a path seamlessly between the couples circling the floor, and yet she felt as though he was entirely focused on her.

And all she could think about was him. The way his eyes rested on her face, the light press of his hand gently curving around her waist. It was such a long time since she'd felt so free, so light, so young.

The band changed tempo, and as the music slowed the shifting crowd of dancers seemed to shrink around them. She felt his hand tighten against her back, the heat of his grip seeping through the fabric of her dress. Their bodies were closer now: too close. She was conscious of the solidity of his shoulder beneath her hand and he smelled so good—a kind of clean, masculine scent that made her long to lean into him.

Only she couldn't let herself do that, for if she gave in to that longing she knew where it would lead. And where it would end. But for some reason, right now, that realisation didn't seem to be carrying any weight.

Everything was snarled up inside her—desire and fear, impatience and guilt, her need to keep her distance clashing with an urge to brush her lips against his.

'I'm losing you.'

'What?'

She glanced up at him, her eyes widening with shock that he could read her so well. White and pink and yellow strobe lights above the dance floor were criss-crossing between them, dappling his skin in gold shadows, highlighting the curve of his jaw and cheeks. He looked like the profile on a coin and she had to hold back from reaching up and touching his face.

'You're tensing up. Just let it go.'

He was staring directly into her eyes, and she felt her belly clench as the rum and his nearness and her own tingling hunger began to curl around her brain. Looking at him hurt—but not so much as wanting him.

'Let it all go,' he said softly.

Her hand tightened against his shoulder and her hips

drew closer to his, their bodies blurring into one. It was as if she was floating. Everything felt soft-edged, enchanted.

Around her the room seemed to be slowing down in time to the music, and the song's chorus was chiming in time to a melting ache deep and low down. It was way past midnight. She'd been alone with him for hours. But if someone had asked her, she would have said it had been no more than minutes.

Her heart jumped. So why did she feel as if they had always known each other?

His head dropped. His face was so close that she could feel his breath coming fast and warm against her cheek. And then his eyes locked with hers, the green of them so deep and unending that it felt as though she were drowning in them.

She could fight it, could push to the surface—but she didn't want to. Blindly, she reached up and ran her fingers over the first rough trace of stubble, seeing, sensing, feeling a need that was as palpable as her own. And then, standing up on her toes, she closed her eyes and kissed him—not gently, but fiercely, forcefully, with a hunger she had never felt for any man but him.

As their mouths touched he pulled her towards him, parting her lips with his, splaying his warm hands across her back.

She moaned softly. Her breasts were aching and she could feel every contour of his hard, muscular body. Only she wanted more. Wanted the touch of his hands sliding over her skin and the frenzied release that she knew they would bring.

She had missed him.

Pleasure danced across her skin. The blood was racing along her limbs as though towards some imaginary finishing line.

And then suddenly something shifted inside her. This intimacy was too much. Her pulse was beating too hard and too fast.

Her heart punching against her ribs, she pulled away. Silencing the tingling heat that was creeping over her skin, she opened her eyes and the room jolted back into focus.

The lights were too bright. She wanted to close her eyes. And her body was humming, the imprints of his hands stinging fiercely on her skin.

'Excuse me—'

She felt dazed, unsteady—and, not wanting to meet his gaze, she spun round and walked swiftly off the dance floor, her legs moving automatically like some wind-up toy.

'Kitty—'

They had reached the table and she turned reluctantly to face him. He was standing beside her, his hand resting on the back of a chair, and she tried her best to rebuild the barriers she had so casually smashed with one careless kiss.

'I'm sorry,' she said. 'I shouldn't have done that.'

He frowned. '"Shouldn't" usually implies a level of duty or obligation to something. Or someone.'

His voice was quiet, but there was a tension there that hadn't been there before—one that matched the set of his jaw.

'I thought you were a free agent.'

He let the words hang in the air between them.

Her throat tightened. 'I am. That wasn't what I meant.'

She clenched her hands. She was making a total mess of what she was trying to say, but she had so little experience of this kind of conversation.

He took a step forward, his green eyes searching her face. 'You look pale. Here, sit down.'

She shook her head. 'It's so hot in here. I think I need some fresh air.'

But it was more than that. She could sense it…just out of reach, in the corner of her mind…like the answer to a crossword clue or a forgotten name that went with a face.

He led her out of the nightclub into the foyer. The cool air restored her a little, but her legs still felt as though they weren't connected to her body.

Incredibly, the ladies' cloakroom was empty.

On another night, perhaps if she'd still been out with Carrie and the other girls, she might have taken a photo and sent it to Lizzie, for the ladies' room was gloriously over the top, with gilt-edged mirrors and a chandelier hanging from the ceiling. But right now she felt too on edge to enjoy the flamboyant decor.

Turning on the tap, she held her wrists under the cooling water and stared at her reflection in the mirror. César was right. Her face did look pale, and her eyes were wide and feverish.

Except she didn't feel ill. Just not herself.

You're just tired, she told her reflection. *You've been working too hard, and it was a shock meeting him like this tonight.*

Her cheeks felt suddenly warm again. And, of course, she'd kissed him. *Again.*

What was happening to her?

She'd hoped that Cuba would bring a change to her

life, but when she was with César she just didn't recognise herself. Gone was the sensible, shy, small-town girl and in her place was a wild, passionate woman who acted without thinking.

But it had to stop here.

It didn't matter that he looked like an angel, or that his touch turned her inside out with ecstasy. In fact, that was a reason *not* to give in to her desire. She didn't want to want this dazzling, uncompromising man who threatened to bring passion and emotion into her world. For emotions were as dangerous and random as life itself, twisting and transforming, so that love turned to loss and passion to pain in a heartbeat.

And she was an adult. She could feel attracted to him and not act on it.

Breathing out slowly, she opened her handbag and found her compact. She tilted her face upwards and dusted some blusher across her cheeks. That was better. Now it just needed some lipstick. Where was it?

Frowning, she felt inside her bag, and then tipped the contents out onto the counter.

There it was.

Picking up the tube, she swiped it carefully across her lips, blotted them with a tissue and then swiped again. That would have to do.

She dropped the lipstick back into her bag and began to pick up the other items, and as she did so her hand froze. Gazing down at the box of tampons, she felt her stomach flip over, and then a rush of panic, cold and dark and swift-moving like floodwater, swept over her skin.

Gripping the side of the counter, she steadied her legs.

She couldn't be.

Probably she had her dates wrong.

With an effort, she worked her way back through the calendar. But there was no doubt. She was at least five weeks late.

Tilting his wrist, César glanced down at his watch and frowned. He didn't usually stand around waiting for women to come out of cloakrooms, and Kitty seemed to be taking an unusually long time, but he felt responsible for her.

The thought jarred. Feeling responsible, feeling anything aside from desire was not something he'd anticipated, but he knew that he had no choice. Right now she was his responsibility.

He wondered again why she was taking so long. Remembering her flushed cheeks, he grimaced. She was obviously embarrassed—or had he been too vehement when she'd pulled away? His chest tightened. Maybe...

But he was only human, and *she* had kissed *him*, leaning into his body so that he'd been able to feel her heart vibrating, her fingers caressing his face. And everything had faded. The lights, the music, the tension in his body—everything had turned to dust, spinning into the darkness. Everything except Kitty.

He thought back to how she'd melted into him, the heat and the hunger of her kiss and the softness of her mouth. His breath caught in his throat. She had made his head spin, made his body ache. And he'd wanted more. Only as suddenly as she'd started it she had pulled away. So, yes, he had been a little terse.

He gritted his teeth. He should never have asked her to dinner. In fact he should never have come back to

Cuba. If he'd just kept to his schedule he would be in the Bahamas, asleep, serene and oblivious.

Instead his body felt as if it was about to fly apart.

Suddenly he saw her, and his heart started to pound. There was colour on her cheeks, still, but she didn't look embarrassed—more stunned.

'Is everything okay?'

She nodded stiffly. 'Yes, it's fine. Thank you.' Her eyes didn't meet his. 'I'm a little out of practice when it comes to going out on the town.'

'Of course.' In other words, she wanted to go home. He felt a momentary pang of regret that the evening was ending, but then pulled out his phone. 'I'll call my driver.'

The drive home to the estate took less than twenty minutes. Usually he liked the clear night-time roads, but tonight he felt a little conflicted, for a part of him wanted to delay the moment when he and Kitty returned to being Señor Zayas and Ms Quested.

Glancing over to where Kitty sat beside him, her eyes fixed on the window, he felt his muscles tighten. Although perhaps that moment had already happened.

Her villa was in sight now. Feeling the car slow, he leaned forward and tapped on the glass behind Rodolfo's head. 'You can drop me with Ms Quested. I need to stretch my legs,' he said in Spanish. 'So I'll make my own way up to the house.'

As the car drove away Kitty gazed up at him warily.

It was not dark. A beautiful pearlescent moon spread a clear white light over the villa. But he'd been raised to walk women to their front doors.

'I'll walk you in.'

'Thank you,' she said quietly.

Inside, the villa was dark, but she switched on a table lamp and instantly a warm yellow glow spread across the room. He waited for her to say goodnight. Waited for her to smile politely and thank him for a wonderful evening. But she didn't speak.

He stared at her tense, set face, trying to interpret her silence. And then he shut the door quietly. 'Look, I'm sorry about what I said at the club.'

He stared past her across the living room and then instantly wished he hadn't as he caught sight of the sofa. His body hardened painfully as an image of the pair of them, half-naked and panting, played inside his head.

With an effort, he forced his mind away from the memory and dragged his gaze back to her face. 'I was out of order.'

'Actually, I kissed *you*, so if anyone was out of order it was me.'

He thought back to the disturbed nights and restless days he'd endured since walking out of this villa. He might have left her in Cuba, but she had never left his thoughts, and had he not been her boss he would have kissed her first in the club.

'It doesn't matter,' he said truthfully. 'We crossed that line seven weeks ago. Left it for dust on that couch.'

'That doesn't make it right.'

Watching her face stiffen, he felt a rush of frustration. A planned life was a life free of complication, because there were rules and boundaries. This kind of twisting, awkward conversation was exactly why he didn't leave his libido in charge of his actions.

Worse, in this room, with the ghost of their passionate encounter still tangible, her remoteness was setting his teeth on edge. Between leaving the dance floor and coming out of the cloakroom something had changed. But what?

He stared down at her uncertainly, reluctant to know more but even more reluctant to turn away. 'Has something happened?'

A quick breath lifted her shoulders. 'I don't know. It might have. Or it might not. I'm not sure—' She broke off mid-sentence.

Beneath his shirt, his heart started to pound. Her words made no sense, but it was her sudden retreat into silence that made the tension in his chest suddenly unbearable. For he had learned from Celia that the unsayable was always worse than anything that could be spoken out loud, no matter how inarticulately expressed.

Gazing down at her pale, set face, he felt his muscles tighten, and suddenly he knew why she couldn't speak. 'I'm sure you'll be fine,' he said coolly. 'But if you're that worried why don't you call your boyfriend?'

He felt a sharp sting of anger just saying the word, but he was grateful to have found out the truth now rather than later.

She was shaking her head. 'I don't have a boyfriend. I told you that—'

'I know what you told me, but that doesn't make it true.'

'I'm not lying to you.' Her eyes were narrowing and a flush of colour was slipping slowly over the contours of her face. 'I'm trying to tell you the truth.'

'It's a little too late for that.'

He knew his anger was disproportionate. They'd had

sex only once, but it was disconcerting to discover that he still had this weakness inside, this impaired judgement.

Her mouth twisted. 'Not really. I only realised tonight.'

'Realised what?'

She hesitated, and his anger flared hotter.

'I'm not about to start playing guessing games, Kitty.'

'I didn't—' She licked her lips. 'I think I might be pregnant.'

Whatever he'd been expecting her to say, it hadn't been that. He stared at her in silence, brain reeling, body rigid with shock. 'How do you—?'

'How do I know?' She bit her lip. 'I don't—for sure. But I'm five weeks late.'

He did the maths inside his head. It worked. Only...

'I thought you said you couldn't have children?'

The accusatory tone and the implied doubt in his words seemed magnified in the small room. He watched her face close over.

'I didn't think I could.' She looked up at him, her eyes too bright, and he could almost see her retreating. 'I'm sorry. I shouldn't have told you.'

His stomach twisted. She looked drained, and young, too young to be dealing with this alone in a foreign country, away from her family. Having wrongly accused her of lying, he could hardly condemn her for honesty.

'No, I'm glad you told me.'

And, despite his shock, he was surprised to find that he actually was. The truth was always preferable to being fed lies. But this was too big a truth to tackle now. Out of habit, he schooled his features into a mask of calm, the CEO in him taking charge.

'Look, it's late. We can't do anything more tonight and you look exhausted.' He glanced across the room. 'You need to go to bed.'

She shook her head. 'I don't think I can sleep.'

'Then just lie down for a minute.'

Gently, he guided her towards the sofa. He watched her sit down. She seemed hardly aware of him, and he realised that she was as exhausted as she looked.

'Come on.' He grabbed a cushion. 'Put your head on this and just close your eyes.'

She slid off her shoes and lay down, curling onto her side, looking up at him with half-lidded eyes.

'We'll talk about this in the—' he began, but she was already asleep, her hair spreading out like a fan of flames over her shoulders. Shrugging his jacket from his shoulders, he draped it carefully over her body.

Dropping down onto one of the chairs, he shifted against the cushions, trying to get comfortable. He thought back to how this evening had started. Seeing Kitty through the car window, following her into the bar, dancing with her...and then that kiss.

It had been the most tantalising foreplay in what he'd hoped would be a night as passionate as that first time. What he hadn't expected was to find out that he might be a father.

His chest tightened. Mixing a night of incredible sex with a complete loss of control had been a cocktail to rival any daiquiri, only now it appeared that there might be life-changing consequences to that explosive encounter on her sofa.

He felt shattered, his head spinning with a dizzying

rush of unanswered questions, but the answers would have to wait until morning.

Tilting his head back, he took one last look at the woman who was going to give him those answers and then closed his eyes.

CHAPTER SIX

SOMEWHERE, SOMEONE WAS singing about her heart being broken.

Shifting onto her side, Kitty lay with her eyes closed, still half asleep, but following the words. It was a song that was playing everywhere in Havana—only why was it playing inside her villa?

Slowly she opened her eyes and sat up.

There was no sign of César but, glancing down, she realised she hadn't been sleeping under a blanket but his jacket, and the chair opposite the sofa had been moved. Her heart gave a leap as she noticed the indentation in the cushion.

He must have stayed the night—only surely men like César Zayas didn't kip on chairs in people's living rooms.

And then she smelled the coffee.

Standing up, she walked into the kitchen. Her coffee pot sat on the counter. She didn't need to touch it to know it was hot. Steam was still drifting out of the spout.

And there on the back doorstep, a cup in his hand, was César.

She almost turned and ran. Last night she might have been brave or stupid enough to share her fears, but this morning she simply wasn't up to facing him. Particularly as she had turned his world upside down over what must surely be a mistake.

She *couldn't* be pregnant.

Last night had been the emotional equivalent of a ride at the funfair. Bumping into him like that, that kiss on the dance floor… She hadn't been thinking straight, and in the cloakroom she'd panicked and put two and two together and come up with a pregnancy. Surely though, there was some other, less dramatic reason for her symptoms. One that she could best identify on her own, in private.

But before she had a chance to move he turned, and her legs unhelpfully stopped working. For a moment he stared at her in silence, and then he straightened up. He was standing on the bottom step, so that his brilliant green eyes were level with hers, and it took every shred of willpower not to look away.

Even though the clean lines of his face were slightly smudged by sleep, the shock of his beauty made her head spin. Her heart was beating so hard that she could feel her ribs vibrating. She knew she had to say something, but her brain seemed to have shut down in sympathy with her legs.

'How do you feel?' he said quietly.

His gaze drifted down over her body and then slowly back up to her face, and she remembered that she was still wearing her clothes from the night before.

But then so was he.

He'd lost the tie, but he was still wearing his shirt and suit trousers, and the crumpled state of the shirt together with the stubble darkening his jawline was the final piece of evidence confirming what she already knew.

'I'm okay. So, you stayed the night?' She paused. 'Did you sleep in the chair?'

He nodded. 'It was fine.' He held up his cup. 'I hope you don't mind—I made myself a coffee.'

She shook her head. 'No, of course not.'

It felt strange. Not awkward, just astonishing that this man might be connected to her by more than that brief but blinding solar flare of passion.

'Would you like a cup?'

She shook her head again. 'No, thank you. I don't really like the taste at the moment.'

A breeze stirred the air between them, loosening her hair, and she tucked it behind her ear, grateful for something to do as his eyes rested on her face.

'We need to talk,' he said finally. 'Shall we go inside?'

She nodded.

He followed her into the kitchen. 'First things first, you need to take a test.' He met her eyes, blank-faced.

She stared at him dazedly. Everything was moving so fast. Her brain kept jumping back and forth—to the past, to England and Jimmy, then back to the present. Too fast.

In all honesty, she wasn't absolutely ready to know the truth yet—but then she could hardly drop a grenade in his lap, as she had last night, and expect him to sit there and hold the pin indefinitely.

'Yes, I do.' She frowned. 'Do I need to go to a doctor? Or can I get one at a pharmacy?'

'You don't have to worry about that. Here.' He reached past her and picked up a nondescript brown envelope from the counter.

'I had one of my people get a test for you. Don't

worry, he's very discreet. He understands this is a personal matter.'

She nodded mutely, unsure whether she was more shocked by the cool-headed speed and efficiency of his behaviour or the fact that this man might be the father of her unborn child.

Her hand trembled slightly as she took the envelope. Despite his dishevelled appearance—or probably because of it—he looked incredibly sexy. Even rumpled, the formality of his clothes seemed to accentuate the raw masculinity of the body beneath, and his hair looked as it had after they'd made love. Although it was obviously him and not her who had run hands through it one too many times on this occasion—and not in passion but through worry.

For a moment she thought he was going to say something, or that she should. It seemed as if something should be said, but what was the correct choice of words for this situation?

'I'll use the bathroom,' she said unnecessarily.

Closing the bathroom door, she breathed out raggedly. Her hands were shaking a lot now, and she tore at the box clumsily. The instructions were written in English—not that she needed them. She'd taken dozens of tests when she'd tried to get pregnant before, but she still read them through carefully, just to make sure. She'd been careless enough already.

There—it was done.

She gazed down at the stick. It seemed unreasonable that such a small disposable object should carry such heavy expectations: hope and despair, excitement and disappointment, all wrapped up in a tiny piece of plastic.

Her heart was beating erratically, and suddenly she badly wanted to ring Lizzie—only her phone was in her bag, and her bag was wherever she'd left it last night.

But even as she reached for the door handle she knew this wasn't something she could share with anyone but the man who was waiting patiently in her kitchen...

He was standing where she'd left him.

'We have to wait now,' she said quickly, putting the stick down on the counter. 'For three minutes.'

His face was impassive. But then he didn't love her, and this hypothetical baby wasn't planned. It didn't stop her wondering, though, how he would have looked if the situation was different? Would he have held her hand as they waited? Or discreetly checked his watch to check the time.

Her throat tightened. And when it was negative would he have pulled her into his arms and told her that it didn't matter? That next time would be different.

'Why did you become a distiller?'

She glanced up at him, startled. Why was he asking her that now?

'I have a chemistry degree.'

'The two aren't necessarily connected,' he said gently.

She stared at him in silence. She'd been planning to do a Masters in polymers after graduating, but then Jimmy had been diagnosed with cancer and it had been a struggle even to finish her degree.

Naturally everyone had wanted to help, and she had been happy...no, *grateful*...to take a step back, to let other people—doctors and nurses, her friends and of course her family—make the decisions and take charge of the situation. They had helped her care for Jimmy, and then to grieve for him.

But after time she'd realised that somewhere along the line she had taken one step back too many. She had never been an extrovert like Lizzie—never been bold or loud. But after Jimmy's death she'd felt diminished, defeated, and so very tired of life. No amount of coaxing and cajoling could persuade her to leave the house.

And then Bill had asked her to help him at the distillery. Lizzie had set it up, of course, guessing correctly that she would always put other people's needs above her own.

Remembering that first winter when she'd started working for Blackstrap, she almost smiled. The former salt shed was made of stone, and the distillery had been freezing. But she hadn't cared. She had been too busy playing with spices, pulling on the knowledge acquired from her degree, blending and tweaking and chasing that elusive perfect flavour.

And working on the rum hadn't just woken her taste buds, it had woken her from a kind of self-imposed hibernation. It had reminded her that she was still alive, and that even if she was alone she needed to live that life. Only now there might be a new life growing inside of her.

'My brother-in-law asked me to help him. It was Bill's idea to set up Blackstrap, but he was having a few problems with the flavour profile. He's got the technical know-how, but he's not very good at focusing.'

'Luckily for him, you are.'

She stared at him in confusion. Why were they talking about her sister's boyfriend? Surely he wasn't interested in Bill and his lack of focus.

And then, as he glanced casually at his watch, she knew why. He had been trying to distract her.

'I think it's probably been three minutes,' he said quietly.

Her heart contracted. Suddenly she couldn't breathe.

'It's okay.' Reaching out, he took her hand and squeezed it. 'Do you want me to look first?'

'No.' She shook her head and picked up the stick.

Her throat tightened and suddenly it was hard to balance on her feet without gripping the counter. For a dizzying second she pictured Jimmy's face, his smile, his tears.

Pregnant 3+

She looked up at César. 'It's positive.'

His expression didn't change by so much as a tremor.

'I'm pregnant.'

She knew that these tests were ninety-nine per cent accurate, but somehow saying the words out loud made it feel more real. It was there—in her hand. She was going to have a baby.

Only the person who was supposed to be the father, supposed to be there with her, was no longer around.

Her heartbeat had slowed; she felt as if she was in a dream. 'I'm pregnant,' she said again.

César's grip tightened around her hand, and as she met his gaze she felt her legs wilt. His eyes were so very green, and for a moment all she could think was that they should be brown.

Her head was swimming. It had taken five years, but most days she was content with her life. She still regretted Jimmy's death, but the acute pain, that hollowed-out ache of despair, had faded a few years ago. Only now this news had reawakened old emotions.

He caught her arm. 'You need to sit down.'

Still holding her hand, he led her into the living room. She sat down on the sofa. The first shock was starting to wear off and panic was starting to ripple over her skin.

'I don't understand how this could happen.'

When she and Jimmy had started trying for a baby he had been so keen he'd taken a fertility test and everything had been normal. She'd been about to get herself checked out when he fell ill, and then there had been too much going on, other more urgent tests to take and so each time she wasn't pregnant she had blamed herself—her periods had always been irregular. Only now it seemed as though it hadn't been her.

César sat down beside her. 'I'm pretty sure it happened the usual way.'

She stared at him dazedly. Her head was a muddle of emotions, but he was so calm. So reasonable.

'You haven't asked me,' she said slowly, 'if the baby could be someone else's.'

In a way, that was more of a shock than her pregnancy. With hindsight—her late period, her sudden craving for fruit juice, her heightened relentless fatigue—all pointed to one obvious explanation, but she knew it was a question most men in his situation would have asked.

He leaned back a little, studying her face. There was an expression in his eyes that she couldn't fathom.

For a moment he didn't reply, and then he shrugged. 'What happened between us isn't something I've found easy to forget. I'd like to believe that you feel the same way. But if you think there's any question over my paternity now would be a good time to say so.'

She shook her head. 'There hasn't been anyone but you.' Her eyes flicked to his face. 'And, yes, I feel the same way.'

As she spoke some of the tension in her shoulders lifted. They hadn't planned for this to happen, to bring new life into the world, and they might not love one another, but those few heated moments had been fierce and important for both of them, and she was glad that this child had been conceived out of such extraordinary mutual passion.

'I don't regret it,' she said abruptly. 'What we did or what's happened.'

Her heart swelled. She had wanted and waited for this baby for so long, and suddenly all those other tests, with their accusatory ghostly white rectangles, seemed to grow vague and unsubstantial.

'Well, it's a little late for regrets.' He paused. 'This baby isn't going anywhere. What matters now is what happens next.'

What happens next?

The options revolved inside her head.

She could go home—and of course a part of her obviously desperately wanted to jump on the next plane to England. But even if César agreed to help support her financially she was going to need a job at some point.

The fog inside her brain was making it difficult to think straight.

'I suppose I should probably get an appointment with a doctor,' she said hesitantly.

He nodded. 'I can help you with that. And I *want* to help.'

He was still holding her hand. His skin was rougher than she remembered, but his voice was soft, gentle in a way that made her throat constrict.

'Thank you,' she said.

His words replayed inside her head. She imagined that a lot of men—particularly wealthy, powerful men, who liked being in control of every tiny detail of their lives—would have got extremely bent out of shape, being confronted by the unplanned pregnancy of a woman they barely knew. But César seemed remarkably unfazed.

Of course, you didn't take charge of a small-time family business and turn it into a global brand before the age of thirty unless you could handle what life threw at you. Even so, finding out you were going to be a parent was a personal and extraordinary milestone for anybody...

'You're being very kind,' she said quietly. 'Very fair.'

His gaze rested on her face. 'What happened wasn't just down to you, Kitty. We both got swept away.'

For a second they stared at one another, wide-eyed, the sound of their breathing punctuating the silence of the room as they remembered.

As Kitty stared at him she felt her heart oscillating against her ribs. The heat of his body, the swell of his muscles beneath his shirt was crowding her mind. He was so solid and male and real, and everything inside her was reaching out to him—only should she be feeling like this? Was it normal or right to feel such a strong physical need for a stranger when her heart was aching for the husband who had missed out on realising his dreams?

'Yes, we did,' she whispered.

'And now we both have to work this out. And we *can* work it out. We can work it out together.'

His eyes were boring into hers. 'If that's what you want.'

She stared at him, mesmerised by the faint trace of stubble on his jaw and the determination in his green gaze. She knew that Lizzie and Bill, and her parents, would be falling over themselves to help her, but she knew César would make this work. She trusted him to do it because managing complex, challenging situations was what he did every day, and it would be wonderful to have his support—not just for her, but for their child.

'I'd like that.'

'Good.' He smiled, and then pulled out his phone. 'I'll call the doctor first, and then I have a couple of contacts who can probably pull some strings...speed up the paperwork.'

Paperwork?

The word scraped against her skin. Presumably he was talking about some kind of financial settlement or an agreement over visiting rights, but—

'Isn't that a little premature?' She gave him a small stiff smile. 'I mean, the baby's not due for seven or eight months.'

He frowned. 'I know—and that's why you need to stop worrying about all this right now. Just concentrate on yourself and our baby, and let me deal with the wedding arrangements.'

Her ears were buzzing.

Wedding? What wedding?

She stared at him in confusion. 'I don't understand...'

His eyes dropped to her face. 'What's there to understand? You said you wanted to make this work.'

He was speaking patiently, but she could feel the tautness in his body vibrating from his fingers into hers. She felt her pulse accelerate. She hardly knew César, and she certainly didn't move in his kind of circles, but she knew enough about the world—his world—to know that making this situation 'work' didn't typically include a marriage proposal.

'I know I did,' she protested, 'and I do. But—'

'But what?'

Gone was the softness in the voice. Now he sounded as she imagined he did in the boardroom, when confronted by bad sales figures. Cool. Distant. Hostile.

'Marriage is the quickest and most efficient way to tie up all the loose ends.'

Loose ends. Was that what she and the baby were?

'I just assumed that you…' She hesitated. 'Well, that you were talking about being involved in the baby's life—not mine.'

Surely he didn't actually mean what he was saying. It must be the knee-jerk reaction of a powerful man who wanted to call the shots.

His eyes locked on hers and instantly she felt the hairs on the back of her neck stand to attention.

'Then you assumed wrong.' He shook his head. *'"Involved"?'* Frowning, he turned the word over in his mouth as though it tasted bad. 'Clearly you've already given this some thought—so tell me, Kitty. What does "involved" actually look like?' he said softly.

Kitty blinked. His hand was still holding hers and, slipping her fingers free of his, she folded her arms protectively in front of her stomach. 'I don't know, exactly, but you travel a lot for work, so I suppose you could come and visit whenever you're in London.'

His green eyes fixed on her face. 'Is that your way of telling me you're leaving Havana?'

Her breath caught in her throat and her heart stopped beating—and then began pounding like a drumroll.

'I'm not leaving Havana. Not yet, anyway.' She frowned. 'Just because I'm pregnant it doesn't mean I want to stop working.'

'But you are planning on returning to England?'

Trying to still the jittery feeling in her chest, she glanced past him at the view through the open back door. It looked so idyllic and peaceful, and it would be amazing to raise a child here in the sunshine, but Havana wasn't her home.

'Yes, of course.'

He was staring at her as if she had taken leave of her senses. 'So how exactly am I supposed to be "involved" in my child's life on that basis?'

A mix of anger and apprehension was creeping over her skin. A moment ago she had liked him, trusted him, thought that she understood him and that he understood her. How could she have got him so wrong?

But what did she really know about this man sitting beside her on the sofa?

She glared at him. 'How could you be involved in our child's life anyway? Last time you walked out of that door you told me that you didn't spend much time in Havana. And you don't. Seven weeks ago you disappeared off the face of the earth—'

'So that gives you licence to disappear off the face of the earth with my child?'

'Of course not,' she said hoarsely 'I'm just saying that I didn't know where you were or when you were coming back.'

'We had sex *once*. Of course you didn't know where I was or when I was coming back.'

The bluntness of his words brought her to her senses. Why was she even having this conversation with him? It was crazy. But he was crazier if he thought she would suddenly agree to marry him.

'I know that.' Taking a breath, she got her voice under control. 'And now I know how you feel about the baby, obviously I would love you to be involved on some level.'

He was staring at her coolly.

'On some level.' He shook his head. 'That's very gracious of you, Kitty. Would you like cash or are you happy with a bank transfer?'

She shook her head 'I don't just mean financially.' With an effort, she tried to blank out the rapid fire of her heartbeat so that she could think. 'Look, I'm not trying to sideline you. I'm just trying to deal with what's real and what's not.'

His jaw tightened. 'Then let me help you. What's real is that we had sex on this couch. Unprotected sex. Now you're pregnant with my baby, and I intend to watch him or her grow up. Not make do with a couple of snatched weekends a year when I'm passing through Europe.' He stared at her steadily. 'I grew up in a loving, family home with two parents. I want that for my child.'

Her heart felt as though it was breaking. She had wanted that too. But marrying César was not going to make that happen.

'I want that too,' she said slowly. 'But that's not an option here.'

'It is if you marry me.' His eyes were as impassive as his voice.

She breathed in sharply. Her head was swimming. She could still remember Jimmy's proposal, the tremble in his hand as he'd taken hers. He'd loved her, and he'd wanted to share his life with her. And he had, and it had been wonderful, and painful and beautiful, and she wasn't going to sully the memory of her marriage with some convenient but hollow pretence.

She shook her head slowly. 'I'm not going to marry you, César. That isn't going to change and I don't want to talk about it anymore.'

'That's not how this works.'

In reply, she stood up and walked stiffly across the room. He stared after her, and his expression of disbelief would have made her laugh—only she didn't feel like laughing.

'Seriously?'

'Yes, I'm serious. I don't want to talk about this anymore.'

'This is ridiculous.' His eyes were narrowed and opaque, like uncut emeralds. 'It's pointless to make things more complicated than they are. You chose to be with me.'

'No, I chose to have sex with you,' she said shakily. 'And, yes, it was amazing. But it doesn't matter how good it was. Sex is not why you get married. And neither is pregnancy. Marriage is about love and loyalty, and I am not going to stand up in front of witnesses and make vows that I don't believe. Because you shouldn't say them if you don't believe them. And we don't. I don't— I can't—'

Her voice snapped and she lowered her face, not wanting him to see the pain she was feeling, or the tears that were so close to falling.

There was a short, stunned silence, and then he took a step towards her. 'Kitty, I'm—'

She held up her hand to stop him. 'Please don't. Please. Can you just go now? Just go!'

There was another short silence, and for a moment she thought he was going to ignore her wishes, but then seconds later she heard the door shut with a click.

Looking up, she felt a sharp stab of relief and regret as she realised that the room was empty.

She was alone.

Breathing out unsteadily, César stared down at his laptop and then abruptly slammed it shut. What was the point? He'd been looking at that document for an hour now, and he hadn't read one word of it.

He gritted his teeth. Had it really just been an hour since he'd left Kitty's villa—or, to be more accurate, since she'd dismissed him? It felt like a lifetime.

After closing the door he'd walked back to the house and taken refuge in his study. There, surrounded by the familiar armour of his working life, he'd assumed that he would be able to block out those last few moments when her voice had started to shake and she'd looked close to tears.

He'd been wrong.

His stomach clenched. It had been a long time since he'd made a woman cry. In fact he knew the date exactly.

Remembering his mother's tears when he'd been forced to confess his stupidity, he felt a hot rush of shame—just as he had that day nearly ten years ago. And now he had made Kitty cry.

He swore softly. He'd handled it so badly. He'd been relentless and insensitive. Pushing his agenda as ruthlessly as he would do in business. But what did being ruthless in business matter if he was a coward in private?

He stood up abruptly, needing to move, wanting to distance himself physically from the truth. But of course there was no escaping what was inside his head.

Celia had played him. Aged twenty-four, he had been emotionally open, happy-go-lucky and painfully gullible. She had lied—not just behind his back but to his face, repeatedly—and he'd believed every word that had come out of her beautiful lying mouth. Because it had been the same beautiful mouth that had kissed him and told him she loved him.

He'd fallen for her, and in so doing he had embarrassed himself, and his parents. And he'd vowed never to let any woman have that power over him again.

Only it crushed him to live like that. To *have* to live like that. And it was a necessity. He could tell himself that it was just common sense or cool, hard logic for a man in his position to keep things flexible. That women were just pieces on the chessboard of his life. But the truth that only he knew and could acknowledge was that it was fear that kept them at arm's length. Fear of the weakness within him—that flaw in his nature that left him vulnerable to exploitation if he allowed himself to care, to feel.

Only he *did* feel something for Kitty. Desire, obviously, but also something protective that—incredibly— had nothing to do with the pregnancy.

He'd felt it out on that road when she'd looked at him, her grey eyes shining with anxiety and anger, and then again in the villa this morning, when she'd looked so stunned, so torn—

It had scared him, feeling like that, feeling anything,

and he'd been angry and frustrated with himself. So it had been easy to latch on to that frustration and turn it towards her. Not for being pregnant, but for being a soft-mouthed, smoky-eyed reminder of the mistake he'd made all those years ago and was trying so hard not to make again.

Kitty had brought chaos and passion and emotion into his world, and marriage was the logical way to restore order, and not just for himself. He knew how much his parents longed to see him married, and if he could marry and give them a grandchild he might finally atone for the pain and distress he'd caused them.

Only Kitty had other ideas. Hearing her talk had made him feel like an outsider—playing a bit part rather than being the central protagonist he so clearly was—but the harder he'd pushed the more she'd resisted.

There was a knock on the door and his heart twitched with anticipation. But almost immediately his pulse slowed as a middle-aged woman with calm brown eyes appeared in the doorway: his housekeeper, Rosa.

'Would you like some coffee, Señor Zayas?'

His chest tightened. Coffee. A conference call, and then some emails. In other words, business as usual. Except that it wasn't: everything had changed, forever.

He shook his head. 'No, thank you, Rosa. I have something I need to sort out.'

Ten minutes later he was standing in front of the door to Kitty's villa.

The garden was well kept, and the paint on the window frames shone in the sunlight. It seemed astonishing that it should look so untouched by what had happened. Surely, given the storm of revelation and confrontation that had passed through the villa that morning, there should be some sign or evidence of that turmoil, but it all looked so serene.

He tapped on the door and waited. After five minutes he tapped again, this time more loudly, but still there was no reply.

Could she have gone out? His heart began to pound, worst-case scenarios flooding his head and spilling over in panicky surges. Had he driven her out of Havana? Out of Cuba?

Pulse accelerating, he turned and walked swiftly away, circling the house towards the back door, his hand reaching for his phone. If he had to, he would send someone to the airport to stop her.

His fingers tightened around the phone—and then his legs started to slow.

On the back porch Kitty was standing with her back to him, watering some flowers. Her hair was loose and damp, probably from a shower, and she was wearing a simple slip dress. Briefly he allowed his eyes to roam over the long, slim legs and the viola-shaped back, and then, stepping forward, he cleared his throat.

She turned, her eyes widening, her expression changing from soft to guarded in a heartbeat, and his own heart began beating fast as she lowered the watering can in front of her body like a shield.

He held up his hands. 'I'm not here to fight.'

She stared at him steadily. 'So why are you here, César?'

She looked calmer, but there was a redness around her eyes and her already pale skin seemed almost translucent.

'I wanted to apologise for before.' He paused. 'I truly didn't mean to upset you. I'm just trying to do the right thing. I want to do the right thing.'

'And marrying someone you don't love is "the right thing"?'

He winced. 'When you put it like that, no, I suppose it isn't. But people marry for lots of different reasons, Kitty, in lots of different cultures. And sometimes they grow into loving one another.'

'And you think that could happen? To us?'

He was about to say yes, but there was a nakedness in her eyes that made it impossible for him to lie. 'I don't know,' he said truthfully. 'I've never been married so I couldn't say for certain. But you haven't been married either, so you can't say that it wouldn't happen.'

There was a silence. Behind her, a few petals drifted through the air like confetti.

'Actually, I have been married,' she said quietly. Her shoulders were braced but her mouth was trembling.

He stared at her, his breath suddenly leaden in his chest. 'Are you divorced?'

'Widowed.'

She looked exactly as she had done after the accident, her face taut with that same mix of strength and fragility that made him want to reach out and pull her against him.

'I'm so sorry. I had no idea.'

She nodded stiffly and, watching her fight for control, he felt an ache inside his chest.

'What was his name?'

'Jimmy.' Her face softened. 'We weren't married for very long. Only a year before he died. But we knew each other our whole lives.' She blinked. '*His* whole life anyway.'

'How long ago did it happen?' he said softly.

'Five years.'

Her answer shocked him more than finding out that she'd been married and widowed. She'd been so young to have her world implode like that.

'It isn't in your file.'

She frowned. 'No, it's not. Because I don't want it to be. It's not a secret—it's just that I don't want it to be how I'm defined.'

He could hear the tangle of emotions in her voice—the pain, the anger, the defiance.

'Do you know what I mean? Have you ever had something happen to you that you don't want to share with strangers? That's private to you?'

Her eyes were fixed on his face and he felt her question resonate through him. Thinking back to his own past, and how desperately he had tried to distance himself from his weakness and stupidity, he nodded. 'You don't have to explain yourself to me Kitty.'

'I know I don't, but I want to.' She took a step forward. 'It's not that I don't believe in love, it's that I can't believe in it. I can't feel that way again. But I don't want to pretend either.'

It took him two strides to reach her. Pulling her into his arms, he breathed out unsteadily, and then, before he even knew that it was what he wanted to do, he was lowering his face, brushing his lips over her hair and inhaling her scent.

'It's okay. I understand,' he murmured.

He felt her body tense, and then she leaned into him. Blocking off the thoughts swirling inside his mind, he rested his head against hers.

'I don't know what to do.' She looked up into his eyes. 'I don't want to be unfair. This is your child too.'

He swallowed. With her face so close to his, and

her warm, soft skin beneath his hands, everything felt possible. No obstacle was too big. Not even her past.

Or his.

'I know. And, however ineptly I expressed it before,' he replied, 'I meant what I said. I want to give my child the kind of loving family home I had. I know we can't do that as husband and wife, but is there any way we could try and find some kind of middle ground?'

'Like what?'

She was trying to be fair, but he knew that one wrong word would cause her to bolt.

'We hardly know each other, and that's only going to make everything harder in the future, when we need to be able to communicate. If you mean what you say about not being unfair, then we can't stay as strangers.'

She nodded. 'So what do you have in mind?'

His heart was beating steadily now. 'Let's spend some time together. I think you should move in to the main house. Just until you go back to England,' he said carefully. 'There's plenty of room, and I'm sure your family would feel happier knowing you were being looked after, so let me take care of you. Just for now.'

He waited, watching her face, trying not to let the tension show in his own, and then his heart began to beat with relief and triumph as her eyes met his and she nodded slowly.

CHAPTER SEVEN

'WOULD YOU LIKE some ham, Señora Quested? Or perhaps a couple of eggs?'

Gazing at her already overcrowded plate, Kitty smiled up at the dark-haired woman standing beside her and shook her head. 'No, thank you, Rosa. Honestly, this is perfect.'

She glanced guiltily at the plates of food surrounding her. It all looked delicious, but even if she was eating for two, she wasn't going to make much of a dent in this spread.

Her heart jerked. But perhaps it was not all meant for her? As though following the workings of her brain, Rosa shook her head.

'Señor Zayas always eats breakfast early,' she said, leaning forward to refill Kitty's glass. 'But he told me that he's hoping to join you for lunch.'

'Oh, right.' Her smile felt suddenly cemented to her face. Were her thoughts that obvious? Swallowing her juice, trying to ignore the heat rising over her throat and cheeks, she met Rosa's soft brown eyes. 'Then I'll see him at lunch.'

She had no idea what César had told Rosa about their relationship. Did a man in his position explain the dynamic between himself and a guest to his staff? Probably not. She certainly couldn't imagine him doing it and she certainly wasn't going to try to do so. Not least because right now she wasn't exactly sure how to explain their relationship herself.

They weren't a couple.

But he was the father of her unborn child.

And now they were living together.

She felt a twitch of guilt. Living with César was supposed to reassure her family, and yet now, two days after moving into the main house, she still hadn't told either her parents or Lizzie that she was pregnant or cohabiting with the baby's father.

But how could she? Why *would* she?

Whatever he might have suggested the other day, they both knew it was only a temporary arrangement. At the moment her pregnancy was new and strange, and César felt guilty and responsible, but once she was back in England he would find it easy to move on with his life.

Carefully she laid her knife and fork side by side on the plate. In a way, hadn't that already happened? She might be living under his roof, but she'd barely seen him. They'd been like moons orbiting a planet: occasionally, unavoidably their paths would cross—

But of course she hadn't seen him. Irritably, she pushed aside the disappointment she didn't want or have any right to feel. He was flat-out unpacking his work schedule—*for her.*

Anyway, at least not having him around meant she was free of the disconcerting undercurrent of tension between them. Her throat tightened. She'd tried hard to pretend that it wasn't there, but it was—and that was another reason not to speak to Lizzie.

She needed to get a handle on this confusion she felt for César. Living with him and being pregnant was obviously a big deal, but so what if she was temporarily sharing his home? Or that right now, at least, he wanted to be a part of their baby's life.

Being a parent was a lifelong commitment that needed solid foundations. All they had was one, brief, explosive sexual encounter that meant nothing to either of them.

And, truthfully, it didn't matter how sublime their passion had been, it had nothing to do with the tenderness or the love she'd felt for her husband and nor would it. Because feeling that kind of tenderness and love for someone, anyone—even the father of her child—was not something she was capable of doing any more.

Her skin tightened as she heard the sound of footsteps—heavy, determined, male—in the hallway, and her eyes darted involuntarily towards the door. But the nervous smile that was pulling at her mouth stopped mid-curve as the man glanced briefly into the breakfast room, nodding politely as he walked past.

Her pulse twitched. It was only César's driver—Rodolfo.

Ten minutes later, having finished her breakfast, she found herself standing aimlessly in the soaring entrance hall. Gazing up the stairs, she chewed her lip. She could go up to her room, but that would mean being alone with her thoughts.

Breathing out, she put her hand on the bannister—and then hesitated. Somebody, maybe Rodolfo, had left the door to the terrace open, and she could see two stripes of vivid contrasting blue where the sea met the sky.

It looked temptingly tranquil—unlike her thoughts—

and so, turning away from the stairs, she began walking towards the door.

After weeks of self-imposed imprisonment in the labs it felt good to feel the sun on her face, but soon the lacy clouds would disperse and it would be too hot. She found a path beneath the shade of some tamarind trees and wandered slowly over the heat-baked ground, always aware of the main house at the edge of her vision.

It would be easy to stay out here in the shade, and part of her still shied away from the moment when she would come face to face with César, but maybe that was just what she needed. Spending time with him was the quickest, surest way to see through the glamour and past the passion and so transform him from overheated fantasy into cool reality. After all, no man could be that desirable twenty-four-seven.

She made her way out of the woods that edged the dunes, drawn to the sound of the waves, her face lowered as she scoured the blindingly white sand for pieces of driftwood. She had half an idea for a mobile for the baby—some part of his or her homeland when they were back in England—but for some reason now that she was here on the beach even just the idea of going home made her body tense.

Sighing, she lifted her face, intending to scan the sea instead and instantly her body and brain froze and her stomach went into freefall.

She was not alone.

César was on the beach with a lean, dark-haired man she didn't recognise. And they were fighting, their breathing loud in the still morning air.

Her heart began pounding like a jackhammer.

They were a couple of metres away, moving quickly

and smoothly in the sunlight like water, their bodies bent forward, legs arcing through the air, wrists twisting and fists connecting with skin and bone.

Seconds later her brain stuttered back to life and she felt her pulse slow as she realised that both men were identically dressed in loose white trousers.

So not an actual fight, then, but some kind of sparring session. Only it looked real, and it looked as if they were actually hurting one another. And yet César's face was calm.

She gazed at him, confusion mingling with irritation. What was it about this man that made him so determined to push himself to the limit? Wasn't it enough that he ran a global business? His day-to-day working life held enough risk and drama for most people, but apparently he needed something extra. Rawer. Unrestrained.

Her legs felt suddenly stiff with the effort of tensing them. She needed to move but wanted to hide.

Breathing in, she took a step back and trod heavily on a stick.

It snapped, and the crack echoed like a gunshot across the sand, bouncing off the trees and the water so that both men turned towards her. She caught a swift flash of green as César's eyes locked on hers, widening with surprise, and then sensing weakness, his opponent curved his leg upwards, and her pulse jerked as César was thrown down and landed heavily on the sand.

Kitty blinked. It had all happened so fast.

Just like on the road.

Only this time her legs simply wouldn't move.

She watched mutely as the dark-haired man held out his arm and pulled César to his feet. They exchanged a few words, shook hands, and then César turned and walked towards her, padding across the sand like a mountain lion.

Her heart was beating in her mouth as he stopped in front of her. He was silhouetted black against the sunlight, his features in darkness, but she could feel his gaze all over her. And then he took a step closer, and as he came into focus she was conscious of her sudden audible intake of breath.

He'd clearly been working hard. His trousers were saturated with sweat around the waistband and his body was stippled with beads of perspiration. The ridges of his muscles were sharply defined, and his skin glowed like lacquered gold. She knew her reaction was showing on her face but she couldn't pull her eyes away, and she gazed at him, dry-mouthed, clamping her hands behind her back so as not to give in to an almost overwhelming desire to reach out and pull the draw-cord loose.

Remembering her careless assumption that living with César would strip him of his glamour, she gritted her teeth. Clearly there was a long way to go before that happened.

'You seem to be making a bit of a habit of this,' he said softly.

She swallowed. 'A habit of what?'

He held her gaze. 'Knocking me off my feet.'

Her skin felt warm. There was a shimmering tension in the air, low and taut, like the hum of an audience waiting for a play to start. Not touching him was an actual test of willpower like not scratching a mosquito bite.

Startled by the strength of her desire, she cleared her throat and said, 'I didn't knock you off your feet. I was over here, minding my own business. You just weren't paying attention.'

He laughed. 'That's pretty much what Oscar just said to me.'

Her heart stumbled against her ribs. Being around César was supposed to be a sobering reality check, but when his mouth turned up at the corners like that, with the sunlight glittering in his eyes, he was irresistible.

'Oscar?' She was trying to control her voice, but she could hear the catch of nervousness.

'My instructor.'

Glancing past him, she breathed out. 'So, what is he teaching you?' Part of her was really interested, but mainly she was just grateful to break away from his deep, green gaze.

'It's called Eskrima. It's a martial art. Shall we…?'

He gestured towards the house and they began walking back up the beach. It was easier talking to him sideways. For starters, she wasn't having to deal with the continuing shock of his beauty, but also the conversation seemed to flow more naturally with each step.

'Is it Cuban?'

He shook his head. 'It comes from the Philippines. I was spending quite a lot of time down there a couple of years ago.' His eyes met hers. 'They drink a lot of rum there.'

'Yes, it's the third largest market in the world.' She matched his easy smile with a small, tight one of her own. 'They have their own brands, don't they? Lizzie and Bill went on holiday there last year, and they brought me back a bottle. It was a limited edition.' She hesitated, groping for a memory of how it had tasted. 'It was dark…quite oaky.'

'Yeah, they char the barrels.' He frowned. 'Sorry, I didn't mean to get sidetracked into talking about work. Basically, when I was there my regular personal trainer, Félix, had an accident, and he recommended Oscar. And Oscar is a Lakan—a black belt in Eskrima.'

He broke off and glanced up, his attention snagged by a low rumble overhead. Her gaze following his, she watched a dark green plane cut through the cloudless blue sky on its way to the US military base at Guantánamo Bay. As it disappeared from view she looked back down and instantly wished she hadn't. He was looking at her intently, and suddenly her hands were trembling.

'I spoke to the clinic.' His voice sounded harsh against the waves. 'They've arranged a scan for this morning and then we'll see Dr Moreno.'

She blinked. 'Oh, okay...'

'Apparently it's to date the pregnancy.'

His eyes were steady, his expression neutral, but she felt a defensive jolt shoot through her. Although had she really thought that a man like him would simply accept her word?

She felt a sudden hot rush of tears, and in an instant her mood flipped.

In the five years since Jimmy's death she'd worked hard to find some kind of peace and equilibrium, only since meeting César she'd felt like a ship at sea, pushed and pulled in every direction by emotional currents and riptides. Emotions she couldn't control. Emotions she didn't understand.

And it wasn't just hormones, she thought with a burst of irrational anger. It was *his* fault she was feeling like this. His fault she was feeling so conflicted. His fault she was remembering how it felt to want someone, and need them. Only she wasn't supposed to feel like that for this handsome stranger.

If only this was Jimmy's baby it would all be so much simpler...

'Kitty—'

She knew her expression must have changed, and that he'd noticed. She could hear it in his voice. But, striving to keep her own voice on an even keel, she cut him off. 'What time is the scan?'

He stared at her, and for a few half-seconds she thought he was going to rewind the conversation, but after a brief silence he said, 'Eleven o'clock.'

'Okay. I'll be ready.' They were inside the house now, and she glanced pointedly upstairs. 'I'm feeling a little tired, so I'm going to go and have a lie-down.'

He stepped back. 'Then I'll let you go. I'll see you at eleven.'

And, turning, he walked away from her towards the kitchen.

She watched him disappear. If he had turned he would have seen the way her eyes followed him. But he didn't turn and, feeling a stab of betrayal that was as baffling as it was painful, she turned and began climbing up the stairs.

Kitty was relieved to discover that the clinic César had chosen looked more like an upmarket hotel than a private hospital. In the car on the way over she had been tense, her stomach knotting as memories of the numerous trips she'd made to hospital with Jimmy kept floating into her mind, but the foyer was clean and modern, and the smiling staff were dressed to match the decor in varying shades of taupe and cream.

And now she was lying on a bed, her bare stomach covered in gel, as the female sonographer moved the probe over her skin, tilting it from one side to the other, her eyes fixed on the screen in front of her.

'There we are,' she said quietly. 'There's your baby.'

Kitty glanced up at the screen and felt her heart contract. The sonographer spoke very good English, which was lucky. Because had she been speaking Spanish, it would have been easy for her to think that something had got lost in translation.

Her breathing was suddenly out of time. She could hardly believe it. The baby was tiny, but it was real. She really was pregnant. It was extraordinary, impossible, miraculous. But, like all real miracles, it was undeniable.

'And this is the head…that's a leg and a foot…and that's the heartbeat.'

The sonographer was smiling at her and she smiled back dazedly. She'd held that positive test in her hand, but up until this moment she hadn't believed it was actually happening, hadn't wanted to believe it was true for fear of disappointment. But it was true. Finally it had happened. And she felt so blissfully and unconditionally happy that it was as though her whole body was filled with light.

'Is everything okay?' she said quietly.

The other woman nodded.

'Baby's CRL is just under three centimetres, so I think we're looking at about nine weeks. When you see Dr Moreno you can discuss booking a second scan. We'll be able to see a lot more detail then, but right now everything looks great. Now, I'm guessing you'll want a photo?'

Kitty found her voice. 'Yes, please—and thank you.'

Her eyes found César. Since shaking hands with the sonographer he hadn't said a word, but she had expected him to echo her thanks, to see a reciprocal joy on his face. Only he didn't speak. He just kept staring at the screen, his expression intense, his eyes fixed on the shifting image.

She was about to prompt him when a low but distinctive buzzing filled the small room.

'Sorry, I need to take this.'

He didn't sound sorry and, glancing over, she saw that he didn't look it either.

Pulling out his phone, he stood up. 'Excuse me. José, *gracias por llamarme...*'

Watching the door close behind him, she felt a slippery rush of panic. She'd pictured this moment inside her head so many times in the past, and it wasn't supposed to look like this.

Her heart was suddenly too big for her chest. But why had she ever thought this would work with him? She didn't know this man, so how could she begin to know how he would react to anything? More importantly, how could she expect to bring up a child with him?

Picking up his coffee cup, César glanced at the darkening sky. The air was hot and sticky. It was going to rain—and it needed to rain to break the tension in the air.

Jaw tightening, his eyes flickered over to where Kitty sat on the other side of the table, her grey gaze fixed on the horizon. If only the rain could also ease the tension between them.

After the scan they had driven to his sugar cane plantation for lunch. He'd told himself that he needed to speak to his estate manager, José Luis, in person, and he'd told Kitty that he wanted to show her a part of Cuba she hadn't seen. But the truth was that he had simply needed an excuse to drive somewhere—to have an actual, achievable destination in one area of his life.

He took a mouthful of coffee. Since leaving the clinic he'd been trying to think it through logically—but no matter that he had a picture of his as yet unborn son or daughter tucked in his jacket pocket, he still couldn't imagine being a father in just under seven months.

Glancing up, he felt his pulse accelerate as he caught sight of his reflection in the veranda window.

You don't need to imagine it, he told himself, remembering that tiny heart squeezing rhythmically on the screen. *Just take a good look at yourself because it's already happened. You are a father.*

A father?

Even just thinking it was like being hit by a truck. It was ridiculous. He wasn't in a relationship, he wasn't qualified, and he certainly wasn't ready—

His face stiffened.

Ready? Just as he hadn't been ready to take over the business?

He felt a familiar rush of shame and regret. When his father had sat him down and told him that it was time for him to step up he hadn't refused outright, but his stunned silence had been enough of an answer, and with a little persuasion from his mother his father had acquiesced to his plea for 'just one more year'.

And it had been the biggest mistake of his life.

He'd been like some puppy, let off the leash for the first time, rushing up to greet each and every stranger like a long-lost friend. No wonder Celia had found it so easy to string him along. The further she'd thrown the stick, the faster he'd had run to catch it and give it back to her. Except he hadn't given her a stick, but a ring. And not any old ring either, but his grandmother's engagement ring.

Blotting out the memory, his hands gripped the coffee cup more tightly. It didn't matter if he wasn't ready. There was no question of him not stepping up this time. How could there be?

It might be a future he hadn't imagined, but this was his child, and he had meant what he'd said to Kitty. He wanted to make this work. He wanted to marry her. And he'd thought—hoped—that the scan, that seeing their baby together, might nudge her towards changing her mind.

His eyes flickered across to where she sat beside him, silent and still. But instead she had retreated further, and it was his fault.

He knew his silence had hurt her, and he knew he shouldn't have taken that phone call. But he'd had no words—or none eloquent or poetic enough to express the swelling tangle of his feelings on seeing his baby's heartbeat. Not to voice the fear or the wonder, and certainly not the fiercely protective urge he'd felt deep in his guts, not just for the baby but for Kitty too.

There had been no filter, no shield to protect himself, and he'd felt horribly exposed. So when he'd felt her gaze on his face he'd ignored it, not wanting to take on the intimacy of that shared moment and all that it implied.

But that baby growing inside her was so much more than just a baby.

It was a test.

A test that so far he'd failed.

He might have succeeded in getting Kitty to live under his roof, but how was he supposed to present that to his parents? They would be confused and disappointed. *Again.*

No, he needed to marry Kitty—only right now she was barely talking to him.

He gritted his teeth. Actually, he had a strong suspicion that she was ignoring him, but what was he supposed to do?

He didn't coax women or chase after them. Not since Celia. Not since he'd made a fool of himself. It had been the first and only time in his life he had felt helpless and exposed, and he didn't want to feel like that ever again. So, even though he hated letting fear dictate his actions, he'd set up his life so he would never have to feel that way with any other woman.

So that he could always walk away.

Only he couldn't walk away this time.

He breathed out unsteadily. He didn't want to walk away this time. Or at least, not alone.

Pushing back his chair, he stood up. 'Let's go for a walk.' She stared at him warily and, breathing slowly, he held out his hand. 'Please, would you come for a walk with me?'

He watched her face, seeing the conflict, the uncertainty, and then finally she nodded.

They walked slowly, side by side. Behind them jagged green mountains rose up to meet the brilliant blue sky and lush vegetation crowded the path, purple and pink flowers speckling the dark leafy foliage like stars in the night sky.

She was wearing the same dress she'd worn the other

day, and its simplicity combined with her loose hair gave her a breakable quality.

'How are you feeling?'

She stared up at him. 'Fine. Just a little tired, really. It's probably the heat.'

He studied her face. Her cheeks were flushed, just as they had been when she'd kissed him in the club—and, feeling his body respond to the memory of where such a kiss could lead, he gritted his teeth.

Persuading Kitty to move in with him had been a compromise—a first step towards getting her to change her mind about marrying him. Only he was starting to wonder if it had been a good idea after all. Being around her was torment enough, but after the passion they'd shared this awkward formality was like a slap in the face.

Pushing aside his frustration, he glanced up at the sky. 'It'll rain soon, and then it'll be cooler. Or we could take a shower. There's a waterfall just down here.'

He held back some overhanging branches and Kitty brushed past him. He heard her soft intake of breath and tucked it away, gratified by her reaction but not quite ready to admit how gratified.

He stared at the waterfall, trying to picture it through her eyes, to feel her wonder as she gazed at the low outcrop of rock and the gentle cascade of water tumbling into the shimmering sapphire pool.

'It's beautiful. So, is this part of your business empire?' Her eyes were clear and grey, but she looked more nervous than curious.

He shrugged. 'In a way. Obviously the business needs cane, and I like knowing the provenance of my raw materials, but having all of this lets me play at being a farmer.' A drop of rain hit the water, then another, and another.

'Here, take my hand.' He led her up to where the rocks overhung the clear turquoise water. 'We can wait here.' He took a breath. 'And while we're waiting we can talk about what happens next.'

Her expression shifted minutely, her mouth stiffening. 'I thought this was what happened next.' She spoke carefully, as though she was confirming a booking at a hotel or restaurant.

'It was, but now that we've had the scan I thought we should think about what we want to tell our families.' He wasn't going to demand that they marry—not after what had happened last time—but their living together hadn't answered all the questions raised by the pregnancy.

There was a silence, and then she cleared her throat. 'The truth, I suppose.' She bit her lip.

He felt his eyebrows draw together in a frown. He'd assumed that she'd already rung her home, but clearly she hadn't. That surprised him, and it stung too—more than he cared to admit.

'Don't you want to tell your family?'

'I do…it's just that I don't know how to tell them.' Her voice was taut, stretched tight like the string of a kite.

'Are you worried they're going to be upset?'

She looked up at him, her grey eyes wide with confusion. '*Upset?* No, of course not.' Her voice was shaking. 'They'll be delighted…' She hesitated. 'They know how much I wanted to get pregnant…how long Jimmy and I tried. All they want is for me to be happy.'

'So what's the problem?' He paused, remembering her shuttered expression when he'd talked to her on the beach. 'Look, I know how it must have sounded earlier, but I'm not questioning my paternity. That's not why I arranged the scan. In fact, I didn't arrange it. The clinic suggested it and I thought it was standard.'

'I know.' She lowered her head. 'It's not you.'

César took a breath. He was caught between the need to know more and the need to keep his distance, but if he wanted to keep his distance then why was he even here? If he'd meant what he'd said then, whatever this was, he couldn't leave her to deal with it alone.

His mind inched forward and then stopped, teetering on the edge of a new and previously unconsidered outcome. 'I thought you said you didn't have any regrets. Have you changed your mind? About the baby?'

He spoke calmly, but he felt pain saying the words out loud—a pain that was equalled by his relief as she shook her head.

'No—no!'

She looked up, her eyes wide with shock and denial, and he could hear the strain at the edges of her voice.

'I want this baby.'

Her shoulders hunched, and he stared down at her, then slowly reached out and took her hand. He wanted to help, or at least to understand.

'So what's the problem?'

'*That's* the problem.' She pressed her knuckles against her mouth. 'I wanted a baby for so long, for Jimmy, for us, only now I'm pregnant and he's not here. And I should be miserable, but I'm not.'

She looked up him, her distress so undisguised that it hurt to look at her.

'Kitty, it's okay.'

Watching her attempt to control her tears was worse

than seeing her actually cry. Unpeeling her hand from her mouth, he pulled her closer.

'Look, you're putting too much pressure on yourself.'

His fingers tightened around hers. Celia's tears had been meaningless, manufactured on demand to manipulate his emotions, and normally if a woman cried he wanted to leave. But Kitty's pain was raw and real, and her grief transcended his need…his wish to stay emotionally detached.

And so what if it did? He was only doing what he did every day as CEO of a global business. Doing what he did best: staying calm, making things happen, finding solutions. And in this case that meant holding Kitty's hand and being strong for her.

'This is all new and confusing, but it's okay to be happy about the baby.'

Her eyes were bright. 'And I *am* happy—I'm so happy. But I just feel so guilty.'

Guilty. The word resonated inside his head as he stroked her back. He knew all about feeling guilty. Guilt had driven his life, overriding all other impulses, good and bad, and changing him into this guarded island—an emotionally autonomous man focused on work.

But his guilt was penance. Kitty's was undeserved.

'For what?'

She hesitated.

'For what?' he asked again. 'For carrying on? For having a future?'

She shook her head. 'I wish it was that. That's what I should be feeling—and I did at first. I want to feel it now, but all I can think about is you. And what happened with you.'

His body tensed as he braced against the memory of

that moment. The spray from the waterfall was warm, but not as warm as the heat licking his stomach—a heat that had nothing to do with his memories and every-thing to do with the woman holding his hand.

'You shouldn't feel guilty about that.'

He was close enough to see the scattering of freckles along her cheekbones and the pulse working at the base of her throat. His body tightened with need.

'I don't. I feel guilty for wanting it to happen again.' Her free hand bunched the fabric of her dress. 'I don't know why I feel like this…' she whispered.

His body stilled, mirroring the tension in hers. 'I'm not sure if that's a compliment or not,' he said carefully.

She bit her lip. 'I wasn't expecting anything to hap-pen—and then, when it did, I thought it was because I was here and because it's been so long since there was anyone…so long since I even wanted anyone. Only it wasn't that. It isn't—'

His breathing stilled. In her villa, he'd wanted her in the moment. He could still remember the intensity of his desire and, more erotically, of hers—the swell of blood, the heat, the way her body had fitted against his.

Now, though, in the face of her honesty, he could admit that it hadn't been enough. That even as he'd turned and walked away he had been craving more, and it was a need that wasn't diminishing.

Need.

The word made his heart beat faster. But why? He wasn't talking about emotional entanglement and nei-ther was she. He was talking about lust. Sex. Desire. An elemental, physical yearning like hunger or thirst.

He shifted just a fraction, feeling the slight swell of her stomach. But this baby—their baby—was a connection that went beyond mere lust. They were bound by DNA now, and that was bigger than both of them, so he didn't have to fight this—just accept it.

She breathed out unevenly and, heart pounding, he stared into her eyes, mesmerised by the longing he saw there…a longing he knew was mirrored in his own green gaze.

He felt a spinning sensation, almost as though he was drunk. In a way he was…drunk on the realisation that he was just a man, and she was just a woman, and they were equal. Equal in their need and their want. And by giving in to that want he would let go of the mistake he'd made and the fear that he'd let control his life for so long. For *too* long.

'I want you,' he said softly. 'And I haven't stopped wanting you since I walked out of your front door all those weeks ago. It's not wrong or right—it just *is*.' He touched her face, brushing his thumb over her bottom lip, exulting in the feel of her skin, the heat of her breath. 'I can't fight this any more. I don't want to fight it.'

She took a deep breath. 'I don't want to fight it either.'

His blood felt like air in his veins as she leaned forward and flicked her tongue over his lips—and then, threading his hand through her hair, his mouth seeking hers, he kissed her fiercely.

CHAPTER EIGHT

THE SOUND OF the water was rushing in time with her breath.

Inching backwards, she stared up at him dazedly. Her head was swimming, and nothing seemed to matter except his taut profile and the urgent, hungry beat of her heart.

'Your jacket…' she whispered. 'It's getting wet.'

'So is your dress.' His voice was hoarse.

Her throat was dry. 'Then help me take it off.'

They reached out for one another, his hand locking in her hair as she grabbed at his shirt, their mouths colliding as they kissed hungrily, tongues probing, lips bruising.

He groaned into her mouth and they broke apart, panting.

'I've been thinking about this for weeks.' His eyes, fiercely green, burned into hers.

'So have I,' she whispered.

His face was taut and she could see the muscles in his arms tensing, as though he was having to hold himself in check. She felt a rush of blood, hot and sudden, at the hunger in his gaze.

'So what are you waiting for?'

His eyes were trained on her face. 'The baby. Is it okay to—? I don't want to hurt you.'

She slid off her sandals, reached out and touched his chest. 'You won't.'

Her head was spinning, her pulse racing. She felt as though she was melting. She wanted him so badly—wanted him as she had never wanted anything or anyone…ever. And this wasn't about some fantasy. This was real. And it was what they both wanted. That was all that mattered.

Reaching up, she slid her hands beneath his shirt, shaking with the freedom of being able to touch him and the relief that she didn't have to stop—that he didn't want her to stop. She clutched at his shoulders, pushing her tongue into his warm mouth as they moved as one, stepping into the shallow water, circling through shafts of raindrops, bodies pressing together in time to the beating of their hearts.

She touched his collar, fumbled impatiently with his tie, her fingers plucking at the knot, jerking it loose, then tugging at the buttons of his shirt.

As her hands touched his warm, bare skin her breath stalled for a moment and she stepped back on legs that shook unsteadily. He was gorgeous, more gorgeous than any man should be allowed to be, and whatever her memory had conjured up the reality outdid any fantasy. He was crazily, stupidly beautiful—all lean, defined muscles and olive skin that was smooth aside from the line of fine dark hair that ran down the centre of his abs, thickening as it disappeared beneath the waistband of his trousers.

Heart pounding, she slid her hands lightly over his chest and, standing on tiptoe, kissed him again gently, delicately, tasting him as she would one of his rums.

He grunted, tugged off his shirt and dropped it, and then, reaching out, he looped his fingers under the thin straps of her dress and slid them over her shoulders, peeling the damp fabric from her overheated skin. She felt it slide over her body and pool at her feet. She wasn't wearing a bra, and above the soft rush of the water she heard him swallow, saw his control snap, sensed the tension in his arms loosen like a spring uncoiling.

'You're beautiful,' he said hoarsely, 'so beautiful.'

He breathed out raggedly and for a moment he just stared at her, his eyes dark and sightless. Her nipples hardened beneath his gaze—and then she sucked in a breath as he reached out and began to stroke them with the palm of his hand.

It was too much. They were too sensitive to touch.

She grabbed his fingers. 'Not there,' she whispered. 'Here.' She pulled his hand lower, pressing it against the ache between her thighs.

He shifted against her, his leg moving between hers, and she felt the hard length of him pushing against her. Only it was not enough. Her hands trembled. She wanted all of him. She wanted—*needed*—everything he had to give.

Her hands moved to his waist, and then to where the force of his desire pressed against his trousers, her pulse jerking as she began tugging at his belt, working the leather through the buckle.

As he breathed out unsteadily her nerves were forgotten and she felt a rush of excitement. His green eyes were fierce and filled with hunger, and she knew that he was fighting for control.

Knowing that he wanted her as much as she wanted him made her feel powerful in a way she had never felt before, and suddenly she wanted to test that power. Holding his gaze, she reached out and rested her hand against the thickness of his arousal.

He let out a hiss of air.

Shaking his head, he swore in Spanish. And then his hands closed around her wrists and he pulled them behind her back. Bending his head, he took her mouth again. Her insides felt hot and tight and she squirmed closer, raising her hips, seeking to ease the pulsing ache between her thighs. But he was holding her still, keeping himself just out of reach.

Her stomach tensed and she moaned in frustration as he wrenched his mouth away. His eyes were trained on her face. For a moment he just stared at her, and then, holding both of her wrists in one hand, he pulled her forward so that the warm spray trickled over her bare skin.

Her heart began to thump as he leaned forward and ran his fingers slowly over her breasts and belly, then lower to the triangle of her panties. As he slid his hand beneath the fabric her stomach flipped over and inside out with need and frustration, and she arched her aching body up towards his, wanting more, *needing* more.

'Please…' she whispered.

He dropped to his knees and she felt an arrow of heat, sharp and low, as he hooked a finger into one side of her panties and tugged gently, drawing them down her legs and tossing them away.

Her nipples tightened painfully. She felt as though she was teetering on the edge of a bottomless drop. A pulse was beating relentlessly between her thighs—and then his tongue pushed between the damp curls and she gasped.

The rain was pounding down now, fat droplets exploding on the rocks behind them, blotting out her heartbeat and his ragged breathing.

Her body was opening out with longing and she was shaking with need, her whole body trembling. A fluttering heat was spreading out from his tongue, growing stronger, more urgent, impossible to ignore. She could feel herself slipping away, the beat of her desire out of sync with her throbbing heartbeat.

Oh, she had never felt like this before. This need was raw and imperative. It felt like water, or air, or sunlight and she could think of nothing other than the tip of his tongue...steady, precise, teasing, merciless.

Her body was screaming now and, tugging her hands free, she grabbed his hair, her fingers biting into his scalp, pulling him closer, opening herself to him as heat exploded in her pelvis.

She breathed out unsteadily as César kissed his way up her body, chasing the aftershocks quivering over her skin. Her hands were still grabbing his skin, clutching and tensing—and then her fingers found the zip of his trousers.

He groaned as she freed him, and she watched his face tighten with concentration as he held himself back from his own release. Curving his fingers under her bottom, he lifted her up so that he could ease her on to his body.

She began to rock against him, her head spinning, and he wrapped his hands around her hips and pulled her closer, his hunger accelerating. Reaching up, he brought her face down and kissed her fiercely and then, gripping her waist, he pushed up inside her. Instantly, she began to move more urgently, breath quickening. His hips were meeting hers...

'*Yes.*' Her lips parted against his mouth. '*Yes...*
Yes...' she whispered.

He breathed in sharply, jerking his mouth away from
hers. Muscles clenching, blood hardening to iron, he
thrust into her, burying his face against her neck to stop
himself crying out. He held her close, and then, easing
himself free, he backed her gently against the wall of
rock, leaning forward to shield her body with his.

Kitty was still trying to catch her breath. He was
calm and solid beside her, his muscles relaxed, his arms
holding her against him, supporting her flushed, shaken
body.

Had they really just done that? Had *she* really just
done that? Was it her hormones? Or was it this place?

She glanced over his shoulder at the lush greenery
and brightly coloured butterflies. It was all so wild and
vibrant—like stepping into some primitive landscape.
Was that why she'd lost all sense of who she was? All
her inhibitions?

But she knew that it was none of those things. It was
him. And her. The two of them together.

Burying her face against his burning damp skin, she
felt the reality of what had just happened overwhelm
her. It had been so fierce, so urgent, so quick. One spark
was all it had taken: her body the flint to his steel.

For a moment she couldn't bring herself to move or
speak, and perhaps he felt the same way—because he
kept his cheek against her face, his breath, still rapid
and unsteady, in her hair.

She leaned into him, enjoying the sensation of his
skin against hers, the warmth of his body and the steady
beat of his heart. She felt fearless: he had *made* her feel
fearless. Even her nakedness felt natural. His body fit-

ted hers with a symmetry that felt predetermined, as though once upon a time they had been joined and then separated, and she wondered why she had fought against this moment.

But it couldn't last for ever.

She pushed at him gently and their eyes met. Scared of what she might see, she looked down to where her fingers were splayed against his chest. She blinked. In the heat of passion she'd barely registered the scars, but now she stared at them intently. They were of differing lengths, some thin and white, one darker and ridged.

'Did you get that one riding your bike?' She ran her fingertip over the puckered skin.

He nodded. 'I hit a bump in the road, came off, and the bike caught me in the chest.'

'And this?' She touched his side.

His eyes were opaque in the sunlight. 'I was climbing and I missed a foothold. I dropped about a hundred feet before the rope caught me, and I got scraped against the rock.'

A hundred feet. 'What happened?'

He shrugged. 'I chalked up my hands and carried on.'

She couldn't think of anything to say to that. But she didn't need to. He was already reaching down to pick up her dress.

They got dressed with difficulty, their wet clothes twisting and tightening against their skin, and then they walked back to the house, not holding hands but not tensing or leaping apart when their fingers brushed together either.

'I don't how that happened,' he murmured.

Looking up into his eyes, she gave him a quick, shy smile and he grinned sheepishly. Around them rainbows danced in the sunlight, taking form in the spray-soaked air.

'I just meant I didn't plan it.' His face was serious, intent, shocked. 'I don't normally act like this, but I've never wanted any woman the way I want you.' His eyes dropped to her throat and, lowering his mouth, he pressed his lips against the tiny beating pulse there. 'Something happens when I'm around you... I feel so frantic.'

'I know.' She pressed her hand against his chest, feeling his heart throb against her fingers. 'I feel the same way. And I didn't plan it either.'

'Was it okay? I wasn't too rough—?'

Looking up into his face, she could see the concern in his green eyes. She shook her head. 'No, you weren't rough. It was wonderful.'

'Wonderful' didn't really do justice to what they'd just shared. It had been sublime. And César was so gorgeous it was no wonder that she'd clawed off his clothes in broad daylight like a ravenous animal. Or that she would gladly do it all again.

But however handsome or sexy César was, that was irrelevant to their future. Her heart was not for the taking and marriage was still not an option.

She felt her stomach tighten. But neither was pretending that something wasn't happening between them: it was. And it wasn't just sex.

But why did it have to be a binary choice between sex and marriage? Was there no room for something in between? Something bespoke—just for them. After all, it was the twenty-first century.

She thought back to César's scars. This was a man who took risks and tested his limits. She, on the other hand...

It wasn't that she hadn't experienced anything in her life. She had: love, marriage, sickness and death. That was a lot more than most twenty-seven-year-olds. Only that was the problem. It had all been too much, too quickly. She had felt passive, powerless, like a passenger in a speeding car.

But César made her feel powerful. She might not want to skydive or free climb, but knowing how she affected him made her feel in control and euphoric in the same way. Plus, whatever happened, they were both parents to this baby growing inside her.

And all that seemed to matter more than trying to classify their relationship status.

Only did he feel the same way?

His hand reached for hers and he stopped beside her. 'Kitty, I've been thinking. About us. About what we're doing. I've been thinking that I'd like it to carry on.'

Watching her eyes widen, he reached out and pushed a curl away from her forehead.

'I don't mean what happened by the waterfall specifically—although that was incredible...'

He smiled, and the slow burn of his gaze made her nipples tighten painfully.

'So, what *are* you suggesting?'

His eyes rested on her face—not just green but gold and amber, like pirate treasure.

'Look, I'm not ready to go back to Havana yet. I haven't had a proper break in a long time, so how do you feel about staying on here for a couple of days?'

Her heart was hammering in her chest. 'I think it sounds like a lovely idea, but I've already taken quite a lot of time off.'

He shook his head slowly. 'You don't need to worry

about that, I spoke to the big boss—he's a great guy, by the way, cool and good-looking and charming—and he said that you can take as much time as you want.'

She bit her lip, trying to stop the smile that was tugging at her mouth.

Sensing her indecision, he reached out and, taking her hand, pulled her closer. 'Please, Kitty. I know I've juggled my schedule, but it's not enough. I owe it to you and the baby to take a step back from the business and not just relocate my office to my home.'

Lifting her chin, she met his gaze. 'And that means what?'

'I don't know.'

The honesty of his answer caught her off guard.

He hesitated. 'I can't in all honesty say that sex hasn't got something to do with it,' he said carefully. 'But it's not the only reason I want to spend time with you. We're going to have a baby...our lives are going to be overlapping for a long time.'

She nodded. 'I know.'

Leaning forward, he kissed her mouth lightly, brushing his lips against hers so that her pulse jumped in her throat.

'That's why I think we should stop pretending. I want you and you want me and there's nothing wrong in us feeling that way—so why act like there is? I know what we have isn't conventional, but that doesn't mean it has to be complicated,' he said quietly. 'We can just keep everything nice and simple.'

She felt his gaze on his face. For a second their eyes were level as they breathed in one another's scent. Who could resist what he was offering? Pure pleasure with no catch. And it was what she wanted too.

Reaching up, she stroked his face. 'I'd like that.'

His eyes were dark with hunger, a hunger that reflected her own, and her body was already starting to melt as he lowered his face to hers and kissed her fiercely.

Mornings had definitely improved, César thought as he leaned back against the pillow.

Three days had passed since their frenzied encounter by the waterfall and the moment when he and Kitty had agreed to stay on at the plantation, and he was lying in bed—the bed he now shared with Kitty—watching her get dressed.

His gaze followed her fingers as they lingered over the buttons of her blouse. For some inexplicable reason he found it incredibly erotic—inexplicable because she was buttoning it up, not unbuttoning it.

But there was something about her focus, the small furrow of concentration in her forehead, that made heat shimmy over his skin. Or maybe it was the way her freshly showered hair was scattering droplets of water onto the fabric, so that he could see her bare skin through the white cotton.

Was it really only three days? Actually it was three days and two nights of pure, blissful pleasure. And yet in some ways it felt as though she had always been a part of his life.

He wasn't complaining. Heat churned in his stomach as he rewound that morning. They'd made love twice—first with the feverish hunger that had characterised their first encounter, and then again more slowly, touching, tasting, exploring each other's bodies.

He couldn't remember wanting a woman so badly, or a time when sex had held such power over him.

Even with Celia.

Now that he could compare her to Kitty, he could see that she had been a youthful infatuation. He'd been a spoilt, handsome young man, used to girls chasing him, and she'd played hard to get. That had been what had really got him hooked. Had she chased him, or responded to his advances, he would not have been so obsessively determined to win her.

But it felt strange to be so fixated on one woman now, given that he'd spent most of his adult life pursuing variety, not commitment. He'd assumed that his fascination for Kitty lay in her unattainability, but now they were having sex and yet nothing had changed. He still couldn't stop thinking about her.

He shifted beneath the sheet, then instantly regretted it; the smooth fabric brushing against his skin was an agonizing reminder of her teasing touch.

But with an eager, responsive Kitty in his bed, it was hardly surprising he was distracted. After so long just fulfilling basic physical hunger, it was a novelty to want someone specifically and repeatedly, to indulge in her feverish touch, to look forward to seeing her.

He felt his spine tense. And, of course, looking forward to seeing someone was natural for lovers—perhaps even more so for lovers who didn't love one another.

And he didn't love Kitty.

But he did want to marry her.

And when it happened—and it *would* happen—it would work for both of them. He would offer her security and the kind of lifestyle she could only dream about for their child, and marriage to her would allow him to present his parents with the 'happy-ever-after' ending they wanted for him.

Or so it would appear, and that was all he needed it to do.

His hand tightened around the edge of the sheet.

He told himself that he was simply being pragmatic. Believing in love as a prerequisite for marriage was a nice idea—but if love and marriage went together like the proverbial horse and carriage why were there so many divorces?

But there was more to his reasoning than just cynicism. The truth was—and it killed him to admit it, even privately—that mostly it was fear. Fear of what would happen if he repeated the mistake he'd made with Celia and allowed himself to muddle lust, or in this case lust and duty, with love.

Kitty turned and gazed down at him, her eyes flaring as they connected with his bare upper body, so that he felt his groin harden.

Why think about any of that anyway? Right now, with access to her delectable body, he was not so much happy as willing to let her set the pace. Rather than pressurising her to change her mind, he was prepared to play a long-ish game—and that meant not just focusing on the present, but laying the foundations for the future and accepting that, for the moment at least, this arrangement was a jump-off point for the next step.

Tipping her head to one side, Kitty scooped up her mass of hair and raised her arms. It was mid-afternoon, the hottest time of the day, and she was sprawled on one of the loungers that were dotted invitingly around the veranda. She'd just detected the slightest of breezes and she let out a long, slow breath. The quiver of air felt blissfully cool against her neck.

Actually, thanks to César, she felt blissful all over.

She stretched out against the cushions, enjoying the ache in the limbs and the sated heaviness of her body. Oscar Wilde had been wrong. Giving in to temptation was not making César any less desirable. On the contrary, every kiss seemed only to intensify her hunger for him, and her pleasure—endless and exhilarating, mindless and insatiable—was nothing like it had ever been before.

She let go of her hair, feeling it cascade over her shoulders.

Nothing like it had been with Jimmy.

But how could she think that sex with César was better than with the man she'd loved and married and watched die?

Her heartbeat slowed, and she waited for the pang of guilt. Only none came. Was she then starting to realise that it was impossible to compare these two men? Or those two versions of herself?

She had never kissed Jimmy as they'd sat down for lunch and then forgotten all about the meal, abandoning the food on her plate in the heat of a different kind of abandonment.

But with Jimmy she had been so young, and in love for the first time. They had both been inexpert, nervous, but at the same time everything had been so familiar. There had never been that spark of hunger, nor any stomach-swooping rush of need because they—and everyone else—had always expected it to happen.

With César she was learning that there was a lot more to sex—and to herself. She was discovering a hot, passionate woman who was living in the moment and enjoying it.

From somewhere inside the house she heard César's voice. He was on the phone and, judging by the mix of affection and exasperation in his voice, she was willing to bet that either he was speaking to his mother or his father.

Picking up her robe, she sat up and tugged it over her bikini. He'd talked about his family, but people were different when they talked *to* their family. Standing up, curious to catch a glimpse of this uncensored version of César, she walked quietly back into the house.

He was wearing his usual dark suit, talking in Spanish, and she allowed herself a moment to enjoy the flow of his words. It was such a romantic-sounding language.

Her chest tightened. Except that César's responses were growing curter by the minute.

Abruptly he hung up and, not wanting to look like an eavesdropper, she said quickly, 'Hi, I was just going to go upstairs and get changed—'

'Okay.'

Crossing the room, he picked up a cup of coffee and drank it swiftly. She stared after him uncertainly. He seemed tense and upset, more so than she'd ever seen him. Except when she'd refused to marry him.

'Who was that on the phone?'

He turned, his green eyes wary. 'My father.'

'Is everything okay?'

He frowned. 'He's fine. He's just annoyed.'

His face didn't change but his voice sounded clipped, distant—the voice of a CEO talking to an employee.

'About what?'

He frowned, glancing away. 'Nothing. It's not important.'

'So why are you upset?'

'Why do you care?'

She stared at him, dumbfounded, winded by the harshness in the voice and by the realisation that this was how he saw her. She might be in his bed and carrying his child, but his thoughts were off-limits.

Avoiding his cool, green gaze, she breathed out unsteadily. 'You seemed upset. I just wanted to h-help.' She stumbled over the word.

'Kitty, please. I'm sorry.' His voice had changed, the harshness fading. 'I shouldn't have said that.' Reaching out, he took her hand, his eyes soft now, contrite. 'I was angry. With my father. Only I took it out on you.' His jaw tensed. 'I don't even know why I said anything. I knew he'd get mad.'

'What did you say?'

'I told him I was thinking about climbing El Capitan.' Catching sight of her baffled expression, he said, 'It's a nine-hundred-metre granite slab. In Yosemite.'

Thinking about his scars, she felt her heart do some kind of complicated two-step against her ribs. 'Your dad's probably just worried about you.'

'Probably.' His forehead creased. 'He can't understand why I'd want to do something like that.'

Kitty stared at him. 'And why do you?'

Now he was staring at her—only she got the sense that he wasn't seeing her, but someone else. Maybe the question had never occurred to him. Probably it hadn't, given that he appeared to divert all his non-work-based energies into riding motorbikes and climbing ridiculously high pieces of rock.

'I don't know.' He shrugged. 'My life is pretty full-on. Sometimes—a lot of the time—it's difficult to switch off. But when you're on a motorbike, or climbing without a rope, the consequences of making a error are so stark you have to concentrate completely, and it's kind of peaceful.'

Peaceful? How could hanging onto a rock face be in any way peaceful?

He gave her a small, tight smile. 'I know it sounds crazy, but time seems to slow right down. Everything disappears. You're just in the moment and it's like you're dancing with the rock. And when you reach the summit you have this euphoria...'

She nodded, but her hand crept over her stomach. How could anything or anyone compete with that? 'It sounds incredible.'

He paused as though he was hunting for words or trying to make a decision. She caught sight of the wariness in his eyes and she waited, half expecting him to close down the conversation.

'And it helps,' he said finally.

'With what?'

'My frustration.' His mouth twisted. 'Not *that* kind. I'm talking about my parents. I love them. They've always put me first and given me everything. But it just frustrates me that I can't give them what they want.'

What do they want? The question formed on her lips but she didn't need to ask it. She knew what they wanted.

Her chest felt tight. Guiltily, she remembered the conversation they'd had about telling their families about her pregnancy. She'd been so wrapped up in her own concerns she'd not even considered his wishes.

'Yes you can.' Reaching out, she took his hand. 'Tell them about the baby. We can tell them now, if you like.'

His eyes met hers, then glanced away, and she pressed her hand protectively against her stomach.

Just for a moment, idiot that she was, she'd thought he was upset at having to keep their baby a secret from his parents, but actually he was worried about them learning the truth.

The shock of this discovery took her breath away.

'I suppose this isn't exactly what they planned,' she said flatly. He didn't reply, and she felt her pulse accelerate. 'Did they have someone else in mind?' She took a deep breath. 'Did you?'

'No—and no. But they had hopes.'

He smiled then, only it was a smile that made her feel hollow inside.

'They've always had hopes for me.'

'Then they must be very proud,' she said quickly, trying to ignore the needles of misery piercing her skin. 'You've built an empire.'

He nodded. 'They *are* proud. But they're very traditional...old-fashioned. To them, money and status is a bonus. It's family that matters.'

Kitty frowned. 'You're giving them a grandchild.'

He nodded, but there was nothing affirming in his body language. He looked taut and unconvinced.

'Is it because I'm English, not Cuban?'

He shook his head. 'My father will probably say that it's fate. That at least now there was a reason for banishing them to *La Yuma*.' Glancing at Kitty's baffled expression, he gave her a small, tight smile. 'The US.'

But it wasn't the slang that had confused her. Clearing her throat, she said, 'What do you mean, "banishing them"? Who banished them, and why?'

'The who is easy, it was me.' He stared down at her

hand entwined with his. 'The why is more complicated,' he said finally.

His voice was offhand, but she could feel the tension pulsing through his fingers into hers. She hesitated. She didn't know what the rules were for this kind of conversation in their kind of relationship. Or even if there were rules for their kind of relationship.

She lifted her chin, felt the pinpricks of panic starting to dissolve. *So you make the rules then,* she told herself.

'No, it's not.' she told him. 'You just start at the beginning and carry on till the end.'

The muscles of his arms trembled, and for half a second or so she thought he was going to pull away, but then he nodded slowly.

'I was twenty-three. I'd just finished my studies and my father wanted me to take over the business. He'd had a lot of health problems and he'd been pretty much holding on, waiting for me to step up. Only I didn't want to do it.' He grimaced. 'I was an only child, the son and heir, and I was spoilt and very much loved. I wanted to have fun and freedom, so I persuaded them to let me go to the US for a year.'

She squeezed his hand. 'What did you do?'

'Not much. I slept all day and partied all night.' He hesitated. 'That's where I met Celia. At a party. She was older than me. Cool. Hard to pin down. Nothing like anyone I'd ever met. I chased her for weeks before she agreed to go out with me.'

His jaw tightened.

'I thought everything would change once we were together, but it didn't. She moved into my apartment but quite often she'd just not come home. One time I got angry and she stormed off. I lost my head. I was so scared that I'd lost her that I ran out into the street in my boxer shorts but she'd gone. And then she wouldn't answer my calls or messages.'

He swallowed.

'The next day I got a call from my mum and I went home. They knew immediately that something was up, so I told them I was in love with Celia and that I was going to marry her.'

Kitty nodded as though she understood, but it hurt, hearing his pain. Hurt, too, knowing that he had been so in love. 'What happened?'

He looked down into her eyes. 'They were appalled. They tried to talk me out of it, told me I was too young. I got angry again and stormed off.' His face stiffened. 'But not before I'd taken my grandmother's engagement ring. I wanted to prove to Celia that I was serious—prove to my parents that I was an adult. When I got back to the US I found Celia and proposed to her, and she accepted. Then I rang my parents and told them I was getting married and staying in America.'

His face was like a mask.

'Two weeks later I came home early and found her in bed with the guy who lived down the hall. At first she cried, and then she got angry and told me it was my fault for being so needy and immature. That's when I asked her to give my grandmother's ring back. Only she said no, so I had to call my father. He sorted it out, but they were devastated and disappointed.'

'They were just worried about you,' she said gently.

He shook his head. 'I was stupid and naive. Too trusting and open. When I came back to Cuba I knew I had to change. And I did.'

She nodded and, reaching out, she touched the dark

fabric of his jacket. 'You wear your suits like armour.' She hesitated. 'So why did you "banish" your parents?'

He held her gaze. 'Being back in Cuba just got harder and harder. I couldn't be myself here.' Looking away, he breathed out slowly. 'You know how it is. We love life. Everyone talks and dances and flirts.'

He smiled stiffly, and she smiled back. 'I'd noticed.'

He shifted against her. 'Only I couldn't be like that anymore. It worked being autocratic and formal at work, but I couldn't be like that with my family and friends, so when my father got ill I used it as an excuse to move them to the US.'

His mouth twisted.

'They don't hate it, but they're really homesick. It would kill them, knowing I'm living here with you and that they aren't a part of it.' He shook his head. 'I've hurt them so much.'

'And that's why you wanted to marry me?' Kitty swallowed, tears forming behind her eyes. 'Not just to tie up loose ends?'

He nodded. 'It seemed like the perfect solution. I was never going to marry anyone for love, but I could be a husband to you, a father to our child, *and* give my parents what they want.'

Kitty swallowed past the lump in her throat. To be young and in love was beautiful, and she'd been so lucky with Jimmy. He'd been sweet and straightforward. But César had been betrayed and hurt so badly that he'd retreated behind a mask.

Only now the mask was gone.

But the scars hadn't. And she wasn't talking about the ones she could see.

'You're a good person,' she said softly. 'A good son.'

He looked pensive. 'I shouldn't have told you. I'm supposed to be supporting you, not the other way around.'

'I'm glad you did.' Reaching up, she stroked his face. 'We're here to support each other.' She took a breath. 'And that's what we're going to tell our families. That we're having a baby and we're taking our relationship one step at a time.'

He gazed down at her in silence, and then he pulled her against him and she felt the tension seep out of him.

'One step at a time,' he repeated. 'That sounds perfect.'

CHAPTER NINE

CLOSING HER LAPTOP, Kitty smiled slowly. Her heart was beating softly. Finally, after weeks of circling through her notes, she was finally making some progress. The characters of the two rums she'd been hired to create were taking form in her head, at least, and she had that same humming in her blood she'd had when she'd been making Blackstrap.

Of course she'd have to do some tastings back in Havana, and run it past César.

She glanced guiltily over her shoulder. True to his word, he had taken a step back from the business, so it seemed unfair of her to be working sneakily, but just like last time she was unstoppable.

Leaning over, she pushed the laptop underneath her lounger. She was lying on the veranda. Above her, an apricot sun was inching lazily across a completely cloudless blue sky. She felt drowsy with heat, and thirsty too, only moving felt like such an effort—and besides, she just wanted to lie there a little longer and keep thinking.

And thinking was really only possible when César wasn't around.

It felt as if he was always around now, even when

he wasn't. She thought back to the moment when she'd woken that morning. They'd woken early and made love, and then he had got up to go for a run and she had dozed, her body enveloped in the heat he'd left behind so that it had felt as though he was still pressing against her, his arm wrapping her tightly in the growing light.

Frowning, she shook her head. Up until yesterday her feelings for him had been neatly filed into categories. For her boss, she felt a mixture of admiration and awe. Alongside that, her body resonated with a fierce, sexual hunger for César her lover, but there was also a feeling of reassurance from the man who was the father of her baby. In some ways it had felt as if she was dealing with three different men.

But since opening up to her about his relationship with Celia and his guilt over his impulsive youthful behaviour he had changed, and now it was as though part of an invisible weight had been lifted. He seemed easier in himself, so that now she was seeing him as a whole person.

Only for some reason getting to know him better hadn't simplified her response, instead her feelings were now a swirl of confusion.

Her heart ached when she thought of how he must have felt when he'd found his fiancée in bed with another man. He had been young and alone in a foreign country, and he'd given his heart to a woman he'd thought felt the same way, only to learn that she'd betrayed him.

Remembering how he'd talked about hanging around on beaches with his mates, she felt a surge of anger. Now that she knew the full story, it was easy to imagine the younger César with his easy smile, messing around with his friends. No wonder he'd been driven to suppress that side of his character. He'd done it to protect himself from further pain, and to spare his family from being hurt and disappointed again. But in doing so he'd had to close himself off from the people he loved most.

Only not any more.

Her heart contracted. They had spoken to her family first. Of course her mum had cried a little, but her happiness had been obvious. She'd sensed that Bill was desperate to engage César with rum-related topics, so it hadn't been a long call, but she'd had a separate, private and more tearful conversation with Lizzie.

It had been so good to talk to her sister. Lizzie was so candid and certain about everything. 'You can't just marry *anyone*, Kitty,' she'd said firmly. I mean, why would you want to marry a jaw-droppingly handsome Cuban billionaire with a string of homes anyway?'

They had both burst out laughing.

'Seriously, though, there's only one reason to ever get married,' Lizzie had said, when finally they'd both calmed down enough to speak again. 'And when you feel it you know where to find a bridesmaid.'

Telling César's parents had actually been easier than she'd expected. They were delighted by news of their forthcoming grandchild, clearly devoted to their son, and prepared to embrace his unconventional relationship with Kitty.

And she'd seen how much their reaction had mattered to César. The tension which she had always taken to be a part of him, like the greenness of his eyes or the clean curve of his jaw, had eased a little. It felt as if together they'd begun to erase their pasts, and she was meeting him for the first time.

Her cheeks began to burn with a heat that had nothing to do with the sun. Except she wasn't about to erase the memory of their first meeting for anything.

'What are you thinking about?'

She glanced up, her heart suddenly beating too fast. César was leaning against the doorframe, his green eyes roaming slowly over her near-naked body. He'd obviously just got back from his run. His black T-shirt and shorts were damp with sweat, and his golden skin and the stripes of shadow and sunlight across his face made him look almost tigerish.

'Oh, nothing really,' she lied.

Unpeeling himself from the wood, he sauntered over and bent down to kiss her. His lips were soft, and instantly her blood seemed to turn to air. As he dropped down beside her on the lounger she took a small breath. Even though it was no longer new to her, his beauty still dazzled her.

'So why are you blushing?' he said softly.

She punched him lightly on the arm. 'I'm not blushing. I'm warm.'

His eyes met hers and then dropped to the veranda floor. 'Were you working?'

Her cheeks grew warm. 'I didn't mean to, but then I thought of something and it all started to come together.'

'I'm happy for you.' He held her gaze. 'I know how frustrating it is when something's just out of reach.'

She frowned. 'I'm not out of reach.'

There was a short silence, and then he smiled. 'No, you're not. And you weren't blushing because you'd been working.'

'I wasn't blushing,' she protested.

'It you don't tell me I'm going to have to read your mind.'

Cupping her face in his hand, he held her gaze, and, wriggling free, she started to laugh. 'Okay, fine—I was blushing. But I don't want to tell you what I was thinking about.'

'Why not?'

He started to nuzzle her neck, his fingers moving lightly over her skin, and she breathed out unsteadily. Now her whole body was growing warm. 'A woman should have some mystery.'

Raising his lips from her neck, he lifted his face. 'But I want to know everything about you,' he said softly.

Her pulse was beating out of time. There had been other moments before when he'd been gentle, like when she'd told him about Jimmy, so why did this feel different?

It wasn't. It shouldn't be.

The fact that he had opened up to her was obviously a positive, but he didn't love her, and she didn't love him, and that was what she wanted—what she needed. Because the flipside of love was a pain she couldn't go through again.

So it didn't matter that his words made her chest feel tight. Nothing had changed between them, and if that wasn't clear right now it was probably just down to what he'd told her yesterday playing on her mind. Even if he was saying things that went beyond the bedroom-based borders of their relationship—a relationship that would end when one of them tired of the other.

Or at least the physical side would end. Her hand slipped down to rest on her stomach. There would still always be this link between them.

Reaching up, she took hold of his T-shirt and pulled him closer. 'I was thinking about the first time we met.'

She watched his face still, as she'd known it would, but not before she caught something flickering across his eyes. It was there and gone before she had a chance to make sense of it, and it was easy to push it aside when his hand was warming her skin. To let herself be distracted by the fine dark hair on his wrists.

'Do you remember?'

'How could I forget?'

She felt his fingers slide over her stomach protectively.

'That evening is burned into my memory. Even when I shut my eyes I can still see you on that sofa.'

She shivered. Her body was starting to ache. 'I can see it too,' she whispered. 'But my eyes are open.'

They reached for one another at the same time.

Later, he re-tied the strings of her bikini and she smoothed his hair into some sort of order.

'It's the least I can do after ravishing you.' She smiled, wanting to tease him, liking the way one side of his mouth curved higher than the other when he smiled back at her.

'Thank you,' he said softly as she leaned back and admired her efforts. Lowering his mouth, he pressed a kiss to her hand. 'How do you feel about *barbacoas?* It's just that I got a call this morning from Pablo. He's a neighbour, and he and his wife Julia are some of my parents' oldest friends. They've invited us over to his estate for lunch.'

'Really?'

He lifted her hand, weaving his fingers through hers. 'I'm guessing my mother must have rung Julia and told her about us, but if you don't want to go it's not a problem.'

'Of course I want to go.' Glancing down at her bikini, she frowned. 'Will it be really formal? Because I don't have anything smart with me.'

He shook his head. 'No, not at all. It'll be fun—just food and dancing and dominos. Pretty much your average Cuban Saturday family gathering. They'll be loads of *niños* running around, the teenagers will all be eyeing one another up, and as soon as we walk through the door you and I will get cornered by the *abuelas*.'

He grimaced.

'You've heard of the Spanish Inquisition? Well, the Cuban *abuelas* have their own version. They'll be grilling me all afternoon and then serving *me* up with the *mojo* instead of the usual hog roast.'

She burst out laughing. 'I thought you said it was going to be fun?'

He grinned. 'I'm joking. I will probably have to answer a few questions—' his eyes gleamed '—but they'll spend most of the afternoon trying to feed you up.'

Two hours later Kitty was standing downstairs, waiting for César to join her. He'd had some clothes sent over for her when they'd decided to stay on the plantation, and she'd chosen a long apple-green dress covered in tiny leaves that Lizzie had bought her for her birthday last year. It was loose enough to wear in the heat, but it felt less casual than wearing a skirt and blouse.

In fact, maybe she could send Lizzie a photo of herself wearing it. She held her phone at arm's length, trying to fit herself into the frame and stay in focus, but it was harder than it looked.

'Do you want me to help?'

She turned. César was strolling towards her, a key fob dangling from his fingers. She stared at him blankly.

He frowned. 'I thought I'd drive—unless that's a problem?'

Her heart thumped inside her chest. She shook her head. It wasn't the thought of him driving that had caused her fingers to freeze around her phone. César was wearing pale green linen trousers and a cream shirt, rolled up to the elbows. He looked both cool and mouth-wateringly sexy.

'You're not wearing a suit,' she said unnecessarily.

He glanced down. 'No, I thought maybe I wouldn't today.'

She swallowed, her eyes snagging on the golden skin and corded muscles of his arms as he took a step towards her, his hand reaching for hers, his green gaze moving slowly from her eyes down to her toes.

'You look beautiful.'

He pulled her towards him, twirling her expertly into the warm solidity of his body, curving his arm around her waist so that the soft green of his trousers seemed to melt into the leaves of her dress.

'We match,' he said softly.

His green eyes were intent on her face and she realised that they were both smiling. She felt that sudden tightening in her chest, except that it wasn't exactly a feeling of tightness but more as though a balloon of happiness was swelling beneath her ribs, so that she could almost feel herself lifting up off the ground.

And why *shouldn't* she feel happy? For such a long time it had felt as if she was just going through the motions. It hadn't even been grief—just a sense that life was passing her by while she was treading water and trying to stay afloat.

But now she had a job she loved in a country that was starting to feel like a second home. She was having a baby, and in César she had a beautiful, tireless lover. That was enough.

It was a short drive to the Montañez estate. As they walked into the garden, he turned and caught her eye and she nearly burst out laughing, because it was exactly how he'd described it—right down to the teenagers eyeballing one another and the hog roast cooking slowly in the afternoon sun.

As predicted, César did get cornered and cross-examined, but even though she couldn't follow every word of the conversation it was clear that he was doted on by the *abuelas*.

Lunch was served in the shade of the house. The centrepiece of the meal was the pork, accompanied by *chicharrones*—bite-size pieces of crackling which tasted incredible with the citrusy *mojo* sauce—but there were also huge platters of avocado and pineapple salad, and of course *congri*, the famous rice and beans dish that was both delicious and comforting.

Leaning back against the extra cushion that her hostess, Julia, had insisted that she have, Kitty gazed down the table, her eyes drawn to where César had been dragged by the other men to smoke cigars.

It was the first time he had left her side all afternoon. When they'd arrived he'd led her between the clumps of guests, introducing her in both Spanish and English, acting as a translator when necessary, and all the time his arm had rested lightly against her back.

She knew, of course, that he was just being polite—

attentive in the same way as when he'd gone and found her a non-alcoholic drink—but even so she had felt herself responding, wanting to draw closer, to lean into him.

Right now he was lounging in his chair, talking, his green eyes dark beneath the shaded canopy, surrounded by men smoking, and sipping *ron*. She watched as he said something and a burst of laughter floated towards her, momentarily drowning out the more sedate sound of the dominos clicking against the tabletop.

He held up his hand, tilting the rum so that the men watching him all tipped their heads to one side, and she found herself smiling. With his gaze fixed on the glass in his hand, and his arm resting casually against the back of the chair, he looked less like a CEO and more like his Roman namesake: Caesar addressing his senators.

Behind them on the lawn some of the children were playing chase, but two of them—a girl and a younger boy, brother and sister maybe—stood side by side eating *coquitos*, their eyes wide as the others zig-zagged past them.

Kitty watched as the boy held up his caramel-covered hand, frowning.

The girl shook her head. *'Puaj! No me toques!'* Turning she tugged the jacket of the man nearest to César—Pablo's nephew, Jorge. *'Papi, Javi está todo pegajoso!'*

Picking up a napkin, the man reached down—but his son was too quick and, laughing, grabbed César's leg and hauled himself onto his lap, burying his face against his shirt.

Oh, no. Kitty held her breath. She could see the sticky smears even from where she was sitting. But, waving away Jorge's apologies, César grinned, and then, gently grabbing the little boy's hands, he held them out to be wiped clean.

Her chest was aching. He was so sweet. His patience, his gentleness, reminded her of Jimmy—and yet for the first time ever she couldn't picture Jimmy in her head. His familiar features seemed to have faded, no longer sharp but blurred and growing fainter.

Around her, the noise of the party faded too, drowned out by the hammering of her heart. She stared at César, mesmerised. This was what he would be like with his own child. The thought made her whole body swell with happiness, so that she couldn't hold in her smile. Only there was a lump in her throat too. For, even though she knew there was no point in thinking it, it was impossible not to imagine that if they were a real couple then together they would be a family—the kind of family that she'd dreamed about for so long.

As though feeling her gaze, César glanced up, his eyes seeking hers. It was the kind of private look that only couples shared—a mix of tenderness and understanding that made her feel dizzy. Except they weren't a real couple. Just two people taking one step at a time...

She managed to keep smiling as César stood up and strolled over to where she sat, concern in his eyes. 'Is everything okay? You look a little pale.'

She nodded, still smiling. 'I'm always pale.'

He sat beside her, his green gaze resting on her face, and then, reaching out, he rested his hand lightly on her stomach. 'If it's a girl I want her to have your hair.'

Ignoring the way her pulse skipped forward, she cleared her throat. 'And if it's a boy I'll let you clean him up when he's been eating *coquitos*.'

Grinning, he leaned forward and plucked a beautiful

white flower from the arrangement on the table. 'Here.' Gently he slotted it into her hair. 'My *mariposa.*'

She felt her heart bump against her ribs. 'I can't be your *mariposa*. It's the Cuban national flower and I'm a foreigner.'

His eyes collided with hers. 'Actually, it's a foreigner too. It comes from India. In the Revolution, Cuban women who helped the rebels used to wear them in their hair.'

'Well, I'm helping you with your rums, so does that make you a rebel?' she asked teasingly.

'Not today.' He grimaced. 'Today I need Julia to report back to my mum that I was the perfect gentleman. Speaking of which—would you like to dance?' He glanced down at his shirt. 'Or am I too sticky?'

She swallowed past the lump in her throat. 'You're not sticky, you're sweet,' she said.

And, standing up, she let him lead her beneath the huge shaded gazebo to where couples were circling to salsa music. Curving his hand around her waist, he pulled her close.

'Everyone's looking at us,' she whispered.

'Not us.' He gazed down at her, his green eyes dark and intent. 'They know me far too well to find me in any way interesting. It's you they're looking at.'

She felt her pulse slow. If only she could freeze time, capture this moment. Heart pounding, she stared at him, wanting desperately to memorise every detail of his face.

'Yes, because I'm with you,' she said lightly. 'Mr Big Shot from Havana.'

Havana—the word reverberated in the air between them. Since deciding to stay at the plantation neither of them had really talked about when they were going to go back. She knew he must be in contact with his office but, true to his word, he'd taken the promised step back from work and it hadn't seemed to come up in conversation.

Only of course they couldn't stay here for ever…

Judging by César's expression, he was clearly thinking the same thing. His next remark confirmed her suspicion.

'Talking of which, I suppose we should think about heading back fairly soon.'

He was staring right into her eyes and she tried to smile, to take his casual remark at face value even though she felt as though her heart had relocated to her throat.

'Yes, I suppose we should,' she agreed.

There was a short silence, as though he was waiting for her to say something more, or maybe to say something else himself, but then finally he nodded.

'Do you want to go today?' She braced herself for his reply.

He frowned. 'No, there's no rush. We can drive back tomorrow.' He paused, his face stilling, and she sensed that he was working through something in his head. 'Actually, I don't think we'll take the car. I don't know if I told you, but I have a yacht—'

She raised an eyebrow. 'Of course you do.'

He grinned. 'It might be fun to sail her down to Havana.'

'Is this a good time for me to tell you that I'm really bad at tying knots?'

'You are?' His eyes gleamed. 'That's a coincidence—so am I. Maybe we should spend tonight in the cabin, practising a few,' he said softly.

* * *

Raising his hand to block out the glare of the sun, César gazed at the turquoise sea. It looked perfect.

He felt a thrill of anticipation—could almost taste the adrenaline. It had been months since he'd had a chance to get out on the water, and it felt great to feel the spray on his face. He felt lighter, as though the chains of his youthful stupidity were no longer restraining him. And they weren't—thanks to Kitty. She had freed him, forced him to let go of the pain and the guilt, and now he felt at peace with his past.

And yet something still felt off-key and unfinished.

He looked across the deck to the waves beyond. Usually being on the yacht transcended his mood, but of course usually he sailed alone. His jaw tightened. Maybe inviting her on to the boat had been a bad idea.

For him, sailing was both a release and a challenge. He loved pitting himself against the strength of the sea and the pull of the wind, and he liked that version of himself.

He pictured Kitty's naked body in the cabin below. Then again…

'You look like a pirate.'

He turned. Kitty was standing behind him, wearing nothing but a bikini and one of his shirts. A couple of weeks of careful exposure to the sun had turned her skin the palest gold, and her breasts had rounded out a little. He felt his body stir.

Grabbing hold of the shirt, he tugged her towards him, a pulse of heat tiptoeing across his skin. 'And you look like some incredibly sexy Girl Friday.'

She screwed up her mouth. 'If that's some misguided attempt to get me to scrub the decks, you can forget it. My talents lie elsewhere.'

He grinned. 'Yes, they do.'

'I was talking about making rum.'

'So was I,' he lied. Lifting his hand, he stroked her face. 'Did you get some sleep?'

She nodded. 'I went out like a light. I think it must be the—' Her forehead creased.

He frowned. 'What is it?'

'I just thought of a name for one of the rums.'

Watching her pupils flare, he felt his blood grow lighter. She was genuinely excited.

'Diabolito—you know…?'

'The pirate.' He nodded slowly. 'I like it.'

'You do?'

'Yes, I do—and, what's more, I've just thought of a name for the other one.' His stomach flipped with a rush of anticipation more intense than any skydive. 'What do you think of Mariposa?'

Her smoky eyes widened and a flush of colour spread over her cheeks. 'I think it's beautiful,' she said shakily.

For a moment they stared at one another, and then she glanced over his shoulder and frowned again.

'Have we stopped?'

He grinned. 'Spoken like a true sailor. It's called dropping anchor—and, yes, we have. I thought maybe we could do a little snorkelling.'

The look of surprise on her face made his grin widen.

'Boring fact—Cuba has the second largest reef in the world after the Great Barrier Reef.'

And exploring it with Kitty would be fun. The fact that it would delay their return to Havana was of course just coincidental.

He could see the longing in her eyes, but she started to shake her head. 'I don't actually know how to.'

'It's easy.' He took her hand. 'I promise. All you have to do is breathe. You'll be great.'

'Will I?'

Her grey eyes looked almost silver in the sunlight, and her expression was so open and trusting that it hurt him to look at her.

'Of course—and I'll be right there beside you.' He pointed across the deck. 'All you need is a mask and a snorkel and some flippers. Try the orange ones—they're a little smaller.'

His heart was thumping against his ribs. The idea had come to him while she was sleeping and now, watching her pick up a pair of flippers, he felt stupidly excited. He didn't know why, but he wanted to be the one to introduce Kitty to the undersea world.

No, that wasn't true. He *did* know why. She'd had such a terrible time. She'd known heartbreak and loss and he wanted to see her happy. He wanted to *make* her happy. And this would be something special just between them.

Turning, he walked over to where Kitty was standing. She had her back to him, her head tilted to one side, and the hem of his shirt was riding high on her thighs as she gazed abstractedly at a face mask.

He stood for a moment and admired the flaring curve of her bottom, and then his gaze stilled as she rotated her hand and he watched her small, delicate fingers cup and caress the mask. Her touch was light, almost reverent, and he felt his felt his body stir, the blood starting to pound hot and fast as he remembered how she had touched him in the same way but for another, more intimate reason just a few hours ago.

'Ready?' he called.

She turned and, smiling shyly, she nodded.

As they swam side by side he felt both incredibly protective and captivated by Kitty's wide-eyed excitement. It had been such a long time since he'd allowed himself to be so open, but with her it was easy—not just to reveal his own pleasure but to enjoy hers. And there was a rainbow of reef life to enjoy in the warm, clear waters: yellow and blue angelfish, coral-coloured parrotfish and zebra-striped spadefish. It was as though the sea had decided to put on a cabaret.

And Kitty looked enchanted.

'I never thought it would be like that,' she said as they enjoyed lunch on deck. 'I thought it would be dark and gloomy and that all the fish would be scared of us. But they're not.'

He smiled. He couldn't imagine anything being scared of Kitty. 'It's because they're still not that used to divers. Probably because it's on our doorstep, Cubans themselves don't bother with diving that much.'

'What's it like if you go deeper?'

He grinned. 'Cold! That's why you wear a wetsuit. But it's amazing—like a whole new world you didn't even know existed.'

She shivered. 'I'm not sure I'm ready for that.'

Watching her face, he felt his throat tighten. He felt like a tuning fork. Everything she was feeling seemed to resonate through him too, so that her happiness was his happiness, her pain became his pain. It was a strange, unsettling sensation, and even though he couldn't give a name to it he knew it was dangerous.

His heart began to beat faster. There were safer ways of seeking danger.

He glanced past her at the still sea. 'Actually, there's a wreck just along the coast from here, and as we're in the area I thought I might go take a look.'

'On your own?'

He heard and ignored the confusion in her voice. He'd solo-dived before. It was a more risky than diving in a group, but right now that was what he needed. He shrugged. 'Even if you weren't pregnant, it wouldn't be safe for a first deep dive.' He hesitated. 'I don't have to go...'

'No, it's fine. I want you to go.' She gave him a quick, tight smile. 'Really.'

They anchored twenty minutes later.

The coastline was more rugged here, and the water was choppier, and he could see from Kitty's expression that she was having second thoughts.

'I'll be fine.' Taking her hands, he pulled her against him and kissed her lightly on the lips. 'I know what I'm doing. I've done a lot of dives and this is pretty shallow.'

'How long will you be?'

'Forty minutes?' He glanced at her face, then at his watch. 'I'll be back up in half an hour.'

He was desperate to go. Desperate to prove that *this* was what his life had been lacking. This rush of exhilaration—part fear, part anticipation. Kitty might be captivating in so many ways, but this was what made his pulse race.

Holding his mask and regulator in place with his palm, he stepped off the side of the yacht into the water.

Watching him disappear beneath the waves, Kitty felt her chest tighten. It was stupid to feel so tense. He knew what he was doing.

She took a breath. It was only half an hour. Thirty short minutes. Shorter than the time it took her to wash and dry her hair.

She glanced down at her phone, at the timer she'd set as he jumped into the water. Twenty-five minutes now.

There was no point in worrying. There wasn't anything she could do if something went wrong down there. But it made her feel dizzy just thinking about all the things that could go wrong.

Life wasn't kind or fair—she knew that—and the ocean was a cruel place. But César was an experienced diver, and the sea had been kind to her.

Thinking back to how a group of beautiful angelfish had swum right up to her mask, she smiled. They had been so gentle, so curious, and the warm water had felt incredibly relaxing and safe. Her stomach gave a little flip. That was what it must be like for their baby.

Resting her hand against the slight curve of her belly, she glanced down at the timer and breathed out slowly. Only ten minutes to go now.

Which was just enough time for her to take a few pictures to send to Lizzie.

She was reading her sister's response to the photos when the timer went off.

Feeling a rush of relief, she made her way to the swim platform. She stood gazing down at the water, her heartbeat filling her head. *Where was he?*

She glanced down at her phone. He was five minutes later than he'd said he would be.

Her heartbeat sped up. An ache was spreading out from her heart—an ache she remembered, an ache she had never wanted to feel again. She glanced back at the phone. Now he was eight minutes late.

Did he have enough oxygen?

A hot and slippery panic was crawling over her skin. She felt sick and scared.

What if something had happened to him?

The thought was unbearable.

It hurt like an actual physical pain, as though a crack was opening up inside her. But why did it hurt so badly? It was completely disproportionate, excessive, unreasonable, and it didn't make any sense. They barely knew one other and they weren't even a 'real' couple.

She thought back to the lunch party, and to the way her eyes had met his along the length of the table.

No, it didn't make any sense, unless—

Unless she loved him.

She breathed out unsteadily. Her heart felt as though it was about to burst out of her chest and her whole body was vibrating with shock and acceptance and joy at her silent admission.

But of *course* she loved him.

Every thought, every action, every feeling she had led back to him. Even when he wasn't there she could conjure him up, fully formed, inside her head.

Only how had it happened? She had never expected to feel this way again. She'd thought that life had given and then taken away everything it had to give. But then this man had stepped into her path—or rather she had stepped into his—and now she could feel love and hope working through her veins as she gazed down at the sea.

And then, just like that, he was there, bursting through the surface of the water, his dark hair sleek against his head. As he pulled himself up onto the platform the blood seemed to drain from her body with relief.

His eyes, so green, so familiar, so necessary, locked with hers. 'What is it? Did something happen?'

She hesitated. Really though, what could she say? *Yes, I just realised I love you.*

She wasn't feeling that brave right now.

'You're late.'

'I know.'

He pulled her against him, and the chill of his usually warm body was a shock.

'I was under the boat and I noticed a couple of dents in the hull.' His hand tightened in her hair. 'I just wanted to check them out.'

His voice was tense, distant, as though he was still beneath the water.

She nodded. She felt exhausted. But he was alive, and he was here, and that was all that mattered.

They reached Havana by mid-evening.

As they followed the inevitable traffic diversion through the centre César had to grip the edge of his seat to stop himself knocking on the glass behind Rodolfo's head and asking him to take them back to the boat.

After the peace and isolation of the plantation the city felt incredibly loud and bright, and maybe Kitty felt the same, he thought as they headed back to the estate. She had been quiet in the car. In fact, she'd been quiet since the dive.

Later, she was quiet during dinner too. But maybe it wasn't just bodies that needed to decompress after a dive. Perhaps emotionally it was hard to adjust to ordinary life when moments earlier you'd been in a thrilling underwater world.

'If you like we could take the boat out next weekend.

There's a nature reserve just up the coast with turtles and stingrays. Sometimes even manatees.'

She stared up at him, her thoughts clearly elsewhere. 'That would be lovely.' She hesitated. 'I'm sorry that you didn't get longer in the water.'

'It's fine.'

His heart clenched as he thought back to the dive, to the moment when he'd realised that something was wrong. Tension had been building in his chest, his blood pulsing inside his head, and at first he'd thought it was his mouthpiece. But of course it hadn't been.

She bit her lip. 'You didn't say much about it.'

He frowned, then rubbed a hand over his face. 'It was different from usual.'

'In what way?'

His heart was thumping now. The tension was back. Earlier, in the water, he'd forced himself to go deeper, to do what he always did, what he'd always done—flee the feeling. Only this time he hadn't run, he'd swum.

But the feeling had stayed with him. And there, in the shifting currents of the Atlantic, he'd realised that it didn't matter how far he swam. For years now he'd kept pushing his body to the limit—diving, climbing, base-jumping—always seeking the next thrill, constantly needing to go deeper, faster, higher. Only for the first time he had asked himself why?

Could it be that all those physical challenges were just an attempt to fill a void? The void left by his decision not to pursue the normal goals of adult life—marriage, falling in love, having a family?

If so, then they were no longer necessary.

He'd reached the wreck and then, using the currents,

made his way over and around it, trying to escape the pressure in his chest, choosing not to give it a name.

Now, though, with her beautiful, serious grey eyes on his face, he didn't want to escape, and he was tired of fleeing.

Reaching out, he took her hand. 'Look, Kitty. I don't know how to say this—'

She stared at him, her fingers stiffening.

'So I'm just going to start at the beginning and carry on to the end.'

'Okay,' she whispered.

'I wanted you from the first moment I saw you, and I tried to stay away only I couldn't. So I came back. And then you told me you were pregnant, and I wanted to be there for the baby, so I asked you to marry me. But I didn't love you.'

'I know.' Her eyes were wide and bright. 'I know how you feel, César.'

His grip tightened around her hand. 'Only today, when I went down to the wreck, I kept expecting to feel how I usually do. A little bit nervous, maybe, and excited. But I didn't.'

His mouth twisted.

'The whole dive just didn't feel right. I kept thinking something was missing. And then I realised...' He paused. 'I realised that it was you. I missed you, and what I was feeling was loneliness. I told myself I was being stupid, that it was the dive talking. Only when I got out of the water I felt better. I felt whole again.'

She cleared her throat. 'What are you saying?'

'I'm saying that I still want to marry you.' He let out a shaky breath. 'But this time it's because I love you.'

'You *love* me?' For a moment she stared at him blankly, and then slowly she withdrew her hand from his.

Striving for calm, he opened his mouth—but his words stayed unspoken as she started to shake her head.

'But I never asked for your love and I don't need it. I don't want it.'

'Kitty—'

He reached across the table, but she jerked backwards.

Still shaking her head, she got to her feet, scraping her chair across the floor. 'I'm sorry, César, but I don't love you.'

The chair fell backwards, and as it hit the floor he watched, heart hammering, body frozen, as she turned and ran from the room.

CHAPTER TEN

KITTY MOVED BLINDLY through the house, the lie echoing inside her head. Her heart was racing, her blood pounding incessantly.

He loved her and she loved him.

So why had she turned and run from him?

But that question didn't need answering.

She thought back to when she'd been waiting for him on the boat.

Waiting.

Worrying.

Hurting.

She stopped at the bottom of the staircase, blinking furiously.

Earlier, when she'd realised that she loved César, it had been a shock. For years she had lived believing that she would never love again. She'd shut down that part of her life. And then she'd moved here to Cuba, and suddenly there had been César, and now she was pregnant, and her world had started to grow warm again, and the ice around her heart had begun to melt.

It had felt exciting, picturing the two of them together, but now she could see that she had just tricked herself into thinking she had moved on and was ready for love.

She wasn't.

All she'd been doing was painting a picture in her head of a fantasy of love in a faraway place with a tall, dark, handsome stranger who made her heart beat faster.

César telling her that he loved her had made it real.

Too real.

She couldn't breathe.

Fantasy love didn't hurt, but real love did—because real love had to exist in the real world, where life was cruel and random. And that was why she had to leave now.

Her feet were moving of their own accord, up the stairs and into her bedroom. If she stayed, she wouldn't be able to resist him; she didn't want to resist him. But she couldn't love a man who lived the way he did. He was a risk-taker, and loving him would mean accepting she could lose him, and that was a risk she couldn't take—a pain she didn't ever want to feel again.

Only it hurt so much to think that she was going to have to leave.

Trying to hold back the tears that were threatening to spill over, she found her suitcase and began grabbing handfuls of her clothes. It was the only way.

'What are you doing?'

César's voice broke into the tumult of her thoughts. Her heart froze. She hadn't expected César to follow her. Why would he when she'd so inexplicably thrown his love back in his face?

Watching the light in his beautiful green eyes dim, she had wanted to take his hand and retract her words, to go to him and pull him close. But she had no right to do any of those things—not now, not ever—and the pain of knowing that, and of knowing that one day another woman would cradle his head in her lap, comfort him at the end of a long day, was her penance. It was necessary and right.

Only now he was here.

'I'm packing. I need to go home.'

'To England?'

The bruise in his voice wrenched at something inside her and, gripping the handle of her suitcase, she felt a tear slide down her cheek.

She swiped it away.

Please let him leave. Please don't make me have to look at him.

'Yes, to England. And nothing you say is going to change my mind.'

'Can't we talk about this?'

'There's no point. There's nothing to say.'

'I can't let you go, Kitty. Not like this. It's late, and you're upset.'

She shook her head and she heard him breathe out unsteadily.

'Then I'll go. I'll get a hotel.'

'No.' She turned. 'Why should you leave? It's your home.'

'It's your home too.'

She tried not to look at him, but she just couldn't stop herself. 'It's not. It never was. It just felt like it could be when we were at the plantation—'

He took a step forward. His green eyes were fixed on her face, and he looked pale and shaken. 'Nothing's changed except our location.'

'No, *everything's* changed.' She felt a flash of panic. She could feel herself wavering, wanting to believe what he was saying, longing to trust the hope in his eyes.

'Because I told you I love you?'

'And I told *you* that I don't believe in love,' she said.

He reached for her hand. 'No, you said you can't believe in love, that you can't feel that way again.'

He was right. She could remember saying the words—saying them when she had been still in shock from finding out that she was pregnant with his baby.

'But you do love me, Kitty. I know you do. And I know we can make this work.'

She tried to pull her hand away, but he didn't let go.

'So why are you running away?'

She didn't reply, and his eyes searched her face.

'Is it guilt? Do you think you don't deserve to be happy again? Because you do. You deserve it more than anyone I've ever known. You've been through so much, and you've been so strong and brave.'

Brave.

The word tasted bitter in her mouth.

Breathing out unsteadily, she looked up at him and shook her head. 'I'm not brave. I'm the opposite of brave. You want to know why I can't marry you? It's because I'm scared.'

He stared at her in silence, his eyes digging into hers. 'Kitty, I don't—'

Tugging her hand free, she took a step backwards. 'I know. You don't understand. And I get that. I get that you need things that I can't give you.' Her eyes caught sight of the thin raised scar on his arm. 'You live your life taking risks. You don't feel fear. I knew that the first time we met.'

Gazing down at Kitty's pale, strained face, César felt his skin tighten. Was that what she believed? He wanted to laugh, except there was something blocking his throat.

He thought back to the years he'd spent masking his easy-going trusting nature—the years he'd spent avoiding romantic attachments. Of course the sexual need had been there, and he'd taken care of that. Only he wasn't just talking about the women who had briefly shared his bed but never his life. Riding bikes, jumping out of planes, diving to the sea bed—they had all been a way to test his limits, to make his heart beat faster.

In a way that didn't actually threaten his heart in the emotional sense.

And somehow, over the years, he'd come to believe that it was enough—that the high of reaching the peak of a mountain was the same as the rush of seeing the face of the woman you loved light up when she saw you walk in the room.

Only it wasn't. And deep down he'd always known that. But he hadn't been able to admit it to himself. Hadn't been able to admit that that he chose to take risks with his life because he was scared of risking his heart. Scared of reaching out. Scared of sharing his life. Scared of trying for happily-ever-after and for ever.

He looked at Kitty.

But he was tired of being scared. And he was going to fight for Kitty even if that meant laying his feelings bare.

'You're wrong,' he said quietly.

'I know all about fear. And not the kind of fear you're talking about.'

His chest tightened. 'Do you remember when we were at the plantation and my father called and we argued about me climbing El Capitan? You asked me why I wanted to do something like that.'

She nodded. 'You said it helped you forget about work and about how you felt you'd let your parents down.'

'That's what I told you.' He cleared his throat. 'And I suppose on some level I was telling you the truth. But it's not the whole truth.' His pulse accelerated. 'After Celia I was scared of being myself. I was scared to trust my own judgement. I was scared of falling in love. And I hated feeling like that. I hated letting fear govern my behaviour. I hated being a coward.'

Reaching out, he took her hand again.

'And that's why I climb rock faces without a rope, why I pushed myself to the limit. It was so I could prove *to myself* that I wasn't a coward. But the truth is I was still a coward. I was still living in the past, hiding behind the bikes and the boats, still scared...'

The concern in her eyes made his heart swell.

'And maybe if you hadn't been out on that road that evening I'd still be scared.' His fingers tightened around hers. 'Before I met you I was living a lie, pretending to everyone that my life was exactly how I wanted it to be. But I wasn't really living. I was just carving up each week into days, and each day into hours, and filling them up so I didn't have to face my fears. And then I met you and everything I thought I wanted was worthless. Meaningless.'

He breathed out unsteadily and, lifting her hand, he pressed it gently against his lips.

'You know earlier today, when I was diving, I realised that nothing makes my heart beat as fast as you do. And all of that, and all of this—my business, my wealth—I could give it all up in a heartbeat. Because it doesn't mean anything unless we're together. You and me and the baby.'

Kitty could hardly breathe.

You and me and the baby.

She stared at him, tears burning her eyes. César wasn't the only one living in the past. And like him she'd been viewing that past selectively as though through the wrong end of a telescope. Her vision had shrunk and her memories had focused on the sadness of losing Jimmy, not on the happiness of loving him, so that she'd become terrified of loving again. Only she'd never stopped loving that whole time. She loved her family, and she loved this baby growing inside her, and she loved César too.

And he was right. It would be the same in England as in Havana. Changing the location wouldn't change how she felt. Nothing could change that.

Her heart was beating out of time, aching with a love she could finally express. 'That's all I want too.'

Her tears were falling now, but she let them fall, and as he pulled her against him her tears mingled with his.

'I love you.' He kissed her fiercely. 'I love you so much.'

'And I love you too.'

For a moment they just gazed at one another, breathing in each other's happiness, and then, reaching down, Kitty twisted his wrist to look at his watch.

'It's the same time in Florida as it is here, so I guess your parents will be asleep, won't they?'

César shook his head. 'Probably not. They still eat late, and they always have a siesta—'

'And what time is it in England?'

He frowned. 'It's about five o'clock in the morning.'

'Then we should probably call your parents first.'

'We should?'

She bit her lip. Her heart was pounding. 'Well, you want to invite them to the wedding, don't you?'

He stared at her blankly. 'The wedding…?'

'Unless you want to wait until after the baby's born?' she said softly.

His eyes, those beautiful green eyes she loved so much, rested on her face.

'Are you asking me to marry you?'

She nodded slowly. 'I wasn't sure you'd ask me a third time.'

Reaching into his trouser pocket, he pulled out a small round box and opened it. 'I was never going to stop asking you.'

She felt her heart backflip. 'Oh, César, it's beautiful.'

She watched, mesmerised, as he slid the sapphire and diamond ring shakily onto her finger, and then putting his hand under her chin, he lowered his mouth to hers and kissed her gently. Breaking away, he stared down at her, his green eyes transparent with love and hope.

'That was a yes, by the way.'

Her eyes met his and she nodded slowly.

'Yes, it was. It is,' she said. 'It definitely is.'

And, stroking his face, she kissed him back.

* * * * *

COMING SOON!

We really hope you enjoyed reading this book. If you're looking for more romance, be sure to head to the shops when new books are available on

Thursday 5th September

To see which titles are coming soon, please visit

millsandboon.co.uk/nextmonth

MILLS & BOON

Coming next month

A PASSIONATE REUNION IN FIJI
Michelle Smart

'Hiding away?' Livia asked.

'Taking a breather.'

Dark brown eyes studied him, a combination of sympathy and amusement in them. Livia knew well how social situations made him feel.

She caught the barman's attention and ordered herself a bourbon too. 'This is a great party.'

'People are enjoying it?'

'Very much.' She nudged him with her elbow and pointed at one of the sofas. Two of the small children he'd almost tripped over earlier were fast asleep on it. A third, who'd gone a pale green colour, was eating a large scoop of ice cream, utter determination etched on her face. 'Someone needs to get that girl a sick bag.'

He laughed and was immediately thrown back to his sister's wedding again.

He'd approached Livia at the bar. She'd said something inane that had made him laugh. He wished he could remember what it was but it had slipped away the moment she'd said it, his attention too transfixed on her for words to stick.

She'd blown him away.

Those same feelings...

Had they ever really left him?

The music had slowed in tempo. The dance floor had filled, the children making way for the adults.

'We should dance,' he murmured.

Her chest rose, head tilted, teeth grazing over her bottom lip. 'I suppose we should...for appearances' sake.'

He breathed deeply and slowly held his hand out.

Equally slowly, she stretched hers out to meet his. The pads of her fingers pressed into his palm. Tingles shot through his skin. His fingers closed over them.

On the crowded dance floor, he placed his hands loosely on her hips. Her hands rested lightly on his shoulders. A delicate waft of her perfume filtered through his airwaves.

He clenched his jaw and purposely kept his gaze focused above her head.

They moved slowly in tempo with the music, their bodies a whisper away from touching...

'When did you take your tie off?' Livia murmured when she couldn't take the tension that had sprung between them any longer.

She'd been trying very hard not to breathe. Every inhalation sent Massimo's familiar musky heat and the citrus undertones of his cologne darting into her airwaves. Her skin vibrated with awareness, her senses uncoiling, tiny springs straining towards the man whose hands hardly touched her hips. She could feel the weight in them though, piercing through her skin.

Caramel eyes slowly drifted down to meet her gaze.

The music beating around them reduced to a burr.

The breath of space between them closed. The tips of her breasts brushed against the top of his flat stomach. The weight of his hands increased in pressure.

Heat pulsed deep in her pelvis.

Her hands crept without conscious thought over his shoulder blades. Heart beating hard, her fingers found his neck…her palms pressed against it.

His right hand caressed slowly up her back. She shivered at the darts of sensation rippling through her.

Distantly, she was aware the song they were dancing to had finished.

His left hand drew across her lower back and gradually pulled her so close their bodies became flush.

Her cheek pressed into his shoulder. She could feel the heavy thuds of his heart. They matched the beats of hers.

His mouth pressed into the top of her head. The warmth of his ragged breath whispered in the strands of her hair. Her lungs had stopped functioning. Not a hitch of air went into them.

A finger brushed a lock of her hair.

She closed her eyes.

The lock was caught and wound in his fingers.

She turned her cheek and pressed her mouth to his throat…

A body slammed into them. Words, foreign to her drumming ears but unmistakably words of apology, were gabbled.

They pulled apart.

There was a flash of bewilderment in Massimo's eyes she knew must be mirrored in hers before he blinked it away.

A song famous at parties all around the world was now playing. The floor was packed with bodies all joining in with the accompanying dance. Even the passed-out children had woken up to join in with it.

And she'd been oblivious. They both had.

Continue reading
A PASSIONATE REUNION IN FIJI
Michelle Smart

Available next month
www.millsandboon.co.uk